# The Treason
# of the
# Ghosts

Paul Doherty

HEADLINE

First published in 2000 by
HEADLINE BOOK PUBLISHING

First published in paperback in 2001 by
HEADLINE BOOK PUBLISHING

10 9 8 7 6 5 4 3 2 1

ISBN 0 7472 6310 8

Typeset by
Letterpart Limited, Reigate, Surrey

Printed and bound in Great Britain by
Clays Ltd, St Ives plc

HEADLINE BOOK PUBLISHING
A division of Hodder Headline
338 Euston Road
London NW1 3BH

www.headline.co.uk
www.hodderheadline.com

To Doreen and Jack Steeb
of Ann Arbor, Saline, Michigan

# Chapter 1

Parson John Grimstone slowly climbed the steps into his pulpit and stared blearily down the parish church of St Edmund's. The grey dawn light filtered through the thick glass windows, even as the morning mist curled beneath the door, moving up the church like a cloud of cold incense. The nave, as usual for Sunday morning Mass, was packed with the burgesses, villagers and peasants of the royal borough of Melford in Suffolk. The wealthy ones sat in their benches and pews, specially bought, carved at the ends with individual decorations and motifs. The not-so-well off, the cottagers and peasants, sat behind them, whilst the real poor were herded at the back around the baptismal font. The rest lurked in the shadows of the transepts, sitting backs to the wall, their mud-caked boots stretched out before them.

Parson John breathed in sharply, trying to ignore the heavy fumes of the previous night's wine. Today, only a few Sundays away from the beginning of Advent, he would talk about death; that silent, sudden messenger which always made its presence felt, particularly in Melford with its history of bloody murder and consequent retribution of public trial and execution. Parson

1

John plucked out the piece of parchment from inside his chasuble, placed it on the small lectern on the back of a carved eagle which soared out in front of the pulpit. He felt cold, the church was gloomy, and he recalled his own nightmares: how those buried beneath the grey flagstones might push the stones aside and stretch out skeletal, claw-like hands to drag him down amongst them – a phantasm, but one which had plagued Parson Grimstone ever since he was a child. His mother had recounted how the dead slept beneath this church, waiting for the blast of Gabriel's trumpet.

Grimstone cleared his throat. He must dispel this feeling of unease. A small, thickset man, with a drinker's red-cheeked face under a mop of snow-white hair, Parson Grimstone considered himself a good priest. He stared down at the people thronged before him. He had baptised their children, witnessed the exchange of vows at marriages and, at least years ago, gone out at all hours of the day and night to anoint their sick and dying.

His parishioners gazed back expectantly. This was one of the high points of the week. Parson John, sober, was a good preacher. He always stirred their hearts, making full use of the paintings on the walls or even the few stained-glass windows St Edmund's possessed. They were now in the autumn season, when everything was dying; perhaps their priest would remember that. He might talk about the horrors of Hell, the perils of Purgatory or, not so interesting, the happiness of Heaven.

Parson Grimstone glanced down at his curate, Robert Bellen, a young, thin-faced man, skin white as milk under a shock of black hair, slack mouth and rather vacant eyes. A good, hard-working curate, yet Grimstone wondered if Bellen was in full possession of his wits: he was a man with a horror of sexual sin. Perhaps that's why he was always tongue-tied in the presence of women. Father Robert, hands on his lap, was staring up at one of the gargoyles, a demon with a hideous face which surmounted one of the squat, rounded pillars which stretched down the church on either side. Father Robert had such an interest in devils and Hell! Parson John's close friend, the former soldier Adam Burghesh, sat in his own special chair to the left of the pulpit. He'd quietly murmured how the young curate must have visited Hell, he knew so much about its horrors.

Burghesh moved in his seat, his long, grizzled face betraying puzzlement at the parish priest's delay in beginning his sermon. Parson Grimstone smiled back and hid his own anxiety. He and Burghesh had grown up in Melford; half-brothers and close friends, they'd gone their separate ways. Burghesh, however, had made his fortune in the King's wars and returned to Melford. He'd bought the old forester's house behind the church. Parson Grimstone had grown to rely on him, even more that he did Curate Robert.

The congregation began to cough and shuffle their feet. Parson Grimstone glanced along the front bench and noticed that Molkyn the miller was absent. His wife, Ursula, was there and the miller's strange, blonde-haired, pale-faced daughter, Margaret. So, where was Molkyn? After all, on a Sunday, the mill was closed, no corn was ground, no flour sacked. Molkyn should be here, especially to hear this sermon.

The parish priest raised his head.

'Death!' he thundered.

The congregation hugged themselves: this would be an exciting sermon.

'Death!' Parson Grimstone continued. 'Is like a bell whose function is to waken Christian people to pray. But lazy folk, after hearing the first chimes, wait for the second: often, they are so heavy with sleep, they do not hear it.'

He glanced quickly at Molkyn's wife.

'Bells have different songs.' He smiled down at Simon the bell-ringer. 'The song of this death bell is: "Remember thy last end and thou shalt never sin." '

Parson Grimstone pulled back the maniple on his left wrist, warming to his theme.

'Death is like a summoner.'

He paused as his congregation nodded and muttered to themselves. They all hated the summoner, that dreadful official of the archdeacon's court, who came-sniffing out sin and scandal. When he found it, be it a married woman playing the naughty with her lover, he issued a summons for the offending parties to appear at the archdeacon's court.

'Ah yes,' Parson Grimstone continued. 'Death is like a summoner and carries a rod, as a sign of his office, more sharp, more cruel than the finest arrow. Death is also like a knight on horseback. He carries a huge shield, cleverly quartered. In its first quarter, a grinning ape, which stands for a man's executors who laugh at him and spend his goods. In the second quarter, a raging lion because death devours all it catches. In the third quarter, a scribe, indicating how all our deeds will be written down and recited before

God's tribunal. And in the fourth quarter . . .'

The door to the church was flung open. Parson Grimstone lowered his hands. The congregation craned their necks. Peterkin, the village fool, a man of little brain and even less wit, came lumbering up the nave. His shaggy, matted hair almost hid his wild eyes, his hose and battered boots were caked in mud.

Parson Grimstone came slowly down from the pulpit. Peterkin was one of God's little ones. He depended on the charity of the parish and slept in barns, or at Old Mother Crauford's, eating and drinking whatever was doled out to him. Parson Grimstone could see he was agitated. In fact, Peterkin had been crying, the tears creating rivulets of dirt down the poor fool's face. The man bared his lips, blinked but the words never came out. The congregation were now agitated at their Sunday morning routine being so abruptly disturbed.

'Hush now!' Parson Grimstone ordered. 'Peterkin, whatever is the matter? This is God's house. We are having Mass. You know that. Are you hungry? Are you thirsty? Or have you had one of your nightmares?'

Peterkin wasn't listening. He was staring to his left and pointed to a painting in the transept. He was shaking and the inner leg of his hose was stained with urine. Parson Grimstone grasped Peterkin's hand.

'What is it?' he demanded. 'Show me!'

Like a child Peterkin led him across into the transept, the peasants and the cottagers making way. Peterkin pointed to a painting on the wall, showing the beheading of John the Baptist. The saint's head was being placed on a platter by a wicked-looking Salome, to be taken to her vengeful mother.

'Have you dreamt of that?' Parson Grimstone asked, curbing his own impatience.

Peterkin shook his head. 'Molkyn!' the grating voice replied.

'Molkyn the miller?'

'Molkyn the miller,' Peterkin repeated like a schoolboy. 'His head is all afloat!'

Those around heard him. Some scrambled to their feet, staring across at Ursula and her daughter, Margaret, who gazed, round-eyed, back. Parson Grimstone took off his chasuble and threw it to his curate. He hitched up his robe under his belt and grasped Peterkin's wrist.

'You must come! You must come!' Peterkin said. 'Father, I do not lie! Molkyn's head swims!'

Leading Peterkin by the hand, Parson Grimstone walked quickly down the nave of the church. The rest of his parishioners, taking their cue, followed close behind. They went down the steps across the graveyard under the lych-gate. Instead of going right, down into Melford, Peterkin turned left towards Molkyn's mill. The morning mist was still thick and cloying, shrouding the countryside. Parson Grimstone was conscious of a gripping sense of fear, a chill which caught the sweat on the nape of his neck. Peterkin's laboured breathing and the clatter of his parishioners behind him shattered the brooding silence. They crossed the wooden bridge over the river Swaile, through the wicket gate which would lead them down to the millpond. The gorse and undergrowth on either side were drenched with rain. Parson Grimstone could see little because of the mist. Peterkin stopped and pointed with his finger.

'Yes, yes.' The parson followed his direction. 'That's Molkyn's mill.' He stared up at the great canvas arms which stretched, like those of a monster, up through the shifting greyness.

'Come!' Peterkin mumbled.

They went up a small hill, then down the other side to the reed-ringed millpond. Again Peterkin pointed. The mist shifted.

Parson John gaped in disbelief. Now he could see it, as the others could behind him. A woman screamed. Molkyn's wife pushed her way forward. Repton the reeve held her fast. Parson John just stared. Peterkin's wits were not wandering. Molkyn's head had been severed clean from his shoulders, placed on a wooden tray and sent drifting across the millpond.

Four nights later, Thorkle, one of Melford's leading farmers, stood inside his threshing barn. He stared down at the sheaves of wheat, the last from that year's harvest. Both doors of the winnowing barn were open. A cold breeze seeped through; Thorkle wanted it so. He wiped the sweat from his brow. He wished this was done.

Darkness was falling, a sure sign of approaching winter. Soon it would be All-Hallows Eve. The inhabitants of Melford would be lighting the fires to keep the souls of the prowling dead at bay. Thorkle repressed a shiver. Melford was becoming a place of the dead. He and the others had known little peace since Lord Roger Chapeleys had been hanged on the great gibbet at the crossroads outside the town. So many dreadful murders! First, the Jesses killer. Those young women, including Goodwoman Walmer, raped and cruelly garrotted. Sir Roger had been blamed and paid with his life: that should have been the end of it.

Now, five years later, another young woman had been killed. And what about Molkyn? His head taken clean off his shoulders and sent floating on that wooden tray? Thorkle and others, at their priest's urging, had climbed the steps and entered the mill where an even more grisly sight awaited: Molkyn's decapitated corpse, sitting in a chair, soaked in his own blood and gore. Yet, like some macabre joke, the killer had placed a half-filled tankard of ale in the dead man's cold, white fingers. What was happening?

Chapeleys should not have died. Thorkle swallowed hard. Molkyn and he knew that. Now what? Sir Maurice, Roger's son, had written to the royal council in London demanding the entire business be investigated.

Thorkle stared at the door at one end of the barn. The darkness was waiting like the mist, ready to creep in. He looked at the two lanterns hanging on their hooks, then down at the corn stalks. The farm was quiet. He wished he had brought his dog but it would be close to the house, hungry for any scraps his wife threw out. He jumped suddenly. Wasn't that a cockcrow? Why should that happen? Or was it his imagination? Didn't the old ones say that if a cock crowed at night, it was a sign of impending violent death?

Thorkle heard a sound deep in the barn. Grasping the flailing stick, a two-piece pole held together by an eelskin hinge, he walked to the door of the barn. Across the long yard, strewn with mud and hay, he glimpsed the candlelight from his house. He heard his wife singing. She had so much to sing about! The cheery, deceitful wife, busy over her butter churn. He walked back into the barn, placed down the flail, scooped up some ears of corn and flung them into the air. The breeze would carry the chaff. The kernel would fall into the leather sheet provided. He'd done it absent-mindedly. It was getting too late to be working.

Thorkle was oppressed by the silence as well as his own fears. Parson Grimstone was right when he whispered so close to Thorkle in the shriving pew and heard his confession. Sin did come back to haunt you. It was so different when he and the rest quaffed ale at the Golden Fleece. They'd feasted in the special rooms provided for the jury before trooping importantly back across the cobbles into the Guildhall. It had been the height of summer: the sun strong and vibrant, the grass growing long and juicy, promising a rich bountiful harvest! Such memories decided Thorkle. He would go across to his house, satisfy his hunger on some bread and meat and go down to the Golden Fleece. He wanted company, life and laughter, a roaring fire, the reassurance of his friends and fellow men.

Thorkle walked to the far end of the barn and pulled across the doors, pushing the bolt back. He stared up at the roof. It was well thatched, no leakages. He would finish all the work tomorrow. He walked back and stopped. One of the lanterns at the other door had been extinguished. Thorkle's throat went dry. A cloaked figure had stepped out of the darkness, a cowled hood over his head. What was he hiding? The flailing stick? Thorkle drew his knife.

'What is it? Who are you?'

'The winnower, separating the wheat from the chaff.'

Thorkle was sure he recognised the muffled voice.

'What is it you want?' Thorkle edged closer.

'Justice!'

'Justice?' Thorkle squeaked.

He stood frozen to the spot. The figure walked quickly forward. Thorkle was confused. He tried to move but the assassin was faster. The flailing stick swept back and its clubbed edge caught Thorkle on the side of the head, sending him spinning to the ground. The pain was intense. Thorkle could already feel the hot blood. He stared up: the flailing rod fell time and time again, shattering Thorkle's head till his brains spilled out.

Elizabeth, the wheelwright's daughter, was frightened of the hobgoblins, sprites and all other hideous dark shapes who dwelled in the shadows but, not today. She dismissed such tales as fanciful, parents' tricks to keep their children away from lonely glades and desolate paths. Elizabeth was in love, or so she thought. She had come into Melford to spend her birthday pennies but, of course, her real reason . . . well, she'd best not think of it. Perhaps Old Mother Crauford was right, the air might catch her dreams and waft them back to her father's workshop or to Mother, busy in the kitchen.

Elizabeth paused at the end of the alleyway and

glanced back. The market was still busy. Adela had tried to question her but that was part of the game, wasn't it? You never told people your secret business. If a hidden admirer made his presence known then why should she share it with the likes of Adela? She'd only go into the Golden Fleece and tell everyone. More importantly, she wouldn't have let Elizabeth go so quickly. She'd demand to know why, how and who. Elizabeth smiled, pushed back her long hair and smoothed down her kirtle. How could she tell someone like Adela? It would only provoke laughter. Elizabeth's smile faded. She wouldn't say how the message was delivered or, more importantly, who was responsible; that would only arouse more curiosity.

Elizabeth turned and ran on. She kept to the shadows. She knew which paths to use so no one would see or accost her. After all, when she returned home, she certainly didn't want to be questioned. Elizabeth had grown up in Melford. She knew its every nook and cranny. She went by the church and glimpsed Master Burghesh busy digging a grave in the cemetery. She ran on. He wouldn't have seen her. He was only interested in Parson Grimstone and that gloomy church. Elizabeth paused to catch her breath. The church spire and the tombstones made her feel slightly uncomfortable, evoking memories of poor Johanna, so barbarously killed near Brackham Mere. Johanna had always been more adventurous: she often went into the countryside, collecting flowers, or so she said. This was different. Two people knew where she was going: the messenger and the sender.

Elizabeth swung her hair and walked more purposefully. She crossed a ditch, slipped through a hedge but paused for a while. She must be early. She had learnt the time from the great capped hour candle in the marketplace so she should wait awhile. She stared up at the sky. To have an admirer, a secret admirer who'd paid to meet her! It was so good to be out under God's sky, away from the busy marketplace and the close, rather oppressive atmosphere of her family, with Mother telling her to do this or that.

Elizabeth stared at the copse which stood on the brow of the gently sloping hill. Did adults know about love? All her father could talk about was Molkyn's head and Thorkle's brains. Elizabeth had never liked either man, Molkyn particularly – and that poor daughter of his, what was her name? Oh yes, Margaret, always so quiet and kept to herself. Ah well ... Elizabeth walked through the grass. She glanced to her right: in the trees far away she thought she had seen a movement. Was someone there? Perhaps a shepherd or his boy? Elizabeth felt a shiver; the weather was certainly turning. She wished she'd brought a shawl or coverlet.

Elizabeth entered the trees. She loved this place. She used to come here as a child and pretend to be a queen or a maiden captured by a dragon. She threaded her way across the cold, wet grass and sat at the edge of the small glade, on the same rock she used to imagine as her throne or the dragon's castle. It was very silent. For the first time since this adventure began, Elizabeth's conscience pricked at deceiving her parents. Her happiness was laced with guilt and a little fear. This place was so lonely – just the distant call of the birds and the faint rustling in the bracken. Elizabeth shut her eyes and squeezed her lips.

I'll only wait here for a short while, she promised herself.

Time passed. Elizabeth rubbed her arms and stamped her feet. She shouldn't have come so publicly, swinging her arms crossing that field. Perhaps her secret admirer had seen someone else and been frightened off? In Melford, gossip and tittle-tattle, not to mention mocking laughter, could do a great deal of harm. She should have come along Falmer Lane and slipped through the hedge at Devil's Oak.

Elizabeth heard a sound behind her, the crack of a twig. She turned, her mouth opened in a scream. A hideous, masked figure stood right behind her: the garrotte string spun round her throat and Elizabeth the wheelwright's daughter had not long to live.

# Chapter 2

Punishment in the King's royal borough of Melford always attracted the crowds, even more so than a branding at the crossroads or a fair on the outskirts. The good townspeople flocked to see justice done, as well as collect scraps of scandal and gossip. Which traders had been selling underweight? Which bakers mixed a little chalk with their flour or sold a load beneath the market measure? Above all, they wanted to discover what house-breakers had been caught, pickpockets arrested.

On that particular October day, the crowds had an even greater reason for flocking in. Word had soon spread, how the murders of Molkyn the miller, Thorkle, not to mention that of poor Elizabeth Wheelwright, whose ravished corpse lay sheeted for burial in the crypt of the parish church, had eventually reached the royal council in London. The King himself had intervened, not by dispatching justices or commissioners of enquiry but officials from his own chamber, a royal clerk, the keeper of the King's Secret Seal, Sir Hugh Corbett and his henchman, Ranulf-atte-Newgate, principal Clerk in the Chancery of the Green Wax. The people of Melford wanted to view

15

this. Oh, they desired an end to the horrid murders. They also wanted to see a King's man arrive, with all his power and authority, to enquire into this or that, to execute the royal Writ, bring malefactors to justice and publish the Crown's justice for all to see.

And, of course, there was the mystery. Who had been responsible for the ghastly murders of Molkyn and Thorkle? Killings took place, even in a town like Melford, but to decapitate the likes of Molkyn and send his burly, fat head across the mere of his mill! Or Thorkle, a prosperous yeoman farmer, having his brains dashed like a shattered egg in his own threshing barn! Surely someone would hang for all that?

And those other heinous murders, the ravishing and slaying of young maidens? They had begun again. One wench had been slaughtered late last summer, her torn body being brought across this very marketplace. Now Elizabeth, the wheelwright's daughter, with her flowing hair and pretty face. She had been well known, with her long-legged walk and merry laugh, to many of the market people. Such gruesome murders should never have occurred! Hadn't the culprit been caught five years earlier and hanged on the soaring gibbet at the crossroads overlooking the sheep meadows of Melford? And what a culprit! No less a person than Sir Roger Chapeleys, a royal knight, a manor lord. The evidence against Chapeleys, not to mention the accounts of witnesses had, despite royal favour, dispatched him to the common gallows. Nevertheless, the murders had begun again and so the King had intervened. What was his clerk called? Ah yes, Sir Hugh Corbett. His name was well known. Hadn't he been busy in the adjoining shire of Norfolk some years ago? Investigating murders along the lonely coastline of the Wash? A formidable man, the people whispered, of keen wit and sharp eye. If Corbett had his way, and he had all the power to achieve it, someone would certainly hang.

The day was cloudy and cold but the crowds thronged around the stalls. Those in the know kept a sharp eye on the broad oak door of the Golden Fleece tavern, where the royal clerk would stay. He would probably arrive in Melford with a trumpeter, a herald carrying the royal banner and a large retinue. Urchins had been paid to keep a lookout on the roads outside the town.

In the meantime, there was trading and bartering to be done. Melford was a prosperous place, and the increasing profits from the farming of wool were making themselves felt at every hearth and home. Silver and gold were becoming plentiful. The markets of Melford imported more and more goods from the great cities of London, Bristol and even abroad! Vellum and parchment, furs and silk, red leather from Cordova in Spain. Testers, blankets and coverlets from the looms of Flanders and Hainault, not to mention statues, candlesticks and precious ornaments from the gold- and silversmiths of London and, even occasionally, the great craftsmen of Northern Italy.

Walter Blidscote, chief bailiff of the town, loved such busy market days. He made a great play of imprisoning the vagrants, the drunkards and lawbreakers in the various stocks on the stand at the centre of the marketplace. This particular day he proclaimed the pickpocket Peddlicott. Blidscote himself had caught the felon trying to rifle a farmer's basket the previous morning. Blidscote was fat, sweat-soaked but very pompous. He drank so much it was a miracle he caught anyone. Peddlicott, however, was dragged across the marketplace as if he was guilty of high treason rather than petty theft. He was displayed on the stand and, with great ceremony, the market horn being blown to attract everyone's attention, Peddlicott's hands and neck were tightly secured in the clamps. Blidscote loudly proclaimed that they would remain so for the next twenty-four hours. If the bailiff had had his way, he would have added insult to injury by tying a bag of stale dog turds around the poor man's neck. Some bystanders cheered him on. Peddlicott shook his head and whined for mercy.

Blidscote was about to tie the bag tight when a woman's voice, strong and clear, called out, 'You have no authority to do that!'

Blidscote turned, the bag still clutched in his greasy fingers. He recognised that voice and narrowed his close-set eyes.

'Ah, it's you, Sorrel.'

He glared at the strong, ruddy-faced, middle-aged woman who had shouldered her way to the front of the crowd. She was dressed in stained brown and green, a sack in one hand, a heavy cudgel in the other.

'You have no right to interfere in the town's justice,' Blidscote said severely. 'Punishments are for me to mete out. And what do you have in that sack?' he added accusingly.

'A lot more than you have in your crotch!' the woman retorted, drawing shouts of laughter from the crowd.

Blidscote dropped the bag and climbed down from the stand.

'What do you have in the sack, woman? Been poaching again, have you?'

Sorrel threw back her cloak and lifted the cudgel warningly.

'Don't touch me, Blidscote,' she whispered hoarsely. 'You have no authority over me. I don't live in this town and I've done no wrong. Touch me and I'll cry assault!'

Blidscote stepped back. He was wary of this woman, the common-law widow of Furrell the poacher.

'Been busy, have you?' he added spitefully. 'Still wandering the woods and fields, looking for your husband? He had more sense than to stay with a harridan like you! He's over the hills and miles away!'

'Don't you talk of my man!' Sorrel snapped. 'My man Furrell is dead! One of these days I'll find his corpse. If you were a good bailiff you'd help me. But you are not, are you, Walter Blidscote? So keep your paws off me!'

Blidscote made a rude gesture with the middle finger of one hand. He went to pick up the bag of turds.

'And leave poor Peddlicott alone,' Sorrel warned. 'The punishment said nothing about such humiliation. Loosen the stocks a little.'

She pointed at Peddlicott's face, now a puce red.

The bailiff was about to ignore her.

'It's true!' someone shouted, now sorry for the pickpocket's pain. 'No mention was made, master bailiff, of dog turds and, if he dies, when a King's clerk is in the town . . .'

Blidscote searched the crowd carefully. He recognised that voice. Master Adam Burghesh, a former soldier, companion to Parson Grimstone, shouldered his way to the front.

'Why, Master Burghesh.' Blidscote became more cringing.

'Mistress Sorrel is right,' Burghesh added. 'There's no need for such humiliation.'

Others began to voice their support. Blidscote kicked the bag of ordure away. He climbed back on the stand and loosened the clamp round Peddlicott's neck and wrists. Burghesh had a few words with Mistress Sorrel; the crowd, their interest now dulled, drifted away.

'Just one moment!' Blidscote called out.

Sorrel turned. Blidscote climbed down and thrust his face close to hers. She flinched at the stale beer on his breath.

'One of these days, Mistress, I'll catch you at your poaching. I'll put you in the stocks and tighten the clamps very hard around that coarse neck of yours.'

'And one day,' Sorrel taunted, 'you may catch moonbeams in a jar and sell them in Melford, Master Blidscote. Why not join me in the countryside?' Her eyes narrowed. 'Perhaps you'll come down to Beauchamp Place. I'll tell you about what I see as I roam the fields, woods and lonely copses. It's wonderful what Furrell and I learnt over the years. Do you like going out to the countryside, Master Blidscote? Chasing young tinker boys?'

Blidscote visibly paled and stepped back.

'I . . . I don't know what you are . . .'

'I do,' she smiled and, not waiting for an answer, pushed a path through the crowd. She shooed away the apprentices who tried to catch her by the cuff, with their shouts of, 'What do you lack, Mistress? What do you lack?'

Sorrel reached the market cross and sat on the high step, the sack between her feet. Most people knew Sorrel and her past. How her man had tried to help the convicted Sir Roger Chapeleys, only to disappear some years ago. Sorrel had become a common sight, roaming the countryside around the town. If anyone ever stopped and questioned her, they received the same reply: 'I'm looking for my poor husband's corpse.'

For some strange reason Sorrel truly believed Furrell had been murdered and his mangled remains buried secretly without a blessing or a prayer. She was a sturdy woman and, despite the disappearance of the occasional rabbit or pheasant, honest in her own way. People, apart from the likes of Blidscote, left her alone.

Sorrel hid her excitement, her heart beating fast, her throat constricted. This was her day of salvation. This was the day she had prayed for before that little battered statue of the Virgin Mary which she kept in her chamber in the ruins of Beauchamp Place. Justice would be done, the King's authority would be felt. This Sir Hugh Corbett would help resolve the mystery and find her husband's corpse. In her wanderings Sorrel encountered tinkers and travelling chapmen, the Moon People, all the travellers of the road. She'd met some who knew about this royal clerk.

'Like a greyhound he is,' one reported. 'Black and lean. He hunts down the King's quarry. He can't be bought or sold.'

Sorrel had longed for this moment. She wanted to catch the eye of the royal clerk, perhaps seek an audience. She glanced towards the entrance of the Golden Fleece. No sign yet. On the corner of a nearby alleyway she glimpsed the shuffling figure of Old Mother Crauford, grasping the arm of Peterkin the simpleton. A strange pair, Sorrel reflected. Old Mother Crauford was as old as the hills and, like any aged one, a true Jeremiah, full of the woes and wickedness of her time. On many occasions Sorrel had tried to draw her into conversation, especially about Furrell. Old Mother Crauford would hint at things, macabre memories, how Melford was always a place of murder, but she wouldn't elaborate any further. Instead she became tight-lipped, sly-eyed and would shuffle away.

Sorrel couldn't blame her for her reticence. The young ones of the town whispered how the old hag was a witch. Is that why she kept Peterkin close to her? For protection? Or just companionship? Sorrel wondered if they were blood kin. She studied the pair carefully. Old Mother Crauford was berating Peterkin, wagging her bony finger in his face. Was she still annoyed at how the simpleton had inter- rupted Sunday Mass? Or was it something else? She noticed the old woman had taken something from Peterkin's hands. The young man's cheeks were bulging. Sorrel smiled. Sweetmeats! Her smile faded.

It jogged a memory. She had seen Peterkin feeding his face on many occasions. Once, out in the countryside, she had come across the simpleton carrying a small box of oranges, a rare fruit which cost a great deal. She'd wondered then, and still did, how Peterkin could afford such a luxury. In fact, he hadn't been so stupid then but sharp-eyed and very defensive. He'd clutched the box and scampered away. How could a witless wonder like him earn silver? True, Melford was growing prosperous and Peterkin was used, especially by the young gallants and swains, to carry messages to their loved ones.

Out of the corner of her eye, Sorrel glimpsed a man sneaking up the steps of the cross, his hand snaking out to grasp her sack. She quickly brought the cudgel down and slapped his fingers. Repton the reeve, his sour face suffused in anger, backed away.

'Don't touch what's not yours!' Sorrel declared.

'I heard about your words with the bailiff,' Repton sneered, nursing his fingertips. 'Stealing again, Sorrel?'

'No, I haven't been stealing. I am an honest woman, Master Repton. I tell the truth, on oath or not!'

The sneer faded from Repton's face. 'What do you mean?'

He glanced quickly to the left and right. The reeve now regretted his action. He had drunk two quarts of ale at the Golden Fleece and knew Adela the serving wench was watching him from a casement window. He had seen the 'poacher's wench', as he called Sorrel, climb the steps to the market cross and loudly boasted he'd find out what she carried in her sack.

Now his fingers burnt and the ale had turned sour at the back of his throat.

'You know what I mean,' Sorrel continued evenly. 'The night Widow Walmer was murdered. My man Furrell told me what he saw.'

Repton made a rude sound with his lips. 'I am not bandying words with you,' he sneered, and he swaggered away.

Sorrel opened the sack, looked inside and grinned. Three fat pheasants: she'd trapped each of them, slit their throats and hung them up for a day. The taverner Matthew Alliot, mine host of the Golden Fleece, would pay good silver for these.

'Here they come!' a man cried.

Sorrel clambered to her feet. Three horsemen had entered the marketplace just as the church bell tolled for the mid-morning Angelus. At first sight they didn't look like royal emissaries: no trumpeter, no herald, just men slouched in the saddle, dark cloaks hitched about their shoulders, cowls pulled over their heads, almost hiding their faces. Sorrel grasped the sack, and pushed and shoved her way through the crowd and past the stalls. By the time she had reached the entrance to the Golden Fleece, the three arrivals had dismounted, and their horses were being led off by an ostler. Like men who had travelled far, they were now loosening their cloaks, stretching to ease the cramp in the small of their backs, thighs and legs. One of them was clearly a groom, smaller than his two companions, dressed in a leather jacket like a soldier; a homely face despite the cast in one eye. The tall, red-haired man with the lithe figure of a street fighter must be Ranulf-atte-Newgate.

Sorrel smiled as she shifted her gaze to Sir Hugh Corbett. Just as tall as his red-haired companion, Corbett was dark-faced, his black hair, streaked with grey, tied at the back. His clothes were of good quality: the jerkin, a white shirt underneath, and hose of dyed blue wool; his high-heeled boots were the best Spanish leather. Corbett carried his cloak over one arm and was busily undoing his sword belt. He was looking up at the Golden Fleece as if memorising every detail before turning to glance across the marketplace. Sorrel liked to compare men to animals or birds. Yes, she thought, you are a greyhound, dark and swift like an arrow, a hunter of souls. Or a falcon? Yes, a bird of prey which soared high, gliding and moving, its eyes always watchful before the killing swoop. Sorrel felt a thrill of pleasure. This man would pursue matters to the bitter end. He was no pompous royal official, dressed in a gaily coloured tabard, proclaiming his every step to the tune of tambour and trumpet. A stealthy man, Sorrel concluded, who would come like a thief in the night and few would know the day or the hour.

Sorrel watched as the arrivals swept into the Golden Fleece, then followed close behind. She was disappointed. She had expected to find the visitors in the taproom but all three had disappeared. Taverner Matthew must have taken them up to their chambers immediately.

Sorrel moved across, past the tables and stools, to a small window seat. A chapman, sitting at a nearby table, was feeding morsels to his pet ferret. Sorrel interrupted this; the ferret, nose twitching, jumped down from the table and sped across to the sack. The man pulled at the string, then yelped as a rat sped out from beneath the wainscoting and scuttled across to the rear door, the ferret in pursuit. For a while chaos and confusion reigned. The tinker jumped to his feet and threatened Sorrel with his fist. She banged the table with her cudgel until he backed off.

'Well, well, well!' Adela, the saucy-eyed tavern wench, came sauntering over, her luxurious hair piled back. Her smock was deliberately too tight for her fulsome figure, the top laces of her bodice carelessly undone. 'Have you come to see the taverner?' She tapped the sack with her sandalled foot. 'He and Blidscote are upstairs with the high and mighty ones.' Adela wiped the sweat from her face with the back of her wrist. 'Come to seek out poachers they have, Sorrel . . .'

'Is that correct, Adela?' came the cool reply. 'Then I'll tell them what I've seen down at Hamden Mere . . .'

Adela's face coloured and she sauntered off, hips swaying.

A short while later the taverner came downstairs, shouting at the potboys to take refreshment to his guests. Sorrel leant back and closed her eyes. The tinker had now regained his ferret and moved to a different table. This corner of the taproom was quiet. Sorrel relished the breeze coming in from the herb garden; the smells from the buttery were especially fragrant. What was the taverner cooking? Roasted capons, fat and succulent, venison, tender and juicy to the bite, and simmering in an onion sauce? She heard a sound and opened her eyes. Taverner Matthew stood over her, a frothing tankard in one hand, a platter of bread and meat in the other. He put these down on the table and allowed two silver coins to slip beneath the platter.

'How many?' he asked.

'Three pheasants,' Sorrel replied. 'And I'll bring two free, next time, if you allow me upstairs to see the royal clerk?'

The taverner sighed and sat down on a stool.

'I would if I could, Sorrel,' he replied kindly, 'but they are tired and busy. They say they have to wash, change and break their fasts. Corbett is already sending out messages: there's to be a meeting up at the church.'

'What will he do, this Hugh Corbett?' Sorrel asked. 'Find the truth, master taverner?'

'I don't know. He doesn't speak much; the red-haired one is his mouthpiece. Corbett's courteous but a man of few words. The first thing he asked me was to describe what happened the night Widow Walmer was killed and what I knew about the other murders.' He blew his lips out. 'What can I tell him? Adela knew young Elizabeth, and the night Widow Walmer's corpse was found, men from the tavern hurried to her cottage.'

'And Molkyn and Thorkle?'

'Now, there's a mystery.' The taverner wiped his hands on his blood-stained apron.

'Both were on the jury, master taverner.'

'Yes, so they were. Others are now frightened. I've even heard whispers that Sir Roger was innocent.'

'Of course he was,' Sorrel retorted. 'My man said he was.'

The taverner tapped her gently on the hand and

shook his head sorrowfully. 'I've heard that song before, Sorrel. I've got business to do.'

He returned to the kitchen and Sorrel greedily drank from the tankard. A potboy came over and, without a word, took the sack. Sorrel drained the tankard and stared across the taproom. Should she try to see the clerk? She shook her head and sighed. No, it would be best if she met him on her own ground. Anyway, she had things to show him, the Moon People to meet. She fought back the tears. Surely he would help her find poor Furrell? Perhaps prove that he'd told the truth and might even have been believed, if the others . . .? Sorrel stared up at the smoke-blackened beam from which flitches of ham and bacon hung to be cured. She would love to show Corbett the bones, the strange things she had seen in her wanderings, such as that eerie Mummer's Man with his grotesque devil's mask and silent horse. But would he believe her? They had laughed at Furrell. And why? Because of the likes of Deverell the carpenter.

Sorrel pocketed the coins and grasped her stick. She noticed the chapman had left his cloak in the corner and recalled his curses. She surreptitiously picked the cloak up, and left by the rear door. She stopped to smell the herbs, relishing the tangy scents of the mint and thyme. She went out through the lych-gate, back into the high street and along to the alleyways which led down to Deverell the carpenter's workshop at the back of his house. The gate was closed so she knocked with her stick.

'Who is it?' a voice called.

So, you are frightened, Sorrel thought, detecting a note of tension.

'I have news, Master Deverell. It's Sorrel!'

'The poacher's woman?' The reply was sharp and harsh.

'Yes, the poacher's woman.'

Sorrel paused. She was sure she'd heard a whisper, as if Deverell was telling someone to keep quiet. She walked around but there was no other entrance. She returned to knock at the high wooden gate.

'Go away!' the voice called. 'I am busy!'

'What are you frightened of, Deverell?' Sorrel taunted.

She went round to the front of the house and stepped into the porchway. She noticed the Judas squint on her right. Deverell must be frightened to be checking on everyone who came here. She pounded on the door but there was no answer so she went back to the gate and knocked again. This time Deverell pulled the bolts back and swung it open. He was a tall, thickset man with a sallow, sharp-boned face, thin-lipped and anxious-eyed. His sparse black hair was covered in dust and he was nursing a cut on his right hand.

'I can treat that for you,' Sorrel offered.

'What do you want?' Deverell sucked at the bloody cut.

'I've seen the royal clerk.'

'And?'

'I thought you would be interested. We can discuss it here in the street or I can shout out what I know.'

Deverell sighed and beckoned her in. He led her across a cobbled yard; stacks of timber lay about.

Sorrel noticed how, near the back fence, the wood had been piled high but then dragged away as if Deverell was anxious lest an intruder climb the fence and use the wood to ease the drop into the yard. He led her into his workshop, a long dark shed containing a work bench, stacks of wood, racks of hammers and chisels. He gestured at a stool but kept looking over his shoulder.

'What's the matter?' Sorrel asked. 'Are you alone?'

'My wife's in the market,' the carpenter replied. 'You call yourself keen and sharp-eyed, Sorrel. You know I have no maid or servant.'

'That's what I want to talk to you about!' Sorrel exclaimed, though that was a lie. She knew little about Deverell's private life but she was intrigued. Deverell was a good carpenter, a master craftsman. Even Furrell had praised his work.

'Why does a wealthy man like you have no apprentice, maid or servant?' she demanded.

'That's the way I like it.'

'Why? What are you hiding?'

'I like my privacy.' Deverell sat on the corner of the table as if he wanted to block her view. 'Now, what's really your business? Why have you come here bothering me?'

'I have seen the clerk, master carpenter! Sharp-eyed he is, with close-set lips. He's going to start asking questions . . .'

'Then I'll give him the same answer I did on oath in court. On the night Widow Walmer was killed, I saw Sir Roger Chapeleys fleeing along Gully Lane. He looked stricken and worried.'

'You have got such sharp eyes at night?'

'It was a clear evening. You can tell from the way a man rides, how he wears his cloak, if there's something wrong.'

'And what were you doing out there that night?' Sorrel taunted.

'I was bringing some wood into my workshop.'

'I thought you had timber delivered?'

Deverell struggled to control his temper. 'I am a carpenter and the King's loyal subject,' he replied. 'If I want to go out to look for a certain type of wood, then that's my business.'

'And that's when you saw Sir Roger? Furrell claimed you couldn't possibly have seen him, stricken, fleeing along Gully Lane.'

'Well, he's not here to contradict me, is he?'

'No, but Furrell gave his testimony in court as well. He claimed to have seen Sir Roger that night, and he looked anything but stricken!'

'Pshaw!' The carpenter waved his hand. 'I thought you had something to tell me.'

'I have. The clerk is going to ask the same questions. Where were you standing? How did you see Sir Roger? What were you really doing that night?' Sorrel leant forward. 'And why should you, who loves to keep a distance between himself and his fellow man, bustle forward so busily to swear away another's life?'

'Sir Roger murdered Widow Walmer.' Deverell stood up. 'He killed those other women. Don't forget, poacher woman, there was more evidence, whilst the jury, not I, found him guilty.'

'Aye,' she replied. 'A jury led by Molkyn and Thorkle, and you know what's happened to them. I

31

have seen the squint hole,' she continued, gesturing with her thumb over her shoulder. 'And the bolted gate.'

Her attention was distracted by Deverell's hands as he pointed towards the door. They were stained, covered in wood dust but she noticed how fine and long the fingers were.

'That's my business. Now, Mistress, you should be gone.'

'Do you sleep well at night?' she taunted. 'Or do you have nightmares about Molkyn's head floating across the mere?'

Deverell grasped her by the arm. 'I think you'd better go.'

Sorrel shook him off. She walked back across the cobbles. The gate was still open and she slipped through. She turned to make some parting remark but Deverell closed the gate behind her, pushing home the bolts.

The carpenter listened to the woman's retreating footsteps, sighed and crossed himself. He went round the yard checking all was well, and felt his hair prickle on the nape of his neck. He really should be more careful. Had his other mysterious visitor gone as silently as he'd arrived?

A low whistle came from the workshop. Deverell walked hurriedly back. He sat on the stool and stared further down the room towards the shadowy recess. His heart beat quicker and he swallowed hard. He should lock everything more securely; he'd been trapped so easily. Was his mysterious visitor still there? His heart jumped as the cowled, hooded figure stepped out of the recess and stood, hands up the sleeves of his voluminous gown. Deverell chewed his lip. He had been busy here, sawing a piece of wood and, when he'd looked up, a man dressed like one of those wandering friars was standing in his workshop, though this one wore a mask as well as hood and cowl. As soon as he spoke, Deverell recognised the voice he'd heard five years ago. Yet, what could he do? How could he protest?

'You heard what was said?' Deverell tried to break the ominous silence. 'That busybody—'

'I'll take care of her,' came the grating reply. 'She's madcap and fey with it. No one believes her.'

'She asked the same questions the clerk will.'

'And you'll give the same answer.'

'How did you get in here?' Deverell made to rise.

'I wouldn't come closer,' the voice replied. 'I just wanted to show you how careful you must be, Master Deverell. I came across your fence. It's not so dangerous or so difficult. Your wife is in the market and you are always by yourself.'

'I did what you asked,' Deverell gasped.

'And you'll do it again,' came the hurried reply. 'You saw Sir Roger that night, hastening along Gully Lane. You took an oath, you gave evidence. What more can you say?'

'But, but Molkyn, Thorkle . . .' Deverell stammered. 'They're dead.'

'Aye, and so they are. Perhaps they didn't keep their word, master carpenter. But, that doesn't bother me. I have come to remind you of the agreement we reached some years ago.'

'I fulfilled my part of the bargain,' Deverell protested.

'And I have mine,' came the hoarse reply. 'I won't bother you again. I just want to remind you of what I know and what I can do. If the clerk comes, and he will, have your story by rote, like a monk knows his psalms.'

Deverell's mouth went dry.

'You have a good trade, Deverell,' the voice teased. 'Your work is admired, and your wife hot and lusty in that great bed of yours? And what do the good burgesses of Melford think of you? A master craftsman! Perhaps one day they will elect you to the council or allow you to carry one of their stupid banners in their processions. It's a small price to pay.'

'I'll do it,' Deverell agreed.

'Good! Come, come, man,' the voice continued. 'Who can recall where you were five years ago on a certain night? That's the attraction of a man like you, Deverell! You keep yourself to yourself, well away from the taproom of the Golden Fleece. You could be on the other side of the moon and no one would know.'

Deverell felt a spurt of anger. 'How do you know about me?' he asked.

'Oh, it's obvious, carpenter: the way you walk, the way you talk. A man who keeps to himself. You have a lot to hide.'

'Who are you?' Deverell snarled.

He would have got to his feet but the self-proclaimed friar took a step back and his hands fell from his sleeves. Deverell glimpsed a long dagger.

'Don't lose your temper,' the visitor warned. 'That would be no use, my brother. Silence is your best protection. Now, I have your word on that? The same story as before?'

'You have my word.'

'Good.' The friar pointed to the gate. 'Go and draw the bolts and I'll be gone.'

The carpenter obeyed. He swung the gate open and returned to the workshop.

'Go into your house, then come and bolt the gate behind me.'

Deverell obeyed. He stepped into a small store-room which adjoined the buttery. He heard his gate creak and went back. The workshop was deserted and so was the yard. He hurried to the gate and stepped into the alleyway but it was busy, thronged with people. Deverell searched but he could see no friar and, thanks be to God, no Sorrel either.

Deverell stepped back into the yard. He bolted the gate and leant against it. His body was coated with sweat. He found his legs wouldn't stop trembling. He slid down to the cobbles, arms across his chest, trying to control his panic. He closed his eyes. All he could see was Sir Roger Chapeleys standing in the execution cart, being taken down from the church, along the rutted track towards the gibbet.

'*O miserere nobis Jesus,*' he whispered.

When he opened his eyes, Deverell noticed the cut on his hand had stopped bleeding. He spread his fingers out like a priest giving a blessing.

'*Pax vobiscum,*' he whispered to the ghosts of his former life thronging about him. 'Peace be with you.'

Deverell got to his feet and, still shaking, returned to his house. He entered the clean, scrubbed kitchen and, grabbing a cup, broached the small barrel of Bordeaux a grateful customer had given him. He filled the cup to its brim and sat at the kitchen table, drinking greedily. He hadn't witnessed Sir Roger's execution but others had described his death throes, how the body had jerked and dangled at the end of the rope. Why? Deverell asked himself. Why was it so necessary for that man to die? He heard a rattle on the front door. He drained the cup, hid it beneath a cloth and went along the passageway. He peered through the squint hole. Ysabeau, his wife, stared bold-eyed back.

'For the love of God and all his angels!' she exclaimed. 'Deverell, this is my house. Open the door!'

He turned the key in the lock and pulled back the bolts. His wife came in. He took her basket from her and put it on the floor.

'What's the matter?' She peered at him. 'You look as if you have seen a ghost!'

'It's the coffin,' he lied. 'The one I made for the young girl, the wheelwright's daughter. It still upsets me.'

'Well, her soul's gone to her Maker,' his wife replied. 'And you've heard the news?' she continued. 'The clerk's arrived!'

'Aye, I know he has,' Deverell almost shouted. 'He'll be asking his bloody questions!'

'Hush, man,' his wife soothed. 'Everyone knows you told the truth.'

'What's he doing?' Deverell asked.

'I've heard from Adela, the clerk has called a meeting up at the church. He apparently wants to question Sir Roger's whelp and the other justice, what's his name?'

'Tressilyian.'

Ysabeau walked down the passageway. Deverell closed his eyes.

'So it's begun,' he whispered. 'God's justice will be done!'

Deverell opened his eyes and stared at the crucifix nailed to the wall. At Sir Roger's execution, he reflected, hadn't the knight vowed, just before he was turned off the ladder, to return from the dead and seek justice?

# Chapter 3

The crypt under the church of St Edmund's, Melford, was cavernous and sombre. Rush lights and oil lamps sent the shadows dancing, turning the atmosphere even more ominous. Sir Hugh Corbett stared at the funeral ledges built at eyelevel around the chamber. Some of the coffins were rotting and decayed, displaying fragments of bone. One entire casket had fallen away and its yellowing skeleton lay on its side, jaw sagging. Corbett thought it was grinning at him like some figure of death, ready to pounce. He waited while Parson Grimstone loosened the lid of the coffin which lay on trestles in the centre of the room. The priest took the lid off and removed the purple cloth beneath. Corbett stared down at the waxen face of the corpse within. Those who had dressed the young woman for burial had done their best. Corbett moved the head with one finger. He stared at the mottled bruises which ringed her throat like some grisly necklace.

'It looks like a garrotte,' he remarked. 'Where was she found?'

'Near Devil's Oak. Her body was tucked away beneath a hedge. Two boys collecting firewood found it and raised the alarm.'

Corbett stared at the priest. Parson Grimstone was undoubtedly nervous – his eyes puffy with lack of sleep, hands trembling. He looked as if he hadn't shaved and his black gown was marked with food stains. The parson placed the lid back on the coffin and walked over to the stone chair built into the wall. He sat down next to his friend Adam Burghesh and put his face in his hands.

'You are very upset.'

Sir Hugh Corbett went to stand over him. The priest looked up and swallowed quickly. He was frightened, not just by the terrible murders which had occurred but by the presence of this royal emissary, with his black hair tied in a queue behind him, the long thoughtful face tense and watchful. Corbett would have been called swarthy except for the peculiar strikingness of his high cheekbones and those brooding dark eyes which never seemed to blink. They stared and searched as if eager to remember every detail. Parson Grimstone didn't like the look of the King's principal clerk of the Secret Seal. Sir Hugh was dressed in a dark grey military cloak fastened at the neck; a brown leather sleeveless jerkin beneath, leggings of the same colour, pushed into black, mud-spattered riding boots on which the spurs still clinked.

Corbett took his gauntlets off and thrust them into his sword belt. Yes, I'm frightened of you, Grimstone thought. Even more so of his companion – what was his name? Ah yes, Ranulf-atte-Newgate: tall, red-haired, dressed like his master. A fighting man despite his status as a clerk in the Chancery of the Green Wax. Burghesh had whispered that he was

Corbett's bullyboy. Grimstone glanced quickly at Ranulf's white, clean-shaven face, those lazy, heavy-lidded green eyes. He reminded Grimstone of a feral cat which stalked the graveyard. A brooding man, Ranulf stood with his back to the door, watching his master, who, in turn, seemed fascinated by this rib-vaulted crypt.

'A strange place to gather.' Burghesh broke the silence. 'Couldn't we have met elsewhere?'

'It's cold,' Robert Bellen complained.

The curate sat hunched in one of the chairs almost obscured by the great central pillar which supported the roof.

'The place reeks of death.' Walter Blidscote, the plump, red-faced, balding bailiff of Melford shook his head so vigorously his jowls quivered: his numerous chins pressed down against the military cloak which swaddled him like a blanket does a baby.

'A good place for justice.' The young, blond-haired Sir Maurice spoke up. He had thrown his cloak on to the ground and sat slightly forward, tapping his gloves against his knee. He shuffled his feet impatiently as if he expected the royal emissary to hold court there, and then declare his dead father innocent.

'Who built it?' Corbett asked. He walked round the circular-shaped crypt, stooping to look into the coffin ledges. 'I have never seen the like of this.'

'There used to be an old Saxon church here,' Grimstone explained. 'It was pulled down in the reign of the second Henry. This used to be a burial place. They built the present church over it. The coffins are those of the previous parsons though the

41

practice of burying them here has now stopped.' He laughed abruptly. 'I will join the rest out in the cemetery.'

'Why did you ask to meet here?' Burghesh demanded. 'You can see Parson Grimstone is not well.'

'For two reasons.' Corbett sat down on a chair. He moved an oil lamp on the ledge behind him and placed his gloves beside it. 'As you know, I am lodged at the Golden Fleece where, I suspect, the walls have ears.' He smiled with his lips though his eyes remained hard. 'Secondly, I wanted to view the corpse. By the way, why is that placed here and not in the church?'

'It's the custom,' Grimstone sighed. 'This is our death house. The poor girl was found last Monday. Her corpse was brought into the church yesterday evening. Tomorrow morning it will be placed before the rood screen. I will sing the Requiem Mass and the burial will take place immediately afterwards.'

'It's certainly a dour place.'

Corbett scratched his head. He licked dry lips. He would have preferred to be back at the Golden Fleece. He, Ranulf and their groom, Chanson, had arrived mid-morning, just as the church bells were tolling the Angelus. Blidscote had been waiting in the taproom. Corbett suspected he had drunk more than was good for him. The clerk had insisted on viewing the corpse as well as questioning certain people more closely. He would have preferred Burghesh to be elsewhere but Parson Grimstone was in a dither. He'd insisted that his friend accompany him from the spacious, well-furnished priest's house behind the church.

'Why has a King's clerk, the keeper of the Secret Seal,' Blidscote now spoke carefully, trying to remove the drunken slur from his words, 'decided to grace this market town?'

'Because the King wants it!' Corbett snapped. 'Melford may be a market town, master bailiff, it's also the haunt of murder – brutal deaths which go back years. What is it today?' He squinted across the chamber. 'The Feast of St Edward the Confessor, October the thirteenth, the year of Our Lord 1303. Five years ago,' he pointed across at Sir Maurice, 'his father, Lord Roger Chapeleys, was hanged on the common scaffold outside Melford for the murder of those maidens and a rather rich young widow. What was her name?'

'Goodwoman Walmer,' Sir Maurice replied.

'Ah yes, Goodwoman Walmer. Sir Maurice was only fourteen years of age but, since he reached his sixteenth year,' Corbett smiled at the young manor lord, 'he has sent letter after letter into the royal chancery, stoutly maintaining his father's innocence, that a terrible miscarriage of justice has taken place. Now the King could do little. Lord Roger was tried by a jury before Louis Tressilyian. Evidence was produced, a verdict of guilty brought. The King could see no grounds for a pardon so sentence was carried out.'

'My father was innocent!' Sir Maurice shouted. 'You know that.' He pointed threateningly at Grimstone.

'How do I know that?' the parson retorted.

'Before he was hanged,' Sir Maurice found it difficult to speak, 'you shrived him. You heard his last confession. Did he confess his sin?'

43

'I cannot tell you what was said under the seal of confession.'

'You can tell us what wasn't said,' Corbett declared.

'You told me!' Sir Maurice shouted.

'It's true. It's true.' Grimstone rubbed his hands together. 'Sir Roger did not confess to any murder.'

'He was held here, wasn't he?' Corbett asked, staring round the crypt.

'Yes,' Grimstone confirmed. 'This sometimes serves as a prison. There is only one entrance, which can be heavily guarded. I did hear Sir Roger's confession but, you must remember, he was held here for two weeks pending his plea for a pardon from the King. He was also visited by an itinerant friar. He may have confessed—'

'Enough,' Corbett declared. 'Let us move to the present, to October 1303. In the summer of this year, a young peasant woman was found murdered. Three days ago,' he gestured at the coffin, 'another victim was slain in the same way by a garrotte, as were Goodwoman Walmer and the other victims five years ago.' He gestured to the bailiff. 'What did the locals call the assassin?'

'The Jesses killer,' Blidscote replied. 'When one of the victims was killed, a local poacher, Furrell, was in the vicinity. He was frightened and hid, said it was pitch-dark. He heard the girl scream followed by the tinkling of bells, like those attached to the claws of a falcon or hawk.'

'And where is this Furrell?' Corbett asked.

'Disappeared,' Blidscote replied. 'No one knows where he went. Some people claim he ran away.

Others that, drunk as usual, he stumbled into one of the mires or swamps. There are enough of those in the woods around Melford.'

'He was probably murdered!' Sir Maurice explained. 'He was the only one who claimed my father was innocent.'

'Now, why should he do that?' Corbett asked.

'I don't know. He disappeared shortly after the trial.'

'Did he speak on your father's behalf in court?'

Sir Maurice flailed his hand. 'Furrell was a vagabond, more drunk than sober. He slept out in the ruins at Beauchamp Place. Who'd give credence to his story? He proclaimed his views in court and the Golden Fleece. He said my father never fled along Gully Lane the night Goodwoman Walmer was murdered.'

'Yes, but your father,' Blidscote spoke up, 'did admit to visiting Goodwoman Walmer that evening. Sir Roger must have passed Gully Lane on his way home.'

'Are you saying my father is guilty?' Sir Maurice sprang to his feet.

'Hush now!' Corbett ordered.

'Well, are you?' Sir Maurice advanced threateningly on the bailiff.

Ranulf-atte-Newgate slipped quietly across the room and put his hand on the young man's shoulder.

'I suggest you sit down,' he smiled. 'If my master says something, it's best if you obey.' He pressed hard. Maurice's fingers went to the hilt of his dagger. 'Don't do that.' Ranulf shook his head. 'I beg you, sir, please!'

Sir Maurice stared into those slightly slanted green eyes and swallowed hard. Corbett he found daunting but this fighting man, smelling of a slight fragrance, mixed with horse sweat and leather, and those green eyes which smiled yet held his unblinkingly . . . Sir Maurice breathed in deeply and retook his seat. Only then did he notice Ranulf pushing the throwing dirk back into the leather sheath beneath his wrist.

Ranulf leant against the door and grinned. Old Master Long Face, he thought, was up to his tricks again. Corbett had gathered them all here for a purpose. Not just to view the corpse or be away from the Golden Fleece. He wanted them to feel free to be at each other's throats. To say things they'd later regret. Old Master Long Face would scoop their words up, write them down and concentrate as if he was playing a game of chess. Corbett ignored Ranulf and stared up at the vaulted ceiling.

'What we have here,' he measured his words, 'are three sets of murders. The young women killed five years ago, this year's victims and, of course, the others. Molkyn the miller, whose head was sent floating across his millpond. Someone struck him a silent, deadly blow. A difficult task, eh? Molkyn, I understand, was a burly oaf: that's how Matthew the taverner, mine host at the Golden Fleece, described him. Strong as an ox with a nasty temper. I would have liked to have seen his corpse but it's beneath the ground now.' Corbett paused to chew the corner of his lip. 'He was killed a fortnight ago. A few days later, Thorkle the farmer was slain.'

'Are you saying all these deaths are linked?' Adam Burghesh asked.

Corbett pulled a face as he studied this veteran of
the King's wars. Burghesh looked sickly, skin the
colour of parchment but the large sea-grey eyes were
steady enough. A soldier's face with a crisscross of
scars on the right cheek, thick bushy eyebrows,
clipped greying hair, moustache and beard. A good
swordsman, Corbett thought, with long arms and
broad chest. He would also have been a good master
bowman, especially with the yew bow the English
troops had brought back from the war in Wales. A
captain of the royal levies, Burghesh had been
warmly spoken of by the King when he and Corbett
had met in the Chamber of the White Wax at Westminster.

'Do you think the deaths are related?' Corbett
asked. 'After all, you were all here when Sir Roger
was executed.'

'Adam has been my mainstay and strength.'

Parson Grimstone spoke up so abruptly Corbett
idly wondered if the priest's wits were wandering.
Had the shock and sudden turmoil broken his mind?
Corbett ignored the interruption.

'Well?' he repeated. 'Are the deaths related? True,
Thorkle and Molkyn weren't maidens. They were not
garrotted.' Corbett ran his thumbnail round his lips.
'They were not ravished. But, both were local men
and served on the jury which convicted Sir Roger.
Isn't this strange: the murders of young women begin
again whilst two of the men who convicted the
supposed killer meet a very grisly fate?'

'Why the King's interest?' Blidscote spoke up.

'I think you've asked that before.'

'But you only half answered.'

'Then listen now.'

Corbett got to his feet. He grasped his gloves and slapped them against his leg.

'Sir Roger Chapeleys may have been a murderer,' he waved the gloves as a sign for Sir Maurice to be silent, 'but he was also one of the King's companions, a good soldier. True, a man who liked his drink and a pretty face but that's not a hanging crime. Otherwise my good friend Ranulf-atte-Newgate would have been hanged a hundred times.' Corbett tapped his fingers on the coffin lid. 'But what happens if Sir Roger was totally innocent? After all, the murderer has returned. Not only to rape and strangle young women but even to carry out dreadful murders on those involved in the unlawful execution of Sir Roger Chapeleys? These are serious crimes, sir: not only gruesome killings but a total mockery of the King's justice. Molkyn the miller and Thorkle were the members, even leaders, of the jury against Sir Roger.'

'As you said,' Blidscote growled, 'they led the jury.'

'But,' Corbett continued, 'why those two? Why not any of the other ten? Or has the assassin only begun? Does he, before long, plan to kill all those involved in Sir Roger's death?'

'In which case,' Sir Maurice Chapeleys scoffed, 'I will follow my father to the scaffold. The finger of accusation has already been pointed at me for carrying out revenge.'

'Yes, that's possible. I'm glad you mentioned it, rather than me.' Corbett retook his seat. 'Can you tell me where you were in the early hours of Sunday morning a fortnight ago? Or the night Thorkle died?'

'I was in church with the rest,' Sir Maurice stammered. 'And, as for the following Wednesday evening,' he swallowed hard, 'I was in my manor house: my retainers will swear to that.' He coloured slightly and shifted uneasily. 'It's cold down here,' he added. 'How long do you intend this to go on?'

'One person is missing.' Ranulf-atte-Newgate swaggered into the pool of light, thumbs stuck in his sword belt. 'Blidscote, you received my master's message. Where is the justice?'

'I asked Sir Louis to be here.' The bailiff shrugged. 'I am not my brother's keeper, certainly not Sir Louis's!'

'Master Blidscote!' Corbett called across. 'For the time being, let us concentrate on the murder of these young women. In the last five years or so there have been six such victims? And that includes Goodwoman Walmer?'

'There's neither rhyme nor reason to it,' the bailiff replied. 'Local women, usually pretty, coming or going to the market or town.'

'Isn't that dangerous?' Ranulf asked. 'The trackways and lanes here are lonely. Copses of woods, dark forests, hiding places for outlaws and wolfs-heads.'

Blidscote stared blearily back.

'That's a good question,' Corbett insisted. 'Why should five young women, not including Walmer, go out by themselves? If I understand correctly from the court record, and the same applies to the two most recent deaths, all five were killed outside the town. Now, if I follow the accepted story, Sir Roger was judged guilty of four of the murders but he can't very well have killed the last two, can he?' Corbett pointed to the coffin. 'Take this poor woman. What's her name?'

'Elizabeth the wheelwright's daughter.'

'And her corpse was found under a hedge?'

'Yes, she disappeared two nights ago.'

'And when was she last seen?'

'I have the father upstairs in the church,' the bailiff replied.

'Then you'd best fetch him!'

Blidscote, breathing heavily through his nose, stamped off. They heard the sound of voices and the bailiff returned, the wheelwright trailing behind him. A burly, fat-faced man, his sallow skin discoloured with warts, he stood in the doorway shuffling his feet, passing the staff he carried from hand to hand.

'Come in, Master Wheelwright!' Corbett invited.

The man wasn't listening. He was staring at the coffin. His shoulders began to shake, tears raining silently down his weather-worn cheeks. He stretched out one great red chapped hand as if he could draw his poor daughter back to life.

'Come in, Master Wheelwright.'

Corbett got to his feet and walked across. He opened his purse and put a silver coin into the man's outstretched hand.

'I know that's little comfort,' he said, 'but I am sorry for your pain. Master Wheelwright, my name is Sir Hugh Corbett. I am the King's clerk—'

'I know who you are.' The man lifted his head and glared balefully at Corbett. 'And I am an earthworm, sir—'

'No, you are not,' Corbett interrupted. 'Master Wheelwright, you are a citizen of this town and the

King's loyal subject. I swear on everything holy,'
Corbett's voice rose, 'I am here to trap the murderer
of your daughter. Then I will personally supervise his
execution.'

'They said that before,' the wheelwright murmured. 'They said there would be no more deaths
after they hanged Sir Roger.'

'Well, they were wrong. But,' Corbett touched the
man's arm, 'if God gives me strength, I shall be right
and your daughter's death will be avenged. Now,
come in!'

He made the wheelwright sit down next to him in
one of the strange carved sedilia. The wheelwright
now became aware of his surroundings and looked
nervously about.

'How many children do you have?'

'Elizabeth and two boys; she was the eldest.'

'And the day she died?'

Corbett waited patiently. The wheelwright's
shoulders hunched and he began to sob again. At
last he coughed and wiped his eyes on the back of
his hand.

'I have a house and yard on the edge of Melford.
Elizabeth was a pretty young thing. It was market
day. She wanted to go into town to buy something. It
was her birthday last Michaelmas. She had two
pennies. You know the way it is with young women?
A ribbon, some gewgaw or perhaps to meet a local
swain?'

'Did she have one?' Corbett asked.

'No.' The wheelwright smiled. 'She was fifteen,
but flighty in her fancy. She went to market.'

'And?'

'I made enquiries. She met the other young men and women on the edge of the square where the maypole is set up. Her good friend, Adela, who works as a slattern in the Golden Fleece, saw her last. She said Elizabeth was, well, rosy-cheeked with excitement. "Where are you off to?" Adela asked. "I must hurry home," Elizabeth replied. This was between four and five o'clock. She wasn't seen afterwards.'

'And did Adela know where Elizabeth was going?'

'She crossed the square in the direction of a lane out of Melford.'

'Did this Adela say Elizabeth was rosy-cheeked, happy, as if she had some secret assignation?'

The wheelwright looked puzzled.

'A lovers' meeting,' Corbett explained. 'Was she a secretive girl?'

The wheelwright closed his eyes. 'No. She had her airs and graces. She wanted to make a good marriage. "I don't want to be a farmer's wife," she would often say, "but marry a man with a skill or trade." '

'And the days before her death? Did she change?'

'At first, when Blidscote asked me,' the wheelwright flicked his fingers contemptuously at the bailiff, 'I said no but, now, yes there was something.' He paused. 'I wouldn't say sly but as if she had a secret, something she treasured. There again, she was always falling in and out of love.' The wheelwright fought to keep his voice steady. 'I never thought it would come to this.'

'Master Blidscote,' Corbett turned to the bailiff, 'when the young woman's corpse was found, you went out?'

'I took the cart. I put the corpse in, brought it back

and sent one of my men for the wheelwright.'

'And the corpse?' Corbett insisted. He patted the wheelwright gently on the shoulder as the man began to sob. 'There was no sign of the killer, or the garrotte he used?'

Blidscote shook his head.

'And did you see anything untoward around the corpse?'

Corbett hid his anger: Blidscote's bleary glance told him he hadn't even looked.

'Where is this spot?' Corbett demanded testily.

'At Devil's Oak. It's a big, ancient tree on Falmer Lane.'

'But that doesn't lead to her father's house?'

'No, it doesn't.'

'So, Elizabeth was found in a place she shouldn't have been. Out in the countryside?'

'Yes, yes, that's right.'

'In which case,' Corbett concluded, 'either she went out to meet somebody or was taken there, either before she was killed or after. Correct?'

Blidscote burped and nodded.

'And the corpse itself?' the clerk continued.

'The young woman's kirtle and smock were pushed well above her stomach,' the bailiff mumbled. 'I think she was killed very near where her corpse was found.'

'And the other murder?' Corbett asked.

'Down near Brackham Mere.'

'And her killing?'

'The same.'

Blidscote was now wiping his sweaty palms on his thick, stained hose. He felt distinctly uncomfortable sitting in a cold crypt before this royal clerk with his remorseless list of questions. All he found were corpses: he'd brought them back but now he realised he had made mistakes: he should have been more careful.

'And that victim?' Ranulf asked.

'Her name was Johanna,' Blidscote declared. 'She was the same age as Elizabeth. They were friends. She was on an errand for her mother to buy something in the market. People saw her, talked to her, then she disappeared until her corpse was found near Brackham Mere.'

Corbett patted the wheelwright on the shoulder and slipped another coin into his hand.

'Go back into the church,' he urged. 'Light a candle for yourself and Elizabeth in the Lady Chapel. When you wish, you may go.'

The wheelwright shuffled out. Corbett stared down at his hands. He waited until the door at the top of the steps closed.

'Parson Grimstone, these two young women – they were decent girls?'

'Yes, of good families. Oh, they flirted and they laughed, but they came to church. Minds full of dreams, of falling in love with some handsome knight. Ever ready to dance and celebrate, whisper secrets to each other. Even,' the parson smiled to himself, 'when they should have been listening to me.'

Corbett got to his feet and stretched. 'Both of these last victims,' he declared, 'were found in places they did not usually go. I suspect they knew their killer. But what would lure a woman out to some desolate spot?'

'Money,' Ranulf replied.

'Are you saying they were strumpets?' Burghesh asked sharply.

'No, sir, they were like you and I, greedy! Acquisitive! They were good country lasses, red-cheeked wenches.' Ranulf tapped his fingers on the hilt of his dagger.

'But they were poor. You heard the wheelwright. To buy a ribbon or a gewgaw . . .'

'And they were prepared to sell their favours.' The curate's thin, pallid face flushed, red spots of anger appeared high on his cheeks.

'I don't mean to insult their memory,' Ranulf retorted, 'but they were country girls. Such as they share the same bedchamber as their parents and their brothers. They know what pleasure the love act gives. It doesn't mean they are strumpets. God forgive us all. It only means they could be easily gulled or tricked.'

'I don't believe this!' The curate sprang to his feet.

'Don't you?' Ranulf snapped. 'You're a priest, aren't you? You should know your own people.'

'Sit down! Sit down!' Grimstone got up, tugging at his curate's robe. 'Our *guest*,' Grimstone emphasised the word sardonically, 'speaks the truth.'

'Just what are you saying, Ranulf?' Corbett asked.

'Here we have two young women, Master. They come from poor families; their little noddles are stuffed with dreams and fancies. They go round the market buying bread and cheese, the necessities of life. Then they pass some chapman's tray or pedlar's stall, with blue and red ribbons, perhaps a brooch, a ring, a bracelet? To us they are trifles, but to them, more precious than the King's jewels. Perhaps the killer lured the bait? A free gift? Buy this, buy that. In return for a kiss? The token is given. The young woman, of course, is sworn to secrecy and so the second trap is laid. Only this time in some lonely, desolate place. The young woman thinks why not? She has never earned such money so easily and so lightly, so off she goes to meet her death.'

Corbett stared at his manservant. 'But where is this money?'

'If our master bailiff,' Ranulf went over and squeezed Blidscote's shoulders, 'went to the houses of both victims and searched from floor to ceiling, I wager a silver coin to a silver coin, that the girls' hiding places would be found as well as the money they were given or what they bought with it.'

'Do that, Blidscote,' Corbett ordered. 'If Master Ranulf is telling the truth, you will find me in the Golden Fleece. And where are you going, sir?' Sir Maurice Chapeleys had got to his feet.

'I have answered your questions, sir,' the young knight replied. 'My father's grave.' He swallowed hard. 'I wasn't given leave to take his body back to our manor but, Parson Grimstone was gracious enough . . .'

Corbett didn't know whether the young knight was being sardonic or not.

'You wish to visit your father's grave?'

Sir Maurice nodded. 'This has provoked memories. If you have further questions, our good parson knows where I am.'

Corbett let him go. He briefly recapped on the meeting's progress and was about to adjourn when the door at the top of the crypt opened and shut with a crash, followed by the sound of running footsteps.

'In God's name!'

Ranulf stepped hurriedly aside as a tall, white-haired knight, swathed in a dark blue cloak, flung himself into the crypt. His face was cut and bleeding, clothes mud-stained.

'I have been attacked!'

'Sir Louis!' Parson Grimstone sprang to his feet.

The newcomer took off his remaining glove and threw it on the ground.

'I was attacked!' he repeated.

'Outlaws?' Corbett asked.

'I don't know.' Tressilyian sat down on a chair, mopping his face with the hem of his gown. 'Thank God Chapeleys isn't here.'

'Why's that?' Corbett asked.

'I'd swear it was his father's ghost!'

# Chapter 4

The justice took some time to calm down. Parson Grimstone went up to his house and brought back a jug of ale as well as a bowl and cloth. Tressilyian quaffed the ale in a few gulps, then wiped his face. He had a cut high on his cheek, small scars on the backs of his hands.

'What happened?' Corbett asked.

'I was coming down Falmer Lane,' the justice replied. He paused. 'You must be Corbett?'

There was more confusion as Corbett made the introductions.

Tressilyian studied him from head to toe. 'I suppose you've already been asked,' he smiled, 'why you are here? The King could have asked me to investigate.'

'Aye, sir, but you were the principal justice who tried Sir Roger. Today's events prove that this is a matter for royal concern. After all, you, the King's justice, were attacked on his highway. You were telling us what happened.'

'I was riding down Falmer Lane,' Tressilyian explained. 'There was a fallen tree across the lane, just a sapling. You know how such things frighten

59

horses? Bare branches, dry leaves? I thought nothing of it. I climbed down, took off my gauntlets to grasp it, that's where some of these cuts came from. Suddenly an arrow came flying through the air.' Sir Louis tapped the cut high on his cheek. 'It missed, just skimming my face. I sheltered in the sapling; its twigs and branches cut me. I had no bow. My horse had become frightened and was skittering away. Two more arrows were loosed. I decided that I wasn't going to wait. I gauged where the mysterious bowman must be, drew my sword and charged as if I was on the battlefield.'

'But your assailant escaped?'

'I never even saw him, just a crackle of bracken and then the voice.' Tressilyian paused, staring across at the coffin. 'God's teeth, Corbett, this is a sombre place.' He flung his hand out. 'And that poor woman!'

'What did your voice say?' Corbett insisted.

' "Remember." That's what it said. A man's voice. "Remember, royal justice, how you hanged an innocent man! You and the others will pay for it." ' Tressilyian shrugged. 'Then there was silence. There was nothing more I could do. I returned to my horse and rode here. I saw young Chapeleys going across God's acre. He's visiting his father's grave?'

'Yes,' Grimstone replied.

'Why did you think it was a ghost?' Corbett asked.

Tressilyian looked at him blankly.

'When you came in here,' Corbett insisted, 'you said you thought you'd been attacked by a ghost.'

'Well, it's obvious,' Tressilyian retorted, his light blue eyes dark with anger. 'A young woman lies dead, another has been murdered. Members of the jury who found Sir Roger guilty have also paid with their lives.'

'Yes, but Sir Roger was hanged?' Ranulf asked. 'You were present at the execution?'

'Yes I was. However, after I had passed sentence, before the cart was taken away,' Tressilyian wiped the sweat from his broad brow and sunken cheeks, 'Sir Roger protested his innocence. He claimed his name would be vindicated. He would make a settlement with God and return to settle with us.'

Sir Louis's eerie words in such sombre surroundings created a tense silence. Grimstone and Burghesh looked at each other. Bailiff Blidscote opened and closed his mouth, smacking his lips as if wishing he could drink, forget what was happening.

Corbett glanced around. Including the justice, these were all nervous men. Sir Roger Chapeleys had been a manor lord, a knight, a warrior, a man who had done good service in the King's armies both at home and abroad. True, a lecher and a drinker but what if he had been wrongly executed?

'Sir Hugh!'

Corbett sprang to his feet at the voice calling from the top of the stairs.

'Master clerk!'

Corbett hurried to the door. Chapeleys, wide-eyed, was halfway down the steps.

'Sir Hugh, you had best come and see this.'

Corbett and Ranulf, followed by the rest, left the crypt and went up into the church, through the coffin door and out across the cemetery. Daylight was fading. The sky was sullen and overcast. The first tendrils of the evening mist were curling about the gnarled yew trees, creating a shifting haze around the crosses and tombs. The silence was shattered by the raucous cawing of rooks in the bare-branched trees. If the crypt was a dismal place, the cemetery was no better. Corbett hid his annoyance at being thus summoned, pulling his cloak more firmly about him. Chapeleys led them along a beaten trackway, down into a small dell in the far corner of the graveyard.

'We call this "Strange Hollow",' Grimstone explained breathlessly, coming up beside Corbett. 'It's where we bury the bodies,' he lowered his voice, 'of executed felons.'

Chapeleys was striding ahead. He stopped at a burial mound. Corbett followed and stared at the weathered lettering on a stone plinth. It gave Sir Roger Chapeleys' name, the dates of his birth and death, with the invocation '*Jesu Miserere*' carved beneath.

'What's wrong?' Corbett asked, quickly crossing himself as a mark of respect.

Chapeleys, standing on the other side, beckoned him round. Corbett quickly looked. Someone had scrawled the word 'REMEMBER'. He touched the still-wet liquid, rubbing it between his fingers.

'It's blood,' he declared. 'And done quite recently.'

'Whose blood?' Grimstone asked.

'I don't know.' Corbett bent down and wiped his fingers on the wet grass.

'I'll have it cleaned up. Perhaps it's some game.'

'It's no game,' Chapeleys retorted. He then went across and clasped the justice's hand, as if they were close acquaintants, the best of friends.

Corbett was intrigued and Tressilyian caught his look of puzzlement.

'There's no bad blood between us, clerk. Sir Maurice knows I simply carried out my duty.' He spread his hands. 'Over the years I have done my best for the lad.' His harsh, severe face broke into a grin. 'Now he repays me by falling in love with my daughter.'

Corbett nodded and stared across the cemetery. He noticed the building work, sections of cut stone, a mound of masonry peeping out from beneath a leather awning.

'What's that?' he asked.

'Oh, it's my work,' Burghesh replied. 'Sir Hugh, I may be a soldier but, in the wild and wanton days of my youth, I became apprenticed to a stonemason. Indeed, I signed my articles as a craftsman. Then the King's wars came.' He shrugged. 'Fighting and drinking seemed more glorious than cutting stone. I do a lot of work round here. I am building a new graveyard cross for Parson Grimstone.'

'It's quite a busy place.' The parson spoke up. 'Perhaps not on a cold October day but we have small markets and fairs as well as our ale-tasting ceremonies. It's a place where the parish like to meet.'

Corbett agreed absent-mindedly. He stared up at the soaring hill tower, its red slate roof and pebble-dashed sides.

'A well-kept church, Parson Grimstone,' he remarked.

'Aye, and my father loved it,' Sir Maurice said. 'It's a pity, Parson Grimstone.' The young knight bit his lip.

'What's a pity?' Corbett asked.

'My father had a triptych specially done and placed in a side chapel.'

'And why is that a pity?'

Parson Grimstone sighed noisily. 'The triptych was kept on a wall. After Sir Roger was executed, someone took it down and burnt it, here in the graveyard.' The parson pushed his hands up his sleeves. 'I'm freezing cold, Sir Hugh. Are you finished here?'

'For the moment,' the clerk murmured. 'The lych-gate is on the far side, yes?'

And, not waiting for an answer, Corbett, lost in his own thoughts, walked away. He stopped and turned.

'I thank you for coming. Sir Louis, I am sorry about the attack. You said it was in Falmer Lane, the same place where poor Elizabeth was found? I wonder if we could ride back there?'

'I'll also come,' Sir Maurice offered.

Corbett and Ranulf said goodbye to the rest and walked back to the lych-gate where Sir Hugh's groom, Chanson, shrouded in his cloak, held their horses. The groom's white face was a picture of misery, the sly cast in his eye even more pronounced.

'Sir Hugh, I am freezing.'

'You should have sung,' Ranulf teased. 'That would have brought everybody hurrying back.' He patted the young groom on the shoulder. 'The King's business.' He added mockingly, 'We are all freezing, Chanson.'

'I have given the horses a good rub down,' Chanson muttered.

Corbett half listened. Chanson hated waiting almost as much as Corbett hated his singing. Chanson wasn't his real name. He'd joined Corbett's

service as Baldock. Ranulf, as a joke, had rechris-
tened him 'Chanson', a mockery of his appalling
voice. Ever since, the groom had insisted that
Chanson would be his new name and refused to
answer to anything else. A fine groom with a talent
for talking to horses, Chanson was also a good
knife-thrower, a skill he used to win prizes at local
fairs.

'Can we go back to the tavern, Master? My toes are
frozen; my balls are freezing!'

Corbett gathered the reins and swung himself into
the saddle. He watched whilst Tressilyian, his hand
on Sir Maurice's shoulder, walked further down the
lane to collect their horses.

'Ranulf,' he ordered, 'take Chanson and warm him
up in some alehouse.'

'And then go snooping, Master?'

Corbett pulled the cowl over his head and narrowed his eyes.

'Yes, I want you to snoop. Find out as much as you
can.'

He lifted his head and watched the others leave the
church, Blidscote, the fat bailiff; the two priests and
Burghesh.

'What are you thinking, Master?'

'I don't know, Ranulf. The pot's beginning to bubble. Perhaps this is a beautiful place on a summer's
day but now . . .?'

A sound behind him made him turn. An old
woman was coming up the lane, resting heavily on
a stick. She approached, back bowed, head down.
Corbett thought she was about to pass them but she
stopped and stared up, pushing away wisps of dirty

grey hair from her wizened face. She munched on her gums and wiped the trickle of saliva from the corner of her mouth. She looked at Corbett with rheumy eyes, as if she could learn from one glance who he was and why he was here.

'Good morrow, Mother.'

Ranulf walked towards her. He opened his purse and took out a coin. The woman snatched it.

'Are you the King's clerk?'

Her voice was strong but rasped on the phlegm at the back of her throat. She turned and spat, hobbled forward and grasped Corbett's bridle.

'You must be the King's clerk?'

'And you, Mother?'

'Old Mother Crauford, they call me. How old am I?'

'Not much older than twenty-four,' Ranulf teased.

The old woman's head turned as quick as a bird's.

'Now, there's a pretty bullyboy. I've seen you all come and go.' She pointed a bony finger. 'How old am I?'

'Seventy?' Corbett asked quickly.

'I'm past my eighty-fifth summer.'

Corbett stared down in disbelief. 'You keep your years well, Mother.'

'Go and read the baptism accounts.' Mother Crauford pointed to the church. 'Born in the autumn of 1218. I remember the King's father coming here. Small and fat he was, hair as gold as wheat.'

Corbett stared in disbelief at this old woman who had seen the King's father in his youth.

'And so you've come to hunt the ghosts, have you?'

she continued. 'Melford is full of ghosts. It's always been a wicked place.'

'So you think warmly of this town?' Ranulf taunted.

'I think warmly of no one, Red Hair! It's true what the preacher says. Men are steeped in wickedness.'

'You mean the killings?' Corbett asked.

'Murders more like it.' The old woman let go of the reins of his horse. 'There have always been murders in Melford. It's a place of blood. No wonder! They say a town was here before even the priests arrived; little difference they've made. Anyway, I wish you well.'

She hobbled on. Corbett watched her go. He'd seen the same in many a town or village. The old, shaking their heads over the doings of their younger, stronger ones.

Tressilyian and Sir Maurice rode up.

'I see you've met Old Mother Crauford,' Sir Maurice smiled. 'The townspeople call her Jeremiah. They heard a sermon given by the parson, how the prophet Jeremiah would always be lamenting the sins of the people. Ever since then she's been called Jeremiah. She hasn't a pleasant word for anybody or anything.'

Corbett watched the old woman retreat into the mist. When I really start snooping, he thought, I'll visit her. It's always the old who know the gossip.

'Sir Hugh?'

'I am sorry,' Corbett apologised. 'Ranulf, Chanson, we'll meet at the Golden Fleece and thaw the cold from our bones.'

He turned his horse and followed Tressilyian and Chapeleys down the lane and on to the high road. The day was now drawing to a close. The market stalls on either side of the thoroughfare were being taken down. Corbett gazed about. Despite Old Mother Crauford's lamentations, Melford appeared to be a prosperous place: well-built houses of stone and timber, freshly washed plaster, windows full of glass. The townspeople were no different from any others in these thriving market centres. They reached the end of the high road and entered the town square, fronted by shops, merchant houses with their high timbered eaves and sloping slate roofs. The square even boasted a grandiose guildhall with steps up to a columned entrance as well as a covered wool market where the merchants sold their produce.

'Why isn't the church here?' Corbett asked.

'Melford's grown,' Sir Maurice called back over his shoulder. 'It began round the old church but all things change.'

Aye they do, Corbett thought, eyeing the two manor lords. Both Chapeleys and Tressilyian were well dressed, in robes of pure wool, edged with squirrel fur, Spanish riding boots, gilt spurs, whilst the saddles and harnesses of their horses were of the best stitched leather, gleaming and polished. Corbett noticed the rings on the men's fingers and the velvet-tipped sword scabbards. Both knights had taken these off and slipped them over the saddle horns. Corbett had heard the King talk of the growing wealth of these country knights, turning their fields of corn and barley into pasture for sheep, whose wool was in sharp demand by the looms of the Low Countries. Melford boasted such wealth. The marketplace was properly cobbled, with a pavement at one end. The stocks and pillories were full of malefactors:

vagrants, drunken youths who spent the days in the taverns and whose raucous voices had threatened the day's trading. Market beadles swaggered amongst the stalls. They carried scales and specially carved knives so as to weigh and test different produce. Outside one tavern the ale-conners, or ale-tasters, had broached a barrel and were busy sampling its contents to see if the taverner was selling lighter ale at the highest prices.

'There's your hostelry!' Sir Maurice called out, gesturing across to the Golden Fleece which stood on the corner of an alleyway. A three-storeyed building, black-timbered, its plaster washed a light pink, the tavern had windows of mullioned glass that gleamed in the light of the lanterns slung on hooks along the beam spanning the ground floor. 'Taverner Alliot serves you well?'

'He keeps a fine house,' Corbett replied. 'Matthew Alliot lives high on the hog.'

'Aye, he does that,' Chapeleys replied sourly.

'He was a witness at your father's trial, wasn't he?'

Corbett edged his horse forward. They were now on the edge of the square. Chapeleys reined in, still staring back at the tavern. Corbett noticed how the noise and bustle of the market, the cries of traders had faded as they entered the square. Oh, there was the usual bustle and shouting, the cries of chapmen, 'What do you lack? What do you lack?' Dogs and children darted in and out. Apprentices, still sharp-eyed for customers, swaggered about but Corbett felt as if many of them were watching. Was it the presence of a King's clerk and a royal judge?

'Sir Hugh?' Tressilyian leant over and gently

touched Corbett on the shoulder. 'I can read your thoughts, master clerk, and, perhaps answer them. The townspeople realise you are here because of the murders. It's trade as usual but people are worried.'

'And can you read Sir Maurice's mind?' Corbett replied. 'It's true, isn't it? Taverner Alliot was a witness against your father?'

'Yes, yes, he was.' Chapeleys broke free from his reverie. 'On the night Goodwoman Walmer was murdered, my father went to the Golden Fleece to slake his thirst. According to Alliot, my father said he was going to the goodwoman's cottage.'

'But that's not a lie, is it?' Corbett asked.

He swore as a dog came yapping at his horse's hoofs.

'No, it's not.' Sir Maurice gathered the reins in his hand. 'Oh, never mind. Let's go on, the light is fading.'

They went down a narrow lane, out along the back streets, past the garden plots, piggeries and outside stables of the cottagers' houses. They turned right up a cobbled track and reached the crossroads, a slight rise providing a good view of the surrounding country-side. A little of this was plough land but most of it meadows, dotted with sheep. Small copses and lines of hedgerow broke the greenery. To Corbett's left, the beginning of a great forest which stretched north. He shaded his eyes and caught a glimpse of the river Swaile.

'Prosperous land,' he murmured. 'Well cleared and watered. It makes me homesick.'

He wondered what Maeve was doing at their Manor of Leighton. Would she be in the kitchen

doing business with the steward and bailiffs, checking their accounts, planning what they were doing
tomorrow? Eleanor would be tottering around whilst
Uncle Morgan would be leaning over the crib-cradle
tickling Baby Edward. Or, if Maeve wasn't looking,
trying to pick him up and play with him once again.

'I hate this place!'

Corbett started. Sir Maurice had moved ahead and
was staring up at the great gallows post, its three
stark branches black against the evening sky. Corbett
had studied a map of Melford. Of course, this was the
spot where Sir Roger had been executed. The scaffold
was immense, its main post sunk deep into the earth
and strengthened by mortar. Sir Louis was also staring up, as if fascinated by the sharp hooks at the edge
of each outstretched beam. Sir Maurice crossed himself and sat for a while, head bowed. The cold breeze
caught their cloaks, tugging at their hoods.

'It was here?' Corbett asked. 'Were you present?'

'No, he wasn't,' Tressilyian whispered back. 'He
was only a lad. His servants kept him at the manor,
Thockton Hall.'

Corbett was about to continue his questioning
when Sir Maurice cursed and jumped down from his
horse. He walked over to the scaffold. Corbett
glimpsed a piece of parchment fluttering on a nail
just above the base of the beam. Sir Maurice snatched
this off and brought it back.

'It's the same as on the gravestone,' he murmured,
handing it to Corbett.

The parchment was a greasy piece of old vellum: in
the fading light Corbett made out the red scrawl:
'REMEMBER!'

'Someone has been busy. Sir Maurice, may I keep this?'

His companion nodded. Corbett folded the scrap of paper and slipped it into his wallet. The clerk stared around. The crossroads and the surrounding fields were not so pleasant now. The breeze was cold, the sky more grey and threatening, the misty haze like a shifting gauze veil. A feeling of dread, of quiet menace pervaded. The lives of many in Melford had been blighted. The secrets they nursed, hidden sins, could surface and manifest themselves in brutal and bloody death, especially on an evening such as this.

At Tressilyian's insistence they rode on, Chapeleys slightly ahead of the others. Corbett considered drawing Tressilyian into conversation about the trial but decided that this was not the time nor place. The justice himself seemed to be in a dark mood, keeping his head down, chin tucked into his cloak, cowl pulled across his face. Corbett realised that Tressilyian must also be alarmed, seriously concerned that he had condemned and supervised the execution of an innocent man. The silence grew oppressive. Corbett could understand why Ranulf, a creature of the alleyways and streets of London, felt fearful in the countryside, especially in this quiet time before dusk as if the creatures of the night were waiting for darkness to fall. The path they had taken was nothing more than a broad, rutted trackway, ditches on either side and high, prickly hedgerows. Every so often this line would be broken by a gate or stile.

Corbett reined in, forcing the other two to stop. 'I am a stranger,' he reminded them. 'I am trying to get my bearings. This is Falmer Lane?'

'Yes.'

'And the village of Melford lies – ' Corbett gestured with his hand – 'to the south? The church stands at one end. We have streets and thoroughfares, the marketplace in the centre, then it curves slightly out into the countryside?'

'You are not such a stranger,' Tressilyian replied. 'But yes, that's a good way of describing the town.'

'So, there are many trackways and thoroughfares out?'

'Yes, I told you. Melford has grown as prosperous, and as rambling, as the fleece on a sheep's back.'

'And Molkyn's mill is at the church end of the town?'

'That's right. There's the mill, Thorkle's farm is nearby. In fact, it's almost a small hamlet. There's the mere, the millpond.'

'And Goodwoman Walmer's cottage?'

'About a mile from the mill.'

'And lanes and trackways aplenty?' Corbett asked.

'Oh, Sweet Lord, yes,' Tressilyian laughed. 'If you read the report of the trial, one witness actually described Melford as a rabbit warren. There are lanes and trackways out. You've seen the gates and stiles. Footpaths crisscross the meadows. God knows,' he sighed, 'as a justice I am always having to rule on what is trespass and what is not. You see, Corbett, the land round here has changed. Sheep, not corn, is the measure of a man's wealth. So woods are cleared, hedgerows planted, fences and gates put up.'

'If I catch your drift,' Sir Maurice said, 'an ideal place for murder, yes, Sir Hugh?'

'Any place is ideal for murder,' Corbett replied. 'Ranulf dislikes the countryside. He claims it's more dangerous than the alleyways of London. For once I agree with him. Once darkness falls, a man who knew his way around here could slip along the lanes and gullys and do what he wished. He'd be as well protected as he would in the dingy slums around Whitefriars or the maze of Southwark alleyways.'

'I have seen both those places,' Tressilyian replied. 'I prefer Melford.'

They continued along the lane. The fields gave way to a copse of woods on either side. Corbett felt as if he was going down a hollow, darkened passageway. The lane rose, dipped, then rose again. Corbett identified Devil's Oak before Tressilyian pointed it out: a great, squat tree once used as a boundary mark. The huge oak had been struck by lightning but its branches, now stripped of their leaves, still stretched up to the evening sky. Corbett dismounted. He looked across the fields to his left: a water meadow which ran down to the banks of the Swaile. Corbett glimpsed the tumbled ruins just near its bank.

'What's that?' he asked.

'Beauchamp Place,' Chapeleys explained. 'It was once a small manor house: piggeries, dovecotes, stables, but the man who built it was a fool. The land is waterlogged. After heavy rains it tends to flood. It's been a ruin for about thirty years now. The last relic of the Beauchamps was a madcap old man, found drowned in one of the cellars. The townspeople still say it's haunted.' He pointed to the oak. 'They say the same about this and poor Elizabeth's ghost.'

Corbett stepped across the ditch. There was a gap in the hedgerow on either side of the oak. Corbett slipped through one of these.

'Elizabeth's corpse was found here?'

'Yes,' Chapeleys replied. 'That's what Blidscote said, to the right of the great oak tree, on the field side of the hedgerow.'

Corbett squatted down. The grass was cold, catching at the sweaty skin on his wrist. He brushed this aside and looked along the hard, gnarled branches of the hedge but could see nothing amiss. Feeling with his gloved hand, he searched the area carefully, digging with his fingers.

'What are you looking for?' Tressilyian asked.

Corbett got to his feet. Tressilyian was leaning against the oak tree, Chapeleys on the far side of the ditch. Corbett repressed the feeling of unease at the atmosphere of danger. He did not like Devil's Oak. Here he was with two strangers in a place of brutal murder. He half wished Ranulf was with him.

'Why is it,' Corbett murmured, 'such places have a feeling of desolation? Is it the imaginings of our own souls, a lack of wit? Or does a spot like this still reek of the terrors which visited it?'

Corbett brushed past Tressilyian and leapt across the ditch. He took the reins of his horse, stroking its muzzle.

'What were you looking for?' Tressilyian asked again.

'I don't know,' Corbett replied. 'I am curious.

Why should a young woman like Elizabeth come to a lonely place like this? She wouldn't, would she? No woman in her right mind would travel so far from her town to meet a man in the open countryside.'

'Are you saying she was killed elsewhere?' Chapeleys asked.

'I know she was killed elsewhere,' Corbett replied. 'You see, when those two young boys found her corpse they would be frightened, yes? They'd run back to the town and bring back Master Blidscote and the other bailiffs. Now they would see it lying there and pull it out ever so carefully.'

'And?' Sir Maurice asked, intrigued by this dark-faced, mysterious clerk.

'The man who raped young Elizabeth wouldn't be so tender. He was brutal. He attacked her, ravished her, then wrung her neck with a garrotte string. Even a man like Blidscote, despite all the ale he had drunk, would have seen signs of a violent attack here at Devil's Oak.' He paused. 'I also expected to find bits of hair, clothing, even some sign of the corpse being pushed under the hedge. Again, Blidscote would have noticed that. But the killer seems to have acted as tenderly as a mother with her babe.'

'You don't believe that?' Tressilyian taunted.

'No, I don't.'

Corbett stared across the field and his heart skipped a beat. Was that a figure of a woman – he was sure of it – flitting through the copse of trees on the brow of the hill?

'Sir Hugh, you were talking about the killer . . .?'

'I don't think he was tender,' Corbett replied, still watching the spot through the gap in the hedgerow. 'I think he brought Elizabeth's corpse here in a sheet and rolled it under.' He gathered the reins and swung himself up into the saddle. 'Call the killer tender? No, no, sirs, we are dealing with a ravenous wolf!'

# Chapter 5

They rode down the hill; the hedgerows and fields gave way to a small wood on either side. They stopped at the spot where Sir Louis had been ambushed. The signs were still there: the sapling which the justice had pushed off the road had apparently been cut down by an axe. Tressilyian found an arrow in the far ditch with its barn snapped off. The gravel on the trackway had been disturbed by the horse's skittering, whilst Corbett could still see the tangle of undergrowth where Sir Louis had charged his assailant. The clerk drew his sword to clear away the briars and brambles and followed the same path.

'I am sure he stood there,' Sir Louis called out.

Corbett followed his direction: a thick ash tree where the undergrowth wasn't so dense. He walked across and crouched down. No grass and the mud was soft from the previous day's rain. Corbett could distinguish the prints of Sir Louis's boot but then noticed the imprint of bare toes and a heel.

'That's strange!' he called back. 'Sir Louis, your assailant was bare-footed!'

'Whatever, he was a will-o'-the-wisp!' the justice replied.

Corbett looked up: a narrow trackway curved through the woods, muddy and slippery. He went back and looked at the arrow and recalled his days in the King's armies in Wales. How the Welsh, with their long bows, used to fight bare-footed to keep a firmer grip on the soil.

'What does it all mean, Corbett?' Tressilyian asked.

'I wish I knew.' The clerk looked at the faint tendrils of mist curling amongst the trees. 'But I've kept you long enough with my searches.'

'What on earth is that?'

Tressilyian walked to the edge of the ditch. Corbett followed. A woman, cloaked and hooded, stood beneath the branches of an outstretched tree. He could make out her pale face, hair peeping from beneath a shabby hood.

'Come forward!' Corbett ordered. He gripped his sword tighter.

The woman stayed still.

'Come forward! We mean you no harm!'

The woman seemed hesitant. Chapeleys grasped his horse's reins and swung himself up in the saddle. The woman hesitated and walked forward: long, purposeful strides, sure-footed. She crossed the ditch and stood wiping the burrs from her patched, woollen gown; the linen undergarment hung shabby and frayed above battered leather boots. She wore a half-cloak, a coarse linen shawl beneath a broad and weather-beaten face – her nose slightly crooked, a pleasant, full mouth and wide, watchful eyes. Her black hair was streaked with grey at the front.

'Who are you?' Corbett asked.

'I am Sorrel.'

'Sorrel?' Corbett laughed. 'That's the name of a herb.'

'That's what Furrell called me.'

Corbett heard an exclamation from Chapeleys.

'Of course, you are Furrell the poacher's woman!'

'I was Furrell the countryman's woman!' she replied, deftly moving her hair from her face.

'What are you doing wandering the woods?' Corbett demanded. 'Unarmed, unaccompanied?'

'I am not unarmed, clerk. Oh yes, I know who you are.' She smiled. 'I have a staff. I have left it amongst the trees with my leather bag. Surely I would be safe with a royal justice, the handsome Sir Maurice and the fearsome King's clerk? And, as for being unaccompanied, now who would hurt a poor beggar woman?'

'I saw you earlier,' Corbett declared, 'in the copse at the top of the meadow where Devil's Oak stands.'

'And I saw you.' Sorrel looked up at the sky and sighed. 'So, it's true what they say. You are a sharp-eyed clerk! Come to chase the devil from Melford, have you? By God and all His angels, he needs chasing!'

'Watch your tongue!' Tressilyian snapped.

'My tongue and my manners are my own!' Sorrel's face took on a pugnacious look. 'You are not in your court now, Sir Louis. Because of you, my man has disappeared, just because he told the truth!'

Corbett looked over his shoulder at Sir Louis, who just shrugged. This was no accident. Sorrel had followed them from Melford. She had even learnt a little about him.

'Sir Louis, Sir Maurice!' Corbett called out. 'I have

kept you long enough. I must return to Melford.'

'You will be my guests?' Sir Louis asked. 'Tomorrow night a dinner at the Guildhall? You and your companions?'

Corbett agreed. He stood and watched both knights leave. The woman didn't move.

'You'd best get your bag and staff,' Corbett smiled. 'I'll wait for you here.'

The woman crossed the small ditch, hurried amongst the trees and came back, the leather bag slung over her shoulder, a stout walking cane in one hand. She also brought a cloak which she'd slung around her shoulders and clasped at the throat. She winked at Corbett.

'I have two cloaks. This one's stolen. It's best not to let the royal justice know that.'

'You want to speak to me, don't you?'

'Yes, clerk, I wish to speak to you.'

'Where do you live?'

'In Beauchamp ruins. Common pasture there. No one exactly knows who owns what so they can't clear me out.' She looked at Corbett's magnificent bay gelding. 'Can I ride your horse? Please. I always wanted to be a lady and ride high in the saddle.'

Corbett helped her up, shortening the stirrups, then grasped the reins.

'Now, you won't ride off,' he joked, 'and claim you found the horse wandering?'

Sorrel leant down and stroked Corbett's cheek with her calloused hands.

'You have a priest's face, olive-skinned and smooth-shaven. You tie your hair back like a fighting man. Your eyes are sad but sharp. You remind me of a trapped falcon. Are you trapped, royal clerk?'

Corbett grinned.

'That's better.' She smiled back. 'You can be quite the lady's man but you'd have scruples about that, wouldn't you?'

'I didn't know it was so easy to read my mind.'

'Oh, I haven't. However, when you sit in the inglenook at the Golden Fleece, it's marvellous what you hear. Your reputation precedes you, Sir Hugh Corbett. The King's man in peace and war. Are you the King's man?'

Corbett recalled Edward's face, harsh and lined, the cynical eyes, the way he talked to him but his eyes would shift to Ranulf as if the Clerk of the Green Wax was more his confidant: the man who, perhaps, would do things not covered by the law.

'I try to be,' Corbett replied. 'But it's getting dark, Mistress. I am cold, I am hungry and you have a tale to tell.'

He urged the horse forward, walking alongside. He glanced up. Sorrel was riding as if she was a lady, eyes half closed, humming under her breath.

'You are comely enough,' he said. 'What's your real name?'

'Sorrel, that's what Furrell called me. That's what I am.'

'And why do you wander the woods?'

'I don't wander, I am searching.' Her voice was hard. 'I am looking for Furrell's grave.'

Corbett paused. 'You are so sure he's dead?'

She tapped her forehead and chest. 'I truly am. I want to find his grave. I want to pray over his corpse. If I can discover his grave, perhaps I can unmask his killer. He was a good man. I was a wanderer. I met Furrell twelve years ago. We exchanged vows under a yew tree in the graveyard. We were man and wife, as close and as handfast as any couple blessed in church. Oh, he was merry. He could play a lute and dance a lively jig. He was the best hunter and woodsman. He could creep up on a rabbit, silent as a shadow. We never went hungry and we sold what we didn't need.'

'Poaching's a dangerous pastime.'

'Oh, the occasional deer or the lonely lamb that no one would miss. But who's going to tell? The peasants we sold it to? Fresh meat in the pot for their children?'

'And all that changed?' Corbett asked.

'Oh, it changed all right. The night Goodwoman Walmer was murdered.'

'Who was she?' Corbett asked.

'She lived in the cottage on the far side of the town. A strange one: pretty as an angel, hair like ripe corn, eyes as blue as the sky. She always wore her gown that little bit too tight. Her face was painted, neck, wrists and fingers adorned with necklaces, bracelets and rings. No one knew where she came from. Geoffrey Walmer was a potter, a very good one. He sold as far afield as Ipswich. He was gone for a week and came back with her. You know how it is, clerk? A marriage between May and December? There is no fool like an old fool in love. Anyway, Geoffrey died and Cecily Walmer became a goodwoman, a widow. She looked even more attractive in widow's weeds. The men clustered about her like bees round a honeypot.'

'Did you like her?'

'We understood each other. You know what she was, clerk? You've heard the story many a time. A prosperous tradesman goes to a big town. He makes a tidy profit, enters a tavern and meets some comely maid selling her favours. She's only too quick to leave the horrors of the alleyways for a peaceful life and anything she wants.'

'Are you talking from experience?'

'Very sharp, clerk. Yes, I am but, enough of that. Now Goodwoman Walmer owned a cottage, a self-enclosed plot with chicken coops, dovecotes, piggeries and, in the fields around, juicy pheasants and partridges. Now, on the night she was murdered, Furrell went down there. Sometimes he would call in for a flagon of ale. He crept through the garden, saw the door open and Sir Roger Chapeleys leave. Now, thought Furrell, there's a satisfied man. The manor lord climbed into his saddle like a man full of ale and pleasure. Goodwoman Walmer stood in the doorway. She leant against the lintel, arms crossed, her hair falling down to her shoulders. Furrell decided to ignore his ale and crept away.'

'So, the widow was alive and well when Sir Roger left?'

'Oh, yes. I don't think Sir Roger killed those women. He was a lecher and a drunkard but he was good to me and Furrell. He knew we poached his lands but, at Christmas, he always sent us a chicken or a goose. I mean, why should Sir Roger, with all the slatterns and maids at his manor hall, go out and assault peasant wenches?'

'He visited Goodwoman Walmer.'

'Ay yes, but she was different,' Sorrel laughed. 'An

accomplished courtesan. Sir Roger knew where he was fishing.'

'Was he liked?' Corbett asked.

'No, he wasn't, by either the priests or the towns-people. Sir Roger kept himself to himself, except one night in the tavern he called all priests liars and hypocrites, though he seemed to have a soft spot for Parson Grimstone.'

'Yet that's no reason why so many people should speak against him.'

'I don't know. Furrell said something strange. The day after Sir Roger was condemned, my man and I , we were having a meal in the ruins. Furrell got slightly drunk and abruptly declared the devil had come to Melford. "Why?" asks I. "Oh," he replies, "to make those people say what they did." '

'You mean the witnesses?'

'Everything,' she replied. 'How a bracelet was found in Sir Roger's house, belonging to one of the murdered women. How Deverell the carpenter was so sure he had seen Sir Roger fleeing from Good-woman Walmer's house.'

'Fleeing?' Corbett asked.

'That's the way he put it. All furtive.'

'But I understand from the records of the trial that they found Chapeleys' dagger sheath there.'

'Furrell didn't believe Sir Roger had left it there. In fact, he said more to me.'

'More?' Corbett queried.

'On the night Walmer was killed, Furrell saw Sir Roger leave but claimed at least three other men, on separate occasions, made their way down Gully Lane towards her house.'

'Three?' Corbett demanded. He stopped and stared up at her.

'He repeated the same in court. According to him, Widow Walmer must have been very busy that night. Yet he was surely mistaken. Whatever she was in a former life, Cecily Walmer acted the role of a widow. If she had acted any differently in a place like Melford, the gossips' tongues would have soon wagged.'

'Your man Furrell said that in court?'

'He swore on oath but no one believed him. They said he was drunk and everyone knew how kindly Sir Roger was towards him. They even claimed he had been bribed.'

Corbett closed his eyes and recalled the trial record: Furrell the poacher had defended Sir Roger.

'What did your man mean about the devil making people lie? Are you saying they were bribed?'

'Bribed? Threatened, what does it matter? A good man died.'

'You should be careful,' Corbett warned.

'Oh, don't worry, master clerk, I keep my mouth shut. I wander around as if I am fey in my wits, a still tongue in my mouth. Old Sorrel sees nothing, she knows nothing.'

'But you believe Furrell's been murdered and buried?'

'I know Furrell has been murdered and buried. I intend to find his grave.'

'After five years?' Corbett queried.

'All I know is that he went out one night and never came back. Melford, and the countryside around it, is crisscrossed by pathways, culverts, brambles, thickets, woods and marshes, but I pray. Every night before I go to sleep, I pray I'll discover Furrell's corpse.'

'And Furrell was murdered because of what he said in court?'

'Perhaps. As I have said, Furrell was a sly one, as stealthy as the night. Even with me, he could be tight-lipped, if he wasn't drunk.'

'So you think he saw something?'

'I wager to God and His saints that he did, so he had to be silenced. After all, he is the only one who ever heard the Jesses killer.'

'Ah yes.' Corbett let the horse snuggle his hand. 'I've heard that. What did Furrell actually see or hear?'

'He was out poaching, not far from here. Night had fallen. He saw a shape and heard gasps, the tinkle of bells. Now Furrell was visiting one of his hiding places where he had concealed some venison. He didn't want to be caught red-handed. He thought it was some local with his leman or one of the towns-people with a doxy. Remember, master clerk, Melford is a small town: its walls and pathways have eyes and ears. If you take a fancy to your wife's maid, she's best enjoyed out in the countryside. Then there's the young with their love trysts and starlight meetings. Furrell scampered away. When Blidscote was asking questions, Furrell told him what he'd heard. Furrell always insisted that was a mistake. He regretted ever opening his mouth.'

'But he did about Sir Roger Chapeleys?'

'Ah, that was different. It was in a court, on oath in front of a royal justice. Furrell thought he'd be safe.'

'And what else do you know? If you travel the woods and forests, you must see things others don't.

You followed me from Melford. You heard about my coming. You couldn't wait to speak to me.'

'I will speak to you, clerk, but I beg you never tell anyone what I say.' Sorrel gazed back down the pathway.

'Are you frightened of Tressilyian, of Chapeleys?'

'No.'

She smiled down at him through the darkness.

'I act my part well. They are great lords of the soil. They'll think that you think as they do. Who would believe poor, mad Sorrel?'

She pulled at the reins of the horse and Corbett stopped. He was aware of how the darkness had closed in swiftly. They had left the wooded area. On either side, hedgerows, fields stretching away in the distance. The sky was starlit, a full moon white and strong.

'Furrell would love such a night,' she whispered. 'Forget all the stories about the darkness. Furrell liked to know where he was.'

Corbett could sense the tension from this woman. She acted fey-witted, the relict of a poacher who had disappeared but she was a woman consumed with the need for justice, a desire for revenge.

'Do you pray, Sorrel?'

'I have a statue of the Virgin,' she replied. 'It's made of wood, rather battered and chipped. Parson Grimstone gave it to me. Every night, every morning, I light a wax candle bought specially from the chandlers. I pray: "Dear Mother, you never lost your husband but I have." '

Corbett smiled at this makeshift prayer.

'Am I your answer, Sorrel?'

She leant down and grasped his shoulder. In the moonlight Corbett could see how, when she was young, Sorrel must have been a lovely girl.

'I want justice, clerk.' Tears glittered in her eyes. 'Is that much to pray for? Can't the good God in His Heaven give out a little justice to me, a poor widow woman? You are the answer to my prayer. When I saw you riding across the marketplace, I thought God Himself had come down to Melford.'

'That's blasphemy,' Corbett teased.

'No, clerk, it's the truth. If you bring justice to poor Sorrel. If you can find out where my man lies. If those responsible can be dispatched to God's tribunal then, every day, I will light a candle for you.'

Corbett repressed a shiver. He had sat in the King's courts at Westminster. He had listened to petitions for redress. He had hunted the bloody-handed sons of Cain but never had he been faced with such passion: a deep desire for justice which sprang from the innermost soul.

'You will help me?' Sorrel asked.

'Have you ever been in a maze, Mistress Sorrel? That's where I am now. Melford's a maze with little culverts, paths, shadowy corners. Shadows twist and turn. We have the deaths of these young women, Mistress Walmer, now Molkyn and Thorkle.'

'I know nothing of those,' Sorrel snapped. 'God forgive me, master clerk: when I heard of their deaths my heart leapt. So it begins, I thought, God's justice.'

'What do you mean?' Corbett demanded.

He stared up and caught the fierce look in her eyes. Was she a murderer? Corbett thought. Was her hunger for justice so great? Did she believe Thorkle and Molkyn were in some way responsible for the death of her husband?

'I know what you are thinking, clerk,' she murmured. 'I said I was glad, not responsible.'

'But why should they die?' Corbett asked. 'Is it possible someone else believes Sir Roger was innocent and is exacting vengeance?'

'I don't know. You really should have words with their widows. I am sure you'll find them together. Molkyn and Thorkle's wives are kinswomen, related by blood, though thinly.'

Sorrel slipped her feet from the stirrups and Corbett helped her down.

'I have ridden enough.'

She thrust her hand into Corbett's, rough but warm. Corbett wondered what the Lady Maeve would think of this: out in the dark countryside, walking hand-in-hand with this strange poacher woman.

'Listen. I have three things to tell you, then I'll be done,' she declared. 'First, I saw you at Devil's Oak. You were looking at where Elizabeth's corpse was found. Yes?'

Corbett agreed.

'I glimpsed her,' Sorrel continued. 'Late in the afternoon on the day she disappeared. Elizabeth had a secret place in the copse of trees at the top of the meadow.'

'A secret place?'

'Oh, master clerk, you were a child once! You lived in a house with your parents, brothers, sisters, dog. You had a secret place. Elizabeth Wheelwright had one as do the other young men and women, places they can meet.'

'So, you were the last to see her alive?'

'Yes, and before you ask, Elizabeth was hurrying. I hid and watched her go by. You could tell from her face she was excited, pleased.'

'In which case,' Corbett confessed, 'I am truly confused. All your sighting proves is that Elizabeth was probably killed somewhere between that copse of trees and Devil's Oak. Her slayer cunningly hid all traces of his foul act. I can only deduce that her corpse was moved from the murder place to where it was found. So,' he sighed, 'I'd be wasting my time searching the ground. What else?'

'In the last five years, six young women, including Goodwoman Walmer, have been raped and murdered around Melford. But they are not the only ones.' She squeezed his hand. 'Remember, I wander the roads but so do others: Moon People, tinkers, chapmen, families looking for work. I get to know them well. They talk.' She shrugged. 'Two, three, of their women-folk have disappeared.'

'But that's not unheard of,' Corbett replied. 'Their womenfolk often—'

'No, no, listen to what I am saying,' Sorrel interrupted. 'Corpses have been found but I wonder how many other murders there have been. Was Elizabeth Wheelwright's corpse meant to be discovered? Have you ever seen weasels hunt, master clerk? They have a store. They hide the flesh of their victims so they can come back and eat it later. This Jesses killer is like the weasel: he kills and hides, though sometimes he's not fast enough.

Question Blidscote, he collects the corpses.'

'You don't like our master bailiff?'

'He's corrupt and he's stupid!' She spat the words out. 'He likes nothing better than holding forth in the taproom, telling his business and everyone else's to anyone who will listen. Don't forget, he organised the search of Sir Roger's house.'

Corbett gripped her hand.

'You are saying he was bribed to find that evidence?'

'I thought you were sharp,' she teased. 'Why should Sir Roger kill a girl, steal her tawdry effects and keep them at his manor? You should think more clearly and act quickly . . .'

Corbett caught the laughter in her voice.

'. . . otherwise Master Blidscote will join Thorkle and Molkyn. They will soon be lowering his fat corpse into the soil.'

'And finally?' Corbett asked.

'Ah, yes. The Mummer's Man.'

'The Mummer's Man?'

Sorrel laughed deep in her throat. 'Once, many years ago, I learnt a little Latin. Do you remember that line from the gospels, clerk, when Judas decided to betray Christ?' She paused. 'It reads something like, "Judas left and darkness fell." Melford's like that. Once darkness falls, all kinds of things happen. That's the problem with people who live in towns. They think that if they can get out into the fields and woods they are alone, but they are not. I see things, some are comical, some are sad. Oh, not just the lusty swain wishing to swive the wench of his choice. Other things. Men like that young curate,

Robert Bellen. Now he's a strange one. I've caught him down near the river Swaile, kneeling naked in the mud, except for his loin cloth, bruising his back with a switch, eyes closed, lips moving in prayer.'

'That is fanciful.'

'No, clerk, it's the truth. Why should a young man, a priest of God, feel he has to punish himself like that?'

Corbett swallowed hard. He'd heard of such practices in monasteries and abbeys, the desire to flagellate, to punish oneself. Sometimes it was just an extreme form of mortification, in others a deep sense of guilt. Did not King Henry have himself whipped through Canterbury for the murder of Thomas à Becket?

'Do you have dealings with Bellen?' he asked.

'Very little but I thought it was a tragic sight, master clerk. Why should a young priest wish to do that? What secret sins does he hide?'

'Could he be the killer?'

'All things are possible, Sir Hugh. He made little attempt to hide himself the day I saw him.'

'And Parson Grimstone?'

'A goodly man. He likes the trencher, his roast pork, his capon served in sauces and cups of claret, but I've heard no whisper of scandal about him. Sometimes short-tempered. He and the other one, Burghesh, they are inseparable, like two old women gossiping with each other.'

'And the Mummer's Man?' Corbett asked.

'It happened just before the killings began again. Furrell had mentioned something about a man with a mask riding a horse but that was years ago. I said he was drunk, deep in his cups. Anyway, the day was quiet, one of those beautiful times when the weather is changing. I was in Sheepcote Lane; it's a narrow path across the fields. I was enjoying the sun, nestling behind an outcrop of rock when I heard a horse. Usually the place is deserted but I looked over and, just for a matter of heartbeats, I glimpsed this man dressed in a cloak. On his head he wore one of those mummer's masks, the sort travelling actors use when they appear in a morality play. This one belonged to the player who takes the part of the devil, blood-red, twisted mouth, horns on either side. I was so shocked I immediately hid. He was past me in a trice. I wouldn't have thought anything of it. Perhaps a young man playing a joke? There is so much revelry here. Then I recalled Furrell's words: how one of the travellers he encountered, passing through, had seen something similar.' She touched Corbett's hand and pointed to a gap in the hedge leading into the water meadow. 'I must go.' She tapped her walking cane on the trackway. 'If you wish, you can join me.' She made a drinking gesture. 'I have some very good wine . . .'

Corbett stared into the darkness. 'You saw Elizabeth Wheelwright going across the fields about Devil's Oak?' he asked. 'Weren't you suspicious? Why didn't you follow her?'

'I saw no one else, master clerk. I do not belong to Melford. Few people like me but, in the main, I am tolerated. I don't want to be accused of snooping or prying where I shouldn't. I saw Elizabeth go into the copse. No one else was around, there was nothing suspicious, so I walked on.'

'So, she must have met her killer? Why,' Corbett insisted, 'should a young woman come out into the lonely countryside to meet someone? How would she know where to go? I wager she could scarcely read.'

'I don't know, clerk, but if you come with me, I might enlighten you.'

Corbett gripped the reins of his horse. 'It's truly dark,' he murmured.

'You are not just referring to the night, are you, Corbett?'

'No, I'm not.' He shivered. 'Do you believe in ghosts, Sorrel?'

'I believe the dead walk and try to speak to us.'

'I hope they speak to me,' Corbett replied. 'All those poor women so barbarously ravished and murdered. Surely it's time their ghosts betrayed this killer.'

# Chapter 6

Corbett, leading his horse, followed Sorrel across the ditch and into the water meadow. The ground was wet but still firm. Corbett felt as if he was walking along a dreamlike landscape: the surrounding trees and bushes were bathed in moonlight; Sorrel was striding in front of him, swinging her cane, singing softly under her breath. A hunting owl flew like a white shadow above them. Corbett's horse started and he paused to let it nuzzle his hand. He couldn't help thinking of Maeve watching her husband, a royal clerk and manor lord, going across night-wrapped fields with this mysterious woman. The owl, which had reached the far trees, now began to hoot, low, mournful but clear on the night air.

'My man,' Sorrel said over her shoulder, 'always claimed owls were the souls of priests who never sung their Masses.'

'In which case,' Corbett replied, 'the woods should be full of such birds!'

Sorrel laughed and walked on.

'What can you tell me about the people of Melford?'

'Oh, I could tell you a lot, clerk, but then they'd

realise you'd been talking to me. I think it's best if you found out yourself. I'll show you what I have and let you think. However,' she paused and waited for Corbett to draw level with her, 'you said you were in a maze so let me help you. Blidscote is fat and corrupt. Deverell the carpenter has a lot to hide and Repton the reeve is cold and hard. That's the problem, master clerk, isn't it? If these men were here, or their wives or sweethearts, they'd tell similar tales about me.'

'Old Mother Crauford?' Corbett asked. 'Melford's Jeremiah?'

'Oh, she and that Peterkin! Let me put it this way, clerk: there may be a Mummer's Man who wears a mask but the likes of Crauford and Peterkin also wear masks. They are not what they seem to be, but what they truly are escapes me. She mutters and moans. He acts fey-witted, runs errands for this person or that and spends his coins on sweetmeats.'

'And Melford's history?'

The woman stopped and tapped her stick on the ground. 'As you can guess, I am not from Melford. I wandered here twelve years ago and met Furrell. He was kind and taught me the ways of the countryside. I thought, what's so bad about this? Better God's trees and meadows than the piss-washed alleyways of—'

Corbett was sure she was about to add 'Norwich' but she bit her lip.

'Furrell claimed Melford was a strange place. A settlement stood here even before the Romans came. Do you know who they were, clerk? Weren't they led by William the King?'

Corbett laughed and shook his head. 'No, no,

different people, different times.'

'Anyway,' Sorrel continued, eager to show her knowledge, 'Furrell believed wild tribes lived here: they sacrificed people –' she pointed to a distant copse – 'on great slabs of stone or hanged them from the oak trees.'

'Do you think that's why Old Mother Crauford believes Melford is a place of blood?'

'Perhaps,' Sorrel murmured. 'I'll show you something tonight. You can also meet my friends.'

'Friends?' Corbett queried.

'Moon People,' she explained. 'They have tales which might interest you. But I want to show you something, clerk, something which intrigues me.'

She walked on more purposefully. They were now going downhill. Corbett glimpsed the river and the dark mass of Beauchamp Place, its jagged walls and empty windows clear against a patch of starlit sky. Corbett recalled memories of a haunted house near his own village when he was a boy. He remembered being challenged to spend a night there and his mother's anger when she found his empty bed.

At last they reached a makeshift bridge which crossed a narrow, evil-smelling moat.

'Sometimes, when the river becomes full, it's drained,' Sorrel explained.

Corbett was more concerned with his horse, nervous and skittish as its hoofs clattered on the wooden slats. At last they were across under the old gatehouse and into the cobbled inner bailey. By some coincidence – perhaps the builder had planned it – the bailey seemed to trap the moonlight, increasing the manor's ghostly appearance.

'A haunted place!' Corbett exclaimed. 'Don't its ghosts trouble you?'

'Oh, people say there are ghosts,' Sorrel grinned. 'And I embroider the stories to keep them away.'

'Aren't you nervous?'

'Of the ghosts!' she exclaimed. 'True, strange sounds can be heard at night. I often wonder if Furrell comes looking for me but it's the living who concern me. And, before you ask, clerk, I am not really frightened of strangers or outlaws. Why should they hurt the likes of me? Especially,' she called out as she crossed the yard, 'as I have a cudgel, a dagger, not to mention a crossbow and bolts.'

She led Corbett into the ruined hall. Most of its roof had gone, leaving the beams open to the elements. Sorrel lit sconce torches and, in their flickering dance, Corbett glimpsed faded paintings on the far wall. The dais at the top had once been tiled but most of the stone had been ripped away.

'You can hobble your horse here,' Sorrel explained.

Corbett did so and followed her across the dais. The door in the wall at the back had been repaired and rehung on leather hinges. The large room inside must have once been the solar, or family room, for the manor lord and family. Its roof was still sound; the plaster had been refurbished. Corbett was surprised how clean and neat it was. There were stools, a bench, trestle table, two large chests, an aumbry and, in the far corner, a four-poster bed shrouded by faded red curtains. Candlesticks in iron spigots were placed round the room as well as sconce torches which Sorrel immediately lit.

'Take your ease,' Sorrel offered.

Corbett looked around and whistled under his breath. 'It's very comfortable.'

'Of course it is,' Sorrel called.

She went into a small adjoining room and wheeled back a metal-capped brazier. Corbett watched as she expertly fired the coals and, taking a small pouch of ground herbs, sprinkled some powder across the top. A warm sweet perfume pervaded the room.

'Who did all this?' Corbett asked.

'Why, Furrell. You see, sir, no one owns Beauchamp Place. People are terrified of the ghosts and, if the river spills, it can be dangerous but, the hall, solar and my buttery are safe.' She added proudly, 'Furrell was a good poacher. I was in Melford earlier with three pheasants for the Golden Fleece. People pay well for good, fresh meat, finely gutted and cleaned. Furrell bought the bed from a merchant who was leaving for London. The other sticks of furniture came from the likes of Deverell. That's how people paid him.'

Corbett noticed the paintings on the far wall. He got up and went across. They had been done in charcoal, filled in with rough paints, small scenes from country life; most of them depicted a man or woman netting a hare or catching conys in the hay. Others were more vigorous: a pheasant burst up from the gorse, its head going back as it was hit by a slingshot; a roe deer, antlers high, knees buckling as an arrow dug deep into its neck.

'Who did these?' Corbett asked.

'Furrell. Don't forget, you may work by day but my man worked at night.'

Corbett continued to study the rough paintings. Sorrel brought in two pewter cups. She filled these with wine and, grasping a small poker, thrust it into a now fiery brazier. She then took it out, warmed the wine and sprinkled each with nutmeg. She wrapped a rag round one cup and handed it to Corbett.

'It's good wine, isn't it?' she said, sitting down on the bench opposite, her eyes bright and expectant.

Corbett felt a little uncomfortable.

'Tell me,' he said. 'Do you really believe that I can discover the truth?'

'You must do.' Sorrel pointed across to a small niche containing a statue of the Virgin, a candle fixed in wax before it. 'Every day I pray to her. You're God's answer.'

Corbett sipped at the wine. It was warm and mellow. He felt relaxed, slightly flattered. Most strangers couldn't stand the sight of him. A royal clerk, particularly the keeper of the Secret Seal, was regarded as dangerous: a man who had the ear of the King.

'Right.' Corbett sipped again. 'Five years ago Sir Roger Chapeleys was hanged. Furrell went before the justices and pleaded on his behalf?'

'I've told you all that.'

'And then what happened?'

'Well,' Sorrel pulled a face, 'Sir Roger was in prison for a while. Sir Louis dispatched pleas to London but the King sent the order back. Sir Roger had been found guilty by a jury.' Sorrel sipped at her own wine. 'The poor man even offered to purge himself by trial by combat but that was refused. Sentence of death was confirmed and he was hanged.'

'Did you attend the execution?'

'Oh no, nor did Furrell.'

'And when did your husband disappear?'

Sorrel narrowed her eyes. 'About a month after Sir Roger's execution. Furrell was a strange one. He had many faults. I wondered if he did lie with other women but, in his own way, he was loyal. As I said, we took a vow under the yew tree and he looked after me. He was kind and tender, never raising his hands to me, even in his cups. He could be garrulous, at other times he would sit and brood, barking out short statements like when he mentioned the Mummer's Man.' She pointed to the wall. 'I think that's why he liked painting. He always had a great fear, did Furrell, that his wits would wander, that the loneliness would darken his mind.'

'And Sir Roger's execution?' Corbett brought her gently back to the matter in hand.

'Ah yes.' She shifted her hair away from her face with her wrist then held the cup against her chapped cheek. 'After the hanging my man was not the most popular person in Melford: dark looks at the Golden Fleece, cold shoulders in the marketplace. Furrell, however, was a ferret of a man: he had his mind set on Sir Roger's innocence. He became obsessed with it. I wish,' she sighed, 'I had listened more carefully to his rantings and ravings. He never changed the song he sang: Sir Roger did not attack Widow Walmer. He left her cottage peaceably, full of wine and love whilst she was alive and hearty.'

'And?' Corbett asked.

'Furrell went back to the widow's cottage. Now, you can imagine what happened after her death. The town council seized her property as tax. It's now been sold to another so you won't find anything interesting. Anyway, Furrell went back there. From the night of her death, the council put guards and bailiffs on her property. You know the way it is: windows and doors were sealed though that didn't stop people rifling her hen coops and taking what livestock they could filch. There's nothing like a funeral,' she added wistfully, 'to bring the greed out in people. Now Furrell made very careful enquiries.' She pointed to the door of her own chamber. 'Much as I boast about my crossbow and dagger, when I sleep at night I draw the bolts across. Wouldn't you, master clerk?'

Corbett agreed.

'Well,' Sorrel continued eagerly, putting the cup on the floor and using her hands to illustrate what she was saying, 'on the night she died Widow Walmer entertained Sir Roger, yes?'

Corbett nodded.

'And when he went, what would she do? She's drunk wine, she's made love, she's tired. If I were her, I would douse the fire and lamps . . .'

'Fasten the shutters and bolt the door,' Corbett finished the sentence for her.

'Exactly! Especially if she was alone. Now, if someone had come to attack, ravish and slay her?'

'They'd force the door,' Corbett declared.

'Furrell found this hadn't happened. No damage to the doors or shutters. So our widow must have known her visitor.'

'I am not a lawyer,' Corbett replied, 'but I would argue that perhaps Sir Roger paid a second visit. Widow Walmer would let him in.'

'True,' she agreed. 'But why leave in the first place?

And, if he was going to kill her, why return, why not do it earlier?'

Corbett cradled the cup in his hands. 'Then let me act the lawyer, Mistress. For the sake of argument let's assume that Sir Roger left and did not return. The killer comes tripping down the lane.' He paused. 'So what would happen? The murderer tapped on the door, Widow Walmer must have been so assured that she opened it and let her assassin in. So sure of him, she probably turned her back and that's when he slipped the garrotte string around her throat. I have seen similar murders in London. It doesn't take someone long to learn how to use the garrotte: it's silent and very quick. I don't know,' he rubbed his face, 'whether he first made her lose consciousness, then raped her, or just defiled her dead body. What I am sure of is that he didn't wear a mummer's mask. Widow Walmer would never have let such a creature into her house. So, whom would she allow in?'

'The list is endless,' Sorrel replied. 'Sir Louis, Taverner Matthew, Repton the reeve, who was sweet on her. Parson Grimstone, Burghesh, Curate Bellen. Even Molkyn and Thorkle can't be ignored.'

Corbett rocked himself backwards and forwards on the stool. Why would a widow, he wondered, open her door at the dead of night? There again, she was respectable. She had the protection of a man like Sir Roger. If her visitor was a worthy burgess or priest from Melford . . .?

'The killer,' he declared, 'must have used some pretext to get into her house.'

'That would be easy,' Sorrel smiled. 'Widow Walmer was full of wine and happiness. Perhaps the visitor posed as a messenger from Sir Roger?' She caught Corbett's sideways glance. 'I know what you are thinking, clerk!'

'What am I thinking, Mistress?'

'Furrell, he was a poacher, wasn't he? Well liked by Widow Walmer. He was near her cottage that night. Widow Walmer would see him as no threat. Furrell had squeezed the life out of many a pheasant or partridge.'

'I am thinking that,' Corbett agreed. 'And you must have thought the same in the days following Sir Roger's execution.'

'That's why I told Furrell to keep his mouth shut. I pointed out how people might begin to think, perhaps regret Sir Roger's death and point the finger at him. I told him I didn't want to hear any more about the business so he kept it to himself.'

'Did he ever hint that he knew the truth?'

'Sometimes. Once he mentioned Repton the reeve but, as I have said, he'd grown secretive.'

'Did he go anywhere? Meet anyone?'

'If he did, he didn't tell me.'

Corbett started as he heard a sound from the hall beyond. His horse whinnied. Corbett's hand went to the dagger in his belt.

'Oh, you are safe,' Sorrel reassured him. 'I've sat here many a night, clerk. I can tell one sound from another. We are alone.' She grinned impishly. 'Apart from the ghosts.'

'And the night Furrell disappeared. You said he left one night?'

'Furrell had stopped talking to me. Oh, we'd discuss the weather, what he'd poached, what goods we should buy. He also avoided the Golden Fleece and drank in other taverns. He'd grown very tense and watchful. He mumbled more and more about the devil. One night he left, all cloaked and hooded.'

'Was he armed?'

'Like me, a dagger and a cudgel. He never returned the next morning. I wondered if he had got drunk and was sleeping it off somewhere. Or had he been caught? I went out into Melford but no one had seen him. A week passed. One night I was praying before that statue. Autumn had come early. I remember a mist sweeping through the hall. Do you know, clerk,' her eyes filled with tears, 'I just knew Furrell was dead and buried somewhere so I began to wander the countryside. I didn't believe the rumours. Furrell wouldn't run away; he wouldn't leave me or his house.' She blinked quickly. 'I am not fey-witted. I don't really believe in visions or dreams but I used to have nightmares of Furrell's corpse lying in some shallow, muddy grave all scarred and unhallowed. I remembered what he used to say. How, when he died, he wanted his body churched and blessed; a Mass sung for his soul.'

'Did you go to see Parson Grimstone?'

'Yes I did. Him and Master Burghesh were very kind. The parson said he'd sing a Mass for him and refused the coin I offered. I still want to find his grave. I've discovered many things – that's what I want to show you – but not Furrell.'

'Many things?' Corbett queried.

'Come with me.'

Sorrel put her cup down. She took a torch from the wall, handed it to Corbett and grasped one herself.

She led him back into the hall, across the courtyard and in through a small stone-fretted door.

'Take care,' she warned as she led him up some weather-worn steps.

Corbett followed warily. The steps were narrow, steep and slippery. They reached a stairwell. Corbett steeled his nerves against the scampering rats. At last they reached a long, narrow room very similar to the hall. The roof was gone, the plaster walls soaked by the wind and rain. Corbett could tell by the shape of the empty windows, the small platform at the far end and the recesses in the walls, that this must have been the manor chapel.

'I want to show you something.'

A bird, disturbed by their arrival, abruptly burst from where it was nesting in the rafters and flew up into the night sky. Corbett closed his eyes and breathed in deeply. He fought back the waves of weariness. He should be back at the Golden Fleece but, on their journey into Melford, Corbett had repeated to Ranulf and Chanson, time and again, how quickly they must act.

'We must take people by surprise,' he'd told them, 'not give them time to concoct stories.'

'Master clerk, are you asleep?'

Corbett opened his eyes. The torch felt heavy, he lowered it and smiled in apology.

'What is it?' he asked.

Sorrel was now taking away bricks from the wall. Corbett joined her; he realised that a recess lay beyond. Sorrel told him to stand back and pulled out a makeshift platter.

'Part of a doorway,' she explained.

She threw back the dirty linen sheet. Corbett stared in disbelief at the skeleton which sprawled there. He lowered the torch. The bones were yellowing with age. The jaw sagged, the blackened teeth had crumbled, faint tufts of hair still clung to the skull. He muttered a prayer, moved the bones and glimpsed the tawdry, green-tinted bracelet lying beneath.

'What is this?' he murmured. 'A former inhabitant of Beauchamp Place?'

'No, no,' she replied. 'All its owners were buried in the parish graveyard. I put this here.'

'Why didn't you tell anyone?'

'Oh come, master clerk.' Sorrel took the bracelet from his fingers. 'You know the old law. Whoever finds the corpse falls immediately under suspicion. You know what they'd say? "Were you involved in this, Sorrel? Is this the work of your man, Furrell? Is that why he fled?"'

'They'll say the same if they come here.'

Sorrel shook her head. 'I'll be sly. I'll say I never knew the bones were here. I know nothing of them. Perhaps they belonged to a lady or maid who once lived here.'

'So, you know it's a woman?'

Sorrel closed her eyes. 'Of course it's a woman, hence the bracelet. I also found a cheap ring, the remnants of a girdle. I kept them as treasure.'

Corbett, still holding the torch, sat down on the cold damp floor.

'But why, Sorrel? What is this skeleton doing here?'

She took the torch out of his hand and stuck it into a niche in the wall; she did the same with hers, then she made herself comfortable before him.

'You'll tell no one,' she warned. 'I won't be troubled because of this. I am as innocent as a child.'

'Tell me,' Corbett insisted.

Sorrel rubbed her face in her hands. 'Furrell was a very good poacher. He knew all the trackways and wood lore. When I used to go hunting with him, he'd always tell me to stay away from this place or that. I asked him why. That's when he told me how Melford used to be, about the sacrifices. He tried to frighten me with stories of the dead wandering the woods.' She laughed abruptly. 'He just wanted me to be safe on dark nights, indoors by the fire.'

Corbett watched her curiously. Here he was in this haunted, unhallowed place, the sky visible through the beams above, the cold wind sending the flames dancing. Before him the remains of some poor woman and this widow telling eerie stories about Melford's dark past.

'Anyway,' Sorrel continued, 'I paid him no heed. I told you people talk about the murders, other women disappearing. I saw it as no business of mine.'

'Until after Furrell disappeared?'

'Yes. Now I reasoned that Furrell would never enter someone's house. The night he disappeared he didn't visit the Golden Fleece or any tavern or alehouse in or around Melford. I reasoned that if he had been killed, it must have been out in the countryside and his corpse secretly buried. I began to search.' She bit her lip. 'Shall we put the remains back?'

'In a while,' Corbett replied softly. 'Continue your story, Mistress.'

'I won't be held responsible?'

'You will not be held responsible,' Corbett confirmed. 'But,' he added wryly, 'I wish you to add flesh to the bones.'

She laughed at the macabre joke. 'Furrell was once an outlaw. He knew all about Sherwood and the other great forests north of the Trent. He told me how outlaws, if they killed a traveller, would never take the body far but bury it near the road or trackway where they'd planned their ambush. The places Furrell told me to stay away from were always near a trackway or path. Now, you have seen Devil's Oak and Falmer Lane. If you were a bird, master clerk, yes . . .' She closed her eyes. 'Imagine yourself a falcon flying above the meadows and fields around Melford. Go on, close your eyes!'

Corbett did so. 'Strange,' he murmured. 'The day is not clear but grey and overcast.'

'Good,' Sorrel agreed. 'Now, remember the fields on either side of Falmer Lane – they roll and dip, don't they? The lanes and trackways are deep, more like trenches through the countryside. That's what Furrell called them.'

'Yes, yes, I've thought of that,' Corbett agreed. 'It's a vision enhanced by the high hedgerows.'

'That's the work of the sheep farmers—'

Corbett opened his eyes. 'What are you implying?' he interrupted.

'A poacher,' she replied, 'always stays within cover. He will, where possible, always scurry along a ditch or a hedgerow. It's common sense. One side is protected and he does not want to be caught out in the open. Rabbits and pheasants do the same. The night Furrell disappeared, he must have followed the hedgerows down to a certain place to meet someone. He was probably killed there.' She kept her voice steady. 'And his poor corpse buried. Good, I thought, that's where I'll begin.'

'But I saw you in a copse well away from Devil's Oak?'

'Patience,' Sorrel murmured. 'I mentioned one path Furrell would take but he also favoured the secret copse, the hidden clump of trees. I searched both places. In my first week, Sir Hugh,' she tapped the skull, 'I found this. It was behind a hedgerow down near Hamden Mere, a place Furrell had warned me to keep well clear of. I was curious. I dug, no more than a foot, and came across the grave, just a shallow in the ground, the remains tossed in. I noticed the ring, bracelet and piece of girdle. I was going to leave it there but my conscience pricked me. Here was I, searching for poor Furrell's corpse yet I couldn't give these pathetic remains proper burial. I don't trust Blidscote, or any of those wealthy burgesses. I thought of going to see Parson Grimstone, but who'd believe me? I took the ring as payment, wrapped the skeleton in a leather sheet and brought it here.'

'This was once the chapel, wasn't it?' Corbett asked. 'In your eyes, a holy place?'

'Yes. I later regretted my charity.'

'Why?' Corbett asked.

'I found two more graves,' she confessed.

'What!'

'I tell you, I found two more graves. That's why I called the killer of those young women a weasel but . . .' She paused.

'What?' Corbett asked.

'How do we know these poor women were murdered? I've examined these bones. There's no blow to the head. No mark to the ribs. Nothing!'

Corbett got to his feet. His fingers felt cold and he stretched out towards the warmth from the sconce torch. What do we have here? he thought, staring into the heart of the flame. Sorrel was an expert poacher. She knew the land around Melford. He'd met similar people on his own estates. They could tell if the ground had been disturbed, what animals had passed along which trackways. Furrell must have discovered these graves scattered around the countryside. Being shrewd and clever, he must have disturbed them, realised what he had found, covered them over and, because of superstition, kept Sorrel well away from them. She, in turn, when looking for his grave, sharp-eyed and remembering what she had learnt, had found one grave: out of respect or superstition, she'd then moved the pathetic remains to this ruined chapel. But were they murder victims?

'What do you think, master clerk?'

'They could be murder victims.' Corbett spoke his own thoughts. 'They could be the prey of the slayer of Elizabeth Wheelwright and the others but, there again, another killer could be responsible, years earlier. Look at the skeleton. The flesh and clothes have all decayed – nothing but brittle, yellowing bone. Indeed, these graves may have nothing to do with murder.' He sat back on the floor. 'In London, Mistress Sorrel, beggars die every night on the streets, particularly during wintertime. Their bodies are buried in the mud flats along the Thames, out on the moorlands or even in someone's garden. Melford is a prosperous place,' he continued. 'Think of the young girls from Norwich and Ipswich, the Moon People and the travellers. A woman sickens and dies of the fever or, frail with age, suffers an accident. What do these people do? They leave the trackway. They don't go very far but dig a shallow grave, place the woman's corpse there in some lonely copse or wood. A skeleton does not mean a murder,' he concluded. 'We don't even know when this poor woman died. Do you still have the ring?'

She shook her head. 'I traded it with a pedlar for needles and thread.'

Corbett examined the bracelet. 'It's certainly copper, the damp earth has turned it green.' He held it up against the flame. 'But I would say . . .'

'What, clerk?'

Corbett took out his dagger and tapped it against the bracelet.

'It's not pure copper,' he confirmed. 'But some cheap tawdry ornament. The same probably goes for the clothes and the girdle.'

He crouched down beside the skeleton and examined it carefully. Sorrel was correct. None of the ribs was broken, nor could Corbett detect any fracture of the skull, arms or legs. He examined the chest, the line of the spine: no mark or contusion.

'The effects of the garrotte string,' he murmured, 'would disappear with decay. How many more of these graves did you say?'

'Two more and the bodies are no less decayed than this.'

Corbett, mystified, replaced the bracelet. He rearranged the bones back on to the board, covered them with the cloth and slid them back into the recess. Sorrel replaced the bricks; Corbett helped her. He tried to recall his conversations with his friend, a physician at St Bartholomew's Hospital in London.

'You found no string? Nothing round the throat?' he asked.

'No, I didn't.'

Corbett was about to continue his questioning when he heard a sound. He got to his feet and moved to the window.

'You have sharp ears, clerk.' Sorrel remained composed.

'I thought I heard a horse or pony, a rider . . .'

'I told you, someone I wished you to meet,' she explained.

Corbett, one hand on his dagger, stood by the window. He heard the jingle of a harness. Whoever had arrived had already crossed the bridge. An owl hooted but the sound came from below. Sorrel went to the window and imitated the same call. She grasped Corbett's hand.

'Our visitor has arrived.'

'The Moon People?'

'They got tired of waiting,' Sorrel explained. 'They watch the hours as regularly as a monk does his office.'

Corbett stared up at the night sky. Aye, he reflected, and I watch mine. What time was it? He had left the church with Sir Louis and Sir Maurice about an hour before nightfall. It must be at least, he reckoned, three hours before midnight and he still had other business to do: Molkyn's widow to speak to for a start! He heard a sound. Sorrel, holding the sconce torch, was standing in the doorway.

'Come on!' she urged.

They reached the cobbled yard. Sorrel's visitor was standing in the middle. Corbett made out his shadowy outline.

'I stood here deliberately.' The voice had a strong country burr. Corbett recognised the tongue of the south-west. 'I didn't want to startle you.'

The man stepped into the pool of light. He was tall. Raven-black hair, parted down the middle, fell to his shoulders; sharp eyes like a bird, crooked nose, his mouth and chin hidden by a black bushy moustache and beard. He was swarthy-skinned and Corbett glimpsed the silver earrings in each earlobe. He smelt of wood smoke and tanned leather. The stranger was dressed from head to toe in animal skins: the jacket sleeves were of leather, the front being of mole's fur, with leggings of tanned deerskin pushed into sturdy black boots. He wore a war belt which carried a stabbing dirk and a dagger. Bracelets winked at his wrists, rings on his fingers.

The stranger studied Corbett from head to toe. 'So, you're the King's clerk?'

'You should have waited,' Sorrel accused. 'I would have brought him.'

The man's gaze held Corbett's.

'I did not want to meet him,' he replied insolently. 'I don't like King's officers, I don't like clerks. I only said I would see him because you asked. What I've got to say isn't much. You said you'd bring him to see me if you could.'

Corbett glanced at Sorrel and smiled. He was intrigued by how much this woman had planned what had happened this evening.

'You find me amusing?' the man asked dangerously.

'No, sir,' Corbett replied wearily. 'I do not find you amusing. You are the leader of the Moon People, aren't you?'

'One of its clans.'

'You came here, not because you're tired of waiting, but because you did not want me in your encampment?'

The man's eyes flickered.

'You don't like court officials,' Corbett continued, 'because they stride amongst your wagons like the Lord Almighty. They steal your goods, bully your men, harass your women. They take your horses and accuse you of crimes you did not commit. They will only go away if you offer silver and gold. Do you think I am like that, sir? I tell you, I'm not!' Corbett undid his purse and took out two silver coins. 'You come here out of friendship to Sorrel. Go on, take these for your pains!'

The man took the coins.

'You are an ill-mannered lout!' Sorrel exclaimed. 'This clerk's no Blidscote.'

The Moon man extended a hand. 'My name is Branway. I've come to tell you something.'

Corbett grasped his hand.

'I'll tell you what I want, here under God's sky. In that way you know I am telling the truth. I belong to the Moon People. We travel from Cornwall to the old Roman wall in the north. We have our carts and our ponies. We have coppersmiths, seamstresses, carpenters and painters. We buy and sell and, yes, when our children go hungry, we steal. We know the King's kingdom better than he does. We arrived here two days ago and we'll be gone tomorrow morning.'

'What do you mean?' Corbett asked.

'We have to use these roads,' Branway explained, 'and we can't help passing by Melford on our way to the coast. But you'll find none of our women wandering the lanes. Over the years some have disappeared.'

Corbett took a step closer. 'You mean disappeared, not run away?'

'Oh, I know what you are thinking, clerk. We have taken into our care some of the poor wenches who flee from your cities and towns. Our women do not run away. It's common talk amongst the Moon People how, over the years, six or seven of our women have disappeared: in the main, young girls stupid enough to wander out, intrigued by what the market holds. They left and never came back. We searched but did not find. I've heard the same amongst other travelling people. That's all I can tell you.'

'But surely you've gone to the Guildhall?'

Branway threw his head back and laughed. 'And get beaten for our pains! No, master clerk, we just avoid Melford, whilst our women are kept within the encampment.'

'And have you seen anything amiss?'

'I've told you what I know: no more no less.'

The man nodded at Corbett, kissed Sorrel on each cheek and walked off into the darkness.

Corbett watched him go.

'I must leave too. I thank you for what you've told me.'

Corbett nodded at Sorrel, bade her good night,

collected his horse and crossed into the water meadow. For a while he paused and looked up at the sky, reflecting on what he'd learnt.

'True,' he whispered into the darkness, 'this is a place of hideous murder!'

# Chapter 7

Walter Blidscote was having nightmares. He wasn't asleep but he wished to God he was. After he had met that terrifying clerk in the crypt beneath St Edmund's Church, Blidscote had strode off wielding his staff of office. He had walked quickly, pompously, with all the authority he could summon up. Once away from prying eyes, he'd slumped beneath a sycamore tree and allowed his fat body to tremble. Sweat had trickled down his back whilst his stomach squeezed and winced so much he had to retreat deeper into the trees to relieve himself.

Blidscote had been petrified.

'I am living in the Valley of Ghosts,' he'd whispered, staring round. He believed he could see shapes amongst the trees. Or was it just the branches in the curling mist? Blidscote felt he was being haunted. He recalled the words of a preacher: how a man's sins, like hungry dogs, can pick up the scent and come howling down the passage of the years. Blidscote's mind trailed back. He couldn't forget the day of Sir Roger's execution: Chapeleys standing on the cart, the noose round his neck. He'd protested his innocence, shouting that one day he would have his vengeance.

Blidscote stared at his hands. Were they covered in blood? Or was it just dirt? He wiped them on his hose and felt the cold mud beneath him. What happened if that keen hunting dog of a clerk started to dig up the bones of the past? This was not some local matter. The King had intervened. The great council at Westminster had issued warrants under the Great Seal. Blidscote knew something about the law. Sir Hugh Corbett may stand in his dark clothing and travel-stained boots but he represented the Crown. He could go anywhere, see anything, ask any questions. God and his angels help any who tried to impede him! Blidscote had so much to hide. Sometimes he sought consolation in being shriven, in confessing his secret sins in church, in vowing repentance, in lighting candles, but still the burden on his back grew heavier.

Blidscote became so frightened, he got up and walked back into the town for company. He'd visited a dingy alehouse. Now he was sickened at what he had drunk so quickly from the polluted vat and the dirt-encrusted, leather tankard. He had enjoyed a quick fumble with a greasy potboy in one of the outhouses but the ale fumes were now dulled, his sense of pleasure replaced by remorse. Blidscote stumbled along the lanes, making his way towards the square and the Golden Fleece. Guilt perched on his shoulder like a huge crow. He'd ignored Corbett's request to visit the families of the victims. They would tell him nothing. Images came and went like fiery bursts in his befuddled mind. Blidscote was a boy again, snivelling-nosed and ragged-arsed, standing before Parson Hawdon, the old priest who had served

St Edmund's Church long before Parson Grimstone ever came.

'Do not lie, boy!' the old parson had thundered. 'A lie echoes like a bell across the lake of Hell and the demons hear it.'

Blidscote paused, wiping the sweat from his unshaven face. He always did have an awful fear of the church: those gargoyles which grinned down at him from the pillars; the wooden carvings, depicting the realms of the dead, the dancing skeletons . . . Blidscote felt so hot, he wondered if it was the glow from the fury of Hell. He paused and leant against the plaster wall of a house, mopping his face with the hem of his cloak. He was about to walk on when he felt the touch of cold steel on his sweaty neck. Blidscote tried to turn.

'Stay where you are, bailiff of Melford!'

The sharp steel dug in a little closer. Blidscote couldn't stop shaking. The voice was low, hollow, muffled, as if the speaker was wearing a mask. Blidscote forced his head round. It was a mask, ghoulish and garish like the face of a demon. Blidscote closed his eyes and whimpered. Was he having a nightmare? Had he died? Was this one of Hell's scurriers sent to fetch him? Yet he recognised that voice from many years ago.

'Well, well, Master Blidscote, we meet again.'

'I have kept faith,' Blidscote muttered. 'And a still tongue in my head.'

'And why shouldn't you, Master Blidscote?' came the cool reply. 'What can you do? Confess all to the King's justice or seek private words with the royal clerk? Will you tell him the truth? You can hang for perjury, Walter.' The tone was now bantering. 'Or haven't you heard the news? How the King's parliament at Winchester have issued a new statute? Perjury is now treason's brother. And do you know what happens to a traitor?'

Blidscote just whimpered.

'Then let me tell you, master bailiff. For we are all alone in the dark. That's what we are, aren't we, creatures of the night? Scurrying rats with our horde of secrets?'

The sword was quickly withdrawn.

'Stay where you are!' the voice hissed, and the demon figure melted away.

Blidscote did. A beggar was coming up the lane, trundling a small barrow heaped with rags and other rubbish he'd collected from the town midden heap. The small wheelbarrow creaked and clattered on the cobbles. Blidscote turned. He would have loved to have run but he knew his tormentor was still lurking in the shadows on the opposite side of the lane. The beggar man drew closer. He recognised Blidscote, put his barrow down and grinned in a display of rotting gums and fetid breath. Blidscote flinched, waving his hand.

'Good evening, Master Blidscote.'

'On your way! On your way!'

The man was about to protest but Blidscote gripped him by the shoulder.

'Get you gone or I'll have you in the stocks for vagrancy!'

The beggar took up his barrow and almost ran down the lane, muttering curses about unchristian bailiffs.

Blidscote took a step forward but the razor-sharp steel nicked his neck.

'The Golden Fleece will wait,' the voice whispered. 'I was telling you about the penalty for treason and perjury. You will be taken to London and lodged in Newgate. Then you'll be fastened to a hurdle behind a horse and dragged all the way to Smithfield. They'll put you up a ladder and turn you off. Your fat legs will dance, your face will go black as your tongue protrudes. Afterwards they'll cut you down, half dead or half alive. Does it really matter? They'll quarter your sorry trunk, pickle it, dip it in tar, fix it above the city gates. Ah, travellers will comment, there's Master Blidscote!'

'I hear what you say,' Blidscote gasped. 'I have told you. I keep a still tongue in my head and will do so till the day I die.'

'I like that, Master Blidscote. So, tell me now, Molkyn's death and that of Thorkle . . .?'

'I know nothing. I tell you, I know nothing. If I did—'

'If you do, Master Blidscote, I'll come back and have more words with you. Now, look at the wall. Go on, turn, look at the wall!'

Blidscote obeyed.

'Press your face against it,' the voice urged, 'till you can smell the piss and count to ten five times!'

Blidscote stood for what appeared to be an age. When he turned, the shadows were empty. A light to the mouth of the alleyway beckoned him forward. Blidscote shook off the horrors of the night and ran. He reached the market square, the cobbles glistening in the wetness of the night. The place was quiet. The houses and shops beyond had their doors and windows closed but lights and lanterns glowed, welcome relief to the darkness and cold. Blidscote realised he had lost his staff. He ran back down the alleyway, collected it and returned to the marketplace. The shock of the meeting with that demon had sobered him. He adjusted his jerkin, pulling the cloak around his shoulders, and strode purposefully across the marketplace. He stopped at the stocks where Peddlicott the pickpocket had his head and hands tightly fastened in the pillory: sentenced to stand there till dawn.

Peddlicott lifted his head. 'Master bailiff, of your charity?'

Blidscote slapped him viciously on the cheek and walked towards the glowing warmth of the Golden Fleece.

Ranulf-atte-Newgate, together with Chanson, sat in the comfortable house of Master John Samler, which stood in a lane on the edges of Melford. Ranulf stared around. The rushes on the floor were clean and mixed with herbs. The plaster walls were freshly washed with lime to keep away the flies, and decorated with coloured cloths. Onions and a flitch of ham hung from the central beam to be cured in the curling smoke from the fire in the open hearth. Chanson sat on the bench next to Ranulf, hungrily eating the bowl of meat stew garnished with spice to liven its dull taste. Ranulf picked up a piece of bread, smiled at his host and dipped the bread into the bowl.

'So, John, you are a thatcher by trade?'

His host, sitting opposite, eyes rounded at having such an important person talking to him, nodded. Beside him, his wife, pink-cheeked with excitement. Their children, supervised by their eldest girl, clustered on the stairs. They reminded Ranulf of a group of owls, white-faced, round-eyed. Ranulf felt uneasy. The thatcher was a prosperous man with a garden plot before and a small orchard behind the house. He had been so overcome when Ranulf knocked on the door, ushering him in as if he was the King himself, serving the best ale his wife had brewed.

'You have five children, Master Samler?'

'Eight in all, two died . . .' The thatcher's voice trailed away.

'And Johanna?' Ranulf insisted. He looked across at the children.

'Yes, Johanna.'

'I understand,' Ranulf continued softly, 'that Elizabeth Wheelwright was murdered a few days ago and your daughter Johanna earlier in the summer. Am I correct?'

Samler's wife began to sob. Chanson stopped eating and put down his horn spoon as a sign of respect.

'She was a fine girl,' Master Samler replied. 'She wasn't flighty in her ways.'

'And the day she died?' Ranulf asked.

'I was out working. Johanna was sent on an errand. She loved the chance of going into the market square to talk to her friends.' He shrugged. 'She went but never came back.'

'Was there anyone special?' Ranulf insisted. 'Anyone at all?' He lifted his head. 'What's your name?' he asked the eldest girl.

'That's Isabella,' Samler replied. 'She's two years older than Johanna.'

Ranulf studied the girl. She was comely enough, with flaxen hair coming down to her shoulders, thin-faced, sharp-eyed. Just a shift of expression betrayed her; perhaps she knew more than she had told even her parents.

'And you know of no reason why she was killed?'

'Why should anyone kill a young woman like Johanna?' the thatcher retorted. 'I have told you, sir, she had no secrets. Oh, she danced and she flirted but there was no one special, was there, Isabella?'

Ranulf smiled across at the young woman, who sat on the stairs above her brothers and sister.

'But she was killed out in the open countryside,' Ranulf insisted. 'Down near Brackham Mere.'

'I have told you what I know, sir,' Samler retorted. 'One afternoon she was sent on an errand to the marketplace and never returned.'

'Will you catch him, sir?' Isabella Samler called out.

'Oh, we'll catch him,' Ranulf replied. 'My master is like a hawk: sharp-eyed and swift. He'll float above Melford and, no matter where the killer hides, be it the thickest bramble bush or the longest grass –' Ranulf got to his feet gesturing with his hand. Isabella watched him – 'he'll swoop, wings back, talons out, and he'll clutch your sister's killer in his tight claws.'

'You are only saying that.'

'No, Mistress, I am promising it.'

Ranulf undid his purse and put a silver coin on the table. The thatcher made to refuse.

'No, no, take it,' Ranulf urged. He patted Chanson on the shoulder. 'For you, your family.'

He walked to the door, gathered up his cloak and sword belt, then looked round. Ranulf felt a tug at his heart. They looked now like a group of rabbits fascinated by a stoat.

'I mean you well, I really do. But you have nothing to say, eh? Nothing more to tell me about Johanna's death?' He glanced quickly at Isabella.

'She was a comely lass.' The thatcher's wife spoke up.

Ranulf put his hand on the latch and turned. 'And she had no love swain?'

'No,' Isabella answered quickly. 'Only those she laughed about.'

'And a secret place?' Ranulf urged. 'Everyone has a secret place.'

'The same as Elizabeth Wheelwright's,' Isabella blurted out. 'They used to visit the copse on the hill overlooking Devil's Oak. It's not really secret.'

'Could you show me the way?'

'It's dark,' Samler replied.

'No, no,' Ranulf smiled. 'I meant if Isabella could show us the lane back to the Golden Fleece.'

Samler's daughter needed no second urging but grabbed her cloak from a peg on the wall. Ranulf made his good nights, as did Chanson, his mouth still full of food. They collected their horses. The lane was dark and muddy. Isabella walked ahead of them.

'Just keep going straight on,' she explained when they reached the end of the lane. She pointed to an alleyway. 'That leads to the market square.'

Ranulf indicated that Chanson walk on.

'You'd best go back then.'

Isabella watched Chanson lead the horses away. She drew closer and stared up at this strange, green-eyed clerk. Isabella Samler had lived a sheltered life. She'd never met a man like this before: tall, slim, smelling of horse, leather and fragrant soap. His white chemise was undone at the neck, allowing the glint of a silver chain, his sword-tip slapped against his boot. She felt frightened yet excited. He was dangerous. If his master was a hawk then so was he.

'Will you really catch him?'

Ranulf chucked her under the chin. 'If you tell me what you should, then it will be sooner rather than later.'

Isabella, in a mixture of fear and flirtation, moved a little closer.

'Did your sister confide in you? Do you know why she went, whom she was meeting?'

'We often lay awake in our bed loft. We'd frighten ourselves with stories about night-walkers.'

'But there are no night-walkers in Melford, are there?'

Isabella swayed slightly side to side as if she was enjoying her riddle.

'You'd be very surprised what walks the streets and lanes of Melford at night. Talk to Parson Grimstone. There's more sin here, under the cover of darkness, than in your great city.'

Ranulf took a silver coin out of his purse and held it firmly between his fingers.

'I gave one to your father but your sister had one, didn't she? Is that why she left? Went out into the countryside? No, no,' Ranulf smiled. He stroked her cheek with a gloved finger. 'Johanna was a good girl but there's not much money, is there? And the tinkers and the chapmen sell such pretty things: a ribbon, a brooch, a bracelet, perhaps a necklace of stones, all polished bright? So, are you going to tell me?'

Isabella looked at the coin and licked her lips.

'My sister had no such coin.'

'Then whom did she meet?'

'I don't know. Perhaps an admirer, perhaps the Mummer's Man.'

'Mummer's Man?' Ranulf asked.

'It's someone I've heard of.'

'You're telling tales?'

'I don't think so.' Isabella stared at the coin. 'I met a travelling girl once. She claimed to have seen a Mummer's Man. He had a mask over his face and his horse moved like a ghost along the lanes outside Melford.'

Ranulf recalled the lonely country trackways they had ridden along on their way to Melford. He felt a prick of fear at this hideous vision of a masked man riding a silent horse.

'I tell you, sir,' she clutched the front of Ranulf's jerkin, 'that's all I know.'

'Nothing else? This travelling girl?'

'It was dusk. She couldn't see much. I didn't think much of her tale till after my sister's death. I daren't tell anyone; I was frightened of getting into trouble.'

Ranulf pressed the coin into her hands. 'Then you'd best get back.'

She took the coin.

Ranulf grasped her wrist. 'Don't go out in the

country lanes, and be careful of the Mummer's Man!'

He released her and she ran off into the darkness.

'What was all that about?' Chanson came back leading the horses. 'Ranulf, I'm tired and I'm cold. Despite what Samler gave us, my belly thinks my throat's slit. My mouth is so dry it's forgotten how to drink. Where's Sir Hugh?'

'Oh, old Master Long Face.' Ranulf took the reins of his horse. 'He'll be riding round the dark lanes, high in the saddle, cowl pulled across his head. He'll be thinking. He broods a lot, does Sir Hugh, turning things over and over in his mind like a water mill. Oh, he'll come back and he'll sit in his chamber staring out of the window, moody and quiet.'

'Is he safe?' Chanson asked. 'I mean, the Lady Maeve told him to be careful.'

'He was attacked in Oxford,' Ranulf replied. 'Took an arrow high in the chest but the King's physicians healed him.'

'Does he love the Lady Maeve? Is that what he is thinking about?'

They reached the end of the alleyway. Ranulf stared across at the poor unfortunate clasped in the stocks. The marketplace was empty, the rubbish had been cleared. Only the occasional flitting shadows: people walking towards the light of the Golden Fleece. Now and again a door slammed, the cry of a child, a dog yapping in its kennels, all the sounds of the night.

'Sir Hugh is a man of great order,' Ranulf declared. 'You serve me, Chanson. Serve me well and, one day, you may become a clerk like I am.'

Chanson quietened the horse, stroking its muzzle.

'Could I really become a clerk, Master Ranulf?'

'Oh yes, there are clerks of the stables, powerful men they are, in charge of the King's horses. Anyway, I am describing to you the way things are ordered. I am a clerk of the Chancery of the Green Wax, next up the rung is Baby Edward and Sir Hugh Corbett's daughter, Eleanor.'

'And after that?' Chanson asked. 'Sir Hugh?'

'Yes, Sir Hugh, then the King, then God.' He grinned at Chanson. 'And, right at the top, the Lady Maeve.'

Chanson looked narrow-eyed but the smile had gone from Ranulf's lean face. In truth, the groom knew he wasn't joking. Ranulf was frightened of no one, Chanson deeply admired him for that. A true bullyboy, Ranulf would swagger into a tavern, the girls would smile and Ranulf would take out his loaded dice and invite all comers. He was quick as a cat, slightly mocking of Sir Hugh. Ranulf, however, stood in dreadful awe of the Lady Maeve even though she was only small and her golden hair framed a face which reminded Chanson of a painting of an angel in the ancient church. Once in his cups Ranulf had confessed how Lady Maeve's eyes frightened him.

'Light blue they are,' he'd slurred. 'Quick and sharp, they miss nothing. Have you ever heard the phrase, "steel in velvet"?' Ranulf had leant back. 'That's our Lady Maeve. I even think old Master Long Face is secretly frightened of her.'

Ranulf began to walk his horse across the cobbles.

'And are you in love, Master Ranulf? I heard mention of a Lady Alicia . . .?'

Ranulf turned swift as a striking snake, lips curled

in a snarl. Chanson jumped so much even his horse
was startled, throwing up its head.

'Hush now! Hush now!' Chanson soothed it but
kept a wary eye on Ranulf, still glaring at him. 'I am
sorry . . .' Chanson muttered.

Ranulf relaxed. 'Ah, it's not your fault.' He beckoned Chanson forward and put an arm round his
shoulder. 'I tell you this: I loved her and she left me.
Gone to a nunnery, she has. Perhaps I'll join her.'

Chanson stared open-mouthed. 'I can't imagine
you in a wimple.'

Ranulf snorted with laughter and withdrew his
arm.

'No, no, Chanson, not a nunnery but into the
Church. I've often thought of that. Can you imagine
Archdeacon Ranulf, perhaps even Bishop Ranulf of
Norwich?'

Chanson, who had seen these powerful prelates,
repressed a smile. Ranulf-atte-Newgate, in gorgeous,
flowing robes, wearing a mitre and carrying a crosier,
processing slowly up the aisle of Westminster Abbey!

'What was that girl talking to you about?' he asked,
changing the conversation.

They stopped at the trough to allow their horses to
drink. Ranulf looked up at the sky, then once more at
the smart front of the market square, its timbered
buildings, lanterns and gleaming paintwork.

'Old Master Long Face will want to know what
we've been doing. So, what do we have here, Chanson? A fat, prosperous town, where everybody makes
a good profit. Lords of the soil, like Sir Maurice and
Tressilyian the justice. Merchants, farmers, millers,
well-fed priests. Look at Master Samler: a thatcher

who does a good trade. He's not prosperous but, in a few years, he'll be sending his sons to the schools in Ipswich.' Ranulf paused. 'During the day the markets are busy, trade is good. Silver and gold change hands, but where there's wealth, corruption, rich and stinking, also flourishes. People have more time on their hands. A man lusts after his neighbour's wife. Secret sins begin to fester like weeds amongst the corn. Rivalries break out, grudges are nursed. All strange sights and sounds appear.'

'What do you mean?' Chanson queried.

'Take Samler's family. Notice the girls, young, plump and well fed. Time is on their hands, not like things used to be when an entire family worked from morning to dusk. They filled their bellies on watery ale and crusts of bread and slept like hogs until the dawn. All has changed. Now, into this little paradise steps a demon, a man who likes to rape and kill.'

'Are there such men?' Chanson looked totally bemused. He was terrified of women and would bask in the smile of the ugliest, greasiest slattern.

'Go into London, Chanson, talk to the ladies of the night in Southwark. They'll tell you about men who like to beat and hurt them, sometimes quite badly, before they can take them.'

'You mean like a stallion has to be quickened before he can mount a mare?'

'I couldn't put it better myself,' Ranulf said drily. 'That's what our killer is. Melford's an ideal place for him: no walls or gates; there must be at least twenty or thirty lanes leading out to the countryside which surrounds the town with lonely meadows, woods and copses. It's so easy,' Ranulf continued, 'for the killer to slip in and out.'

'Even on horseback?'

'You work with horses,' Ranulf replied. 'Tell me, Chanson, what if I wanted to dull the sound of my horse's hoofs?'

'Sacking or straw,' the groom replied. He bent down and lifted his horse's foreleg. 'You can't take off the shoe – that will hurt the animal, make it lame. However, if you took small sacks, filled them with hay or grass, then tied them over the hoofs like buskins, it would be fairly quiet. Why, has the girl seen someone?'

'What she called the Mummer's Man, masked, riding a horse.'

'That would be easy enough,' Chanson confirmed. He climbed into the saddle and gathered the reins. 'If I put sacking on my horse's hoofs, I could ride this horse across the cobbles and you wouldn't know I was there.'

Ranulf grinned up at him. 'But pretend I'm a comely maid. If I met you, Chanson, riding along a lane, wearing a mask, I'd run, flee for my life.'

The groom pulled a face and eased himself out of the saddle. 'I hadn't thought of that.'

'In fact,' Ranulf quipped, 'mask or not, any country wench would take one look at you and flee for her life.'

'I can't help my eye.' Chanson coloured. 'It's the way I was born!'

'I was only joking.' Ranulf patted him on the shoulder. 'But think, Chanson. You're the horseman. I'll tell you what.' Ranulf pointed across to the

Golden Fleece. 'You solve the riddle and I'll buy you the juiciest pie and a tankard which froths and glitters as if it is full of angel mead.'

Chanson wetted his lips. 'You'll keep your word?'

Ranulf lifted his left hand. 'As your horse has a tail.'

Chanson climbed back into the saddle, gathered the reins and stared hungrily around. Then, digging his heels in gently, he rode to where Peddlicott the pickpocket dozed quietly in the stocks. The groom dismounted, took the water bottle off the horn of his saddle and held it to the grateful man's lips.

'Listen,' he said, opening his wallet. He took out a piece of dried meat and gave it to the astonished pickpocket to gnaw on. 'Give me the name of a tavern wench.' He gestured at the Golden Fleece.

'Try Matthew's daughter, Adela. She's buxom enough.'

Chanson thanked him, left his horse and walked back to Ranulf.

'So, you say I am ugly, Master Ranulf?'

'Well, not in so many words,' Ranulf laughed, 'but I've seen prettier gargoyles.'

'A tankard, a pie *and* a silver piece,' Chanson threatened.

'For what?'

'That I can bring a comely wench out from the tavern.'

'But they already know you,' Ranulf retorted.

'No, they don't. They have seen only you, Lord High-and-Mighty, and Sir Hugh Corbett.'

'Wager accepted.'

'On second thoughts,' Chanson came back, 'two silver pieces.'

Ranulf shrugged in agreement. Chanson, full of righteous anger, disappeared through the doorway of the Golden Fleece. Ranulf, ignoring Peddlicott's cry for more salty bacon and a dish of water, stood bemused. Chanson knew everything about horses but his fear of the fairer sex made him quite hopeless with women and they were as frightened of him.

'I know what he's going to do,' Ranulf murmured. 'He's going to sing. They'll hear a few notes and that tavern will empty as if the rushes have caught alight.'

He was about to walk across and have words with Peddlicott when, to his amazement, the tavern door swung open: out sauntered Chanson holding a young, red-haired woman by the hand. They walked across the cobbles like a love swain and his doxy. The girl had a pretty, cheeky face, snub nose and an insolent mouth. She looked at Ranulf from head to toe.

'Well, yes, I know you. What's this?' She let go of Chanson's hand and rubbed her arms. 'It's cold, I've got jobs to do. You promised me a piece of silver.'

Ranulf looked at Chanson's triumphant smile, sighed, opened his wallet and handed across a piece. The wench grabbed it, giggled and fled back to the tavern.

'And the other piece?' Chanson demanded. 'I'm also tired of standing here.'

Ranulf reluctantly tossed it across.

'You should thank yourself,' Chanson smiled. 'Remember what you told me about the girl Johanna? No country wench can resist a piece of silver.'

'What did you do?' Ranulf demanded.

'I went into the tavern and called Adela. She sauntered over, pert as a robin. "You're Adela?" I asked. "Why?" she replied. "There's someone out there who wants to give you a silver piece." ' Chanson shrugged. 'She almost pushed me out of the door.'

'Of course.' Ranulf closed his eyes. 'That's how the Mummer's Man might have done it. He wouldn't approach her. He'd just call out, "Elizabeth Wheelwright, Johanna Samler, I have good fortune for you!" ' Ranulf opened his eyes and clapped Chanson on the shoulder. 'He'd promise to leave a piece in a certain place and so lure them to their deaths. Can't you see that, Chanson?'

'I'm the one who proved it.'

'If I told any girl in this town,' Ranulf declared, 'how there's a silver piece lying beneath Devil's Oak, specially for them, they'd laugh, they'd be intrigued, but they'd also be curious.'

'And wouldn't tell anyone else.'

'No, of course they wouldn't,' Ranulf murmured. 'In a town like Melford people would kill for a piece of silver. And that's the truth of it!'

# Chapter 8

The church of St Edmund's lay in darkness. Only a red sanctuary lamp glowed, a small pool of light against the encroaching night. The carved face of the crucified Christ stared down whilst those of His mother and St John gazed up in anguish. The mist had seeped through crevices in the windows, under the door, slipping like steam into the church, turning the paving stones ice-cold. Mice scampered in the transept searching for morsels of food or pieces of candle wax. No one was there to witness the anguish and agony of Curate Bellen as he knelt on the prie-dieu in the chancery chapel. He had taken his robe off, his hose, his boots. He knelt in the cold as an act of mortification. He gazed up at the statue of the martyred King of East Anglia. Bellen's hands were clenched so tight his knuckles hurt. He prayed for protection, wisdom and forgiveness.

'So many sins,' he murmured. Evil he'd never imagined! Ordained by the Bishop of Norwich, Curate Robert Bellen was unused to the wickedness and wiles of this world. He only coped by keeping his eyes firmly on the next. He, too, was sure Satan had come to Melford, and wasn't he as guilty as the rest?

Bellen sighed and, muttering under his breath, got to his feet. He took off his shift and stretched out on the cold paving stones. Better this, he thought, than the freezing shores by the lakes of Hell. What could he do except pray and atone? The chill caught his hot body and he shivered, quivering as his mind fought against the creeping discomfort. He clutched his Ave beads more tightly. He would pray, do penance then penance again. Perhaps St Edmund, patron of this church, would ask God to send an angel to comfort him. But were there angels? Was God interested in him?

The curate closed his eyes. He should have been a monk. Bellen tried to clear his mind by chanting phrases from the Divine Office. He stared up into the darkness. Carvings gazed back: angels, demons, the faces of saints, even the carved representations of priests and curates who had served here before him. What should he do? Write to the Bishop? Make a full confession? Yet what proof did he possess? Or should he go in front of that sharp-eyed clerk? He was a royal emissary but also a man; he would understand.

Bellen heard the wind creak and rustle the twisted branches of the yew trees outside. Then a sound, like the click of a latch. But that was impossible! Surely he had closed the corpse door behind him? He sighed and got to his feet. He walked out of the chantry chapel and down the transept to the side door. The latch was still down. Shivering, feeling rather foolish, Bellen lifted this and pulled the door open. The cold night air rushed in. Outside God's acre lay silent in the moonlight. He was about to close the door when he looked down and his freezing back prickled with fear. He could see the boot stains. Someone had come into this church, like a thief in the night, had stood in the shadows and watched him.

Sir Hugh Corbett reined in and stared across at the church. The lych-gate was closed, but in the moonlight he could make out the path, crosses, carvings and burial grounds. The grass and gorse were already glinting under a frost. Corbett felt tired and cold. An owl hooted deep in the cemetery. Corbett smiled. Next time he told a story to little Eleanor, he would remember this place with its shadows, dappled moonlight, the haunting silence and the ominous sound of a night bird. Corbett also felt hungry. He closed his eyes and thought of the parlour in Leighton Manor. He'd sit in his high-backed chair or on cushions before a great roaring fire, watching a poker heat red in the flames: he'd then pluck it out and warm posset cups for himself and Maeve. She would be singing softly under her breath, one of her sad Welsh songs. The logs would splutter and crackle, the flames leap higher . . . Corbett opened his eyes.

'Oh Lord,' he prayed, 'the wind is cold, the night is hard. I wish to God I were in my bed, my lover's arms around me.'

Corbett laughed softly. Maeve would call him a troubadour. His horse snickered and, lifting a hoof, struck at the hard trackway. Corbett patted its neck.

'There now! There now! Good lad!' he soothed. 'You've ridden hard and done fine work. It will be oats and a fresh bed of straw for you tonight.'

The bay threw its head back and whinnied as if it

could already smell the tangy warmness of its stable at the Golden Fleece.

Corbett had left Sorrel and spent the greater part of the last hour riding the trackways and lanes around Melford. He wanted to take his bearings: on a number of occasions he had become lost.

'It's a maze,' he muttered.

Melford was not like those ancient towns along the south coast, or the royal boroughs around the Medway, with their walls and gates. Melford had begun as a village, then spread as the wealth from its sheep increased. A murderer could slip easily in and out of such a town. At one time Corbett would be amongst cottages and houses, he'd then take a turning down a muddy lane and be out in open countryside. But at last he had a map in his mind and was already sifting possibilities. How and where the murderer had carried out his crimes was still impossible to deduce. Corbett could only form a vague hypothesis. Now he was intent on visiting Molkyn the miller's widow. He wanted to proceed quickly. The longer he stayed in Melford, and the more time he gave people to reflect, the more they'd say what they wanted him to hear rather than the truth.

Corbett urged his horse forward, passed the church and, following the direction he had taken earlier, rode down a muddy lane. He entered the miller's property and reined in before the mere glinting in the moonlight. Corbett could imagine the tray or platter bearing Molkyn's severed head floating and bobbing on its glassy surface. He dismounted and led his horse round the mere. Above him the great mill soared, its canvas arms stretched out to the night. He glimpsed a light and went on up the lane towards the house. A dog came snarling out of the darkness. Corbett paused, stretching out his hand.

'Now, now,' he whispered. 'No need for that.'

The dog barked again. A door opened and Corbett glimpsed a shadowy form holding a lantern.

'Who's there?' came the challenge.

'Sir Hugh Corbett, King's clerk! I would be grateful if you would call your dog off!'

A low whistle broke the darkness. The dog slunk away and Corbett went on. The man carrying the lantern was young, broad-faced, red-haired, pugnacious and aggressive. He was dressed in a cote-hardie which fell to his knees. Both that, and the leggings beneath, were dusty with flour.

'What do you want?'

'A civil welcome!' Corbett snapped. 'I carry the King's commission.'

'Ralph, Ralph,' a woman's voice called from the doorway. 'Take our visitor's horse.' The voice was low and warm. 'You'd best come in, Sir Hugh Corbett, King's clerk, the night is freezing.'

The young man led off the horse. Corbett undid his sword belt and cloak and followed the woman into the warm, stone-flagged kitchen, a long, sweet-smelling room. The windows at the far end were shuttered, a fire blazed merrily in the hearth and the air was rich with the smell of baking from the ovens on either side of the fire. The woman who welcomed him was blonde-haired and slender, with a smiling, pleasant face. Behind her two other women sat at a table. One was undoubtedly Molkyn's daughter. She had fair hair and a sweet face. The other had coarser features: a flat nose, podgy cheeks, a watchful, hostile gaze. Her grey hair was hidden under a dark blue veil, now slightly askew. She sat, the sleeves of her grey gown pulled back, a sharp pruning knife in her hands. She was helping cut up some vegetables. She dropped these in the pot on the table, her gaze never leaving Corbett's face.

'I am Ursula,' the welcoming woman said.

'The miller's widow?'

Smiling-eyed, she studied Corbett intently. 'Yes, I am the miller's widow whilst you're more handsome than they said.'

Corbett felt himself blush. The woman laughed deep in her throat. She must have seen Corbett's surprise at the green gown she was wearing.

'Widow's weeds are for mourning, master clerk. Molkyn's dead and buried so that's the end of the matter. This is my stepdaughter, Margaret, and the lady staring so boldly at you is another widow, Lucy, Thorkle's wife.'

Corbett felt uneasy. Here were three women who had lost their men. Two their husbands, the young one her father, but there were no funeral cloths against the wall. No purple drape covered the crucifix, chests or cupboards. The kitchen looked like one in the royal household, sparkling clean, scrubbed and washed.

'I do not wish to intrude.'

'You are not intruding.' Ursula's blue eyes remained steady. 'We've all heard of your arrival. We've had King's commissioners here ready to steal our corn but never a royal clerk. We are greatly honoured! We will be the talk of the parish. Come on now!'

Ursula led him by the elbow across to the chair at the far end of the table. She wouldn't take no for an answer but served him freshly baked bread, pots of butter and honey and a pewter tankard of ale from a barrel in the far corner.

Her son Ralph returned. Corbett reckoned he must be about twenty summers old and had apparently taken over the running of the mill. He sat surly and ungracious on the bench, moodily sipping at the drink his mother poured. Thorkle's widow and Margaret continued to slice the vegetables. Ursula sat on the bench to Corbett's left.

'You've come to talk about Molkyn?'

Corbett chewed the bread carefully. He felt this woman was quietly mocking him.

'I haven't really come about Molkyn. More his killer. I've passed the scaffold at the crossroads. Before I leave I want to see his murderer dangle there.'

'And my husband's?'

'Yes, Mistress. I think the killer of both your husbands is one and the same!'

'What makes you say that?' Ursula demanded.

'Here we have,' Corbett now glanced at her, 'two noble burgesses in the town of Melford: a prosperous miller and an equally prosperous yeoman farmer. Someone cut Molkyn's head off, put it on a tray and sent it floating across the mere. The same killer, later in the week, went into Thorkle's threshing shed, took a flail and beat your husband's brains out.'

'An evil man.' Lucy's face had a stubborn look on it.

'Who said it was a man?' Corbett demanded. 'In Wales I have seen a woman take a soldier's head with a shearing knife.'

Lucy looked at the one she was holding and put it down on the table.

'And a flail can be used by anyone.' Corbett shrugged. 'A powerful weapon. Now,' he continued, 'why should someone want to kill your husbands? They belonged to the same parish, their wives are related but they've got more in common than that, haven't they? Molkyn was a foreman, and Thorkle his deputy, of the jury which convicted Sir Roger Chapeleys of horrid murders. Because of their verdict, one of the King's knights was executed on the common gallows.'

'And rightly so.' Ralph slammed his tankard down. 'I was in my fifteenth year. I attended the trial. Sir Roger was a drunkard and a lecher. He had the blood of those young women on his hands.'

'You are sure of that?' Corbett asked.

'We were all sure of it,' Ursula coolly replied. She glanced quickly at Lucy. 'Molkyn and Thorkle often discussed it. Never once had they any doubts about his guilt.'

'Now, there's two brave men,' Corbett retorted. 'They see a knight hang—'

'What difference if he was a knight?' Ralph interrupted. 'That's what knights do, isn't it, kill? Just because they are lords of the soil doesn't make them special.'

'No, it doesn't,' Corbett agreed. 'But Chapeleys was

a King's knight. He'd sworn an oath to uphold the law and he died protesting his innocence. Strange that your father and Thorkle never wavered in their decision.'

'The evidence was there.' Lucy picked up the paring knife.

Corbett noticed how the young woman Margaret hardly looked at him but kept her pallid face averted as if she found his presence distasteful.

'What evidence?' Corbett insisted. 'Why were they so convinced Sir Roger was a murderer?'

'He visited Widow Walmer on the night she died. He was seen by Deverell the carpenter, fleeing along Gully Lane. His house was searched, a bracelet from one of the girls was found amongst his possessions. He was well known for his lecherous ways.'

'With whom?' Corbett asked.

'Widow Walmer for one.'

'But the women in the town?' Corbett queried. 'Did any come forward and claim he had accosted them?'

'He was well known amongst the chambermaids and slatterns of his manor.'

'True,' Corbett agreed, 'but that's not what I asked you. Why should a manor lord, with maids of his own to chase, attack, ravish and slay young women from the town?'

'Perhaps it was the slaying he liked?' Ralph declared sourly.

'Then why the widow woman? Sir Roger had declared in the taproom of the Golden Fleece how he was going down to see Mistress Walmer. Why should he proclaim that he was going to slay someone? What

I'm saying,' Corbett continued, 'is that the evidence against Sir Roger was not final and complete.'

'But it was.' Lucy rubbed the bone handle of the knife between her fingers. 'Master clerk, you must understand women of this town have been killed. Sir Roger was seen near Walmer's cottage. When his house was searched, belongings of the dead women were found, not to mention his knife and sheath left in Widow Walmer's cottage.'

Corbett stared down at the table, he had forgotten that.

'I have my doubts,' he declared. 'Yet you are certain neither Molkyn nor Thorkle ever raised a question about anything amiss?'

'You have your answer,' Lucy smiled insolently.

She thought Corbett was going to look away but he caught her sly-eyed glance at young Ralph, mouth slightly open, tongue between her teeth. You are lecherous, Corbett concluded. Something was very wrong here. These were not two widows mourning their husbands. The same went for Ralph and his sister. They were conspirators, pretending to be sad but secretly rejoicing. Was there a relationship between the saucy-eyed Lucy and this young miller? And why wouldn't Margaret look up, catch his eye? She sat silent as a deaf mute, cutting the vegetables like a dream-walker, almost unaware of what she was doing. On a few occasions Corbett had done business in towns like Melford. He had warned Ranulf and Chanson what to expect: tangled relationships, secret fears, lusts, grudges and grievances. These could abruptly manifest themselves in a lunging dagger or hacking axe.

'Are you tired, Sir Hugh?'

Ursula's mocking coolness rubbed salt into the wound. He felt as if he was knocking at a door knowing full well that those inside heard but refused to answer. He pushed the tankard away. He wanted to be blunt, tell them what he thought but he sensed a trap. They were not grieving, yet that was their business. If he challenged them they would only lie. Were they the killers? It wouldn't be the first time the demon Cain entered a family. And the same went for Lucy, sitting smug at the end of the table as if savouring some secret joke. Had she gone into that threshing barn, picked up the flail and killed her husband so she could lie with Molkyn's son? He pulled back the tankard.

'I am not tired,' he replied, 'just gathering my thoughts.'

'I am busy,' Ralph said.

Corbett undid his wallet and took out the royal warrant displaying the King's Seal. He was wary of this young man whose resentment was so tangible. He was acting the role of the busy, tired miller but his surly looks were as much a threat as his dog which had come snarling out of the darkness.

'I'm also busy,' Corbett said softly. 'The King is busy. You, sir, will sit here, or anywhere I choose, to answer my questions.'

'We do not wish to give offence.' Ursula played with the tendrils of her blonde hair. 'But, Sir Hugh, you come here and ask about a jury which sat five years ago. They only returned the verdict. Sir Louis Tressilyian passed sentence.'

'I will ask him in due time,' Corbett retorted. 'Five

years is a long time, but a few days a mere heartbeat, eh? Your husband Molkyn was a good miller, rich and prosperous?' He gestured round the kitchen. 'What do you have in the house? A parlour, store-rooms, a writing office and bedchambers above stairs?'

'Aye, and a bed as soft as a feather down.'

'And were you lying there,' Corbett asked, 'the night your husband was so barbarously killed?'

'Molkyn liked his ale,' came the tart reply. 'On a Saturday afternoon, he closed the mill down. In spring and summer he played quoits or would go jousting on the Swaile, a little hunting with the dog or cockfighting down at the pit behind the Golden Fleece.'

'And in autumn and winter?'

'He'd take a small barrel of ale, sit in the mill amongst his wealth and, quite honestly, sir, drink himself into such a stupor he'd piss himself.'

Corbett flinched at the coarseness.

'And God help any man, Sir Hugh, who disturbed his pleasure. That included me, his son and his daughter.'

'I never went there.' Margaret looked up, eyes blazing in her thin, white face. 'I never went there. You know that, Mother.'

'Hush now!'

For the first time since they had met Ursula seemed disconcerted, begging Lucy and Ralph with her eyes to assist with Margaret.

'Why didn't you go there?' Corbett asked. 'Come on, girl!'

'I am not a girl.' Margaret made no attempt to hide

152

her hate. 'I am a young woman. My courses have already started. I don't like the mill.' She paused briefly. 'I've never liked the mill! Those grinding stones, the scampering of the mice, and that mere – even in summer it looks dank.'

'My daughter is still upset,' Ursula intervened quickly.

Corbett nearly replied she was the only one that was, but bit back the reply.

'So,' he continued, 'we have Molkyn relaxing after his labours on a Saturday afternoon with a firkin of ale. Surely you became worried when he didn't stagger into bed?'

'Why should I object?' Ursula smiled. 'He stank like a pig and snored like a hog.'

'Surely you'd send someone across to the mill to see all was well?'

'He had a bed there. Why should I ask him to soil clean sheets?'

'Did this drinking become worse after Sir Roger's execution?'

'No. For a while Molkyn seemed happy, if that was possible, that Sir Roger was gone.'

Just for a moment the woman blinked quickly, a slight quiver to the mouth. Corbett went cold. It was the way Ursula had pronounced Sir Roger's name – not harshly, not dismissing him as a great killer. Corbett decided to change tack.

'Mistress, did you ever meet Sir Roger?'

The laughter disappeared from her eyes.

'Did you?' Corbett insisted.

'I – ' she glanced quickly at Ralph – 'I saw him sometimes in church.' She shook her head. 'Now and again in the town. He was someone I knew by sight.'

Again a lie, Corbett thought. More pieces of the puzzle; at least, he was making sense of it. Ursula was a hot-eyed woman, well favoured and comely. No wonder Sir Roger had been dispatched to the gallows. How many other men in Melford had he cuckolded, planting pairs of horns on their heads? A charming, sweet-tongued knight, Sir Roger could ride round the town and pay courtesy to any lady of his choice. They would be flattered. Perhaps open to seduction. Was that why Molkyn had decided on the verdict? Revenge against both Sir Roger and his wife who had cuckolded him?

Ursula got up and, without asking, took Corbett's tankard and refilled it. She came back and in one look Corbett knew he had the truth. Despite her petty errand, the blush still tinged her cheeks.

'Who empanelled the jury?' Corbett asked.

'Ask Blidscote,' Lucy sneered. 'Isn't that the task of the chief bailiff?'

'But he doesn't choose them,' Corbett insisted. 'According to the law, it's supposed to be done by lot.'

'Is it now?' Lucy asked sardonically. 'All I know is that they gathered in the taproom of the Golden Fleece. The names of those on the electoral roll were inscribed on pieces of parchment. Twelve were drawn out. Molkyn and Thorkle first. Surely,' Lucy added sweetly, 'such a system cannot be corrupted?'

Ralph put his head in his hands and quietly snorted with laughter. Lucy was openly mocking Corbett.

Time and again the royal council had issued denunciations of the empanelling of juries, and their corrupt management. Such practices were a constant theme of strident petitions by the Commons. Corbett scratched the sweat on his neck. He certainly looked forward to his meeting with Sir Louis Tressilyian the following evening.

'So, Molkyn was killed, his head sheared off and placed on a tray, which was pushed out on to the mere? He was a strong man?'

'He was drunk as a sot.' Ralph got to his feet. 'Are you a numbskull, master clerk?'

Corbett gazed at him steadily.

'The mill is some distance away. The dog only barks if someone approaches the house. I'll take you there if you want.'

Corbett shook his head. 'So, what do you think happened?'

'Molkyn was lying like a pig on his bed,' Ralph explained. 'Sometime in the early hours the killer walked up the steps and entered the mill. He carried a sword, an axe, a cleaver. He sliced off my father's head,' he pointed to Lucy, 'as she slices an onion. One swift blow. The head was put on a tray, the body thrust up into a chair, a tankard between his hands. The killer left. As he does, he takes the tray with Molkyn's head on it and sends it floating across the mere. That's where poor Peterkin later found it.' The young man, hands on the table, pushed his face close to Corbett's. 'God forgive me, master clerk. I know what you are thinking. We do not grieve. Do you know why? Because we are not hypocrites! Molkyn was an oaf, quick with his fists or his cudgel. As for enemies, go down to Melford, knock on each door, particularly the bakers'. They'll tell you about

Molkyn's false weights and measures, the dust and chalk he added to the flour. The way he short-changed farmers and fixed his prices. He wouldn't give a cup of water to a dying man. I am pleased he's dead. As far as I am concerned he can rot in Hell!'

The young man stormed out, slamming the door behind him.

'Does he speak for you all?' Corbett asked.

'Yes he does,' Margaret replied swiftly and incisively. 'He certainly speaks for me.' She glared defiantly at her mother.

'And you, Mistress?'

Ursula ran a finger along her lower lip. 'Margaret,' she commanded, 'leave those, go upstairs! Make sure the warming pans are ready!'

The girl was about to refuse.

'I said go!'

The young woman threw the knife down and flounced out as angrily as her brother.

'They are not my children,' Ursula explained.

'I beg your pardon, Mistress?'

'I am Molkyn's second wife.'

'His first wife died in childbirth?'

Lucy stifled a laugh. Corbett refused to look in her direction.

'She fell.' Ursula pointed to the stairs. 'An unfortunate accident.'

'Do you know, Mistress, I *am* tired.' Corbett sipped from the tankard. 'Of lies, of hidden laughter, of shadow games as if we are children. She didn't fall, did she? There is a suspicion that she was pushed. Is that what you are saying?'

'Molkyn was free with his fists. His first wife fell,

bruised her face and broke her neck. Molkyn claimed he was working at the mill when it happened.'

'But you don't believe that, do you?'

'No, sir, I don't. He was a bully: he would have done the same to me. I fought back. I told him that I would stand on the market cross and proclaim what he really was and – I'll be honest – if he ever hit me, one night I'd slip across to that mill and slit his drunken throat. But,' she tossed back her hair, 'before you ask, I didn't. Molkyn may have been a big man but he had the mind and belly of a greedy child. Of course, I don't grieve for him. As for bed sport,' she hid a giggle behind her hand, 'I'd have a better game with that whey-faced curate of Parson Grimstone's.'

'And is that the view of Thorkle's widow?' Corbett asked.

Lucy sliced a vegetable, then wiped her mouth on the back of her hand.

'If Molkyn was a roaring dog,' she replied, 'Thorkle was a mouse of a man. And, as for his death, come down to my farm, master clerk. Or even better, ask young Ralph. He was in my house when Thorkle was killed, sitting in the kitchen, talking to me and my children. I don't know why Thorkle died. Like a little mouse he kept his mouth shut. He always was in fear of Molkyn.'

'And your daughter, Mistress?' Corbett asked. 'She's not upset?'

'Ah!' Ursula got to her feet, wiping her hands slowly on the breast of her taffeta gown. 'If she's upset, master clerk, it's because you mentioned Widow Walmer. Didn't you know she often acted as her maid?' She laughed at Corbett's surprise. 'Well, not maid – don't forget she was only a young girl of twelve – more as a companion. She often slept there, spent the evening, kept the good widow company.'

'And the night Sir Roger supposedly murdered her?'

'Well, the widow was expecting company, wasn't she? Margaret was told to stay away, that's all she knew and that's all I can tell you.'

Corbett stared across at the fire. He'd learnt enough. He had picked up pieces which he must arrange in some form of order, but, perhaps, not tonight. He pushed back his stool, picked up his cloak and sword belt, thanked his hosts and went out into the yard.

# Chapter 9

The wind had picked up, whirling the branches, scattering the dry leaves. Clouds raced across the moonlit sky. Corbett dug his heels in, guiding his horse across the bridge and up the lane leading back to the church.

'The devil's night,' Corbett whispered.

He recalled boyhood stories. His mother used to sit him on her knee and talk about the wild woodman, all tangled hair and glaring eyes, who supposedly lived in the forest, an arrow-shot from their farm. Corbett closed his eyes and smiled. Such stories! Every tree, every bush, hid a fantastical world of evil goblins, malignant forest people; dragons, griffins and man-sized hawks. He'd started telling the same to Baby Eleanor but always in a whisper. Maeve had clear ideas about such legends.

'Uncle Morgan used to frighten me to death as a child!'

'He still frightens me,' Corbett had whispered.

Uncle Morgan had arrived years ago for a 'short visit' but settled down and didn't show the slightest inclination to return to Wales. On a night like this, however, Corbett was glad Uncle Morgan was at Leighton.

Corbett was tightening the reins when the figure came whirling out of the darkness. A rustle in the undergrowth, a slithered footfall, Corbett glimpsed the club coming back, aiming for his leg. His horse whinnied and started. Corbett cursed, going back in the saddle, fingers searching for the hilt of his sword. Then his attacker had disappeared, quietly and mysteriously.

'What on earth . . .?' Corbett pulled himself out of the saddle, patting his horse, talking to it reassuringly. The bay, however, refused to be quietened, going back on its hind legs, threatening to rear, shaking its head and expressing its annoyance in sharp whinnies. Corbett held on to the reins, talking softly as Chanson had taught him.

At last the animal calmed. Corbett allowed it to nuzzle his hands and face before remounting. Of all the attacks he had ever endured, that was the most surprising. A man on foot could really do little harm to a rider. The blow had been directed towards his leg; only sheer luck had saved both him and the horse from considerable pain. But why?

Corbett emerged from the woods and stared up at the moon-washed church. He breathed in deeply, quietening his mind, calming his temper. He'd had enough. He had been out in the dark too long! He urged his horse into a canter and was pleased to reach the square and the glowing warmth of the Golden Fleece. He went round the side of the tavern and gave his horse to an ostler.

'I want him treated really well,' Corbett ordered. 'A good rub down. You have the blankets? Make sure he's fed and watered.'

The sleepy-eyed boy promised he would. Corbett tossed him a penny, took off his sword belt, grasped his saddlebags and walked through the rear door and along the passageway into the bustling taproom: a welcome relief from the cold and darkness.

The taproom was busy, lit by lanterns and candles, and warmed by a roaring fire. The air was thick with the smell of candle grease and wood smoke. Somewhere a shepherd played a lilting tune on a lute. Corbett's mouth watered at the spicy smell from the side of pork being tended on the spit by two red-faced boys crouched in the inglenook. They turned it slowly, basting it with herbs soaked in oil. Mastiffs lay before the hearth and slavered at such pleasant odours. Slatterns, their hands full of tankards of frothing ale, pushed their way through, slapping away the wandering fingers of chapmen and tinkers. Ranulf and Chanson were seated in the corner, surrounded by locals. Both of them looked well fed and relaxed. Ranulf sat like Herod amongst the innocents, those precious dice in his hand, inviting his 'guests' to lay a wager.

'You've returned at last!'

Corbett glanced behind him. In a cooler, darker part of the taproom sat Blidscote and Burghesh. Burghesh was the same as ever, Blidscote looked bleary-eyed and red-nosed as if he had drunk too much, too fast. Burghesh waved Corbett over.

'I recommend the quail pie and some of that pork.'

Matthew the taverner came bustling across. Corbett ordered food for himself and ale for his companions. He did not have to wait long. The taverner served the food personally: a broad, wooden platter with half a steaming pie, strips of crackling pork and vegetables diced and covered in a cheese sauce. Corbett took out his horn spoon and the small dagger kept in a sheath above his right boot. He ate quickly, hungrily, savouring every mouthful. He half listened to Blidscote and Burghesh's chatter: about the change in the weather and the arrangements for All-Hallows celebrations.

'A busy day, Sir Hugh?' Burghesh asked once the clerk had finished eating. The old soldier toasted him with his tankard.

Corbett responded. Blidscote might be a toper but Burghesh's broad face was friendly: clear grey eyes and smiling mouth. Corbett wondered how much this veteran of the King's wars knew about Melford.

'I'll tell you this, Master Burghesh.' Corbett wiped his mouth on the back of his hand. 'If the French ever invade, Melford will be a hard town to take. You'd have to surround it with a circle of steel.'

'Ah, but the French will never come,' Burghesh smiled. 'That's one of the joys of this place, Corbett. You can wander in and out.' He lifted the tankard. 'God knows there are enough people in this taproom who will keep an eye on what you do and where you go.'

'But what about the chapmen and tinkers?'

Corbett pointed across to where a group of these sat with their trays carefully stacked on the floor beside them. One was busy feeding a pet squirrel, a small red ball of fur on his shoulder which prettily gnawed on the offered scraps. Now and again the squirrel would break off to chatter at the vicious-looking ferret held by another.

'I mean,' Corbett continued, 'they can wander in

and out when they like and not pay the market toll.'

'They can try,' Blidscote slurred. 'But who'll buy from them? They'll only get reported, put in the stocks and banned for a year and a day. They are only too willing to come into the market square and pay the tax.'

'And you are responsible for that?' Corbett asked.

He studied the chief bailiff's fat, sweaty face, weak chin, slobbery mouth and bleary eyes. Corbett recalled his conversation at the mill. Blidscote was a dangerous man: weak, boastful but, if threatened, dangerous in a sly, furtive way.

'I'm chief bailiff,' Blidscote replied. 'I do my job well.'

Corbett sipped from his tankard. 'And you were one of the first to see Widow Walmer's corpse?'

'Aye.' The bailiff shook his head. 'I'll never forget that evening. I was here in the taproom, wasn't I, Burghesh, with you and Repton the reeve?'

'Tell me exactly,' Corbett demanded.

'I'll do it,' Burghesh offered. 'Do you remember, Blidscote, we gathered here early? There was you, me, Matthew the taverner and Repton.'

'Who's this Repton?' Corbett asked.

'He's over there.'

Corbett followed his direction.

'The fellow with the lank hair, thin as a beanpole. A widower, he had lustful thoughts about Widow Walmer – wanted to marry her, he did.'

Repton was tall, thin, angular; a sallow, bitter face, lank brown hair down to his shoulders. He was dressed in a dark green cote-hardie. A choleric man, he was deep in heated discussion with his fellows.

'Anyway,' Blidscote continued, 'Repton was talking about visiting Widow Walmer. "Ah," says Matthew the taverner, "Sir Roger Chapeleys is fishing in that pond tonight." '

'And how did Matthew know that?' Corbett demanded, though he suspected the answer.

'Why, Sir Roger had been here earlier in the day and said as much in his cups!' Burghesh took up the story again. 'Anyway, Repton was all a-sulk, muttering to himself for some time. He wanted to go and see her. The reeve had been acting strangely all evening. He went out and then came back.'

'How late was this?'

Burghesh pulled a face. 'Oh, it must have been between ten, eleven o'clock at night. I remember looking at the hour candle.' He pointed to where it burnt fiercely under its bronze cap near the kitchen door. 'Repton was in his cups. He asked me to go with him.' Burghesh sipped from his tankard. 'So I agreed. It was a pleasant enough evening. We went down Gully Lane. I realised something was wrong as we approached the cottage: the front door was off its latch, one of the shutters was still open. Inside, Goodwoman Walmer was lying on the kitchen floor, a dreadful sight! Dress and petticoats all askew, legs stuck out, head strangely twisted, her dress had been torn, dark blue marks round her throat. In Scotland I'd seen men who had been garrotted with bowstrings. She was the same – face a bluish-black, eyes popping, mouth all twisted. I told Repton to stay there and came back for Blidscote.'

'Master bailiff?' Corbett interjected.

'I'd drunk a good bit,' the man confessed. 'I took

some of the men from the tavern and went down. It was, as Burghesh described: hideous and ghastly. I was sick outside. We searched the house. Nothing was stolen but, under the kitchen table, we found Sir Roger's knife, a small stabbing dirk with his arms emblazoned on the ivory handle and sheath.'

'And what did Sir Roger say when this evidence was offered?'

'He said he'd given it as a gift to Widow Walmer.'

Corbett hid his disquiet. Any theory that this corrupt bailiff, or anyone else, had deliberately left incriminating evidence was to be rejected, though anyone knowing she'd received such a love token could have used it to incriminate Sir Roger.

'You are sure of that?'

'As the Good Lord lives, yes.'

'And then what happened?' Corbett insisted.

'The next morning,' Blidscote replied, 'I travelled to see Justice Tressilyian. At first he wouldn't believe what we told him, then he swore out warrants. I went to Thockton Hall. Sir Roger, of course, denied everything but I showed him the warrants. The armed posse I'd brought searched his chambers. They found a bracelet and a brooch in his private coffer: these had been taken from two of the dead wenches.'

'And Sir Roger denied having these?'

Blidscote smiled craftily and tapped the side of his nose. 'What are you implying, Sir Hugh? That someone in my *comitatus*, my posse, placed those trinkets there? No, no, Sir Roger confessed they'd been sent to him in a small leather sack as a present. He'd put them in his coffer and hadn't given them a second thought.'

'You mean as some sort of love token?'

'That's right, master clerk, some sort of love token! We asked him about the knife. He made the response as I have described. Then we asked him about the three young women who had been killed. Again, Sir Roger confessed that one of them had worked at Thockton Hall and he had tumbled the wench.' Blidscote blew out his cheeks. 'He claimed he was innocent of the murders. I told him that was a matter for a jury. Justice Tressilyian came down to the Guildhall, two others with him, but he was the principal judge. A court was held and depositions taken.'

'And there were plenty of hostile witnesses. Sir Roger was not liked?'

'No, he wasn't.' Burghesh took up the story. 'Melford is a prosperous town, Sir Hugh. The old ways are dying. People resent a manor lord, a knight, winking at their women, acting the great lord of the soil. Sir Roger had a temper, and when angered he told people what he thought. Now people had a chance to reply.'

'But that's not evidence?'

'No, Sir Hugh, it isn't. I admit there was a lot of chatter and gossip, then Deverell the carpenter came before the justice. He took an oath: how he had seen Sir Roger fleeing up Gully Lane, all dishevelled and troubled.'

'And what was Sir Roger's response to that?'

'He dismissed Deverell as a liar, the son of a whore.'

'But what was Deverell doing in Gully Lane at night?'

'Oh, he was returning to Melford with a supply of wood.'

'So.' Corbett cradled his tankard. 'We have the knife, the brooch and the bracelet. We have Sir Roger Chapeleys certainly visiting Widow Walmer as well as confessing to a relationship with one of the murdered women.'

'There was other evidence,' Blidscote offered. 'Sir Roger could not produce any proof of where he was when those three women were killed. Time and again he was asked. His reply was simple and stark: he couldn't recall.'

'And the parchments he burnt?' Burghesh added.

'What?' Corbett queried.

'Ah yes.' Blidscote leant forward, waving a finger. 'When I arrived at Thockton Hall with my warrants, Sir Roger's retainers raised the alarm. There was a bit of a struggle; we had to push by them. Sir Roger was found in his bedchamber, his hands and fingers black from soot. He had burnt some papers. I examined the fragments. They were love letters, some record of his conquests.'

'And Sir Roger's response?'

'He said he could do what he liked with his own property. Justice Tressilyian was very fair. "Tell us, Sir Roger, what you burnt," he said. "Private papers," was the reply.'

Corbett turned and shouted across to the slattern to bring fresh ale.

What if I had been Tressilyian, he thought, and this evidence had been laid before me? It certainly looked bleak. Sir Roger had had a case to answer and had failed to do so. He had denied none of the evidence except Deverell's, but he had had one friend . . .

'Sir Hugh?'

Corbett glanced across at Burghesh.

'What are you thinking?'

'About Furrell the poacher. Why wasn't his evidence believed? He claimed he saw Sir Roger leave Widow Walmer alive, that he even glimpsed others going down to her cottage.'

'Furrell was a poacher,' Blidscote jeered. 'He loved his ale.' The bailiff's face turned puce as he realised the hypocrisy of what he was saying. 'Even more than me,' he muttered. 'He was also in Sir Roger's pocket.'

'What do you mean by that?' Corbett asked.

'Well, Sir Roger was kind. I think Furrell knew more than he should have done about Sir Roger. Our good knight didn't go to church often – more interested in matters of the dark.'

'Are you saying he was a witch or a warlock?' Corbett scoffed.

'There's some truth in that,' Burghesh interjected.

'Oh, come, come!' Corbett sipped from his tankard. 'If I'm to believe you, Sir Roger had no virtues. Are you now claiming he danced with the Queen of the fairies in moonlit glades? Or made bloody sacrifices to the demons of the woods?'

Burghesh grinned. 'No, no. Sir Roger was interested in magic: in those twilight areas where the light and dark are not so pronounced. He would sometimes talk about it in here.'

'But Furrell's evidence?' Corbett demanded, steering the conversation on to firmer ground. 'Here was a man prepared to go on oath that Sir Roger left Widow Walmer alive and well.'

'He could have gone back,' Blidscote replied.

'But Furrell also hinted that he glimpsed others going down Gully Lane towards Widow Walmer's cottage.'

'Ah well.' Blidscote grinned over the tankard. 'How do we know it wasn't Sir Roger returning? We have also got Deverell the carpenter's evidence.'

'And the jury?' Corbett decided to change tack.

'They were selected as usual by ballot here in the taproom.'

'But, isn't it strange, master bailiff, that the foreman and the deputy of that jury . . .' Corbett paused, '. . . well, certainly Molkyn, was no friend of Sir Roger?'

'What are you implying?' Blidscote's face turned ugly. 'That I am guilty of embracery?' The bailiff stumbled over the official term for the corruption of a jury. 'The ballot was open and fair. Sir Roger had no friends, I've told you that. Moreover, I'm only the bailiff, not the justice. Sir Louis Tressilyian could have sent Sir Roger for trial before King's bench in London.'

'Yes, yes, he could have done.' Corbett cradled the tankard. 'I wondered about that.'

When Corbett had met the King at Westminster, he had asked the same question: Edward, who loved arguing about the subtleties of the law, had simply shaken his head.

'I think Sir Louis,' the King had replied, 'tried to do that but I refused. It sets a precedent, Corbett. Can you imagine what would happen if every murder case was referred to Westminster? The courts would be as clogged as a wheel on a muddy day.'

'Sir Hugh Corbett! Sir Hugh Corbett!'

The clerk turned. A royal messenger, his surcoat emblazoned with the snarling leopards of England, stood in the doorway, boots and spurs caked with dirt. He carried a wallet in one hand, his white wand of office in the other.

'I am here!' Corbett called out.

The man wearily made his way forward. He thrust the wallet into Corbett's hand.

'Messages from Westminster,' he declared.

Sir Hugh looked at the man's red-rimmed eyes. 'What's your name?'

'Varley, sir.'

'Well, Varley?' Corbett then called across the taverner.

'I'm to be away at first light,' the messenger added warningly.

'At this moment I have no reply to make,' Corbett declared. 'Master taverner, give this man a clean bed, something to eat and drink.'

'All our beds are clean,' the taverner replied, his square, red-whiskered face breaking into a grin. 'But I know what you mean.'

He led the messenger off. Corbett broke the seals and undid the wallet. The first roll was a copy of Sir Roger's trial which he had asked for before leaving Westminster. The second was from the Chancery of the Secret Seal, giving details of Sir Roger's military service in Gascony and along the Scottish/Welsh march. Corbett demanded a candle and read this carefully. He grunted and thrust it back into the wallet. He stared across the taproom at Repton. The reeve lifted his head. Corbett flinched at the hostility in the narrow, close-set eyes. He glanced at Blidscote.

'It's time I walked with Master Repton. After all, he did start this dance.'

Blidscote eased himself up and sauntered across. Corbett waited. When he felt the presence of the man beside him, he glanced up.

'Sit down, Master Repton,' he offered. 'Have some ale.'

The reeve pulled across a stool.

'I drink with my friends.' Close up Repton's face was even more sour.

'Do you now?' Corbett drained his tankard. 'And you were drinking here the night Widow Walmer was killed?'

'That's correct. I was here with my friends whilst that killer raped and choked the woman I loved.'

'And did she love you?'

The reeve blinked. 'I never had the chance to ask, clerk, did I? But, if she had responded, I would have met her at the church door to exchange vows.'

Corbett studied the reeve. His cote-hardie was of good cloth. The brown belt strapped around his narrow waist of good leather; his leggings of dark blue worsted; even the boots were the work of a craftsman. A prosperous man, Corbett concluded. He would act as reeve, steward of lands held by the town. He would also have his own holding: producing for the market as well as for the pot.

'What's the matter, clerk?'

'I am wondering why you are so hostile. You've told your tale a thousand times. Surely, you can tell it once more?'

'Fine, I'll tell you my tale.' The words came out as a snarl. 'I was drinking here. I wanted to visit Widow Walmer. I asked Burghesh to accompany me.'

'No, no, that's not true, is it?'

'Are you calling me a liar?' Repton's hand went to the knife in its sheath.

'No, I am just saying you are rather forgetful. You were drinking here and you decided to visit Mistress Walmer. However, the taverner Matthew had announced how the widow was receiving another guest that night.'

The reeve swallowed hard. Corbett was aware of how quiet the taproom had fallen.

'That's my first question,' Corbett smiled. 'Why, in the late hours of the night, did you suddenly decide to visit a woman whom you knew was entertaining someone else? She would not have liked it and Sir Roger would have objected. A feisty man, Sir Roger. I don't think he would have liked someone else a-calling?'

'That's why I took Burghesh.'

'Ah,' Corbett sighed. 'You always take a companion when you visit a lady friend?'

The reeve grasped the corner of the table. 'What are you implying?'

'I am implying nothing, master reeve. I am trying to get to the truth of the matter. Had you visited Widow Walmer before? Well, had you?'

'Yes, but that's my business.'

'Fair enough and had you asked someone to accompany you?' Corbett leant closer. 'Give me one occasion, name one companion.'

'That night Sir Roger was there I needed—'

'Did you really? But, surely, it was very late? Sir Roger may have left?'

'I don't know what you are implying.' Repton leapt to his feet. In one swipe he drew his dagger from its sheath. He backed off and stood slightly crouching, legs apart.

You've fought before, Corbett thought: you're a taproom brawler.

'What's this nosy clerk doing here?' Repton glowered round the quiet taproom.

His question provoked a murmur of agreement.

'Who do you think you are? Chapeleys was a murderer!'

A chorus of approval greeted his words.

'He killed Widow Walmer and those other women. So he was hanged for it. Now his whelp sends whining letters to Westminster.'

'Sit down, master reeve,' Corbett ordered. 'Put your knife away and sit down!'

'Do you think I'll do what you say, clerk?' Repton raised the knife. 'Or is that all you are good for? A long nose with a clacking tongue? This is Melford, not Westminster. You won't be the first to be sent packing!'

Some of the other customers were now jeering.

'Come on!' Repton waved his hand.

'I carry the King's warrant.'

'I carry the King's warrant,' Repton mimicked.

This provoked further guffaws of laughter. Corbett looked across at Ranulf, shook his head and got to his feet.

'I want to talk to you, Repton, that's all. I want the truth. The King wants the truth.'

'I've told you the truth. You're not in the Schools of Oxford now, clerk.'

'I'm trying to be reasonable.' Corbett took a step forward. 'I wish you no ill.'

Corbett watched the man's eyes. Repton had drunk deep. He was beyond reason.

'Look,' Corbett played with the chancery ring on his finger, 'I apologise. I am sorry if I have upset you.'

The laughter grew. Repton couldn't resist the audience. He came up, the knife moving away. Corbett lashed out with his boot, catching the unfortunate full in the groin. Repton screamed with pain and fell to his knees, the knife clattering amongst the rushes. He tried to crawl forward but Corbett gently placed his heel on the back of the man's hand.

'I am the King's clerk!' he proclaimed. 'I wish no man ill but, if I wanted, Repton could hang for treason. So I shall tell you why I am here. Five years ago Sir Roger Chapeleys was executed for the murder of at least four women.' He stared round the taproom. 'Good, I now have your attention. If Sir Roger was guilty then he deserved to die. But there's the riddle. Not only have the murders begun again but two members of the jury responsible for convicting Sir Roger have also been killed in a barbarous manner. I will have the truth either in Melford or in the King's own prison at Newgate!'

Chanson was staring open-mouthed. Ranulf, grinning from ear to ear, was busy pocketing his earnings.

'Now, Master Repton,' Corbett pressed the heel of his boot till the man flinched, 'do you not accept my apology?'

'Yes,' the man gasped.

'And will you not accept a tankard of ale?'

'Yes.'

Corbett helped the reeve to his feet. He now looked woebegone. He didn't know whether to nurse his hand or his groin. Corbett lifted the stool and ushered the man to it. Burghesh and Blidscote sat fascinated, as if they couldn't understand what was happening. Corbett ordered more tankards of ale. He thrust one into the reeve's hands.

'The pewter's cold.' Corbett urged, 'Hold it against your groin, it will ease the pain.' He leant forward. 'You are a fool!' he hissed. 'You could be hanged for that!'

Repton caught back a sob.

'You are not angry, are you?' Corbett continued. 'You are frightened.'

He was aware of Ranulf and Chanson joining them, taking stools and sitting behind the reeve.

'What do you mean?' the reeve stuttered.

'You came into the Golden Fleece that night twice, didn't you? You had been drinking all day. You learnt from Taverner Matthew how Widow Walmer was entertaining so off you staggered, along Gully Lane to Widow Walmer's cottage?'

'I didn't do it,' the reeve whispered, and sipped from the ale. 'I swear to God I didn't do it!'

'Did what?' Blidscote queried.

'You reached the cottage, didn't you?' Corbett ignored the bailiff. 'And the door was open?'

'Yes, the door was open.' The reeve spoke as if learning a lesson. 'Widow Walmer was lying on the floor.' He clutched his stomach. 'I could tell what had happened, her dress had been pulled down at the

175

top, those hideous marks round her throat. Body and legs twisted. I was frightened. I thought the killer could still be there. I panicked. What if they accused me?'

'So you came back to the Golden Fleece,' Corbett explained, 'where you drank some more, turning over and over in your mind what you had seen. Once your courage returned, you asked Burghesh to accompany you. So, both of you went along.'

'That's right,' the reeve slurred.

'You didn't tell us this,' Blidscote stated.

'How could I?' The reeve blinked. 'But I didn't kill her!'

'And Sir Roger's knife?' Burghesh asked.

'I told you. I stood in the doorway. I touched nothing. Just one glance was enough. I went outside and was sick in the bushes. Then I came back here.'

'Did you see anything of Sir Roger?'

The reeve shook his head. Corbett pushed away the tankard; he picked up his leather wallet, cloak, sword belt and saddle panniers.

'You see,' he smiled at Blidscote. 'I am here for the truth, but now I am tired.'

He bade them good night, went across the taproom and up the stairs.

'Your master is a strange man,' Burghesh declared.

'Old Master Long Face is strange enough,' Ranulf grinned, getting to his feet. He leant over the table, raising his voice so it carried across the taproom. 'He's a strange one, is Sir Hugh. He nags and nags at the truth. He never gives up. But,' he raised his eyebrows, 'tonight he was in a good temper.'

'Why?' the reeve asked. 'Would he have killed me?'

'No.' Ranulf grasped the reeve by the shoulder. 'Sir Hugh wouldn't have killed you but I would have done!' He pushed his face closer. 'And, if it happens again, I will! Do tell that to the people of Melford!'

# Chapter 10

'An exciting day, Master.'

Ranulf, perched on a stool, grinned over his shoulder at Chanson, who squatted near the door. Corbett sat on his bed beneath the small casement window. He stared around his bedchamber, a comfortable, sweet-smelling place. He was particularly intrigued by this large four-poster bed with its ornate tester and curtains of mulberry-coloured wool.

'You'd think it was a bridal chamber,' he murmured. 'Certainly comfortable; even rugs on the floor.'

'At least our taverner knows how to treat a royal clerk,' Ranulf laughed.

'I am that tired,' Corbett replied, 'I'd sleep in a pigsty. Don't be too hard on the good citizens of Melford: they are frightened.'

He watched the capped brazier in the corner, its coals glowing through the narrow slits. Every so often he would catch the flavour of spring from the herbs sprinkled there. Corbett had not demanded such luxury but he was appreciative of it.

'Nothing like a well-aimed kick, is there, Master?'

'Repton was a fool, yet I couldn't let it pass. Well, I

know what you found and you now know what I've learnt.'

They'd spent at least an hour exchanging information. Corbett was particularly intrigued at how Ranulf's story about the Mummer's Man corroborated what Sorrel had told him.

'Oh, what was that information from Westminster?' Ranulf asked.

'A record of the trial from the court of King's Bench. The rest was a little research I'd organised. Never once,' Corbett waved a hand, 'was Sir Roger, whilst serving with the King's forces in many places, ever accused of attacking or raping women. As you know, when troops are in hostile country those who love to abuse women seize such opportunities with relish. I've seen at least five or six hanged in Wales for rape and abduction.'

'What do you mean, relish?' Chanson asked.

'When we return to London, Chanson, Ranulf may take you down to the stews of Southwark, introduce you to some of his lady friends.'

'You mean whores? Ranulf's talked about them.'

'No woman is a whore!' Ranulf snapped. 'I call them my ladies of the night. A prettier bunch of damsels you've never clapped eyes on.'

'You should talk to them,' Corbett continued. 'They will tell you about a certain type of man who can only enjoy intercourse after he has beaten a woman. The ladies of the night make them pay for such a privilege. Last Michaelmas we entertained Monsieur de Craon, the French envoy. When he's not busy plotting for his master, Philip of France, or trying to steal secrets or kill our spies, de Craon is used, like I am, to track down killers. He mentioned a particular case near the royal hunting lodge of Fontainebleau. About two summers ago, young women were attacked, raped and murdered. De Craon eventually caught the killer and watched him broken on the wheel at Montfaucon. He was fascinated by how the man enjoyed what he did. De Craon described him as an animal; a human wolf, who liked to prey: he enjoyed the violence more than the kill.'

'And this is what we have in Melford?'

'Yes, Ranulf, but I can't make sense of anything we have learnt.' Corbett leant forward. 'Let me tell you a story.'

Chanson drew nearer and sat cross-legged next to Ranulf.

'Once upon a time,' Corbett smiled at his companions, 'we have the King's market town of Melford, a very prosperous place where crops are no longer sown but the fields are grassed over. Sheep are raised and the wool is sold for a fat profit. You've seen the effects of this: good, stout buildings, a tavern like the Golden Fleece, Guildhall, shops, luxury items, brought in from the merchants of London. Now all is pleasant in this little Eden until five years ago . . .'

'So, who came here five years ago?' Ranulf asked.

'I've scrutinised that,' Corbett replied. 'No one did. Most of the characters we are dealing with, including the Chapeleys, have been here at least ten years, as have the vicar, his curate and Burghesh, Molkyn the miller and so on. However, I know what you're implying. The first murder took place five years ago but, according to Sorrel, there have been others: the womenfolk of traders, chapmen, tinkers, Moon People. The latter now avoid this place like the plague. However,' Corbett continued, 'five years ago, in the space of a few months, three townswomen were attacked, raped and garrotted; their corpses found in different parts of the countryside. Now you have seen this town, it lacks walls and gates. An army could slip in and out and not be noticed. I have ridden around it: at one time you are in a busy, prosperous market town, the next lonely countryside. It's a landscape our killer would love: it dips and rolls. Part of the forest has been cleared away but copses and woods still survive.'

'And there's no ploughing,' Ranulf declared.

'Good man, Ranulf! We'll make a farmer of you yet. When fields are ploughed, you have a constant stream of labourers moving in and out: harrowing, fertilising, sowing, reaping. Meadow land is different, that's why raising sheep is so profitable. The longer the grass grows the better. The sheep are put out to pasture and who looks after them? A shepherd with, perhaps, his boy and dogs? Because sheep wander, hedgerows have been planted along the narrow lanes. In places the trackways are like trenches. Someone could move along them and not be seen by a shepherd boy dozing under a tree – a perfect killing ground. However,' he tapped his foot on the floor, 'we do have one perplexing problem. Why should a young woman wander out into such countryside to meet this assassin? Yes, Chanson, I accept how you bribed the tavern wench to come out and meet Ranulf. But, would she have gone into the countryside, to a lonely place like Devil's Oak? And this Mummer's Man, riding his silent horse? Is he the murderer? If so, his victim would have to be out in the countryside to begin with. And, bold as she might be, Adela would not approach such a strangely garbed figure on a lonely country lane.'

'But for silver?'

'Oh, I accept the logic of what you say, Ranulf. If I told any of the serving girls below that a silver piece was out at Devil's Oak, they wouldn't tell anybody in case they lost it. They'd keep it quiet. I could understand Adela going out for a second time, if her first journey had been profitable. But, what inducement would she be given first?'

Ranulf snapped his fingers. 'Master, the Mummer's Man was seen riding the country lanes?'

'Yes, that's what Sorrel told me.'

'So, he may have been going to put the silver in the secret place, travelling to meet his victim? Or even returning after the murder?'

'And?'

'I'd wager,' Ranulf continued excitedly, 'the killer first approaches his victim here in the town, a narrow lane, a dark alleyway. He calls out a name. Perhaps he coats the trap with honey? Says so-and-so admires her. Perhaps that Mummer's Man, if he is the killer, doesn't give a name but just says a silver piece will be in a certain place?'

'I agree. Few young women could resist such an approach. The victim would be curious, wondering if it was true or not. So she plucks up her courage and goes out to some desolate spot. The silver piece is there. Perhaps she is killed on the first occasion, the assassin lurking nearby. Or, maybe she has only to go a short distance that first time, and, the trap laid to ensure greater compliance, it's the second time he strikes, luring her further away to an appropriate place.'

Corbett half cocked his head and listened to the sounds from the stable yard, the cries of farewells as the taproom was cleared.

'Anyway, let me continue my story. Our killer lusts after young women. Wearing a disguise and mask, he makes his approach. The victim is lured out into the lonely countryside and killed. For all we know, there may be women who were not tricked so easily but that might be difficult to establish. Now, so far,' Corbett continued, rubbing his chin, 'the story is simple, it's like luring a child with sweet-meats. I suspect this Mummer's Man is the killer. He roams the countryside lanes and trackways looking for possible victims like a fox hunting rabbits. Remember, the corpses of these victims have been found because relatives became worried. But, what happens to other victims, the wandering womenfolk? Their relatives might believe the wench has run away, gone somewhere else. Or don't even care? In the area around Whitefriars in London, God forgive us, you can buy a girl of twelve for a penny.'

'But Widow Walmer doesn't fit this pattern.'

'No, Ranulf, she doesn't. Here's a pretty widow who has probably seen the world, knows its wicked-ness and has the wit not to be trapped. She lived by herself though Margaret the miller's daughter served as her companion. On the night she died she expected Sir Roger, that's a well-known fact, so young Margaret was told to stay at home.'

'How would the killer know that?'

'By deduction, Ranulf. If Sir Roger, God bless him, was trumpeting in the taproom how he was going to visit the widow and the killer heard.' Corbett pulled a face. 'That's not the real problem: the riddle is why? Why Widow Walmer?'

'It would appear, Master, she almost had to die?'

'What do you mean?'

'If she hadn't, Sir Roger wouldn't have been trapped, his house wouldn't have been searched. The carpenter wouldn't have remembered seeing him in Gully Lane.'

Corbett sat and reflected. 'Are you implying, Ranulf, that Widow Walmer was murdered because she knew something? Or that she was deliberately killed to trap Sir Roger?'

'Possibly both, but I would choose the latter.'

Corbett shook his head in disbelief. 'You are a man of cunning wit, Ranulf. I hadn't thought of that. Let's follow that path. Sir Roger suspects who the true killer of the young women is. Perhaps he hints at this knowledge. So, our mysterious Mummer's Man spins his own murderous web to catch this knight. The only weakness of this argument is Sir Roger was a man of hot temperament. Why didn't he just accuse the killer openly? Have him arrested? Drag him before Justice Tressilyian?'

Ranulf, who had been preening himself at Corbett's praise, stared blankly back.

'No, no.' Corbett leant over and patted him on the knee. 'I accept your hypothesis. Let us return to Widow Walmer. Sir Roger goes for his evening of love, then leaves. We have to believe that Furrell was telling the truth but the poacher also claimed he saw other people slipping down Gully Lane towards Widow Walmer's cottage. One of these could have been the killer, the other two must have been Repton's comings and goings.'

'Do you think Furrell really was telling the truth?'

'Yes, Ranulf, I do. It makes sense. The killer knew that Sir Roger would leave Widow Walmer. The goodwoman probably insisted that he not spend the night there. So the killer goes down, he murders Widow Walmer, and finds, by good luck, Chapeleys' knife and sheath which had been given as a gift. Those are left on the floor and he flees into the night. Repton goes down once and, having fortified himself with ale and the company of Master Burghesh, returns. The murder is known and the hunt is on. What happens next is what you'd expect. They visit the local justice and warrants are sworn out. Thockton Hall is searched where more incriminating evidence is found.'

'I don't understand.' Chanson, who had been carefully following the argument, spoke up. 'What was a manor lord doing with gewgaws from wenches of the town?'

'If, my dear horseman, our noble Clerk of the Green Wax is correct, then I believe the killer sent these to Sir Roger, who mistakenly thought they were keepsakes of some woman he had tumbled. It's like young Adela in the taproom below sending me a ring or a brooch—'

'Lady Maeve would have your head!' Ranulf broke in.

'Yes, yes, she would,' Corbett smiled. 'But if I was

Sir Roger, I wouldn't want to throw them away. I'd toss them into my coffer and not give them a second thought, which is what happened. Now, it's Sir Roger we must concentrate on.' Corbett scratched the back of his head. 'He didn't help his case one whit. He was disliked and he was blunt but three things he stoutly denied: the murder of the young women, the slaying of Widow Walmer and Deverell the carpenter's evidence.'

'We should have visited him first,' Ranulf declared.

'He'll not change his story. This is not Repton the reeve. Deverell went on oath; he swore a man's life away. If he changes his story now he'll hang tomorrow and he knows that. I suspect that's why he wasn't in the taproom tonight.'

'He's hiding from us?'

'As well as from the real killer. I'll come to him in a moment.'

'So,' Ranulf spoke up, 'we have the allegations laid and Sir Roger under arrest in the crypt. Justice Tressilyian sweeps into Melford, takes his seat at the Guildhall. Popular feeling is running high against the imprisoned knight and a jury is empanelled.'

Corbett tapped the roll of the court with the toe of his boot. 'The record will give us the other jurors' names. Tressilyian is under orders to gather them together for me to question. However, I do think it's a remarkable coincidence that the jury was led by a man who hated Sir Roger.'

'Even so,' Ranulf declared, 'the evidence against the knight was impressive.'

'Except in one matter: the garrotte – that was never found. But you are right, Ranulf, the evidence is impressive and the trial takes its course. Justice Tressilyian tries to have the matter referred to King's Bench at Westminster but this is refused. Chapeleys is found guilty. There's only one sentence the justice can pass, though, once again, letters are sent to Westminster, this time pleading for a pardon. The King, advised by his own Chief Justice, refuses to grant a pardon and Sir Roger is hanged.' Corbett paused. 'My feet are killing me,' he groaned. He eased his boots off and threw them into a corner. 'Melford goes back to its peaceful existence. But,' Corbett paused, 'that doesn't mean the murders cease. I am not too sure how many other women, the kin of wandering folk, this assassin has killed.'

'And don't forget Furrell the poacher.'

'No, we mustn't forget him. All the evidence indicates Furrell saw something, knew more than he should have done. He would have to be silenced. I believe Sorrel. Furrell's cold in his grave, God only knows where that is. Sorrel knows this countryside like the palm of her hand but, there again, her husband's corpse may lie at the bottom of the Swaile, weights and stones attached to its legs. Anyway, back to Melford. In appearances, all is quiet. The murders have been avenged, the King's justice carried out, then the murders begin again.'

'Why?' Chanson asked. 'That, Master, doesn't make sense.' He smiled. 'It's not logical.' He quoted Corbett's oft-repeated phrase.

'What do you know about logic?' Ranulf asked crossly.

'About as much as you know about horses!'

'Hush now! Chanson has made a good point.

There were certainly no killings amongst the towns-women for five years. There must be reasons for that. First, it had to be seen that Chapeleys was responsible. Secondly, we must understand the soul of the killer. Here is a man who knows he does wrong but, like a dog returning to its vomit, cannot restrain himself. Over the years his frustration grows. He walks the lanes and streets of Melford and sees this pretty face, a soft neck, well-turned ankles. He lusts in secret. Eventually the demons return. And, finally . . .' Corbett stared across the chamber.

'Yes, Master?'

'We have hunted killers, Ranulf, those who plot murder, the taking of lives. One trait of these children of Cain always fascinates me: their overweening arrogance. They are like pompous scholars in the Halls of Oxford. They think they are different from anyone else, more intelligent, more cunning. They enjoy the game, they truly believe they cannot be caught. In a sense, the killer is mocking Melford, ridiculing the townspeople. "Look," he is saying, "I killed before and I escaped. Now I'll kill again and what can you do?" '

'Of course, we could be wrong,' Ranulf said. 'There is the possibility that Sir Roger was guilty and some-one is now copying these murders.'

'True,' Corbett smiled. 'But logic indicates the same killer, using the same method. Young Elizabeth, the wheelwright's daughter, a lovely, young woman, is teased and enticed by the Mum-mer's Man. Maybe he's already tested her and she's taken the bait. Now she goes out to her secret place somewhere near Devil's Oak. The first time she collected a piece of silver but the second time her killer is waiting: it was money well spent for the enjoyment he gets.'

'And the other murders? Molkyn and Thorkle?' Ranulf asked.

'Ah yes, that precious pair. Let's discuss them as well as Blidscote and Deverell the carpenter. Let us say, for sake of argument, that all four were corrupted. How could that be done?'

'Money!' Chanson spoke so loudly Ranulf jumped.

'I'd like to agree,' Corbett replied. 'But we are no longer talking about young women. These are wealthy, responsible burgesses of Melford. They would have to be bribed heavily to participate in corruption which would lead to an innocent man's execution. They would also know that if they were ever discovered, the most gruesome death awaited them.'

'Blackmail?' Ranulf queried.

'That would seem the most logical explanation. But, there again, who would know so much to put the fear of God in all four? We must also remember they were halfway down the Judas path: they disliked Sir Roger and so were receptive to any approach.'

'That means they must have known the killer?' Ranulf rubbed his hands, enjoying himself. He loved to follow his master's tortuous mind. It reminded him of a hunting dog snaking and curling amongst the bushes, refusing to give up the scent, determined to track down its quarry. 'Perhaps,' he suggested, 'we should collect Master Blidscote and Deverell and cart them off to London.'

'I doubt it.' Corbett loosened the cords on the neck of his shirt. 'The most they would tell us is that they were corrupted. The killer, the blackmailer, probably approached his victims in a silent, secretive way.' He sighed. 'Now, as for the killer of Molkyn and Thorkle, we have two choices. First, the Mummer's Man could have silenced them. Perhaps both were having qualms of conscience, feelings of guilt, although there is no evidence of that. Indeed, the little I know of Molkyn, it's highly unlikely.'

'And secondly?' Ranulf asked.

'That there's a second killer in Melford. Someone who now knows Sir Roger was innocent either because they found evidence or, more simply, because these murders have begun again. This man, or woman, realises what a heinous miscarriage of justice has been committed and is determined to avenge Sir Roger's death. Molkyn and Thorkle die and Sir Louis is attacked.' Corbett chewed the corner of his lip. 'Yes, it must be an avenging angel, hence the warnings daubed on Sir Roger's tombstone and at the gibbet.'

'And who could this avenging angel be?' Chanson asked.

'Well, the list is endless. Perhaps the priests, they may have heard something in confession. Chapeleys' son, Sir Maurice, eager to avenge his father's name. Oh, God knows! It could have even been their wives.'

'Their wives!' Ranulf exclaimed.

'I told you. I met them tonight. Believe me, Ranulf, if some assassin cut my throat, and the Lady Maeve showed as little grief as those two,' he smiled, 'I'd be tempted to come back and haunt her! I have never met widows like that. God forgive me, they were almost happy to have their husbands cold in their graves. I believe Ursula may have known Sir Roger more intimately than her husband would have liked. There is no doubt that Lucy, Thorkle's wife, is dewy-eyed about the miller's son. The one I would love to have questioned, and intend to do so, is young Margaret.'

'Why?'

'Why, Chanson, because I am suspicious. Somehow or other she knows a great deal. She was Molkyn's daughter, a companion to Widow Walmer and she hated her father.'

'So many theories,' Ranulf whispered. 'So many paths. Which one do we follow?'

'I don't know.' The clerk spread his hands. 'So many possibilities. Is the murderer of five years ago responsible for these last two young women's deaths? Is he responsible for the killing of Molkyn, Thorkle, the attack on Tressilyian, those secret messages? Or are there two, perhaps even three, killers? Are the Jesses killer and the Mummer's Man one and the same? How did this assassin, despite all our theories, entice his victims out to some desolate spot? Why was Walmer killed? What happened to Furrell? Were Blidscote, Deverell, Molkyn and Thorkle corrupted? If so, why and by whom?'

Corbett got to his feet, undid his jerkin, went across to the lavarium and splashed water over his face. He took a linen cloth and dried himself.

'We should question Master Deverell but it will be as informative as talking to this bed post. I could go back to the mill and, of course, there are those two priests. Tomorrow, Chanson, Ranulf will come with me. You seek out Master Blidscote. Take him to the Guildhall. I want to know if there have been other reports about young women disappearing over the last ten years.'

'And us?' Ranulf asked.

'We are going to the dawn Mass at St Edmund's.' Corbett looked down at the floor. 'I was attacked tonight. I don't see the logic behind that, or indeed what happened to Justice Tressilyian. Beneath the serene surface of this town seethe bloody passions and murderous urges. I need the Mass. I must take the sacrament.'

Ranulf watched his strange master.

'In a matter of days,' Corbett continued, 'we celebrate All-Hallows Eve. They say the ghosts of the dead come back. When I was a boy, we used to light fires, a circle of bonfires around the village, to ward off the ghosts. Well, the ghosts have come back to Melford to haunt, to seek justice, perhaps even revenge. We not only deal with treasons of the living, Ranulf, but the treason of the ghosts. Old lies, deeply embedded, ancient sins quickened and festering. We should be careful as we walk. Perhaps that's the last time I'll journey around Melford under the cloak of darkness.' He sat on the edge of the bed. 'It's best if we sleep. The morning will come soon enough.'

He bade his companions good night and ushered them out.

Ranulf led Chanson back to their own chamber at the end of the gallery overlooking the stable yard.

'He's in a sombre mood,' the groom declared as they settled for the night.

'He's always in a sombre mood,' Ranulf answered, sitting at the table, busily lighting more candles.

'Aren't you going to sleep?'

'I have a letter to write,' Ranulf declared proudly.

He opened one of the panniers and took out a sheet of vellum and laid it on the desk, then his portable writing-tray, quills, inkpot and pumice stone. Ranulf heard Chanson's chatter but he wasn't listening. He wanted to write to Alicia in that lonely convent in Wiltshire. This would be the sixth letter he had written and still he'd received no reply. Each occasion Ranulf found it more difficult. Was he writing because he missed her? Because he truly loved her? Or because he rejoiced in his new-found skills? He was now Master of the Cursive Script, the elegant phrase: Ranulf had a passion for scholarship. One day he would be a senior clerk in the Chancery of the Secret Seal.

He wrote the words: 'My dearest Alicia,' and then paused. Would he be a senior clerk? He smiled at his secret ambition: to take Holy Orders! And why not? He was a King's man, wasn't he? Time and again, old Edward at Westminster would take him aside, grasp him by the arm as if Ranulf was one of his boon companions. The King would share his sorrows and troubles; flatter Ranulf with praise and promises of things to come. It was the one part of Ranulf's life he never shared with Corbett. Yet, sometimes, more frequently now than ever, Corbett would sit and stare at him. Was it mockery? Cynicism? Or sadness?

Ranulf sighed. He told Chanson to go to sleep and continued with his letter.

In his chamber Corbett lay on the bed, hands

stretched out, staring up through the darkness at the embroidered tester. The wind rattled the shutters. Distant sounds of the tavern settling for the night drifted up. Images came and went: Maeve dressing for bed; little Edward, plump and pink, snoring softly in the cradle well away from window draughts; Uncle Morgan downstairs, busy baiting the servants. Corbett let these images go. He was standing under the Devil's Oak in Falmer Lane. He was watching a young woman slip through the meadow to that copse of trees at the top of the hill. The Mummer's Man or the Jesses killer would be waiting.

'The bells!' Corbett whispered to himself. 'It wasn't jesses. The Mummer's Man wore a mask with bells on either side. So, who would do that? And why?'

Only a few streets away, Ysabeau, wife of Deverell the carpenter, was also concerned about the hideous murders which had taken place out in the countryside. She lay in bed staring into the darkness, straining her ears for sounds from downstairs. Since Sir Roger's trial, nothing had been the same! Deverell, a surly man, had only grown more grim and withdrawn. He had never discussed his evidence but, when asked, would repeat it by rote like a *chanteur* telling a story. Had her husband told the truth? Why had he been so insistent he had seen Sir Roger that night? She could never understand Deverell's unhappiness. He was a carpenter, a craftsman. He had done work as far as Ipswich. Merchants and burgesses visited his workshop. Why was he always sad? What did he have to hide?

Deverell had come to Melford some seven years ago. A travelling journeyman, he possessed skill with the hammer and chisel that had soon established him as a craftsman. He was definitely learned. He could read and write and, at times, betrayed a knowledge of Latin and French. On one occasion, in his cups, he had even discussed Parson Grimstone's sermon on the body and blood of Christ. He was a good husband, loyal, faithful and, even when drunk, he never beat her. So why this great fear? And why now?

News had swept through Melford of the arrival of the King's clerk. Deverell had grown pale and withdrawn. He had spent more and more time in his workshop. When she brought him food and drink, Ysabeau found he had almost turned it into a fortress, shutters and doors all closed, locked and barred. It was the same with the kitchen below. Deverell had even replaced the door and built a Judas squint in the wall. He never told her the reason why. Now he refused to come to bed but sat in his great high-backed chair in front of the fire, drinking and brooding. If anyone knocked on the door, he went to the Judas squint and peered through to see who was standing in the porch.

The carpenter's wife stirred. Wasn't that a tapping on the door? At this hour? She threw the blankets back and sat up. Yes, someone was tapping. She could hear it. She swung her legs off the bed and, putting on a pair of soft buskins, stole across to the latticed window. She opened it and looked out.

'Who's there?' she called.

She could still hear the tapping but she couldn't see anybody because of the porch recess. Whoever was there was well hidden. She closed the window and went across the bedchamber. She heard a sound like that of a groan, the crash of a stool, even as the rapping on the door continued. She waited no longer but fled down the stairs, along the passageway and into the kitchen. Lanterns and candles still glowed, the door was still barred but Deverell lay sprawled near the fireplace. A crossbow bolt had smashed him full in the face, shattering skin and bone. Blood pumped out of the terrible wounds, spilling out of the half-opened mouth.

Deverell's wife grasped the back of a chair and stared in horror. She couldn't breathe. She could hear screaming and realised it was herself, just before fainting away.

# Chapter 11

'*Ecce Corpus Christi*. Behold the Body of Christ!'

'Amen!' Corbett murmured.

He received the sacred wafer on his tongue and returned to kneel just inside the rood screen. The flagstones were icy-cold. Corbett ignored the distraction as he closed his eyes and prayed. Ranulf joined him. Parson Grimstone returned to the altar and the Mass proceeded to its conclusion. Grimstone picked up the chalice and the paten and walked off to the sacristy. Corbett crossed himself and looked around. A few parishioners grouped around the sanctuary steps. He noticed with amusement how Burghesh had his own personal prie-dieu and, once the priest had left the sanctuary, the old soldier hastened up to extinguish the candles and remove the sacred cloths.

Old Mother Crauford and the slack-jawed Peterkin were present: huffing and puffing, the old woman got to her feet. She grasped her cane in one hand, Peterkin's arm in the other, nodded at Corbett, went through the rood screen and out by the corpse door.

Corbett crossed himself and, followed by Ranulf, walked down the nave. The church was cold and dank but well kept and swept. The benches were neatly piled in the transepts. The oaken rood screen, the sanctuary chair, furniture and wooden statues were clean and polished. No cobwebs hung round the pillars and considerable monies had been spent on a series of eye-catching wall paintings. One in particular showed Christ, after his crucifixion, going down amongst the dead: the Saviour stood on the shores by the lake of Hell, gazing sorrowfully across at the armies of the damned.

'Very imaginative,' Corbett murmured. 'Every church has its paintings, Ranulf. Because local artists are hired the pictures are all different.'

He stopped to admire a triptych: Christ as a child, Mary on one side, Joseph on the other. Corbett smiled at how the town in the background looked remarkably like Melford. He walked back into the sanctuary. The three stalls on either side had their seats up, displaying misericords carved below. The artist, as usual, had carved local scenes or incidents: a wife beating a drunken husband; a dog with a leg of lamb in its mouth; a parson with a tankard to his lips. The sanctuary was the centrepiece of the church: coloured glass glowed in the windows behind the altar; a silver-gold pyx holding the sacred host hung from a filigree chain; candlesticks of heavy brass gleamed and winked in the light of the sanctuary lamp; more paintings on the walls; soft carpets on the altar steps whilst the altar itself was of pure oak, polished and smoothed.

With Ranulf wandering behind him, Corbett left and entered the Lady Chapel. The statue of the Virgin seated, holding the baby Jesus, reminded him of the shrine at Walsingham. Corbett slipped a coin into the heavy box and bought a number of candle-lights. He lit them with a taper, murmuring: 'One for Maeve, one for Eleanor . . .'

He had hardly finished when Parson Grimstone, accompanied by Curate Robert and Burghesh, joined them.

'Would you like to see the church?'

Corbett agreed and the parson proudly led them around, explaining the paintings, the different items bought by parishioners. How the rood screen was new and the baptismal font near the front door needed to be refurbished. He then took them into the bell tower with its narrow, winding steps, coloured bell ropes, the deep, sloping window recesses on the outside wall.

'This is the old part of the church,' he explained.

Corbett looked at the arrow-slit windows at the far end of the recesses.

'It reminds me of a peel tower,' he declared, 'on the Scottish border. Soldiers would climb into such recesses to defend it.'

'This is Curate Robert's domain,' Parson Grimstone declared, his rubicund face creased into a smile, though his eyes were watery and nervous. He proudly clapped the curate on the shoulder.

In fact Bellen looked anything but proud: dressed in his black gown with a white cord round the middle, the curate stood white-faced and heavy-eyed. Now and again his lips moved soundlessly as if he was talking to himself.

'I understand,' Grimstone said flatly as they left the bell tower, 'that you met some of my parishioners last night and made the personal acquaintance of Repton the reeve?'

'It was interesting,' Corbett replied. 'Parson Grimstone, you have a fine church here. Do you have a Book of the Dead?' he added sharply.

'Why, yes.' The parson became flustered. 'It's in the sacristy.'

He led them back down the church and into the small, oak-panelled room with its cupboards and chests. It smelt fragrantly of incense and beeswax candles, and was dominated by a huge black crucifix nailed to the wall above the panelling. Parson Grimstone, hands shaking, unlocked the parish coffer and sifted amongst the documents and ledgers. Beads of sweat coursed down Grimstone's face: he quietly rubbed his stomach, whilst his search was clumsy.

You're nervous, Corbett thought, but you are also a toper. Corbett had seen the same phenomena amongst clerks in the chancery who spent their nights in the alehouses and taverns: an unexplained flush to the face, a tendency to sweat, whilst their hands shook as if they were afflicted by palsy. He noticed how the curate stayed near the door. Burghesh was solicitous, going to help the parson like a mother would a child. Grimstone at last found the silver-edged ledger and pulled it out. The pages inside were thick and crackled as he opened it.

'It's the work of a binder in Ipswich,' he remarked. 'It's about a hundred years old but well sewn together with twine. Why the interest, Sir Hugh?'

'Elizabeth the wheelwright's daughter's name is in this?'

'Oh yes, oh yes,' Parson Grimstone said, flustered. 'Of course, she is. We celebrate her Requiem Mass at noon today, followed by interment.' He pointed to the black and gold vestments laid out over a chest. 'Robert will sing the Mass. He has a fine voice. He knew the girl better than I did.'

'In what way?' Corbett asked sharply.

The curate walked forward, scratching at his mop of hair. He's not as nervous as he looks, Corbett thought. Bellen's eyes were troubled but steady.

'She came to me in the confessional pew.'

'But you never met her outside your priestly duties?'

'No, Sir Hugh, why should I? I am a priest, sworn to celibacy. I heard her petty sins and shrived her. You know Canon Law, clerk.'

'I know Church Law, priest! I have no intention of asking you what you heard under the seal of confession. It is a sacred seal, is it not?'

The curate smiled with his eyes.

'I mean no offence.' Corbett took his gloves off and pushed them into his war belt. 'But the poor girl lies dead.'

'Aye, Sir Hugh, she does but her soul's with God. Elizabeth Wheelwright was guilty of no serious sin, at least none that she confessed to me.'

'And Sir Roger Chapeleys?' Corbett queried, glancing at Grimstone.

'We've had this conversation before, Sir Hugh. I've told you what I know. Sir Roger's last confession was heard by a visiting friar but he did say that Sir Roger had not confessed to any murders.'

'You think he was innocent?'

'No man is innocent.'

'You think he was a murderer?' Corbett demanded.

'I don't know.' Parson Grimstone sat in a high-backed chair between two chests. 'I know nothing about Sir Roger. I would not describe him as a man of God. Oh, he attended Mass on Sundays and when he had to. He gave a triptych to the church which was later burnt.'

'Why was it burnt?' Ranulf asked.

'You've asked me that before. Perhaps a member of my parish resented anything from a Chapeleys hanging in this church.'

'Were Molkyn the miller and Thorkle churchgoers?'

'Thorkle more than Molkyn,' Grimstone replied. 'The miller feared neither God nor man. He did not like priests.'

Corbett came over and took the Book of the Dead from the parson's fingers. 'You are a priest, you hear confessions?'

'Yes, both in the shriving pew and elsewhere.'

'Father,' Corbett crouched down to hold his gaze, 'there's a killer loose in Melford. He has killed Widow Walmer and other women. I believe he was responsible for the grisly execution of an innocent man. Don't you know anything that can help me?'

'Ask me,' the parson stammered. 'Ask me anything you wish.'

Corbett tapped the Book of the Dead. He got to his feet and glanced at the curate.

'Melford is a busy place. It trades in wool, is well served by roads and trackways. People come and go. Has anyone ever knocked at your door and asked about a missing girl? Tinkers' families, traders, Moon

People?' He smiled at Burghesh. 'Even professional soldiers who move their families from castle to castle?'

'We have had a number,' the curate replied, 'over the years. But, there again, I am not too sure whether the girls returned or whether they had run away. Sometime last spring I met a group of chapmen with their gaggle of women and children. They were asking about some wench who'd gone missing. I listened, but how could I help?'

'Curate Robert is correct,' Burghesh added. 'For the love of God, Sir Hugh, go to Ipswich. You will find the alleyways and streets packed with young women who have fled their family or master. Widow Walmer is a good case in point.'

'Did you know her?'

'No, Sir Hugh, but I would have liked to.'

Corbett flicked through the book, with its close-marked entries. He accepted what Burghesh said. If it was true of Ipswich, it was certainly true of London. The brothels of Southwark were always on the look-out for runaways. The purveyors of soft flesh were constantly searching for what was new; it was so serious a matter even the King's council had debated it.

He glanced at Ranulf, standing near the door, and hoped that he hid his unease. It was comfortable to sit in his bedchamber and spin theories like some master in the Schools at Oxford but what he needed was evidence, proof.

'Let me ask you another question.' Corbett walked over to the small latticed window so as to study the entries more carefully. 'The parish of St Edmund's serves most of Melford, yes? In your graveyard you have a plot called the Potter's Field?'

'That's right,' Parson Grimstone declared. 'It's that area of God's acre which is reserved for the corpses of strangers, the victims of sudden violence and contagion. Often we don't even know their names. We have such deaths in Melford: a tinker falls ill of the sweat or a beggar is crushed under a cart.'

'And the corpses of unknown women?' Corbett demanded.

Grimstone chewed on his lower lip and stared beseechingly at the curate.

'Robert, I can't remember, can you?'

'There was one,' Burghesh declared, taking the book from Corbett's hand. 'About two years ago. A young woman's corpse was fished out of the Swaile.'

'Ah yes, I remember.' Parson Grimstone clicked his fingers. 'That poor creature. She had been in the water for so long, she was sheeted immediately for burial.'

'There!' Burghesh had found the entry.

Corbett followed his stubby fingers across the page and translated the Latin entry.

'Buried, the corpse of an unknown woman: the feast of St John the Baptist, 1301.'

'And this book?' Corbett handed it back to the parson. 'It contains no other entries which might provoke suspicion? Where was this unknown corpse found?'

'Down near Beauchamp Place,' Burghesh replied. 'We think poachers had been out on the river and probably dislodged it. It was found floating amongst the weeds.'

'Poaching?' Corbett smiled. 'I met Sorrel yesterday, Furrell the poacher's wife.'

'Oh, that poor, benighted thing.'

'Did Furrell ever come and see you?' Corbett asked. The parson shook his head.

'Yes, he did!' Robert the curate declared. 'And it was just after Sir Roger had been executed.'

'And what happened?' Parson Grimstone asked.

'Don't you remember, Father,' the curate insisted, 'you met him in the parlour.'

Grimstone blinked. Corbett stared at him closely. The parson's face was vein-streaked around the nose. Corbett noticed three dark blotches: one on his neck, the other on his forehead, the third on his right cheek. Corbett recalled what his physician friend had told him in London – how such blotches were the mark of an inveterate drinker.

'Yes he did.' Parson Grimstone asserted himself. 'He came in and told fantastical stories of how Sir Roger was innocent. I didn't believe him. In fact, I only half listened but he did say something interesting – about a Mummer's Man. But Furrell was always full of tales.'

'Why does Sorrel still search for his corpse?' Burghesh asked. He came over and stood beside the chair and patted the parson on the shoulder.

'What do you mean?' Corbett asked.

'Well, I'm not a countryman,' the old soldier replied, 'but you have seen the land round here, Sir Hugh. Every piece is grassed over, whilst Furrell and Sorrel knew the woods like the backs of their hands.'

Corbett followed his drift. 'Of course,' he murmured. 'A newly marked grave might be ignored by a stranger but someone like Sorrel would find it soon enough. Whilst, if you dig a plot on meadow land, a shepherd or labourer would notice it, not to mention wild animals, who can sniff decaying flesh and dig it out.'

'So his corpse must be well hidden,' Ranulf declared.

'Aye, that's what convinces me about Sir Roger's innocence,' Corbett continued. 'Furrell spoke in his defence and Furrell disappeared.'

'He could have run away.'

'Nonsense!' Corbett glared at Curate Robert. 'God knows Sorrel loves him and, undoubtedly, he loved her. She believes that he has been murdered and I accept that. Let's go back to Molkyn the miller.' Corbett sat down on one of the chests. 'Do you remember those puzzles we used to play as children? Jumbled words which carry a message? Or pieces which, rearranged, form a picture of a knight on a horse or a maid in a castle? My mother, God rest her, always taught me to look for one particular word or piece, that was the key.'

He rubbed his boot against the shiny wooden floor and gazed under his eyebrows at Ranulf, who had his head down, trying to stifle a laugh. Whenever old Master Long Face indulged in whimsy, it was a sign that matters were becoming dangerous. The Clerk of the Green Wax wondered what curious dealings were forming in his master's teeming, busy mind.

'And Molkyn the miller is such a piece?' Curate Robert asked.

'Very good, sir! Very good indeed!' Corbett breathed. 'Molkyn the miller – an oaf, a wife-beater, a bullyboy.'

'That's no way to speak of the dead!' Parson Grimstone snorted.

'Very true, sir. But that's not what I say, that's his family's opinion. I visited the mill last night. A less grieving group of people couldn't be found, especially his young daughter, pretty Margaret. How old is she – eighteen, nineteen summers? Did she ever come and ask to be shriven?'

'Robert spends more time than I do in the shriving pew.'

'And I am bound by the seal of confession.'

'So you are, so you are.' Corbett crossed one leg over the other and played with the rowel of his spur. 'And her father, Molkyn the miller? A man who feared neither God nor man.'

'We've told you about him.'

'And I am asking you again, on your loyalty to the King. Did Molkyn the miller ever come here and speak to you about matters not covered by the seal of confession? Curate Robert, God knows you are an honest priest and your face is like an open book.'

'Aye, he came one afternoon, about five years ago, around the same time Sir Roger Chapeleys was arrested. He knocked at the door of the priest's house and said he wished to see the Bible.'

'The Bible!' Ranulf exclaimed.

'Yes, he asked about certain verses from Leviticus. I was surprised but he was so insistent. Now Molkyn could read but not Latin. It was about ten verses in all. I can't remember the actual chapter but it was the Mosaic prescription about a man not sleeping with his brother's wife, animals, you know.' Curate Robert waved his hand. 'I went through, translating the

209

verses for him. Molkyn listened very carefully then spun on his heel and walked out.'

'And why do you think he was so interested in Leviticus?'

'I don't know.'

'Didn't you ever wonder why a miller was so curious about obscure verses from the Old Testament?'

'Sir Hugh,' the curate replied, 'if you knew how many odd requests are made of us ... But, at the time, yes.'

'Well, here's a strange thing ...' Corbett got to his feet and walked to the door leading out to the garden. 'We have a miller,' he continued, 'who couldn't give a fig about church. However, about the same time he became foreman of a jury which would send a man to the gallows, he became very curious about obscure verses from Leviticus. Now, wouldn't you say, sirs,' Corbett spoke over his shoulder, 'that the miller knew what God's teaching was? Good Lord, the humblest peasant in the kingdom, unlettered and unschooled, knows you don't sleep with your brother's wife or his sheep or goat. So why should Molkyn make his way up here and ask such a question?' He turned and stared.

Grimstone was still shaking. Curate Robert's face was ashen. Burghesh stood mouth gaping.

'We could,' Corbett whirled his fingers, 'turn this round and round like a spinning top. I wager if I went down to the Golden Fleece, no one would recall Molkyn talking about scripture.'

'What are you implying?' Parson Grimstone demanded querulously. 'Sir Hugh, you go up and down like a hare caught in the garden.'

'This is my theory,' Corbett replied, 'and I have yet to reflect on it. I think Molkyn the miller was threatened. Someone brought verses from the Book of Leviticus to his attention. Molkyn was frightened. A surly man, he wouldn't have given a pennyworth of flour for what people thought, but this was different. So he comes up to this church. Molkyn's no dullard. He doesn't give the actual chapter and verse but a whole collection of verses which he asks Curate Robert to translate.'

'And in that passage?' Ranulf asked.

'In that passage,' Corbett replied, 'was a warning: that's what disturbed Molkyn. It's like me leaving a quotation from Scripture on the table beside Curate Robert's bed: Matthew's Gospel, Chapter thirteen, Verse five. You'd be intrigued, wouldn't you?'

Curate Robert nodded.

'And that's interesting.' Corbett smiled. He emphasised the points with his fingers. 'Who would warn Molkyn the miller? Why should they warn him? And how many people know the Book of Leviticus?'

'You are not accusing the priests, are you?' Burghesh's face flushed.

'Hush, man,' Corbett remarked. 'Even if I was, it wouldn't make them murderers.'

'No, it doesn't,' Burghesh replied hotly. 'I am tutored and schooled in the Bible. So are many people in Melford: Sorrel can read; Deverell the carpenter; Master Matthew the taverner—'

'All I am saying,' Corbett interrupted, 'is that someone said something to Molkyn which disturbed him. It doesn't make that person a murderer but it is interesting.'

'I am confused.' Parson Grimstone rested his head in his hands. 'Sir Hugh, are there any other questions? I don't feel well.' He got to his feet. 'Master Burghesh, if you could look after our visitors... Robert?'

And, without waiting for an answer, the priest, helped by the curate, left the sacristy.

'Is Parson Grimstone a well man?' Ranulf asked.

'Oh, he's well enough,' Burghesh replied, picking up the Book of the Dead. He put it back in the chest and secured the lock. 'He's a little older than me, past his fifty-fifth summer, and sometimes his mind becomes forgetful.'

'He drinks, doesn't he? Quite heavily?'

Burghesh got to his feet and came back.

'Yes, master clerk, he drinks. He's a priest, he's lonely, he's made mistakes, he becomes confused. But, he has no woman, he does not dip his fingers into the poor box. He goes out at night to anoint the dying. Parson Grimstone tries to be a good pastor but, yes, he drinks. In his youth he was a very fine priest.' Burghesh's eyes brimmed with tears. 'A very scholarly man. He could have become an archdeacon, even a bishop. He has a fine house but he lives sparsely as a soldier. His one weakness is the claret, a petty foible; his parishioners allow it.'

'Do you know him well?' Corbett asked.

'Hasn't anyone told you?' Burghesh laughed. 'We are half-brothers. Different names but the same blood.' He grimaced. 'I know there's no likeness between us. We grew up here – well, not in Melford itself, but in a farm nearby. Our father married twice. John's mother died in childbirth. We were both sent to school in Ipswich. I always wanted to be a stone-mason. I remember when they finished part of this church. I used to come up here and help the builders until a soldier's life beckoned. I became a master bowman, a sergeant-at-arms. I helped myself to plunder, gave my money to the Lombards and, when I'd seen enough of fighting, came back here.'

'You were married?' Corbett asked.

'Many years ago. But she died and that was it. You get tired of death, don't you, Sir Hugh? One night eating and drinking round the campfire with your friends, the next morning the same man takes an arrow in his gullet. I came back here, oh, about twelve years ago. I bought the old forester's house behind the church but, if the truth be known, I returned to look after John.'

'And Curate Robert?' Corbett asked.

'Oh, he's what you described him as, an open book. A good priest but anxious, ever so anxious.'

'What about?' Corbett asked.

'He likes the ladies.' Burghesh's voice dropped to a whisper. 'Oh, there's nothing wrong with that. Many a priest can cope with it. Curate Robert has gone the other way. He is constantly sermonising about the lusts of the flesh. It's a joke amongst many of the parishioners.'

'But a good priest?' Corbett demanded.

'Oh yes, he has a gift, especially with the young. A gentle man, his severe face hides a kind heart.'

'Could someone like Margaret the miller's daughter have approached him?'

'It's possible. But come, Sir Hugh, you haven't broken your fast. Let's leave Parson Grimstone.'

He took them out into the graveyard. The sun was now breaking through, turning the hoar frost on the grass to a glistening dampness. Birds swooped above the tombstones; somewhere a rook or raven croaked. They passed the half-finished cross. Corbett noticed the barrow, hoe and mattock, the freshly dug grave, the brown earth piled high beside it.

'Poor Elizabeth!' Burghesh murmured. 'That will be her last resting place.'

'You dug it?' Ranulf asked.

'Yes, I did. I act as verger, general handyman round the parish. I have to. Trade is good, everybody is busy, no one has time to spare. Oh, we have church ales, the paying of the tithes, but why should a man dig graves if he can earn more raising sheep?'

They passed the priest's house and followed the path round, across a small yard housing stables, hen runs, chicken coops and a small dovecote. At the end of this yard stood a small orchard of apple and pear trees.

'They give good fruit in summer.' Burghesh stopped and stared at the branches. 'But they need pruning.'

He led them through the orchard, which gave way to a small field. At the far end, flanked on either side by trees, stood the forester's house. It was narrow but three-storeyed, with white plaster and black beams. Its windows had been enlarged and filled with glass, the roof was newly tiled.

'It's what I used to dream about,' Burghesh confessed.

He led them along the path, took a ring of keys from his belt and opened the front door. The passage inside was stone-flagged but clean and well swept. The plaster walls were lime-washed and there were shelves holding pots of herbs. Corbett smelt lavender, pennyroyal, agrimony and coriander.

'I'm a keen gardener,' Burghesh declared.

He took them through, past the comfortable parlour, kitchen and buttery into the physician's garden at the back. This was formed in a half-moon shape, ringed by a red-brick wall. Burghesh proudly pointed out how he had arranged the herbs according to their uses: herbs for bites and stings, herbs for the kitchen and household. He then led them back and made them sit at the thick wooden kitchen table whilst he served them home-brewed ale and freshly baked bread.

'Are you a cook as well?' Ranulf asked, enjoying himself.

'No, I sell the herbs to the apothecaries and buy my bread.'

'Are you a hunter?' Corbett asked.

Burghesh threw his head back and laughed.

'I'm as clumsy as a dray horse.' He supped at his ale. 'I understand we will be meeting again tonight?'

'Oh, yes,' Corbett recalled. 'Sir Louis Tressilyian has invited us to supper.'

'And Parson Grimstone. We'll all be there.'

'Tell me about Curate Robert's peccadilloes.'

Burghesh hid a smile behind his tankard. 'Who's been talking?'

'Well, no one has, but,' Corbett smiled at his half-lie, 'I think you know. The flagellation?'

'Yes, Parson John's often talked about it. He put a stop to it here. But,' Burghesh sighed, 'Curate Robert has been seen out in the countryside. God knows what sins he thinks he's committed. We all have our secrets, eh, master clerk?'

Corbett was about to reply when he heard the sound of hurrying footsteps and a hammering on the door. Burghesh went down the passageway. Sir Louis Tressilyian, cloaked and spurred, Sir Maurice Chapeleys behind him, strode into the kitchen.

'Sir Hugh, you are needed in Melford.'

'What's the matter?' Corbett got up.

'We met your man Chanson. Haven't you heard? Deverell the carpenter has been murdered.'

# Chapter 12

Deverell's house stood in its own ground between two alleyways: a broad, two-storeyed building with a garden plot and workshops. The area was thronged with people as Tressilyian and Chapeleys ushered Corbett through the front door into the kitchen. The curious, despite the best efforts of Blidscote and Tressilyian, had their faces pressed up against the window. Ranulf cleared the kitchen except for Deverell's wife. She sat, white-faced and hollow-eyed in a chair, staring down at the bloodstain on the stone-flagged floor. Standing beside her was a neighbour who, by her own confession, had come to borrow some honey. She'd knocked and rapped but the carpenter's wife had refused to open the door. The neighbour, a prim, self-composed woman, had taken one look through the crack in a shutter and raised the alarm.

'I was in Melford,' Tressilyian explained, 'to summon the jurors who served at the trial. Blidscote found us in the marketplace. Sir Maurice searched for you.' He pointed at Chanson sitting at the foot of the stairs. 'He told us you had gone to the morning Mass.'

'What happened?' Corbett demanded.

'Last night Deverell refused to go to bed. Apparently he was much disturbed by your arrival, Sir Hugh; drawn and fearful, as he had been over the last few days. He sat here, brooding and drinking, staring into the fireplace. Now his wife claims . . .'

Corbett raised his head and studied the carpenter's wife. She was pretty, with her long, black hair, but her face was piteous, grey and haggard, her eyes circled by dark rings. She sat, lips moving, talking to herself, almost unaware of what was going on around her. Now and again she seemed to catch herself, stare around, then go back to her own thoughts.

'Continue,' Corbett demanded.

'Ysabeau,' Tressilyian gestured at Deverell's widow, 'retired to bed. She could do nothing about her husband. He had locked and bolted the door, the same with the shutters. She was lying upstairs wondering what to do when she heard a knock at the door. She got up and went to the window. You've seen the porch in front of the house? The door is in a recess and she couldn't see the visitor. She then heard a crash even as the knocking continued.' Tressilyian paused. 'Well, God save us, Deverell took a crossbow bolt just beneath his left eye. Killed instantly. His wife came hurrying down, took one look and fell into a deep swoon.'

'Clerk?' Ysabeau was staring at him with hate-filled eyes.

'Yes, Mistress?'

'Are you the royal clerk?'

'I am.'

'He feared you.' Her upper lip curled. 'He didn't

want you to come to Melford.'

'Why not, Mistress?'

'He never said. A man of secrets, my Deverell.' She moved her dark eyes to Sir Maurice. 'And you are the Chapeleys whelp? He was never the same after they hanged your father.' She eased herself up in the chair. 'Never the same,' she repeated.

'There was more found.' Blidscote opened his wallet and handed across a scrap of parchment squeezed into a ball. 'Apparently Deverell held that. It was found near his corpse.'

Corbett undid the parchment: it was yellowing and dirty, tattered at the edges. The scrawled words were like letters from a child's horn book.

'It's a quotation,' Corbett murmured. 'From the commandments.' He smiled at Ranulf. 'We seem to be having many of these. Have you read it, Master Blidscote?'

'Aye, Sir Hugh.'

'What does it say?' Sir Maurice demanded.

' "Thou shalt not bear false testimony." '

'He didn't.' Deverell's wife half rose from the chair, her face a mask of fury. 'He didn't bear false testimony.'

Her neighbour coaxed her back, patting her gently on the shoulder.

'There's a true mystery,' Blidscote continued, 'about Deverell's death.'

'Explain!'

'Well, Sir Hugh, the shutters were still barred, all the doors to this house were locked. So how was Deverell murdered? How did the killer manage to pass this message to the victim?'

Corbett stared at the pasty-faced bailiff. It was still early morning yet Blidscote had been drinking even though he hadn't recovered from the previous night's bout. You are frightened, Corbett thought: at the appropriate time I'll squeeze your ear like a physician would a boil and see what pus comes out.

'I mean, I had to force the door,' Blidscote stammered.

Corbett looked behind him and saw the lock buckled. He walked across, opened the door and stood in the porch. On either side rose plaster walls. He glimpsed the Judas squint high on the right side.

'Apparently Deverell refurbished this door,' Blidscote explained. 'It took a battering ram to force it.'

'And there's no other open entrance to the house?' Corbett demanded, aware of the others joining him in the porch.

'I tell you, Sir Hugh,' the bailiff whined, 'the back door and the shutters were all locked. The neighbour became concerned. She peered through a crack in one of the shutters and saw the body lying on the floor. She pounded and yelled. Eventually Ysabeau unlocked the door and the alarm was raised.'

'So, why did you have to force it?' Corbett asked.

'Deverell's wife was in a frightful state. She claimed the killer would come back for her. She relocked the door. We shouted and we reasoned.' He pointed to a half-burnt timber lying on the cobbled yard. 'We had to force an entry.'

'The killer could have used the Judas squint,' Corbett reasoned. 'Look, it's a handspan across and the same deep. You could rest an arbalest against it. A crossbow bolt would take whoever stood on the other side full in the face.'

'I know,' Tressilyian replied. 'But, according to Ysabeau, the knocking continued even after her husband was killed. She remembers that distinctly. She was in the bedchamber, heard the rapping on the door, the crash of her husband's fall but the knocking continued.'

Corbett stood by the Judas squint. Try as he might, pretending to hold a crossbow in one hand, he couldn't knock at the door: it was too far.

'There would be another problem.'

Corbett peered through the Judas squint at Ranulf standing on the other side.

'What's that, Clerk of the Green Wax?'

'Well,' Ranulf's voice sounded hollow, 'Deverell was killed in the dead of night. It would be dark. How would you know when I appeared at the Judas squint? That's why these spyholes exist, isn't it? You'd only be allowed to loose one bolt and Deverell would be warned.'

Corbett asked them all to go back inside. He had the front door closed and stood in the porch. He knocked on the door. At the same time he pretended to hold a crossbow aimed at the Judas squint. Now he couldn't reach that.

'I can't do both at once,' he murmured.

He then told Ranulf to act the part of Deverell but this only complicated matters. He never knew when the soft-shoed Ranulf stood at the Judas squint. It would be even harder at night, Corbett confessed to himself. He opened the door and walked back into the kitchen. Were there two killers? he wondered. One who knocked at the door, the other positioned at the Judas squint, crossbow primed? But how would the killer know when Deverell approached?

'You are sure,' Corbett demanded of Blidscote, 'that the knocking continued even as Deverell was killed?'

'That's what Ysabeau said.'

Corbett picked up the crumpled piece of parchment and turned it over. He noted the faint streaks of blood.

'That's Deverell's?'

'Oh yes,' Blidscote replied.

Corbett walked back to the front door and stared out. The curious still thronged at the mouth of the alleyway. From where he stood Corbett could hear the hustle and bustle of the marketplace. Old Mother Crauford was standing in the front of the crowd, one hand resting on her stick, the other on the arm of the lank-haired, empty-faced, young man.

Peterkin, Corbett thought, the one who had found Molkyn's head floating on the mere. The old woman raised her cane in greeting. Corbett was about to reply with a wave, then closed his eyes and laughed.

'Master?' Ranulf was standing behind him.

'What I want, Ranulf, is a long piece of fire wood, a cloth and a small cup of wine.'

He followed his bemused companion back to the kitchen. Ranulf searched around and brought a long piece of kindling, a wet rag from the buttery and a pewter cup half-full of ale.

'I couldn't find a wine cask,' Ranulf apologised.

'Sir Hugh?' Tressilyian, sitting on a bench near the fireside, got up.

'Please sit here and see what happens,' Corbett invited him. 'Ranulf, you pretend to be the carpenter.

When I knock on the door, do what you think Deverell did last night. Don't flinch or delay.'

Ranulf agreed. Corbett went outside, pulling the door closed. He put the cup of ale down, rolled the wet cloth in a ball and pushed it down the Judas squint as far as he could. He then grasped the piece of kindling in one hand, the cup of ale in the other. He stood by the spyhole and used the stick to rap on the front door. He heard a movement within followed by Ranulf's exclamation. The piece of rag was removed and, as it was, Corbett threw the contents of the cup into the spyhole. Ranulf's curse was long and colourful.

'That's how it was done,' Corbett declared, coming back into the kitchen. 'There weren't two killers, just one. He put that piece of parchment into the spyhole and brought the primed crossbow up to rest on the ledge, the bolt aimed to hit anyone who stood on the other side. It was dark, the killer knew about Deverell's fears so he kept tapping insistently on the door with a stick or a cane. He wouldn't hear him come to the spyhole but he'd hear and see the parchment being removed. Once it was, he let slip the catch and the crossbow bolt took Deverell full in the face.'

'Is that possible?' Blidscote stammered.

'It's logical,' Corbett replied. 'And very easy. Imagine Deverell being frightened. He hears a constant rapping at the door. He thinks he's safe. Deverell knew his own house: you can't knock on the door and stare through the Judas squint at the same time. He doesn't realise the killer is using a cane. He goes to the spyhole to stare out but becomes confused. His view is blocked by that ball of parchment. He naturally pulls it out: that's the sign for the killer. He sees a pale reflection of light from the kitchen, knows that Deverell is standing there, the crossbow bolt is primed. One simple touch of his finger and the bolt is sent speeding through. Deverell wouldn't have known what was happening. He is still curious about the piece of parchment. Perhaps he thinks it's a message. He has been drinking, his wits are dull, he doesn't move away. In a few heartbeats he's dead, staggering to collapse on the kitchen floor. The crumpled piece of parchment rolls out of his fingers. He didn't even have time to read it.'

Sir Maurice clapped his hand gently. 'Well done, Sir Hugh, but who is the killer and why?'

'I don't know who but I do know why. Deverell gave evidence at your father's trial, how he saw Sir Roger fleeing along Gully Lane on the night Widow Walmer was killed. Sir Louis, I truly believe that was a lie and an innocent man was executed.'

'So soon?' Sir Maurice's face had paled. 'You have reached that conclusion so soon?'

'Sir Maurice, you don't have to be a scholar of great wit or learning: Molkyn and Thorkle have been murdered, now Deverell.'

'Why?' Sir Maurice asked.

'I don't know,' Corbett replied, 'whether it's to punish them or to close their mouths for ever. What we have is a continuation of the horrid murders of young women and now the grisly deaths of some of those who played a prominent part in your father's trial.' Corbett rubbed his chin. 'I don't know whether we are dealing with one killer or two.'

'And there was the attack on me,' Tressilyian said sharply.

'Yes, Sir Louis, there was.' Corbett slapped Blidscote on the shoulder. 'If I were you, master bailiff, I'd walk most warily at night. Sir Louis, you have the other jurymen?'

'I told them to meet in the taproom of the Golden Fleece. There should be ten but only five remain. In the last few years the others have died.' His face broke into a cold smile. 'Oh, don't worry, Sir Hugh, apart from Molkyn and Thorkle, they died of natural causes.'

Blidscote was now moving from foot to foot, nervously clasping at his groin.

'Am I in danger, Sir Hugh? I did nothing wrong!'

Corbett went across. 'Of wetting yourself, Master Blidscote,' he whispered into his ear. 'For all our sakes, if you wish to relieve yourself, go!'

Blidscote hurried down the passageway. Corbett wondered if he should question the bailiff now, but what proof of corruption or complicity did he have? Blidscote would deny any wrongdoing. He had to or he'd hang.

The clerk went and squatted down beside Ysabeau. She seemed more composed now, no longer talking to herself. She lifted her eyes and smiled slyly at him. Corbett was chilled by the look. The woman's wits were certainly disturbed. Corbett felt a pang of grief, of deep regret. Deverell had died because of the King's clerk's arrival in Melford. Justice had to be done but the price would be heavy.

'I am sorry,' Corbett murmured. 'Mistress, I deeply regret your husband's death. God be my witness, I did not want his blood on my hands!'

Ysabeau just glanced at the bailiff, who'd returned.

'Tell me,' Corbett looked up at the neighbour, 'how many people knew about the Judas squint?'

'Not many,' the neighbour answered. 'Deverell, God rest him, was a man who kept to himself but, there again, people did call to place orders.'

Corbett looked over his shoulder. 'Master Blidscote, did you know about this?'

'I did and I didn't,' came the defensive reply. 'True, I visited here but I'd always forget it.'

'Sir Louis? Sir Maurice?'

Both knights shook their heads.

'Have there been any strangers at the house?' Corbett asked.

Ysabeau's gaze didn't shift.

'I glimpsed a friar,' the neighbour replied. 'One of those wandering priests, ragged and dirty. He came here recently. Deverell called him a nuisance. He only left when he was given some food and drink.'

'Anyone else?' Corbett demanded.

The woman shook her head.

'I'll look upstairs,' Corbett declared. 'I want to view the corpse.'

He left the rest and climbed the broad polished stairs to the small gallery. The door to the bedchamber was open, a well-furnished room with gleaming furniture which matched the carved woodwork of the four-poster bed. Corbett went across and looked through the window. A crowd still gathered below. Burghesh had joined them. The church bell began to toll and Corbett realised St Edmund's would be getting ready for the funeral of

Elizabeth the wheelwright's daughter.

He moved back to the bed and pulled aside the drapes. Deverell's corpse was hidden beneath a bloody sheet. He carefully peeled this back and flinched at the terrible wound. The crossbow bolt had been shot very close, reducing one side of the carpenter's face to a bloody pulp. The bolt had entered just beneath the eye: a piteous, hideous sight. Corbett murmured the requiem. Surely God would have mercy on this man, so full of fear, sent so quickly into the dark?

Although Corbett felt a deep regret, he knew the root cause of Deverell's murder was Sir Roger's death. Deverell had certainly lied at the trial, but why? What had forced this wealthy craftsman to perjure himself, to send a man to the gallows? Who in Melford could exercise such power, exploit fearful nightmares? Had Deverell himself begun to regret his sin? Was he the one who had daubed Chapeleys' tomb, pinned the notice to the gallows post? Indeed, had Deverell been the stranger who had so mysteriously assaulted him the previous evening, a fearful man who had lashed out but then panicked and fled?

'A terrible death,' Corbett murmured, pulling over the blood-soaked sheets. He heard a sound behind him; it must be Ranulf. 'I've seen many corpses but each time is different.'

Again the floorboard creaked. Corbett whirled round. Ysabeau was creeping towards him, a broad-bladed knife in her hand. Corbett was trapped by the bed behind him. He moved sideways. She moved with him. She shifted her grip. Those black eyes never left Corbett. The clerk knew he was in mortal danger. Ysabeau had one thought only: to kill the man responsible for her husband's death. Corbett moved away. She moved with him. He feinted to draw her in but she kept on the balls of her feet like a dancer. Corbett had no choice. He moved closer. Ysabeau was quicker, the knife snaking out, but he caught her wrist: her strength surprised him. He put one hand on the wrist holding the dagger. He tried to cup his other hand beneath her chin to force her away. She was tense and taut as a bowstring.

Corbett began to panic. He wanted to defend himself but, try as he might, he could not hurt this woman. She was no footpad or outlaw, only demented with grief. He pushed her back against the half-opened door.

'Ranulf!' he screamed.

Ysabeau, eyes blazing with hate, suddenly brought her other hand round and clawed Corbett's face. The clerk hit her, sending her out on to the gallery to collide with Ranulf. She turned. Ranulf lashed out with his boot, kicking the knife out of her hand. Others were hurrying up the stairs as Ranulf seized her in a vicelike grip, pinioning her arms to her side.

'You whoreson!' The froth flecked Ysabeau's lips. 'You gallows bird!'

She struggled against Ranulf. The clerk held her fast. The neighbour appeared, a cup in her hand. Ranulf dragged the unfortunate woman down the gallery, kicked open the door to a chamber and threw her in. The neighbour, accompanied by Blidscote, followed, slamming the door behind them. Corbett heard the bolts being drawn. He dabbed the cut on his face, then picked up the knife and tossed it down the stairs.

'I am sorry,' Sir Maurice gasped. 'One minute she was sitting there, then she said she wanted to view her husband's corpse and apologise to you. She must have had the knife hidden away.'

'It's all right. It's all right,' Corbett breathed.

He went back to the bedchamber, splashed water over his hands and face, drying himself on a linen cloth.

'It's only a small scratch,' Ranulf declared briskly. 'It will make you look more handsome.'

'Thank you, Ranulf.'

Corbett wiped some water from his eyebrows.

'She was strong. Sir Louis, you are the local justice, yes? I want you to send Chanson downstairs for an apothecary or physician. The woman needs a sleeping potion. She should be guarded day and night. At least,' he added drily, 'until I leave Melford. I am also going to search this house.'

'You can't do that,' the justice retorted. 'You have no warrant.'

Corbett tapped his pouch. 'I have all the warrants I need. You can wait for me in the kitchen below. Ranulf will be your host.'

Once they had left, Corbett closed the door behind them and began his search: coffers, aumbrys, chests, but they contained nothing untoward. Most of what he found was connected with Deverell's trade: receipts, ledgers, as well as different purchases. The bedchamber yielded nothing.

Corbett went downstairs. Ignoring the rest, he searched the kitchen and the small parlour. He found a little chancery or writing office behind it. The door was locked. Ranulf found the keys and Corbett went inside.

A narrow, dusty chamber with one small window high in the wall; a tall writing-desk and stool. Corbett lit the candles. He had to force the desk, but again nothing. The small coffer beneath it, however, with its three locks, looked more interesting. A search was made and the keys found in the dead man's purse. Corbett undid the three locks and pulled back the lid. It contained a small breviary, a Book of Hours, not a collection of prayers but the Divine Office: Prime, Matins, Lauds. The writing was the careful script of some monk, the pages well thumbed.

'A carpenter who understood Latin?' Corbett murmured.

There was also a white cord with three knots in it and a brown scapular, two pieces of leather on a coarse string. Corbett slipped this over his own head, allowing one piece of the leather to lie on his chest, the other on his back. The cord looked well used, slightly fraying in places. He went through the other items: a medal, Ave beads, a small pyx for carrying the host.

'So, that's what you were?' Corbett declared. 'No wonder you kept yourself to yourself!'

He took off the scapular and put all the contents back in the coffer, closed and locked it and returned to the kitchen.

The two knights and Ranulf were sitting at the kitchen table. Chanson came through the front door, a stout man striding behind him who introduced himself as a local physician. He brusquely told Corbett to get out of his way and went upstairs to see his patient.

'We should be gone,' Corbett declared, picking up his cloak.

'Did you find anything?' Sir Maurice asked.

'Is Blidscote still here?' Corbett asked Chanson.

'Oh yes, but he prefers to be as far away from you, Master, as possible.'

'I'll have words with him soon,' Corbett replied.

'What have you found, Corbett?' Tressilyian demanded.

'Deverell may have been a carpenter but, once upon a time he was a monk.'

'A monk!' Sir Maurice exclaimed.

'A defrocked priest,' Corbett replied. 'A monk who ran away from his monastery. It's not so unusual. He could never really close the door on his past so he kept a few mementoes: Ave beads, the scapular some monks wear beneath their robes, his psalter and his cord with the three knots symbolising the vows of Chastity, Poverty and Obedience. I suspect Master Deverell, as a monk, showed tremendous skill as a carpenter. Perhaps he got tired of his vocation. Perhaps he quarrelled with Father Abbot. So he fled. He arrived in a prosperous town like Melford, married and settled down.'

'And what has this got to do with my father's death?'

'A great deal, Sir Maurice. Remember Deverell was a craftsman, a worthy burgess of this town. His word would carry a great deal of weight.' Corbett lowered his voice. 'On oath his evidence would be believed by a judge and jury. Yes, Sir Louis?'

The justice, tight-lipped, nodded. Corbett glimpsed the anger in his eyes. Judges and justices made mistakes. Sir Louis would not be the first, and certainly not the last, to regret a sentence passed.

'I appreciate, sir, this is difficult for you,' Corbett apologised.

'In the end, Sir Hugh, justice will be done. If Deverell gave false testimony, and any others, then let it be upon their heads. I can only accept the verdict of the jury. God knows, I pleaded for Sir Roger's life.'

'I know.' Corbett glanced over his shoulder towards the stairs. 'Deverell, God rest him, lied and perjured himself. But why? Gold or silver?' He pulled a face. 'A man like Deverell wouldn't risk his life and reputation for that. No, Deverell was being black-mailed. Someone here knew he was a runaway monk, which means his marriage wasn't valid. The summoner could arrive from the Archdeacon's court: Deverell could either be excommunicated or dragged back to his monastery to do penance on bread and water.'

'So, Deverell perjured himself?'

'Yes, he perjured himself. The problem is, who knew his secret? I wonder about Deverell,' Corbett continued. 'Was he the one who sent Molkyn the miller that verse from Leviticus?'

'What verse?' Sir Louis asked.

'I'll tell you later,' Corbett replied.

They walked out into the sunshine. Corbett heard his name called. Sorrel came out of one of the alleyways.

'So, Deverell's dead!' she murmured, eyes gleaming. 'Fitting punishment for a perjurer.' She offered Corbett the coin he'd given her the previous evening. 'I shouldn't have taken that.'

'Why not?' Corbett steered her away from the rest.

'I didn't tell you,' she confessed. 'I'm well furnished with silver.'

'How?'

'Three times a year,' she said, 'at Beauchamp Place a silver coin appears wrapped in a piece of parchment. No messages: it's been the same since Furrell died. Every January, Easter and Michaelmas.'

'Keep it.'

Corbett closed her fingers round the coin. He was about to join the rest but Old Mother Crauford hobbled forward, cane tapping the cobbles, one hand grasping Peterkin. She shooed a scavenging cat out of her way.

'More deaths, royal clerk. They should rename Melford, Haceldema.'

'The Field of Blood,' Corbett translated. 'Why do you say that?'

'Always been deaths,' she declared.

'What's the matter?' Corbett glanced at Peterkin, who was jibbering with fright.

'He lives with me,' the old woman explained, 'and he's all a-feared. He thinks you've come to take him away to a house of simpletons, where he'll be fed bread and water and given the whip.'

Peterkin's face was dirty and unshaven, his eyes full of terror, his lower lip quivering. If Old Mother Crauford hadn't held him by the wrist, he would have bolted like a rabbit. Corbett took a coin out of his wallet and, grasping the man's hand, made him accept it.

'I have not come to take you,' Corbett said softly. 'Peterkin is my friend. Old Mother Crauford is my friend. Buy some sweetmeats, a hot pie or join me in the Golden Fleece. Have a tankard of ale.'

The change in the simpleton's face was wonderful to behold. He shook himself free and danced from foot to foot, humming under his breath.

'Peterkin's rich! Peterkin's rich!' he slurred.

'Aye, Peterkin's a friend of the King,' Corbett added.

He was about to walk away when Mother Crauford caught him by the fingers.

'That was kind of you, clerk,' she whispered. 'But, be careful as you walk through Haceldema!'

# Chapter 13

The jurors were a nondescript group of petty trades-men and farmers. They sat in a corner of the tap-room, shuffling their feet, looking rather woebegone, frightened of meeting the royal clerk. They had fortified their courage with stoups of ale. Tressilyian cleared the taproom of everyone else. Sir Maurice Chapeleys sat some distance away, feet up on a stool, drumming his fingers on the table. Chanson went to check on the horses. Ranulf sat beside Corbett. Tressilyian took charge. He introduced the clerk and smiled sadly.

'Time passes quickly,' he declared. 'Five of the jury which tried Sir Roger Chapeleys have died.' His smile disappeared. 'Two have been murdered. Now, you remember the days of the trial well, yes? The trial took place in the Guildhall?'

They all nodded like a group of obedient mastiffs.

'I've never asked you this,' Tressilyian continued. 'The deliberations of the jury are usually secret but why did you return a verdict so swiftly, in less than an hour?'

'It was your summing up.' A burly tradesman, a butcher by the blood on his apron, spoke up.

'Yes it was,' Tressilyian conceded. 'Your name is Simon, isn't it? You are a flesher?'

'That's right, my lord.'

'Please answer my question!'

'I can't remember every detail,' the flesher replied, 'but the evidence was clear: Sir Roger went down to Widow Walmer. He was seen by Deverell the carpenter – and yes, we now know he's dead.' He gazed round at his companions. 'And, by the way, what protection do we have? It wasn't our fault Sir Roger was executed.'

'No one said it was,' Corbett replied. 'Do continue.'

'Sir Roger was seen hurrying away from the widow's cottage. He possessed belongings of the other women who had been murdered.'

'What I'm interested in,' Tressilyian declared, 'and what Sir Hugh wants to know, is what happened in the jury room after you retired. Molkyn was your leader, Thorkle his deputy?'

'Well, I'll be honest,' Simon replied. 'Molkyn was a bugger. I didn't like him alive, I don't like him dead. He was all hot for Sir Roger being hanged. Guilty, he said, as soon as the door was closed. Thorkle, of course, followed suit.'

'And the rest of you?' Corbett asked.

He stared round at these men with their chapped faces and raw red hands. He felt sorry for them. It was common for juries to be intimidated but, there again, they could prove surprisingly stubborn, particularly when a man's life was at stake.

'Some of us objected. I am not going to say who. Rein in your horse, we told Molkyn. You could see he didn't like Sir Roger.'

'It was Furrell.' One of Simon's companions spoke up. 'I was very concerned about Furrell's evidence. He claimed Widow Walmer was alive after Sir Roger left. He also hinted at how others were seen going down to her cottage.'

'Ah yes.' Simon took up the story. 'But Molkyn told us to shut up. He alleged Furrell had been bribed by Sir Roger. The knight could have gone back, whilst the people Furrell had glimpsed going down to Widow Walmer's cottage were probably Repton the reeve and others who discovered the corpse.'

'How did you vote?' Corbett asked.

'By a show of hands.'

'And what convinced you?'

Corbett moved on the stool. He wished Ranulf, sitting beside him, would stop humming softly under his breath. His manservant glanced at him and winked. Corbett wondered what was wrong. He turned back to the flesher.

'The evidence? You mentioned the justice's summing up at the end of the trial. I asked how you voted?'

'It was Deverell's testimony.' The flesher sighed. 'The visit to Widow Walmer and the goods being found in Sir Roger's manor. Molkyn was urging us on; eventually we all had to agree.' He shrugged. 'The verdict was returned.'

'And since then?' Corbett asked.

'Oh, we've discussed it – when the murders began again.' Simon nodded. 'Yes, we wondered if an innocent man had been executed.' The flesher shuffled his feet and looked at the floor.

'What is it?' Corbett asked. 'You have something else to say, haven't you?'

Simon wiped his sweaty brow on the back of his wrist. 'I'd like to make a confession.' The words came blurting out. 'Sir Louis, I should have told you this before.'

'What?' Corbett asked.

'About two years after the trial I was in an ale-house, the Gooseberry Bush at the far end of the town. Molkyn came in. He'd just made a delivery of flour and was drinking the profits. Now most times, Molkyn was a surly bastard, always looking for a fight – fists like hams he had. He calls me over. I was delivering some meat. He was quite insistent so I joined him. He was deep in his cups. We talked about this and that. "Do you believe in ghosts?" Molkyn suddenly asked. "What do you mean, Molkyn?" I said. "Sir Roger Chapeleys," he replied. "Do you think he can come back and haunt us for what we did?" Now I was troubled, I didn't like that sort of talk. "He was guilty," I replied. "What if I say he wasn't," Molkyn jibed—'

'I beg your pardon?' Corbett interrupted. 'Molkyn said that?'

'Aye. I became frightened. I questioned him but Molkyn grew all coy and sly, tapping his fleshy nose and winking. He then told me about a quarrel he had had with Furrell the poacher. "What quarrel?" says I. It appears that after the trial, Furrell had approached Molkyn, saying Sir Roger was innocent and he could prove it. Molkyn told him to go hang. Furrell also accused Molkyn of being a perjurer, then Furrell said something very strange. He claimed there was proof in Melford who the real killer was and that it was plain as a picture for anyone to see.'

'And?' Corbett asked.

'That's all Molkyn told me. He was fuddled in his wits and deep in his cups so I left him.'

'Is there anything else?' Corbett demanded.

A chorus of denial greeted his question. Corbett thanked them and the men left, eager to be away from the sharp-eyed clerk and his probing questions.

'You are rather quiet, Sir Maurice?' Corbett asked.

The young man gazed sullenly back. 'Sir Hugh, what can I do? I was only a boy when my father was hanged. How can I go round Melford asking questions?' His face became hard. 'I can see it in their eyes, Sir Hugh. They still regard him as a killer, an assassin.' His gaze softened. 'But I have trust in you. Justice will be done.'

'Sir Louis,' Corbett glanced around to make sure there were no eavesdroppers: Matthew the taverner, however, had the sense to keep his slatterns and tapboys well away, 'at Sir Roger's trial, were you uneasy?'

'Of course, but what could I do? The only evidence Sir Roger truly denied was Deverell's.'

'And Furrell's evidence?' Corbett asked.

Sir Louis sighed and sat down on a stool opposite. The justice hadn't slept well; his eyes were heavy and red-rimmed.

'Sir Hugh, Furrell was patronised by Sir Roger.' He lowered his voice. 'And there's something else. Three young women were killed before Widow Walmer's death, yes?'

Corbett nodded.

'Now, whatever Sorrel has said to you, and I saw you talking to her, Furrell was a rogue. He was a thief. He poached on my land, as he did on everybody else's but, of course, we ignored him. He only took what he wanted and there was little malice in the fellow. Except,' Sir Louis continued, 'Furrell was a lady's man himself. When it came to maypole dancing or mummery on the green, Furrell, in his cups, was hot and lecherous as a sparrow. Now, when these murders occurred both Blidscote and I investigated. The finger of suspicion pointed strongly at Furrell. He was well known for talking to the girls. He did solicit, albeit well out of sight of Sorrel, and, above all, he knew the country roads and lanes.'

'But Furrell's dead.'

'Is he, Corbett? Where's the corpse? What sign or proof do we have of his death? How do we know that he is not living in the forest or hidden away at Beauchamp Place? He could return to his killing spree. He may be responsible for the deaths of Molkyn, Thorkle and Deverell. Furrell knows this town, its bylanes and its trackways. He was often knocking on this person's house or that: he'd know about Deverell's spyhole.'

'But could he kill a man like Molkyn?'

Corbett was intrigued by Tressilyian's line of argument.

'Oh, our miller was a brawny oaf but a man in his cups. You could take his head like swatting a fly, whilst Thorkle was a frightened rabbit.'

'If I follow your argument,' Corbett recapped, 'Furrell therefore spoke on Sir Roger's behalf, not only out of kindness but because he knew the truth. At the same time Furrell secretly realised his evidence wouldn't be taken too seriously.'

'And afterwards,' the justice added, 'Furrell almost confessed as much to Molkyn before he realised what he had said and disappeared. Like any outlaw, he hides but, when all is quiet, he begins his killings.'

'I would accept what you say,' Corbett declared, 'though there's one other individual I have yet to meet.'

He quickly told Tressilyian and Sir Maurice about the Mummer's Man.

'I've never heard the like of it,' Tressilyian whispered. 'But that could be Furrell.'

Corbett stared across the taproom. He could hear Matthew shouting from the kitchen, the bustle and noise from the yard outside as people angrily wondered why they were being kept away from the tavern.

'We'll talk about this tonight at the Guildhall,' Sir Louis said, 'just after vespers.'

Sir Louis and Chapeleys made their farewells whilst Corbett led his two companions up to his chamber.

'Do you think Tressilyian's theory is possible?' Ranulf asked.

'All things are possible,' Corbett replied. He took his boots off and lay down on the bed. 'What I do think is that Furrell knew the truth. I find it difficult to accept he's the killer. Sorrel's no liar. Sir Louis may be right: Furrell may be the key to this mystery but I still believe the poor man's dead. That flesher also spoke the truth; he had nothing to hide.'

Corbett paused. Then: 'What were Furrell's words to Molkyn? That it was all as plain as a picture?' He stared up at the emblems on the tester cloth above the bed. 'Plain as a picture,' he repeated. He turned on his side. 'Chanson, you made careful enquiries at the Guildhall?'

'I didn't find much,' the groom replied. 'Every year someone is reported missing.'

Corbett stared at a small triptych on the wall. 'I want you to do me an errand.'

'Yes, Master.'

'A message for Sir Maurice.'

'But he's just left.'

'I know and I apologise.'

Corbett got up and went to his writing-desk. Ranulf glared at Chanson, shaking his head as a warning not to protest. Corbett wrote quickly, took a piece of wax and sealed the note.

'Give that to Sir Maurice personally. He is to tell no one what I ask, nor is he to mention it tonight, except to say yea or nay. Do you understand? Now drink a tankard in the taproom below and be off.'

Chanson took the message and left.

'And what were you so pleased about in the taproom?' Corbett asked. 'Humming and singing under your breath?'

'Adela. She's quite a chatterbox,' Ranulf replied. 'She told me that—'

'Told you?' Corbett intervened. 'When did she tell you, Ranulf?'

His manservant coloured. 'Ah, last night I grew thirsty. Chanson is not the most ideal companion: he not only snores like a horse, he smells like one as well.'

'So, you went downstairs and paid court to the fair

Adela. Ranulf, if you become a priest, these midnight trysts will have to end.'

'Well, she has taken a silver piece off me.' Ranulf pulled a stool across and sat down. 'Tavern wenches are a source of gossip. Grimstone likes his wine. Burghesh is the priest more than he is, a veritable busybody. Sir Louis Tressilyian doesn't like the townspeople, whilst Sir Maurice, before he fell in love with Sir Louis's daughter, would often vow terrible retribution for his father's death. The miller was an oaf, a bullyboy. His wife is certainly hot-eyed and may have entertained Sir Roger when her husband was absent—'

'All this we know,' Corbett interrupted. 'This is a town, a parish. Go to any town in the kingdom . . .'

'Master Blidscote,' Ranulf retorted.

'Oh, our good master bailiff.'

'He's unmarried.'

'For some men that might be happiness. I suppose he has an eye for the wenches?'

'Yes, Master, and for the boys.'

'You're sure?'

'So it's rumoured.'

'Children rather than men?'

'So rumour has it,' Ranulf replied. 'There's even a story that Sir Roger had to have words with him years ago about his own son, Maurice. They also say Blidscote's corrupt. A coward at times, a bully at others, his soul is constantly up for sale.'

'So, Ranulf, a man easily blackmailed. Blidscote harmed Sir Roger by ensuring Molkyn was on that jury whilst the rest were people who would give way to the burly miller.'

'Does the trial record reveal anything?'

'No, Ranulf. They call it a transcript, but in truth, it is a summary; it contains nothing new. The prosecution was presented by a sergeant at law from Ipswich, a royal lawyer attached to the city council: he had an easy task.'

'Will we trap the real murderer?'

'I don't know,' Corbett murmured. 'You see, Ranulf, everything we learn is what people tell us. And, as you know, that can be easily controlled. Some people forget, others conceal, a few tell us what we want to know. Then, of course, there are the downright lies. Of course, the killer, or shall I say killers, may make a mistake.'

'So, we are dealing with two?'

'Oh yes. The first likes to terrify young women, ravish and murder them. The second – I don't know: he or she – wages bloody war against those who sent Sir Roger to the scaffold.'

Corbett recalled Old Mother Crauford's words about Haceldema. He sat and half listened to the sounds from the taproom below.

'What happens if we can't prove anything?'

'Then, Ranulf, we can't prove anything. The King has given us little time. He's calling a great council at Winchester shortly after the feast of All Saints and we have to be present. Look, go across to the church. Ask Parson Grimstone if I can borrow the Book of the Dead.'

'Why?'

'Because I want it.'

Ranulf pulled a face and went out. He closed the door behind him and made a rude gesture in its direction. Ah well, he thought, old Master Long Face will sit and brood and then leap like a mouse-hunting cat. But will the murderers be so easily trapped?

Ranulf clattered down the stairs. He was so immersed in his own thoughts he didn't even bother to stop and flirt with Adela.

Back in his bedchamber Corbett lay on the bed. He tried to conceive a map of Melford, the sprawling town, the silent, secretive countryside around. Tressilyian was correct in one thing: a man like Furrell could hide out there – but these murders? He tried to put himself in the place of young Elizabeth, whose corpse was now buried in God's acre. A young woman full of romantic notions, probably resenting the close confines of a family house, Elizabeth would be ever ready to run on an errand to the market, any excuse to talk and chatter to others. No, he decided, the Mummer's Man wouldn't make contact in the town. Would Elizabeth Wheelwright stop because of a shadowy voice calling from a doorway? But she would be even more terrified if she met such a creature out on a country lane. No, there was something wrong with that. He had to ford that gap in his logic. Somehow Elizabeth, like others, is lured out into the countryside, some desolate spot where the killer is waiting. He enjoys himself like the demon he is, then hides the body, or tries to. Five years ago something went wrong. Perhaps Sir Roger began to suspect the true identity of the killer. Sir Roger was trapped, accused of the murder of Widow Walmer. An easy task for, if rumour was correct, Sir Roger was lecherous as a sparrow. The killer prepared the trap well. He not only slew young women but had gathered information about the residents of Melford which he could use. He also sent belongings taken from his victims to Sir Roger. Corbett pulled himself up against the bolsters. But that wasn't enough: Blidscote, Molkyn, Thorkle and Deverell were blackmailed. They were forced to dance to the killer's tune and Sir Roger's fate was a foregone conclusion.

'He enjoys it,' Corbett declared. 'The killer enjoys the power.'

They call him the Jesses killer, Corbett reasoned, the Mummer's Man, but he's more like a chess player. He regards other people as pieces to move as he thinks fit. He likes to see them do what he wants. But who would have such power? Sir Louis? Sir Maurice? They were both manor lords. They would have spies and retainers listening to the chatter. But Sir Louis himself had been attacked. He also had played a major part in Sir Roger's execution. And Sir Maurice? A man dedicated to clearing his father's name, he'd have little love for the people of Melford. But which killer was he thinking about? Corbett shook his head. Then there were the others: Parson Grimstone with his drinking, his seclusion; Curate Robert with his hidden anxiety and deep feeling of guilt. Or Burghesh? Could Blidscote be a killer? A man who may not even like women? Or was it someone he had forgotten? Corbett beat his fist against his thigh. Two killers, he thought, or one? The murder of Molkyn and the rest had only occurred after the killings of the young women had begun again. So, what did that mean? Corbett sighed as he heard footsteps outside. Ranulf entered with Burghesh behind him.

'I brought the Book of the Dead myself,' the old soldier declared. He took it out of the leather bag and placed it on the stool beside Corbett's bed.

'I really shouldn't allow it but,' he grinned, 'you are the King's clerk. If I stay in the taproom below and take it back later . . .?'

Corbett's hand went to the purse in his belt.

'No, no,' Burghesh said. 'I can pay for my own ale. Sir Hugh, I'll be downstairs.'

Ranulf closed the door behind him. Corbett picked up the book and began to leaf through it.

'Well, Chanson's galloping after Sir Maurice,' Ranulf remarked. 'You are going down amongst the dead.'

Corbett smiled over the book. 'If you were involved in Sir Roger's death . . .?' Corbett paused. 'No, let me put the question another way. Who has the most to fear?'

'Sir Louis?'

'But he's a manor lord.'

'Then Blidscote,' Ranulf remarked.

'I agree, and there's little we can do to save him. But, go round Melford, Ranulf, see if you can track our fat bailiff down, then bring him back here for questioning.'

'Anyone else?'

'Ask young Adela to come up. Tell her she has nothing to fear.'

'If the Lady Maeve got to know? Shouldn't I stay,' Ranulf teased, 'and act the chaperone?'

'Ask her to come up,' Corbett repeated. 'She has

more to fear from the messenger than the message he carries.'

Ranulf collected his cloak and sword belt and went down the stairs. A short while later Adela tapped on the door of the chamber. She slipped in, nervous but still bold-eyed, pretending to stand in a docile fashion, hands hanging beside her.

'Sit down.' Corbett gestured to the stool. 'I believe you know Ranulf?'

The tavern wench looked for sarcasm but found none. This clerk's gaze was not lustful or mocking but rather gentle and sad.

'What do you want, Master?'

'Just a little of your time. I am sorry about the game Ranulf and Chanson played with you, bringing you out of the tavern,' he added hastily.

Adela shrugged one shoulder.

'What harm can a man do in a busy marketplace?'

'Has any man tried to harm you, Adela?'

She smiled sweetly. 'Most men are babies: they think with their codpieces.'

'Do we now?' Corbett laughed. 'But you are able to look after yourself?'

'A swift slap and an even swifter kick, Master, is a good defence.'

'You were the last to talk to the wheelwright's daughter, Elizabeth?'

'Aye, but I have answered this. She was in a hurry to get away. I thought she was going home.'

'Did she ever talk of the Mummer's Man or any other creature?'

'No.'

'Tell me, Adela, if you met a man out in the

countryside, riding a horse, wearing one of those masks they use in a miracle play . . .?'

'I'd run and hide,' she laughed.

'And if this evening you were going home and a voice called "Adela" from the shadows?'

'I'd stop, if there was someone with me.'

'And if this voice said that you must go to such and such a place, where some admirer was waiting for you or a gift had been left?'

'I wouldn't believe it. I certainly wouldn't stand there. I'd see who it was.'

'And if that man was wearing a mask?'

'I'd scream and run. Why these questions? I've learnt my lesson about—'

'What do you mean?' Corbett asked sharply.

'Oh, about four months ago, that fool Peterkin – well, he's not as dull-witted as he looks – he brought me a message.'

'What did this message say?'

She closed her eyes. ' "A gift awaits for the one I love at Hamden Mere. After the market horn, it will appear." '

Corbett asked her to repeat it.

'It's doggerel poetry,' he murmured.

'Peterkin's like that,' Adela remarked. 'Hurrying hither and thither like a little rabbit. Ask the taverner: even as a lad, Peterkin was used as a messenger by lovesick swains.'

'And did you go to Hamden Mere?'

'Yes. It's a marsh in a copse of wood on the south side of the town. I was impatient. I wanted to know who it was: the tavern becomes busy after the horn is sounded and the market's ended.'

'Why Hamden Mere?' Corbett asked. 'Why not Devil's Oak or Gully Lane?'

She smiled. 'It's where I used to play as a child.'

'And where you take your love swain?'

'Yes, but don't tell Taverner Matthew: he's always boasting how he runs a good house.'

'And what happened?' Corbett demanded.

'I went and waited. I searched and I looked but there was nothing – a cruel jape – so I came back.'

'Did you later question Peterkin?'

'Yes I did, quietly. I didn't want to make myself look as big a fool as he is. He just gaped at me, said it was a poem he had learnt and didn't say any more.'

'But you believed him the first time?'

'He showed me a coin: said he'd been paid to deliver it.' She shrugged. 'That convinced me.' Adela became all nervous.

'You know what I'm going to ask,' Corbett said softly. 'Is that how Elizabeth was trapped?'

'But I had no proof,' she hissed. 'I was frightened. I did not want to become a laughing stock. The tap-room would never let me forget the day I believed simple Peterkin. Even if I had said something – who would believe me? What proof did I have?'

Corbett took a coin from his purse, went across and pushed it into the wench's hand.

'What's that for, Master?' she asked cheekily.

'Your company,' Corbett replied. 'If I were you I'd go across to the church. I'd buy a candle and light it.'

The young tavern wench looked puzzled. Corbett opened the door. She slipped out, he closed and locked it behind her.

'You danced with death,' he murmured, 'and were allowed to walk away.'

Corbett went to the window and stared down at an ostler cooling horses off in the yard below.

Of course, Corbett thought. Poor Peterkin! Frightened of being taken away, so easily terrified, so quickly bribed. Who would pay much attention to him? The man may be a dullard but the same doggerel would have been taught to him time and time again, only the place changed. Corbett wondered how many other young women in the town had received such an invitation? Some would ignore it, dismissing Peterkin as mad as a March hare. Others, like Adela, would go, perhaps at the wrong time, and find nothing. Poor Elizabeth was not so fortunate. Of course, she'd tell no one. She wouldn't want anyone to know about the secret or, as Adela said, be made to look a fool if there was nothing there.

Corbett turned his back on the window. No one would ever connect the two: daft Peterkin and these murders. He was weak and helpless; a wench like Adela would find him no threat. Corbett smiled grimly. The killer was clever: love trysts, messages . . .! As Adela had proved, young women did not like their elders to know about such things – a conspiracy of silence which the killer exploited.

Corbett picked up the Book of the Dead.

'He didn't strike twice,' he murmured. 'He just did it the once!'

Elizabeth was lured to some place where the Mummer's Man was waiting. Peterkin, he concluded, would be the perfect messenger. Probably after a day or so, the message and the memory would fade and, if the simpleton realised there was something wrong, how could he proclaim what he had done? Corbett vowed to have words with Peterkin. In the meantime . . . He opened the Book of the Dead and, going back twenty years, began to read. He recalled lines from a poem:

> Amongst the dead I have walked,
> And amongst the dead I have found the truth.

Corbett closely studied the Book of the Dead and found what he was looking for: unexplained deaths. He closed it and sat back. Melford was truly a place of bloody slaughter! He recalled Beauchamp Place and that pathetic skeleton stowed away in the old chapel wall.

'Some are left,' Corbett murmured. 'Some are buried, which means not all have been discovered!'

He recalled what Tressilyian had said about the poacher. Was it possible?

'Two assassins!' Corbett murmured.

He thought of Furrell and Sorrel: one a lecherous poacher, the other committed to what? Justice? Vengeance? Both knew the countryside, and what did Furrell mean about 'the truth being plain as a picture'?

Corbett pushed back the chair, got to his feet and reached for his cloak and war belt.

# Chapter 14

Sorrel stared at the paintings on the wall of the solar at Beauchamp Place. Now and again she would turn and listen carefully to the sounds outside. People, occasionally, came to buy fresh meat. She'd heard rumours of an important banquet at the Guildhall that evening.

'Best time for a little poaching,' she murmured.

Sorrel walked across to the niche where the statue of the Virgin stood. She reached behind it, plucking out the greasy scroll, a piece of vellum Sorrel had bought in Melford marketplace. She took this to the table, smoothed it out and studied the names scrawled there. Sorrel knew her letters. After all, she was a merchant's daughter with book-learning who had the misfortune to fall in love only to be spurned by both suitor and family. The names were not correctly written, the letters ill formed but Sorrel could recognise them. She ran her fingers down: Tressilyian, Molkyn, Thorkle, Deverell, Repton . . .

'Aye,' she whispered. 'And a few others.'

She took her dagger and etched a rough cross beside the names of those who had been killed. She picked the vellum up. One name caught her attention.

'Walter Blidscote!' she said. 'But your time will surely come.'

Sorrel revelled in Deverell's death, sucked at her teeth and wondered what progress the clerk was making. She had not told him everything. Oh no! She put the parchment back and moved a piece of tapestry hanging on the wall. The crude drawing etched there was not Furrell's work but her own: a rough map of the countryside.

Melford stood in the middle of a circle of copses and woods. The circle's rim was etched with crosses to mark where Sorrel knew other corpses lay, at least seven or eight in number. Sorrel studied it carefully. She now accepted why the Moon People stayed well away from the town and its lanes. She couldn't tell the clerk all this. Sometimes Sorrel herself had doubts. What if Furrell was alive? He could glide through the trees like a ghost. A hunting owl made more sound than Furrell. She put the tapestry back: her eye caught the red-draped four-poster bed. Furrell wouldn't do that! He was normal in his swiving. She recalled their love wrestling on the bed. Furrell was as vigorous as a stallion in heat. Why would he prey on lonely young women? She just wished she had listened to Furrell more carefully during those weeks following Sir Roger's execution.

Sorrel heard a sound and froze. Had that come from the hall? Was she alone? She took the crossbow from where it leant against the wall. She opened the coffer and took out a small pouch of quarrels. She slipped one into the groove and clumsily winched back the cord. Perhaps the sound was just the wind, nothing to be frightened of. Sorrel left the solar. Faint tendrils of mist were seeping through the hall.

'Is there anyone there?'

A wood pigeon nesting in a crevice flew up in a burst of whirring wings. Sorrel took comfort from that. If anyone else was here, the bird would have been disturbed already. She walked down the hall and into the cobbled yard. Nothing amiss. She turned and went through the gatehouse, stared at the wooden bridge, and froze. She hadn't been across for hours: in places the wood was bone white, scoured clean by the wind and rain so the fresh damp patch caught her eye. Somebody or something had crossed fairly recently. She whirled round. Had an intruder slipped stealthily into Beauchamp Place? The practice in the countryside was always to shout a greeting to allay any fear or suspicion. Sorrel found she couldn't stop her hands trembling. She walked back into the gatehouse and stared up through the murder holes: small passages so defenders could loose arrows or drop fire if the enemy broke through the main gate. No sign of anyone in the hedges around them. A weakness of Beauchamp Place, Sorrel reflected, was that it was a warren of broken walls and crumbling steps. A group of outlaws could take refuge and, if they were stealthy footed, hide for hours before discovery.

Sorrel primed the crossbow but the lever hadn't been oiled properly and she found it hard to winch the cord tighter. She walked across the cobbled yard. A sound, a footfall? Sorrel broke into a run. In her panic she did not go into the hall but up the steps to the chapel. She reached the stairwell then turned, not going in, but climbing higher to the storeroom above. Furrell used to call this his lookout post. Sorrel darted inside, slammed the battered door and leant against it, heart racing, panting for breath. She tried to calm herself, wiping the sweat from the palms of her hands as she listened for any sound of pursuit. She waited for the footfall, the door being tried but nothing happened.

She crossed to a window and looked out over the countryside in the direction of Melford. Her eye caught movement, a rider coming down Falmer Lane, but who was it? She left the crumbling windowsill and returned to the door, listening carefully. After a while she relaxed, cursing her own stupidity. She gingerly opened the door and went down the steps. She could see no trace of any pursuer. The chapel was empty. She grasped the crossbow more firmly as she reached the bottom step and entered the cobbled yard. No one. She sped across the hall.

Sorrel didn't fully understand what happened next. One moment she was hurrying forward, the next a shadow moved from her right. The attacker had been hiding behind a buttress, waiting for her to return. She glimpsed the white cord going over her head and instinctively brought her hand up to prevent the garrotte string being lashed tightly round her throat. The harsh cord dug into her hand. Sorrel tried to go forward but the attacker was pulling her back. She realised she must go with him, lessen the tension in the garrotte string, and with her one free hand she lashed out behind her. The string was now cutting her hand, the pain intense. Sorrel thought she couldn't breathe, then realised it was her own terror rather than any constriction round her throat. Backwards and forwards she swayed. All Sorrel was aware of were hurried gasps, a knee pressing into the small of her back. Sorrel, using all her strength, pushed backwards, driving her assailant into the corner of the buttress. At the same time she brought her free hand up, clawing at his arm. The garrotte string was loosened. Sorrel was free. She lurched forward and glanced over her shoulder: her assailant had slumped against the wall, bruising both shoulders and the back of his head. He was dressed like one of those wandering friars, a dark cloak and hood with a cloth mask over his face.

Sorrel didn't wait but fled down the hall. She reached the dais and stumbled. Sounds of pursuit echoed behind her but she was up through the solar door, slamming it shut and drawing across the bolts. She crumpled to a heap on the floor before it, aware of the pain throbbing through her. The left side of her neck was badly gashed, the palm of her hand lacerated, the small of her back ached as if she had been hit by a cudgel, whilst her arms weighed so heavy. She heard her assailant try to force the door but it held firm.

'Go away, you whoreson!' Sorrel screamed.

The thudding stopped, replaced by a scratching as if some wild animal was clawing with long nails. Sorrel got to her knees. Yes, that was what he was doing! Her assailant had drawn his dagger, seeking the crevice between the door and lintel to see if he could work loose the leather hinges. Sorrel gazed around; she'd dropped the crossbow. She ran over to the chest, pulled out the long stabbing Welsh dirk and grasped her cudgel. The scratching continued. Sorrel returned to the door and studied the hinges, thick wedges of leather. It would take some time to work those loose. She looked towards the window. She could try to escape. Perhaps if she reached the woods she could lose her attacker. She drew breath in and tiptoed across.

Pulling back the shutters, she stared to the left and right. She was about to draw her head in when she saw a dark shape stepping out through the large gap in the hall wall. Her attacker had studied the place carefully. She withdrew quickly, pulling the shutters closed, and brought down the bar. Sorrel stood, listening intently. The clawing had stopped. She heard a sound and started as the shutters rattled. He was now trying to get in through there. Sorrel ran across. The shutters were of heavy oak, their hinges strong but there was a gap where they met. She saw the dagger glide in. Her assailant was trying to lift the bar. She lashed out with the cudgel, the dagger withdrew.

Sorrel was now coated in sweat. What if the attacker laid siege, waiting for nightfall? Then she heard the shout, a loud hallo echoing through Beauchamp Place, followed by her name.

'I am here!' Sorrel screamed.

She sank down on a stool: her assailant appeared to have disappeared but Sorrel was so frightened she didn't have the strength to rise. She sat in a half-daze, aware of the throbbing pain in her hand, the wrenching ache in her neck. Only after a while did she become aware of the hammering on the door. She picked up the cudgel and knife.

'Who is it?' she called weakly.

'Sir Hugh Corbett.'

'I don't believe you.'

'Sorrel, for heaven's sake, what is the matter?'

Sorrel closed her eyes and tried to think. The voice sounded familiar, but was it a trick?

'To the right,' she said, 'in the hall, there's a large gap in the wall. Step out into the open.'

'Sorrel, what is this nonsense?'

'Step out!' she ordered.

She heard a curse. Sorrel went to the shutters.

'Come to the window!' she shouted through the crack. 'Just stand there!'

She heard the click of high-heeled riding boots. It must be the clerk. She narrowed her eyes and pressed her face against the gap in the shutters. Sir Hugh Corbett stood there, cloak thrown back, hand on the hilt of his sword. Sorrel drew up the bar and opened the shutters.

'In God's name!' Corbett exclaimed.

He ran back into the hall even as Sorrel drew the bolts, threw open the door and almost collapsed into his arms. Corbett picked her up, took her across and, shouldering aside the curtains round the bed, laid her down gently on the faded blue and gold cover. He filled a bowl of water from a jug, dabbing at the cuts on her hand and side of her neck. She started to shiver so he pulled the coverlet up around her.

'Who attacked you?'

She grasped his hand. 'Don't leave me,' she pleaded. 'He could slip by you.'

Corbett reassured her. Following directions, he went to the buttery, lit the brazier and, cursing and coughing at the smoke, wheeled it into the solar. He then heated some wine. By the time he had finished, Sorrel was sitting on the edge of the bed.

'You would not make a good housewife,' she smiled weakly, 'but I thank you, Sir Hugh.' She gulped the wine.

'The attacker?' Corbett demanded.

'I don't know. I was here by myself. I knew someone had entered Beauchamp Place. I was in the bailey. I heard a sound I didn't recognise and fled in the wrong direction.'

She told her story in halting phrases, looking wild-eyed at Corbett.

'How do I know it wasn't you?'

'Don't be foolish.' Corbett pulled a stool across. 'I have served you mulled wine, not threatened you with a garrotte string!'

He went across and barred the shutters.

'Bolt the door behind me,' he ordered.

Corbett went out into the hallway. He could detect, in the dust on the dais and at the entrance to the hall, the signs of a struggle and pursuit. He went out to the gatehouse and stared across the makeshift bridge. Corbett looked over his shoulder where he had hobbled his horse. The attacker must have been on foot. He'd heard Corbett's approach, let him come in and slipped over the bridge. The long grass and trees would hide him. He could be back in Melford by now.

Corbett rejoined Sorrel in the solar. She had recovered, a small jar on the table before her. She was carefully rubbing some paste into her hand and the side of her neck.

'The juice of moss,' she explained, 'mixed with cobwebs and dried milk. It's a sovereign remedy.'

Corbett thought of his own old wound in his chest.

It had healed but occasionally, as now, the muscles and bone twinged in pain.

'You are most fortunate.'

'I saw you,' Sorrel smiled, 'when I took refuge in the room above the chapel. I glimpsed a rider coming down Falmer Lane. If you hadn't come . . . Did you find my crossbow?'

Corbett shrugged. 'I wasn't looking for it. Did you see your attacker? Did you recognise anything about him?'

She shook her head. 'Are you sure he has gone?' she demanded.

'Oh, he has gone all right, like the silent assassin he is. I wonder why he came here in the first place.'

'Why did you?'

'Well, there are two reasons, Mistress, just as I believe there are two murderers in Melford. Oh yes, we have two assassins. The first is the Jesses killer or Mummer's Man, the ravisher and slayer of women. As you told me, he has been hunting these lanes and trackways like a weasel. Sometimes he attacks tinkers' girls, women like yourself, wandering from the towns seeking a new life, work, a crust of bread and a penny. They are easy victims.' Corbett paused to choose his words. 'Now and again, however,' he continued, 'this killer can't control his lust. Somehow he entices young women from the town out into the countryside where he rapes and garrottes them.'

'And the second killer?' she asked tersely.

'Oh, the second one is not interested in rape or murder, but, strangely enough, justice. Someone who believes that the wrong man was hanged: that Sir Roger Chapeleys was innocent, that his trial was a mockery, a mere mummery. So now he –' Corbett paused, 'or she – is waging a vengeful bloody campaign against those responsible. Tressilyian is attacked on his way into Melford. Deverell takes a crossbow bolt in his head. Thorkle's brains are dashed out. Molkyn is decapitated. Strange, isn't it,' he mused, 'how all three suffered wounds to the head? Now, two people,' Corbett continued, 'believe Chapeleys was innocent: Sir Roger, but he has now answered to God—'

'And my man, Furrell.'

'Yes, Sorrel, your man, Furrell.'

'But he's gone to God as well.'

'Has he?' Corbett asked. 'Or is he still in hiding, moving like some silent vindictive ghost through the trees? Loosing arrows at Sir Louis, visiting Deverell at the dead of night, not to mention his old enemies, Molkyn and Thorkle. Come on,' Corbett urged. 'It's possible. After all, who does leave you that money? Could it be Furrell, guilty at deserting you?'

'No, he wouldn't do that. I think the money comes from young Chapeleys, in gratitude for what we tried to do for his father. I tell you, clerk, Furrell's dead.' Sorrel tapped her chest. 'Oh, yes, sometimes I have wondered myself but I know he's dead, buried in some unmarked grave.'

'For the sake of argument,' Corbett moved on his stool, 'let us say that's true.' He paused. 'By the way, have you seen Blidscote? Ranulf is searching for him. Furrell didn't like Blidscote either, did he?'

'No one likes Blidscote!' Sorrel snapped. 'Especially the tinkers with their little boys. I tell you this, clerk: if Furrell had wanted to kill Blidscote, he could have done it years ago. Perhaps he should have done. Our bailiff's a turd of a man.' She moved her head and winced at the pain in her neck. 'But Furrell's dead.'

'In which case, Sorrel, we come to you.'

She gaped at him.

'Don't act the innocent,' Corbett murmured. 'You are a strong and capable woman, Sorrel. You know the countryside around Melford. You can use a bow, you are strong enough to swing a sword or a flail. You can slip across the fields and no one will notice you. You hated Molkyn and the rest because they mocked Furrell, disparaged his evidence. Because of them Sir Roger was hanged and Furrell later went missing. Your pleasure at Deverell's death was obvious.' He watched her intently. 'I wonder if one of them killed Furrell. Did he become such a nuisance that they murdered him? Perhaps his corpse lies buried under Molkyn's mill? Or on Thorkle's estates? You kept well clear of both of them, didn't you?'

Sorrel's head went down.

'Look at the evidence,' Corbett persisted. 'When Sir Louis Tressilyian rode into Melford to meet me, he was attacked. Everyone, apart from you, was in the crypt of that church.'

'Repton was not there.'

'But why should Repton attack a royal justice?' Corbett pointed to her weather-beaten boots. 'You could slip them off, take a bow and quiver of arrows and try to kill Tressilyian.'

'Why? I have no grievance against him.'

'But he was responsible for Chapeleys' hanging and, indirectly, Furrell's disappearance. Perhaps you suspected him of murdering Furrell? Did your man persist in reminding Sir Louis of a miscarriage of justice?'

'I saw where the ambush took place,' Sorrel retorted. 'If I had loosed an arrow at Sir Louis, I would not have missed. Perhaps the first but certainly not the second.'

Corbett stared at a point beyond her head. He hadn't thought of that. Moreover, hadn't Sir Louis talked of a man's voice taunting him?

'But you were roaming the meadows and woods that afternoon. You must have seen someone. This mysterious archer who, perhaps, was the same person who daubed messages on Sir Roger's tombstone and elsewhere.'

Once again, Corbett privately wondered about the true whereabouts of Furrell the poacher.

'I wasn't roaming anywhere, clerk. I went to Melford to watch you arrive. I visited Deverell.' She bit her lip.

'I'll come to him by and by,' Corbett declared.

'I then went and waited on the outskirts,' Sorrel continued. 'I dogged your footsteps from the moment you left the crypt and, before you ask, I never met any mysterious archer, though, I concede, Sir Louis was attacked.'

'So you visited Deverell? You knew about the porch, the front door and the Judas squint?'

'Yes I did.'

'And you were there when I examined the corpse?'

'So was half of Melford. It doesn't make me the murderer. Are you going to say I killed Thorkle and Molkyn?'

'It's possible,' Corbett replied. 'You could have

taken both men by surprise. One blow would be enough.'

'But I didn't,' Sorrel protested. She got to her feet. 'And why do you accuse me?'

'As I said, two assassins are at work in Melford. Now we come to the attack on you today. Perhaps the Mummer's Man resents your interference in his bloody affray and came to silence you.'

'I can't prove my innocence.' Sorrel walked to the window and pulled back the shutters, eager to breathe fresh air. 'I have never killed anyone, master clerk.'

'Haven't you, Sorrel? Never lifted your hand in violence?'

She stood by the window, shoulders shaking.

'Isn't that why you fled Norwich?' Corbett continued remorselessly. 'Perhaps a customer became too rough? Why all the secrecy, the change of name?'

'Yes, in self-defence, I killed a man.' Sorrel turned and leant against the sill. 'He wanted to hurt me, cut at my body, watch me squeal with pain. He was drunk. In the struggle I took his knife and plunged it into his heart. I don't know who he was or where he came from: it was in some filth-strewn alleyway. I was just a whore fumbling with a customer. I left Norwich within an hour of his death and never returned. Why, master clerk, are you going to arrest me?'

Corbett shook his head. 'Some men bring about their own death. I am more concerned with the present.'

'And so am I, clerk! I did not murder anyone. Oh yes, the thought crossed my mind on a number of occasions. But, take Sir Louis Tressilyian, for example. Do you really think, master clerk, I would have missed? And why should I kill Deverell, Thorkle or Molkyn?' She walked back and stood over him. 'I prayed for your day. I would have loved to have seen such men appear at the bar of justice and be questioned, like you are now questioning me.'

Corbett stared closely at the woman. He always prided himself on his logic and his reason but, as Maeve often advised: 'Follow your heart, Hugh: truth has its own logic.'

'Very well.' Corbett grasped her hand. He folded back the fingers and examined the white linen cloth wrapped round the wound. 'I believe you, Sorrel. So I must still ask myself, why should the Mummer's Man – and I think it was he – come out to Beauchamp Place to murder you?'

'And the answer?'

Corbett chewed the corner of his lip. 'When we first met, you said you had much to say about Melford but you'd let me draw my own conclusions. Perhaps the killer realises this. Perhaps he suspects that you know more than you do and wants to silence you once and for all.' Corbett snapped his fingers. 'Or something else.' Corbett got to his feet. 'Perhaps Furrell told you something? Shared knowledge which brought about his own mysterious disappearance?'

Sorrel shook her head. 'If I could, I'd recall it.'

'No,' Corbett urged. 'I spoke to one of the other jurors. He met Molkyn in his cups. Our good miller confessed that Furrell had declared how the truth about the killer was plain as a picture. Do you know what he meant by that?'

'Furrell said many things,' she answered softly. 'But not that. Or, if he did, I never heard it. I want to show you something, clerk.'

She went across and took down the piece of tapestry and described the crude map she had drawn.

'I didn't tell you the full truth,' she explained. 'But this is Melford. Here is Falmer Lane.' She pointed to the roughly etched map. 'Devil's Oak. These crosses mark the places Furrell told me to stay away from.'

Corbett studied the painting. The map was very crude. He wouldn't have understood it if she hadn't explained each symbol. He shook his head.

'I don't think Furrell was talking about any map!'

He walked over to the other paintings and began to study them carefully. Sorrel joined him.

'I can see nothing,' Corbett shook his head, 'nothing at all. Where else would there be paintings, Sorrel?'

'In a church, though Furrell rarely went there. The Golden Fleece, Chapeleys' manor, the Guildhall, Sir Louis Tressilyian?' Sorrel spread her hands. 'Furrell roamed all over the countryside. He even carried out errands for Sir Roger, travelling as far as Ipswich and the coastal towns.'

Corbett stared round the room.

'And Furrell had no Book of Hours, a psalter?'

'No.' Sorrel laughed abruptly. 'He knew his letters like I do but he was no scholar.'

Corbett walked to the door. 'Let's go back to the chapel,' he demanded. 'I want to re-examine that skeleton.'

Sorrel shrugged and took him across the yard. Corbett paused to see that his horse was well. By the time he'd climbed the steps, Sorrel had removed the bricks and pulled the skeleton out.

'What are you looking for?' she asked.

Corbett picked up the skull, feeling its texture.

'I have a friend,' he said, 'a priest, who is also a subtle physician at the great hospital of St Bartholomew in Smithfield in London. He often talks to me about the property of things.'

Corbett glimpsed the puzzlement in Sorrel's face.

'The way things are and how they change. The bones of this skeleton are dry, yellowing, which means it has lain in the earth probably more than five or six years.' He tapped the skull. 'This is thin, the flesh is gone, the bones are dry. If they'd been allowed to lie, they would have eventually crumbled to a powdery dust. Now, my good friend,' Corbett continued, 'has also been given special licence by the Church to examine the cadavers of men hanged on the nearby gibbet.' Corbett picked the skull up. He walked to the window and, holding it up, looked inside. 'When a man is hanged,' Corbett explained, 'if he's lucky, the fall will break his neck. Death is instantaneous. If he's not, he'll slowly strangle.'

'Like the garrotte?'

'Yes, Sorrel, like the garrotte. Now, according to this physician, the humours in the brain break down and the skull is filled with blood like an internal wound.' Corbett tapped the skull. 'This fills like a swollen bruise, the fetid blood leaving a mark.' Corbett peered closer. He glimpsed a faded russet stain.

'And this one?' Sorrel asked.

'There is certainly a mark here but whether it's blood or the effect of decomposition I don't know.'

'What are you trying to prove?'

'Old Mother Crauford's right. Melford is a place of blood. I suspect young women have been murdered here for many a year. Some bodies are found, others are hidden out in the countryside. The questions are who and how?' He placed the skull tenderly back. 'Now, Mistress, I have to return. You are to come with me.'

'I'll be safe here,' Sorrel replied. 'The killer will not strike again.'

'Come with me,' he urged.

Sorrel agreed. 'I have friends I can stay with.'

She pulled a pair of battered saddlebags from the chest and hurriedly began to fill them. Corbett sat and, to break the silence, hummed a hymn, the 'Ave Maria Stella'.

'You have a fine voice.' Sorrel dropped the saddlebags. 'That's it!' she exclaimed. 'My man, Furrell, always sang, sometimes filthy songs.' She stood, mouth open, suddenly remembering. 'In the weeks following Sir Roger Chapeleys' execution, he was always singing the same words, as if he was intent on reminding himself.'

'What was it?' Corbett asked.

Sorrel, finger to her lips, stood and stared at the statue. She wouldn't take that, she thought: if she moved the statue, this sharp-eyed clerk would notice the piece of parchment. Sorrel did not want to excite his suspicions. 'That's it!' she exclaimed. 'About being between the devil and an angel. I never asked him what it meant.'

Corbett walked to the door. 'We'd best hurry,' he said. 'The day is drawing on. Tonight I feast with the high and mighty.'

He went back into the yard and unhobbled his horse. Sorrel joined him. It was still early afternoon but the mist was curling in thickly now, and the breeze was colder. A bird shrieked as it wheeled against the sky. Corbett, holding the reins, stared across at the river, which wound its way through thickets and tall grass. He was glad he had come here. Had he not, Sorrel would have been killed. Two assassins were busy in Melford but what was the solution? He'd go to the banquet tonight but tomorrow . . .? If only Ranulf could trace Blidscote. The bailiff had last been seen at Deverell's house, but as Corbett set out for Beauchamp Place, Ranulf had reported him missing. Corbett scratched his chin. But what good would such questioning do? He felt a little guilty. It was easy to interrogate the likes of Sorrel, but Blidscote? The bailiff would scarcely confess he'd perjured himself and convened a corrupt jury. And what about the two priests? If Corbett questioned them and really pressed matters, they would protest about their rights under Canon Law. The English Crown was ever conscious of Thomas à Becket's martyrdom and the Church's resolute defence of the rights of priests. Perhaps Burghesh could be persuaded?

'No, no,' Corbett whispered. 'He'd never betray his friends.'

He felt Sorrel beside him.

'You are becoming like me,' she smiled, 'talking to yourself. We could make a good countryman out of you, royal clerk.'

'I doubt it,' Corbett replied. 'There was something else I wanted to ask you but, for the moment, it escapes me.'

They walked across the bridge, their clatter shattering the silence. Corbett stared down at the filth-strewn moat. Sorrel let go of his hand and went before him. She reached the end and suddenly tripped, sprawling into the grass. Corbett's horse shied, going up on its hind legs. For a few seconds Corbett wondered if both of them would plunge into the moat but the horse was well trained. Sorrel stood up, nursing her ankle.

'That whoreson murderer!' she shrieked.

Corbett's horse trembled.

'Quiet,' the clerk soothed.

He stood for a while until the horse calmed down. Sorrel took a knife out of her bag and cut something at the end of the bridge.

'It's safe!' she called.

Corbett led his horse across and allowed it to graze.

'An old poacher's trick,' Sorrel declared, holding up the strong twine.

Corbett knelt beside her: because of the undergrowth on either side of the bridge, this place couldn't be seen from the old manor house.

'An old poacher's trick,' he confirmed, 'and quite a deadly one. The twine is strong and taut.'

'Was it meant for me?' Sorrel asked.

'No,' Corbett replied. 'You were attacked, I came in to Beauchamp Place, the assassin slipped by me across the moat. He expected me to follow in full pursuit. And,' he smiled thinly, 'years ago I might have done.' He pointed back to the empty gatehouse. 'I would have come charging through there and across the bridge: my horse would have tripped and I would have been thrown, wounded, even killed. The assassin was protecting himself whilst also hoping I'd suffer some hideous accident.'

Sorrel, limping, got to her feet. Corbett grasped her by the arm.

'Come, my lady, you'll enter Melford like a princess, led by the King's own clerk.'

Sorrel allowed him to help her up. Corbett grasped the reins and they made their way back across the meadow.

Who could the killer be? Despite the loneliness, Melford was only a short distance. Corbett studied the land and recalled Sorrel's words: the assassin could creep stealthily along the lanes or hedgerows. He could reach Beauchamp Place without breaking cover. Corbett strode on.

'You are thinking, clerk?'

'I think,' Corbett replied. 'You watch. If the assassin struck once, he may well strike again.'

# Chapter 15

An hour later, another visitor arrived on the banks of the Swaile. Master Blidscote, chief bailiff of the town of Melford, was about to die but he did not know it. He had been summoned out to the great water meadow fringing the river. The local inhabitants called it 'The Ferry' but this had long disappeared, swept away in some storm. Blidscote obediently stood on the bank, staring into the reeds, the muddy water swirling amongst them. A desolate place, the silence only broken by the raucous cry of birds.

Blidscote felt as if his life had been taken over by a swiftly rushing river. The arrival of that royal clerk meant justice and vengeance. Blidscote was trapped. Over the years he had taken bribes, tapped his nose and winked and turned a blind eye to this or that. He'd only kept his position by being pliable to those in power and bullying those who weren't. The scrawled message thrust under the door of his small house in Fardun Street had told him where to come. Blidscote felt nervous. He didn't like the countryside – the green, cold fields, the trees, their branches black against a grey lowering sky. He had attended the Wheelwright funeral; that had only deepened his pessimism. He shouldn't have come but what choice did he have? He had followed instructions and ensured the jury which tried Sir Roger would return a verdict of guilty. For such a crime Blidscote could hang. Even if he didn't, he would be turned out of his living and what could he do then? Beg? Become the brunt of the petty cruelties of the townspeople? Many would seize the opportunity to settle grudges and redress grievances.

Blidscote wiped his lips and stared back up the hill. Was that a horseman? His belly curdled on the ale he had drunk so quickly. He whimpered with fright. The countryside brought back memories of his bullying, hectoring ways with the boys of the travelling people. Had someone seen his secret heinous sin? He glanced back at the river. He heard it again, the drumming of hoofs. Blidscote turned and moaned in horror. A black-garbed rider, cloak swirling, a figure from the Valleys of Hell, had stopped on the brow of the hill. He was having difficulty with his horse. Was it the clerk? Had that damnable Corbett brought him out here to be questioned? The rider urged his horse forward. The horse's head was bobbing up and down, hoofs thundering, the rider's cloak billowed round him. Blidscote remembered his childhood nightmares. Death was thundering towards him. Blidscote stood rooted to the spot. He wasn't aware of the squelching mud beneath his battered boots, the strident cry of the birds, the slithering ghostly sound of the river. Only this rider from Hell, this living nightmare charging straight towards him.

Blidscote expected the rider to rein in but he didn't. The bailiff moved to the right then the left, no escape. He staggered back. He was amongst the reeds now, the mud oozing up above his boots as he floundered about. The rider followed him in. Blidscote tried to seize the reins, only to receive a sharp vicious kick. Further and further the rider forced him back. Blidscote stared up at the face but the rider was hooded and cowled.

'My old companion, Blidscote.'

The bailiff now was in mortal terror. He was on the edge of the reeds. He could feel the current of the river tugging at him. He tried to turn. The rider brought the club he wielded sharply down on the bailiff's head. Blidscote fell, face forward, into the river. The cold dirty water filled his mouth and nose. The rider dismounted and, leaving his horse to find its own way back to the bank, dragged Blidscote's body into the shallows. Going quickly along the bank, he brought heavy stones which he thrust down the jerkin and wrapped in the bailiff's squirrel-lined cloak. He pushed the body out as he would a small skiff. The unconscious bailiff was taken out midstream. He floated for a while and then slowly sank beneath the surface. The rider waited. He stared around to ensure he was still alone and, mounting his horse, made his way back across the meadow.

The banquet at the Guildhall proved to be prestigious. Corbett and Ranulf, in their rather travel-stained clothes, felt out of place amongst the costly garbed burgesses and their wives. Sir Louis Tressilyian, in a cote-hardie of dark murrey, soft buskins on his feet, welcomed them at the top of the broad stairs. He escorted them into the main chamber.

Corbett thought he was in a church, so many torches and candles had been lit. The windows were long, most of them filled with coloured glass. The table of honour was on a dais dominated by a gorgeous silver-cast salt cellar bearing the town's arms. The royal charter, which had granted Melford its privileges, was in the centre of the room on a table covered with turkey cloth. The burgesses came up and were introduced: a dizzying array of names and faces. Corbett shook hands and, with Ranulf walking beside him, made his way to the table on the dais.

Sir Maurice arrived, dressed in a blue and gold gown over a white open-necked shirt. He introduced Alianor, Louis's daughter, a small, pretty-faced young woman. She had blonde hair and light cornflower-blue eyes and was dressed exquisitely in a dark red gown and white wimple. She was much taken with Ranulf. Corbett had to stand on his companion's toes, a harsh reminder that the young woman was almost betrothed to Sir Maurice. Ranulf whispered he would be on his best behaviour, except he intended to take some of the choicest pieces of food for Chanson: the groom, with the other servants, was left to his own devices below stairs.

Parson Grimstone and Burghesh also joined them on the dais. The priest intoned the grace, blessed the assembly and all took their seats. White wine and fish food were served first: lampreys in a special sauce; portions of tender carp with special relishes and spices. Toasts were made and speeches delivered. All emphasised the growing prosperity of Melford and how honoured they were by the presence of the King's clerk. Sir Hugh sat bemused. This was such a contrast to the silence of the countryside or his own secluded chamber in the Golden Fleece.

Other dishes were served, to a blare of trumpets and shouts of approval: fried loach with roses and almonds; roast salmon in onion wine sauce; smoked pike; salad in pastry; pheasant in strawberry cream sauce. The hall shimmered with light as silver plates and trenchers, different cups and goblets were placed before the guests.

Corbett ate little and drank even less. He chose to ignore Ranulf's stealthy theft of food as he listened to a plump burgess chatter like a magpie about the King's taxes on wood and the need for better protection in the Narrow Seas. Corbett tried to appear so interested, his face ached. He would have liked to have excused himself but that would be insulting. So, he listened to the burgess but his mind wandered. He'd found the Book of the Dead a treasure house of information. He desperately needed to question Peterkin whilst he had been concerned by Ranulf's failure to find Blidscote.

'Do you think he's safe?' Ranulf had asked.

'No I don't,' Corbett had replied as he'd finished his preparations before leaving for the Guildhall. 'Like the poacher Furrell, Master Blidscote may never be seen again . . .'

'And the King's war in Scotland, Sir Hugh?' The burgess was now eager to prove himself an expert in military strategy. Corbett repressed a sigh; he listened to the good citizen's carefully worded denunciation of the King's war in the north, its disruption of trade and drain on the Exchequer.

Corbett was relieved when the burgess had to give

up playing Hector as more dishes were served. The burgess was about to launch himself into a second sermon when Corbett heard the bell of St Edmund's tolling; it echoed through the Guildhall, silencing the noise and chatter.

'It's the tocsin,' the burgess murmured. 'In God's name, what's happened now?' He glared down the table at Parson Grimstone.

The good priest was already deep in his cups. He tried to stagger to his feet but Burghesh gently pulled him down.

'I will go,' he declared. 'Something's wrong at the church, but I am sure it's nothing.' And, dangling a set of keys, he hurried out.

His departure was followed by dark scowls and muttered conversations. Corbett repressed a smile. He had seen the same thing happen in many a prosperous town. The burgesses grew wealthy, they no longer were in awe of the priest or his church whilst Parson Grimstone was, perhaps, not the man they would have chosen to be their pastor. These wealthy burgesses would eventually build their own church, create a separate parish. They would lavishly adorn their new house of prayer, using it to emphasise their own power and dignity. Corbett grasped his wine cup and listened to the burgess's ill-concealed attack on the King's military ambitions.

'He should capture Wallace, hang him and then negotiate. If there is peace in the north it will create new markets . . .'

The bells of St Edmund's tolled again, just for a short while. The assembled merchants simply grinned at each other. The festivities continued unabated, as did the warlike burgess, who now delivered a long speech against the Scottish rebels.

'Aye.' Ranulf stopped his thieving to intervene. 'But catching the Scottish rebel is like trying to trap moonbeams in a jug. Everyone says it can be done but no one knows how to do it.'

Corbett winked at Ranulf in grateful appreciation. Ranulf continued his teasing for a while. Corbett was about to intervene when the door was flung open. Burghesh entered, shouldering the liveried servant aside.

'Sir Hugh!' he shouted. 'You'd best come!'

Corbett made a sign for Ranulf to follow. Burghesh hurried up and whispered at Sir Louis to look after Parson Grimstone. He led the two clerks down the stairs, not saying anything until they were out in the cold night air.

'It's Curate Robert,' he whispered. 'He's hanged himself.'

They hastened across the marketplace and through the dark entrance of the church. Burghesh grasped a spluttering sconce torch just inside the porch and led them into the bell tower. In the poor light the curate's corpse, swaying slightly on the end of a bell rope, sent the shadows dancing.

'I didn't cut him down. I came in, lit the torch and . . .'

Corbett ordered Ranulf to bring candles from the sanctuary. These were hurriedly lit to reveal the full garish scene. Curate Robert dressed in his gown and sandals, hung, hands down, neck twisted. His face was pallid, mouth open, tongue slightly out, eyes staring in a look of horror. Corbett went up the steps and pulled the swaying body towards him. The knot had been expertly tied behind the curate's left ear.

Using his dagger, Corbett prised the knot loose. Ranulf and Burghesh took the corpse and laid it out on the cold flagstones outside the bell tower. Corbett grasped a torch and moved further up the steps. The tower was dark and freezing. He heard the squeak of rats, their scampering feet further up the darkness. He looked into a large window embrasure and, going back down, carefully examined the other three bell ropes. Each had a heavy weight tied to the bottom to keep it secure. The one Bellen had used had its weight removed. Corbett found this behind the door of the tower.

'Master!'

Corbett went out. Ranulf handed him a piece of parchment.

'This was up the cuff of his gown.'

Corbett undid the piece of crumpled parchment.

'It's a quotation from the Psalms,' he remarked. ' "I have sinned and my sins are always before me." '

He went and knelt over the corpse, made the sign of the cross and said a quick prayer.

'Is it suicide?' Ranulf asked.

'It must have been.' Burghesh pointed to the door of the bell tower, a set of keys hung in the outside lock. 'He must have waited till we'd gone, came in, locked the door behind him and went up into the bell tower. He removed a weight, tied the rope round his neck and then simply jumped off the steps.'

'And that caused the bells to ring?' Corbett asked.

Burghesh nodded. 'It would be swiftly done. Look!'

He led them back into the bell tower, grasped the

rope and climbed the steps. He then jumped down, clearing three or four steps, holding on to the rope and, as he did, the bell clashed and clanged above him.

'You probably heard them ring again,' he added. 'That's when I came in. I tugged on the corpse, feeling for a life pulse in his neck or wrist. There was nothing so I hastened back to the Guildhall.'

'He'll need the last rites,' Corbett declared. 'You'd best get Parson Grimstone.'

'He's in his cups.'

'He's still a priest,' Corbett replied. 'And he's the only one we have. Master Burghesh, I would be grateful if you'd do what I ask!'

Corbett waited until he had gone and closed the door behind him. He went back into the bell tower and scrutinised the bell rope and steps before returning to kneel beside the corpse. He examined the red weal round the neck and then the curate's wrists. The corpse was not yet cold.

'Do you think it was suicide?' Ranulf asked.

Corbett turned the body over. He could find no other wound or cut except that ugly scar round the throat.

'It must have been,' he declared. 'Bellen came in here.' He sniffed at the man's mouth. 'He'd drunk some wine, then God knows what happened. Perhaps this cold darkness finally tipped his wits? There was no struggle, no sign of binding round the wrists or a blow to the head. Master Burghesh is correct, Curate Robert must have come in here intending suicide.' He tapped the piece of parchment lying beside the corpse. 'He put this into the cuff of his sleeve, made sure the church door was locked and went into the bell tower.' Corbett paused. 'He then removed the weight from one of the ropes, tied the rope round his neck, climbed the steps and jumped: that's the bell we heard. Burghesh came across and discovered the corpse.'

'Could Bellen have been the murderer?' Ranulf declared. 'He was strong enough to kill Molkyn and Thorkle and, being a priest who visits parishioners, would know about the squint hole in Deverell's house. He was also a flagellant, punishing himself for secret sins, maybe such as the murder of those young women. Perhaps,' Ranulf added, 'the Mummer's Man was Curate Robert in disguise? Or, there again, a woman might go out to the countryside to meet a priest?'

'True,' Corbett murmured. 'Bellen also heard confessions. He'd know all the secrets of the parish and could blackmail as he wished.'

The door swung open. Tressilyian and Sir Maurice, Parson Grimstone between them, followed Burghesh into the church. Grimstone was near collapse. He took one look at his curate's corpse, groaned and had to be helped to sit on a stone plinth. Burghesh sat next to him, talking quietly.

'Suicide?' Tressilyian asked.

'It would appear so,' Corbett replied. 'Sir Maurice, my groom, Chanson, brought you a message?'

'I can't find it.' Sir Maurice shook his head. 'I have searched my father's records but . . .' He spread his hands.

Corbett hid his disappointment. He had hoped to discover details about the mysterious painting Sir

Roger had given to the parish church.

'Ah well,' he whispered. 'Let's tend the dead.'

Burghesh left them. He brought back the holy oils and gently persuaded Grimstone to whisper the words of absolution and anoint the dead man.

Corbett watched. It was a truly piteous sight: the young priest sprawled on the flagstones, his face still twisted by his violent death.

'Burghesh,' Corbett murmured, 'I need the keys of the house. I must search Curate Robert's chamber.'

'But is that right?'

'No, it isn't,' Corbett agreed. 'But Ranulf thinks that young priest is responsible for all the murders in Melford. He may well be right. Except . . .'

'Except for what?'

'Nothing,' Corbett replied. 'Not for the moment. I'll take the keys.'

Burghesh reluctantly handed them over. Corbett gestured at Ranulf to follow. They left the church and went round to the priest's house. Corbett unlocked the door and went into the sweet-smelling passageway. The walls were half panelled, the wood gleamed and smelt of a rich polish. Corbett, having lit more candles, pushed open doors and looked around. A comfortable place, high-backed quilted chairs, tables, stools and benches. He even espied some books, tied by a chain to a shelf in the small parlour. The stairs to the bedchambers were broad and polished with small pots of herbs in the stairwell. The windows were lead-lined: some were even filled with coloured or painted glass.

Corbett went up. There were three chambers along the gallery; Bellen's stood at the end. Corbett unlocked the door and went in. The room smelt of sweat, candlewax, rather musty, so he pulled back the shutters and opened the window. He waited whilst Ranulf lit the candles. The small cot bed under the window was unmade. Clothes and robes were scattered about. A wineskin, now empty, lay on the floor, an overturned cup beside it. On a shelf above the desk were calfskin-bound books: a psalter, a ledger containing the Calendar of Saints and the order or ritual for different Masses as well as a Book of Hours, rather tattered and faded.

Corbett sat down at the desk and sifted amongst the different pieces of parchment. He noticed some, like the parchment found on the dead priest, were inscribed with quotations from the Old Testament about sin and forgiveness. Corbett searched on. He moved his foot and kicked a small chest beneath the table and pulled this out. He emptied the contents on to the floor: a small, thick hairshirt, a flagellum or whip with strips of sharpened leather strapped to a bone handle.

'Poor man,' Ranulf murmured. 'He seemed more aware of sin than he was of God's grace.'

Corbett searched on.

'Strange,' he whispered.

'What is, Master?'

'Well, Bellen was an educated man but there are no letters or written sermons. After all, Bellen served here for a number of years. I know priests. They have homilies, commentaries, they write letters to friends and colleagues. Bellen, apparently, did none of these.'

He picked up the psalter and shook it. A piece of parchment fell out, yellow, dark with age.

'Now, here's one,' Corbett declared. 'It's a draft letter to his bishop.' He pulled the candle closer and studied it.

Apparently Bellen began the letter but didn't finish it. There were the usual salutations and then the line, 'I have something to confess in secreto . . .' but Bellen had not continued.

Corbett heard Ranulf moving around at the other side of the room.

'He may not have been a letter writer, Master, but Bellen did like to draw.'

Corbett looked round. Ranulf had pulled out a small coffer full of rolls of parchment. He went across and watched as Ranulf sifted through them. Most of them were drawings of the church, rather clumsy and childish: the face of a gargoyle, a pillar, the entrance to the rood screen. Corbett glimpsed one and seized it. Then, hearing footsteps on the stairs, he quickly folded this up and thrust it into his wallet. Burghesh tapped on the door and came in.

'Have you finished, Sir Hugh?'

In the light of the lantern he carried, Burghesh looked haggard and worried.

'Yes, yes, I have finished.'

'And is there anything? I mean,' Burghesh stammered, 'anything to tell us why Robert should take his own life?'

'I don't know.' Corbett smiled thinly. 'But Ranulf and I have to return to the Golden Fleece. The burgesses of Melford will have to do without our company tonight.'

He and Ranulf stepped by Burghesh, went along

the gallery and down, out through the half-open front door.

'Was it suicide?' Ranulf asked. 'It must have been, surely? We were all in the Guildhall.'

'The assassin could be someone else,' Corbett replied evasively.

'Such as?'

'Peterkin; Ralph, the miller's son.'

Ranulf caught his master's arm. 'You don't believe that, do you? Look around, Sir Hugh.'

He gestured across the dark, misty graveyard, the long wet grass, the slanted crosses, chipped headstones and the dark mass of the church beyond, its door still open, the steps bathed in a small pool of light.

'Only the dead can hear you,' Ranulf murmured. 'You don't believe Bellen committed suicide, do you?'

'No,' Corbett replied, 'I don't. Get into the mind of the man, Ranulf. Bellen may have been this and he may have been that but he was still a priest, a man of God. He had a heightened sense of sin: despair and suicide are the greatest sins. Bellen was anxious but self-composed. I think he knew a lot more than he told us.'

'But he died,' Ranulf insisted. 'Burghesh did find him swinging on the end of that bell rope. If Bellen was a man of God, who would regard suicide as a sin, the same is true of murder. He was strong enough; he wouldn't have gone to his death like a lamb to the slaughter.'

'Aye.'

Corbett stared at a hummock of grass which almost shrouded a small headstone. For a brief moment he wondered if it really mattered. All living beings on the face of God's earth ended their lives in places like this. Elizabeth Wheelwright, Sir Roger Chapeleys, all sleeping that eternal dream.

'It's cold,' Corbett declared.

'I didn't find Blidscote. He may have had a hand in this.'

'I doubt it,' Corbett replied.

He gathered his cloak around him, putting on his gloves. He listened to the lonely hoot of an owl in the trees at the far end of the graveyard.

'I wager a tun of wine to a tun of wine, Ranulf, that Blidscote is as dead as any that lie here.'

'Just because I didn't find him?'

'I wonder if we ever will. But come, Ranulf, I need to think, sit and plot.'

They went through the lych-gate. Corbett looked down the lonely lane, ghostly in the pale moonlight. He was tempted to go and see Old Mother Crauford and Peterkin but then he heard voices. People were coming up towards the church as the news spread. He needed to impose some order on what he had learnt.

They returned to the Golden Fleece, to be greeted by scowls and unspoken curses. Corbett ignored them as he stood looking around.

'Whom do you want?' Matthew the taverner came up.

'Master Blidscote – I don't suppose he's been in tonight?'

'No, Sir Hugh, he hasn't.' The taverner glanced at him sly-eyed. 'But the news about Curate Robert is known by all. They are calling you the Death Bringer.'

'I'm not that!' Corbett snapped. 'Master taverner . . .' Then he thought better of what he'd been about to say. 'I'll be in my chamber if anyone wishes to see me.'

Ranulf stayed, determined not to be bullied by the dark looks and seething hostility of the taproom. Once he was in his chamber, Corbett lit a candle and prepared his writing desk. He took out the scrap of parchment from the curate's chamber and studied the outline of the triptych.

'I wonder . . .' he murmured.

He smoothed this out, took a piece of vellum and began to write down everything he had seen, heard or learnt since arriving in Melford. The first afternoon in the crypt; the conversation there; the daubed markings on the grave; the piece of parchment pinned to the gibbet. He wrote down a list of names and, taking each one, carefully recalled how they had looked, what they had said.

An hour passed. Ranulf came up but Corbett was so immersed he simply mumbled good night and went back to his studies. The taproom below emptied. Corbett lay on his bed for a while, thinking, trying to study each person, each death. Blidscote could have helped.

'That was a mistake,' Corbett murmured. 'I should have questioned him before. But, there again, he wouldn't have told the truth.'

He returned to his writings: slowly but surely a pattern emerged.

'Let's take one murder,' he murmured. 'Deverell's. No.' He shook his head.

He wrote down Molkyn's name. Molkyn the

miller? A drunkard, an oaf, frightened by a verse from Leviticus? Corbett was now certain two assassins were loose in Melford: Molkyn was the bridge between them. He had been specially elected to that jury, therefore he must have been blackmailed. But was he killed to keep his mouth closed? Or executed for his role in Sir Roger's death? Corbett underscored the word 'executed'. He sat and reflected, half dozing. He slipped into a dream and woke with a start. For a moment he was back in the cold, stark belfry with that grisly corpse swinging by its neck.

He got up and splashed water over his face. He had his suspicions but who could help? Peterkin? He would have to wait until the morning. Matters, however, were proceeding too fast. The hostility in the taproom might spill over and, as the news of Bellen's death spread, people would say the murderer had confessed and hanged himself. So, why should this clerk be poking his long nose into other people's affairs?

Corbett was about to strap on his sword belt and go out but then thought of Maeve, her face pale and anxious, eyes studying him. Her departing words echoed in his mind. She had whispered them as she put her arms round his neck and kissed him on the cheek.

'Be careful of the shadows,' she'd murmured. 'Remember, if you hunt murderers, they can hunt you.'

Corbett paused, hand on the latch, and changed his mind. Instead he went to sit on the bed and thought of that bell tower, the hanging corpse and those other ropes with the weights at the end. If he could resolve that, he might trap the killer and, with the help of Molkyn's daughter, bring these deaths in Haceldema to an end.

Corbett returned to his studies. He put Bellen's murder to one side for the moment and returned to his theory of two murderers loose in Melford.

'Not Furrell and his wife,' he murmured – he was now sure of that – so who? He examined, once again, the parchment from Bellen's chamber and recalled Furrell's song about the angel and the devil. What else had Sorrel told him? If she was not exacting vengeance then who? There was something about her story? Corbett worked on and, as he did so, the mystery began to unravel.

# Chapter 16

'Who is the Mummer's Man?'

Corbett sat in Old Mother Crauford's small, mud-packed earth cottage. It was smoky and dark. The fire in the makeshift hearth was lacklustre, the green logs gently resisting the licking flames. Old Mother Crauford put down the bellows and looked over her shoulder at Peterkin sitting on a three-legged stool. The simpleton was cradling a bowl of leek soup on his lap. He dropped his horn spoon with a clatter, frightened eyes still on Corbett. He slowly put the bowl on the ground beside him.

'What nonsense is this?' Old Mother Crauford asked. 'It's barely dawn and you come knocking on my door? We have nothing to do with Haceldema.'

'I know why you call it that, Mother,' Corbett replied. 'No, no . . .' Corbett put out a hand.

Peterkin was now staring at the doorway but that was blocked by Ranulf.

'You mustn't run,' Corbett said gently. 'I'll only catch you. Hush!' He held up a hand to fend off more questions from the old woman. 'Look, Peterkin.' Corbett held a silver coin between his fingers.

The slack face relaxed. Peterkin smiled, opening

his mouth, tongue coming out as if he could already savour the sweetmeat he'd buy.

'He's a poor, witless fool,' Mother Crauford mumbled.

'He's not as stupid as you think,' Corbett retorted. 'You know that, Mother, and so does he. It's not really foolish Peterkin, is it? Or simple Peterkin? Or witless Peterkin?' Corbett caught it – just a shift in the eyes, a gleam, a knowing look. 'You understand what I am saying, don't you?' Corbett continued.

'Peterkin does not know.' The reply was low, throaty.

'Yes you do. I'll tell you and Mother Crauford a story. But first I do wonder where you have your secret place, Peterkin? Where do you hide the coins the Mummer's Man gives you?'

'What secret place?' Mother Crauford demanded. She pulled across a stool and studied Peterkin rather than Corbett, as if the clerk's words had jolted a memory.

'What I'll do,' Corbett declared, 'is tell you my story, then I'll threaten. I'll bully you with all sorts of dire punishments, Peterkin, but, if you help me,' he smiled, 'it will be a silver coin for wise Peterkin. St Edmund's parish in Melford,' Corbett continued. 'Well, it's a strange place for a man like you, Peterkin. People are growing wealthy, travellers arrive, merchants, traders, pedlars and chapmen. Your world is changing, isn't it, Mother Crauford? Forty years ago, who cared about Melford, when the plough ripped the earth and the peasants spent every hour wondering what the harvest would be like? Now it's all different: broad meadows cut off by hedgerows where sheep graze and everyone becomes fat on the profits. Peterkin has to be careful. He has no family: people say he has no wits. He acts the part but Peterkin is quite cunning. He has to protect himself from the goodly, newly rich people. Peterkin is frightened of one thing: that he will be taken away and put in some Bethlehem house. No one knows this better than the Mummer's Man. Where does he meet you, Peterkin? Does he come to this desolate lane? And has he taught you a poem?'

Mother Crauford was now staring at Corbett.

'He did, didn't he, over the years – take a message to this or that young woman? How a lover or admirer has left a gift, a token of their appreciation near Devil's Oak, Brackham Mere or some place along Gully Lane. Peterkin takes the message. Everyone ignores you, running up and down, backwards and forwards across the marketplace.'

'That's true,' Mother Crauford intervened. 'But it's only poor Peterkin. He often talks to young women yet he means no harm. No one takes offence.'

'Of course they don't,' Corbett replied. 'Look at him: innocent as a lamb. He wants to be accepted and chatters. Our killer recognised this. So, five years ago, young Peterkin is approached. He's taught the doggerel, given the message—'

'And why should he obey?' Mother Crauford broke in.

'Because the Mummer's Man is frightening. He has a hideous mask. He threatens: if Peterkin doesn't do what he says, the masters of the Bethlehem house will come with a cart and a whip. Poor Peterkin has seen that, haven't you? When the parish gets rid of some beggar? Peterkin's frightened.'

Corbett paused and glanced at Ranulf. In this dank cottage everything he had concentrated on the previous night now hung in the balance. He studied Peterkin's sallow, unshaven face. The mouth hung slack but the eyes were not so frightened, more watchful.

'Peterkin is also rewarded. Because the Mummer's Man holds a rod in one hand but a coin in the other. All Peterkin has to do is go into Melford, seek out a certain young woman and deliver the message. Peterkin may have refused but, there again, why should you? Never, in all your woebegone days, have you earned a penny so quickly. You are given simple instructions. You are to approach the young woman when she is alone, never in a group. You are to tell her to keep quiet but, there again, she's not going to tell anyone, is she?'

'Oh my God!' Mother Crauford groaned. 'Oh, sweet Mary and all the saints!' The old woman was now following Corbett's logic.

'A simple ruse,' Corbett continued, pressing his point. 'Peterkin delivers the message. A short while later that young woman's corpse is found out in the countryside—'

'Peterkin wouldn't hurt a fly,' Mother Crauford interrupted.

'I didn't say he did but Peterkin is now truly trapped. He must have remembered the victim was the same young woman to whom he delivered the message. But you can't tell anyone, can you, Peterkin? The Mummer's Man, the next time he approached you, reminded you of that. Ah well.' Corbett sighed. 'Peterkin is now very frightened. This dreadful

Mummer's Man truly has him by the neck. If he confesses what has happened, who will believe Peterkin? People will start pointing the finger. You wouldn't be the first man, Peterkin, to be strung up like a rat on the town gibbet.'

Peterkin's jaw was now trembling. He started to shake, one hand going out towards Mother Crauford.

'He's just a fool,' the old woman repeated.

'Not as dull as you think, Mother Crauford. And you know that! Haven't you ever wondered why Peterkin is eating a pie or a sweetmeat? Or how he bought some gewgaw from the market stalls?'

'People are kind,' she retorted.

'Oh, I am sure they are,' Corbett declared. 'But let's go back five years. Sir Roger Chapeleys was accused of the murders. He died on the gibbet. The murder of the young women abruptly ended and so did the visits from the Mummer's Man, or at least I think they did. But, late in the summer of this year, the Mummer's Man reappears. Peterkin has no choice but to obey his instructions. Somehow or other you took the message to Elizabeth the wheelwright's daughter, didn't you?'

Mother Crauford seized Peterkin's hand, rubbing it between hers.

'You have no proof of this,' she whispered to Corbett. Her hand went out and clutched Peterkin's face.

Corbett wondered about the true relationship between these two. Some blood tie? Some kinship? Everybody in Melford acted their roles. Blidscote, the pompous master bailiff, Adela the bold-eyed tavern wench. Why not Mother Crauford and Peterkin? She, the old crone, but in reality her mind and memory were sharp and fresh as anyone's, as Corbett's study of the Book of the Dead had proved. And Peterkin? In truth, he led quite a comfortable life: dull in his wits but not the fool he pretended to be.

'They could hang you.' Ranulf spoke up, wondering how his master had discovered this information.

'What do you mean?' Mother Crauford snapped. 'They couldn't hang Peterkin!'

'They would,' Ranulf retorted. 'And you beside him. Don't you understand the word "accomplice"? Sir Hugh is correct. Some people might even allege Peterkin's the murderer. You can tell from his face he is being confronted with the truth.'

'You could hang.' Corbett leant forward. 'You must have known what the Mummer's Man really intended. But, there again, you were frightened, weren't you, whilst, after the first murder, you had no choice.' He glanced at Mother Crauford. 'And I wonder how much you knew? Did Peterkin ever tell, or begin to tell you, what had happened? Did you press your finger against his lips and so help the Mummer's Man in his murderous games? Oh, you knew Peterkin wouldn't hurt a fly. After all, such murders were taking place in Melford long before Peterkin was born. Yet, I tell you this,' Corbett concluded briskly. 'If Peterkin tells the truth he gets rewarded. Some coins and a letter, with the King's Seal on it, proclaiming he is never to be troubled by anyone. And when the new priest arrives . . .' Corbett paused: he could have bitten his tongue off. 'In future years, perhaps, even a small annuity for Peterkin and Mother Crauford from the parish chest?'

Peterkin stopped his gibbering, a calculating look in his eyes.

'And, before Mother Crauford starts talking about the truth,' Corbett added, 'Peterkin must also be puzzled: sometimes he delivered the message but nothing happened because the young woman concerned didn't go or went too soon or too late.'

'Like whom?' Mother Crauford demanded.

'Adela the tavern wench.'

'Oh no.' Mother Crauford tightened her grip on Peterkin's hand. 'Not that bold-eyed, loud-mouthed hussy. It's a wonder she wasn't suspicious.'

'Nothing happened to her,' Corbett smiled. 'So why should she be? And everyone knows Peterkin. Isn't it true, Mother Crauford, some years ago, long before this spate of murders began, Peterkin was used by love swains to take messages to their sweethearts? That's why the Mummer's Man chose him in the first place. However, if I went back to the Golden Fleece and told Adela the true story . . .'

'Peterkin's been stupid,' the simpleton mumbled, head down. 'Peterkin's been wicked.'

'Look at me!' Corbett ordered.

The man raised his head. Corbett judged the woe-begone look genuine: beneath the dirt and stubble, Peterkin's face had paled.

'Where did he meet you?' Corbett demanded.

'He'd wait for me,' came the stumbled reply, 'at the bottom of the lane. At first I was curious.'

'How tall was he?' Corbett asked.

'I don't know. He made me stand behind an oak, he was on the other side. Sometimes his face would peep round. The mask was hideous, red like blood.

He carried . . .' Peterkin imitated a bracelet round his wrist.

'A cord?' Corbett asked. 'With a bell on it?'

'Yes. That's why I knew he was there. I'd go out early in the morning. Most times there's a mist. I'd hear the bell tinkle. At first I thought it was some silly jape. He told me how he knew who I was. He said he had the ear of Justice Tressilyian. Yes.' Peterkin licked his lips. 'That's how he put it. He knew about the way I spied on the young women. How in summer I followed couples out into the countryside. He also claimed I had stolen things: that he'd tell Master Blidscote, who would put me in the stocks.'

'So, he taught you the rhyme?' Corbett asked.

'Yes, he did, but no name was mentioned at first. He returned a few mornings later; ting-a-ling, ting-a-ling his bell would ring. He asked me to repeat the rhyme and I did so. Then he told me to take a message to this person or that.' He shook his head. 'I forget who.'

'Then, eventually, the name of his first victim?'

'Yes.' Peterkin blinked. 'I thought it was all a harmless game. Poor Peterkin.' He clasped his hands together and stared beseechingly at Corbett. 'Poor Peterkin didn't know.'

'And what did the Mummer's Man order you to do?'

'I must find the young woman by herself: I had a great secret for her so she was to tell no one. Only when she had solemnly promised and crossed herself did I give the message.'

'What happened?' Ranulf asked, getting up and

coming forward, intrigued by how this cunning murderer had worked. 'What happened?' he repeated. 'Young Elizabeth, the last victim – what did she do?'

'I found her in the lane coming from the marketplace.' Peterkin closed his eyes. ' "Elizabeth," I said, "I have a great secret for you." "Oh, Peterkin, don't be silly," she replied. "No, no," I whispered. "It's true." '

'Then you showed her a coin, didn't you?' Corbett asked.

Peterkin, now terrified, nodded.

'You said how an admirer had given you that coin so Elizabeth knew you weren't jesting? Yes?'

The simpleton agreed. ' "Oh, Peterkin," she said. "Who is it?" I shook my head. I was sworn not to tell her. I delivered the message and ran away.'

'Skilful,' Corbett murmured. 'Everyone's trapped. Peterkin must deliver the message. He's told to show the victim a coin so she'll believe him. Now, do you understand, Mother?'

'I do.' The old woman's eyes brimmed with tears. 'God knows, poor Elizabeth wouldn't dream of telling anyone else. They'd either follow her to the place or race her to it. Of course, no one really believes poor Peterkin. It might be some madcap notion. She wouldn't want to appear foolish . . .'

'Yes, but Elizabeth, like the other victims, had her curiosity whetted. Peterkin's message was so clear yet so mysterious. The town's simpleton had been paid to carry it so it must mean something. She wouldn't dare tell anyone and so sealed her own fate.'

'What was his voice like?' Ranulf asked.

'I don't know,' Peterkin wailed. 'A soft voice.'

'Have you ever heard it before?'

'For God's sake, Sir Hugh!' Mother Crauford exclaimed. 'The man wore a mask!'

'Did you ever follow him out?' Ranulf asked.

Peterkin, eyes terrified, shook his head.

'After the first death what could I do?' he wailed. Peterkin rubbed his hands together, tears streaking his dirty face. 'I was frightened, I was frightened. Where could I go to? Poor Peterkin!' He beat his chest.

Corbett glanced at Ranulf and shook his head. Peterkin acted more stupid that he really was but what he said possessed its own logic. He was like a trained dog, governed by greed and fear, sent hither and thither on his master's commands.

'You'll catch him.'

Mother Crauford glanced up at Corbett, who now got to his feet, tightening his war belt.

'Oh, I'll catch him. Like a bird in a net. And then I'll hang him, Mother Crauford, on the scaffold outside Melford, like the cruel soul he is.'

Corbett walked to the door. He put his hands on the latch.

'And now you know why I call this place Haceldema?' she called after him.

'Oh yes, Mother, I do.'

Corbett glanced back. Mother Crauford had dried her tears.

'You had your suspicions from the start, didn't you?'

Mother Crauford blinked away her cunning look.

'Couldn't you have done something?' Corbett asked.

'I am an old woman, clerk. I haven't got a bullyboy.' She plucked at her dusty gown. 'I don't carry
sword and dagger. Nor can I produce the King's Writ,
with a piece of wax on the end, telling everyone to
stand aside and bow their heads. You talk of help?
How could I mumble my suspicions? Have you ever
seen a woman burnt for witchcraft, Sir Hugh?
Watched her old body hang above the flames whilst
her eyes bubble and her skin shrivels like that of
rotten fruit? Don't act the preacher with me!'

Corbett smiled grimly and nodded in agreement.
They went out to where Chanson was holding their
horses. Corbett refused to answer Ranulf's questions
but swung himself into the saddle, riding ahead
during their short journey up to the mill.

This time Corbett did not stand on ceremony.
When Ralph the miller came out, shouting and ges-
ticulating that he was a busy man, Corbett rapped
out an order. Ranulf drew his sword and brought the
flat of its blade down on the young man's shoulder.

'Keep a civil tongue in your head!' the Clerk of the
Green Wax warned. 'My master has a terrible temper.'

Corbett swung himself out of the saddle, gave the
reins to Chanson and pushed open the kitchen door.
Ursula was standing by the fire. She was not fully
dressed but wearing a dark-brown robe fringed with
squirrel fur, tied round the waist by a cord. She didn't
look so pretty now, her face heavy-eyed with sleep.
She pushed the hair away from her face.

'I thought you were Molkyn,' she said archly. 'He
used to come charging in like that.'

'Molkyn's dancing with the devil!' Corbett
snapped. 'And what a dance it will be, eh, Ursula?

Your husband was corrupt, a dishonest bullyboy, and those are just his petty crimes.'

'What do you mean?' Ursula's face paled.

'Why did you send Margaret to be Widow Walmer's companion? To get her out of the house? Away from Molkyn?'

'Why?' she stuttered.

'I've been to many towns and villages, Mistress. I have seen what happens to men who commit incest with their daughters, who abuse their own children! A sin which stinks in the eyes of God and man!'

'How dare you?'

'Oh, I dare,' Corbett replied. He stared round the kitchen. 'You are Molkyn's second wife, aren't you? How old was Margaret when Molkyn lurched into her bedchamber? Twelve, thirteen?'

'How do you know all this? It's a lie!'

'Is it?' Corbett asked. 'Molkyn may have killed his first wife. He certainly abused his daughter and, when you married him, you stumbled on his little nest of hideous secrets. But you are a good woman, aren't you, Ursula, behind the bold glance and pert reply? You protected Margaret. You warned Molkyn. Someone else learnt the miller's secret. When Molkyn was chosen by that lazy, dishonest bastard Blidscote to sit on the jury and try Sir Roger Chapeleys, the time of retribution had arrived. Molkyn was blackmailed: find Chapeleys guilty or all of Melford would discover his secret sin.'

Corbett sat down on a chair at the table.

'And what else was Molkyn told? Suspicions about his first wife's death? Or that his second wife, pretty and winsome, had entertained Sir Roger on more than one occasion when Molkyn was away?'

Ursula swayed slightly on her feet. She went across to a cupboard and, opening it, splashed wine into a goblet. She drank it greedily, the drops running down her chin.

'I wonder who knew,' Corbett said. 'For the first time in Molkyn's life, he was trapped. Motivated by fear and the lust for vengeance, he hammered the nails into Sir Roger's coffin, he and Thorkle.'

Ursula sat down and clutched the table.

'It's a pity Lucy isn't here.' Corbett rose and slammed the door shut. 'She has a lot to hide as well, doesn't she? Molkyn was told other secrets. How Lucy lusted after young Ralph, Molkyn's son. Thorkle was more pliant. No man likes to be proclaimed a cuckold. Molkyn wanted Sir Roger's death and he had been given information about Thorkle. I can imagine it happening. Do what I say, Molkyn would bully Thorkle, or they'll be planting cuckold horns on you for as long as you live. I don't think Thorkle would need much persuasion. He, like Molkyn and the rest, had no love for Sir Roger.'

'You have no proof.' Ursula tried to reassert herself.

'Yes he does, Mother.'

Margaret, in a nightshift, a cloak about her, sandals in her hands, had crept quietly down the stairs to stand in the shadows. She came forward and crouched by the fire, stretching out her hands.

'You are well, master clerk?'

She looked over her shoulder, her pale face lit by a smile. Her beauty looked fragile in the morning light, blonde hair cascading down to her shoulders.

'When you first came here I thought you'd be back.

The King's crow, ready to pick at the rottenness in our lives. Oh yes, that's what they call you,' she smiled. 'The King's crow: dark-eyed and sharp-beaked, eh?'

She got to her feet and sat on the bench between Corbett and her mother.

'Our Father who art in Heaven,' she intoned. 'Do you know what my idea of a father is?' Margaret's blue eyes filled with tears, lips quivered but she controlled herself. 'What was your father like, Corbett? Did he come to tuck you into bed at night? My father joined me in mine. Molkyn with his big, burly body and heavy hands.'

'And you confessed this?' Corbett asked. He hid his own sorrow at the hurt in this young woman's face.

'I felt dirty. When Molkyn married Ursula I told her. Who else could I confide in?'

'And I protected you,' Ursula retorted. 'Whenever I could, I sent Margaret hither and thither. Widow Walmer helped. I think she suspected.'

'I liked it there,' Margaret continued dreamily. 'She was very pretty. I think she was in love with Sir Roger and he with her.'

'So you think he was innocent?'

'I do.'

'And did you tell your father that?'

'I never spoke to my father. We were strangers. When someone cut his head off, I was glad that this terrible stranger was dead.'

'Widow Walmer –' Corbett tried to ease the tension – 'who do you think killed her?'

'The day she died,' Margaret replied, 'she sent me a message not to come that night. I half suspected the reason why. I also knew about Sir Roger's gift to her. After she was killed, I just thought Melford was a wicked place where people commit mortal sins.'

Corbett studied the girl closely. He wondered if the terrible abuse had slightly unhinged her wits, turned her mind.

'Molkyn's dead,' he murmured. 'He'll answer to God for his crimes. Whom did you tell?'

'I nearly told the priest, the young one, the one who died last night.' She shook her head. 'But who would believe me?'

'I did,' Ursula declared.

Corbett placed his elbows on the table. 'And?'

'I let you speculate, clerk, on my relationship with Molkyn: a drunk, a beater, an oaf, a man who abused his own daughter. Sometimes I felt as if I wanted to be sick in his face.'

'That's why you refused to go across to the mill on Saturdays?'

'Of course! Let Molkyn drink, let him sleep like a hog. Do you know something, clerk, sometimes I considered killing him myself and setting the whole place alight. I used to pray that one evening he would stagger out and fall in the mere.'

'And whom did you tell? Did you ever accuse Molkyn openly?'

'I hinted at it.'

'You confessed, didn't you?' Corbett murmured. 'You found all these burdens too heavy: your marriage with Molkyn, Margaret's abuse, Lucy and Ralph?'

She nodded. 'Six years ago, on Ash Wednesday, I went to the shriving pew.'

'With Curate Robert?'

'No, no, he was too young. He was frightened of me,' she added with a half-laugh. 'There was a visiting friar but he wasn't there so I sat in church crying. Parson Grimstone came in. I told him everything: my marriage, Margaret, Molkyn, Ralph and Lucy.'

'And would he tell anyone else?'

'How could he? He was under the seal of confession.'

'Did Molkyn ever accuse you of telling anyone else?'

'No.' She placed her hands on the table. 'But sometimes I'd catch that murderous look in his eyes. He'd sit where you are, glaring down at me. It was a matter we never talked about and I never went back to Parson Grimstone.'

'And the night Molkyn died?'

'We've told you the truth,' Ursula replied. 'We were happy. Molkyn went over to the mill, finished his work and settled down like the pig he was to drench his belly in ale. Someone came in, took his head and placed it on a tray which was sent floating across the mere. I am glad he has gone. So is Margaret.'

'And have you,' Corbett turned back to where the girl sat listlessly, 'ever discussed your secret, Margaret?'

'Never!' Her head snapped back, eyes blazing with anger. 'Do you know something, master clerk, I feel as if I've come back from the tomb. Molkyn's rotting in his grave. I want to meet a good man and marry. I don't want my shame proclaimed throughout Melford.'

Corbett got to his feet. 'In which case I shall not trouble you again.'

He walked round, crouched beside the bench and took Margaret's fingers in his. 'Your hands are cold,' he said softly. 'Rest assured, your secret's safe with me. Parson Grimstone will be leaving: God's justice is going to be done and so is the King's.'

He let her hands go, got to his feet, kissed her on the top of the head and went out into the yard.

'Where's Ralph?'

'Locked himself in the mill,' Ranulf smiled. 'Said he had better things to do than argue with busybody clerks.'

'And we are busybody,' Corbett smiled.

They mounted their horses and went back along the trackway. Corbett was about to round the bend when a figure stepped out of a thicket so swiftly, Corbett's horse shied. Corbett talked to it quickly, patting its neck.

'I am sorry. I am sorry . . .' Sorrel pulled back her hood. A crude bandage covered the gash on her neck.

'You've been hunting?' Corbett asked, pointing to the sack she carried.

'Rabbit snares.' Her weather-beaten face creased in concern. 'Another murder, clerk? Curate Robert? They say he's hanged himself. Did he kill my poor Furrell?'

'No, I don't think he did. Tell me, Sorrel,' Corbett grasped the reins and leant down, 'couldn't Furrell's corpse have been hidden in a mire or swamp? I meant to ask you this yesterday.'

'Spoken like a townsman,' Sorrel retorted. 'The swamps and marshes round here aren't all that deep. And what goes down eventually comes back. Why?' she asked. 'Do you know where he's buried?'

'Yes, yes, I do. I know the exact place.'

'Where?' Sorrel dropped the sack and grasped the reins, her other hand clawing at Corbett's knee.

Corbett smoothed the hair away from her face.

'Trust me,' he whispered. 'Let me play this game out. Until then, stay in Melford!'

Sorrel let go of the reins. Corbett urged his horse forward and, followed by Ranulf and Chanson, rode along the trackway back into the town. On its outskirts, just past the church, Corbett reined in.

'Ranulf, Chanson, I'll break my fast in the Golden Fleece. You are to go out to Sir Louis Tressilyian and Sir Maurice Chapeleys. Bring them both to me. Tell them they must come on their loyalty to the King.'

'Chapeleys and Tressilyian!' Ranulf exclaimed.

'Just bring them,' Corbett declared. 'Tell them I have matters to discuss!'

# Chapter 17

Corbett returned to the Golden Fleece where he broke his fast on salted pork, freshly baked bread, slices of cheese and a tankard of light ale. The taproom was fairly empty though, as he finished, others entered, calling in on their way to the market. The usual travellers: a relic-seller, with his tray of so-called blessed goods; tinkers selling ribbons attached to a pole; a travelling coppersmith; two hucksters with a badger, hoping to bait it against a dog. Strangers to the town, they shuffled in and kept to themselves. When Repton and others entered, Corbett decided it was time to leave. He went back up to his chamber and sat at the table, going through the conclusions he had reached earlier that morning. He'd only had a few hours' sleep: his mind couldn't settle but he felt pleased at the way his plan was unfolding. He was sorry for Margaret. Her pain he could not truly understand, but he might have brought her some measure of peace. Corbett thought about little Eleanor and wondered how any father could abuse his own daughter. To distract himself, he prepared the room for his visitors, ensuring both sword and dagger were within easy reach.

For a while Corbett dozed and was awoken by Ranulf's loud tapping on the door. Chapeleys and Tressilyian entered. Both men were hurriedly dressed, unshaven, their hair tousled. Ranulf brought in stools and Corbett asked them to sit. Neither of them protested. Chapeleys looked nervous. Tressilyian had a half-smile on his face as if he knew what was to happen.

'You have news?' Sir Maurice began. 'It must be urgent?'

'No, I don't have news,' Corbett retorted. 'I have reached conclusions. Your father, Sir Maurice, was guilty of no more than drinking and lechery. He didn't murder Widow Walmer. He didn't rape and garrotte women of this town. He was sent to the gallows by a cunning and evil assassin. You have petitioned both Court and Chancery for an investigation, even a pardon for your father. One will be issued.'

'What is this?' Sir Maurice whispered.

'Now, four men knew your father was innocent,' Corbett continued. 'You, himself, the assassin and Sir Louis Tressilyian.'

Maurice looked startled at the justice.

'Five years ago,' Corbett continued in a matter-of-fact voice, 'Sir Louis, quite rightly, was summoned to the Guildhall: he took depositions and evidence against your father. He may have had doubts but, on the basis of the evidence supplied, Sir Roger seemed guilty. Sir Louis probably hoped that a jury, as is their wont, would give the prisoner the benefit of the doubt. He was certainly surprised when they did not. He delayed your father's execution. He wrote to the

King. However, the significant aspect of a jury's verdict is that it is also seen as the verdict of the community. If Sir Louis continued his protests, the finger of accusation would be pointed at one manor lord protecting another. I am correct, Sir Louis?'

'I listen to what you say,' the justice replied.

He spoke so evenly, Corbett wondered if his conclusion was truly correct: Tressilyian seemed so unperturbed.

'Your father died,' Corbett pressed on to Sir Maurice. 'The murders stopped. Sir Louis must have taken comfort from this: he did his best for you, treating you like the son he never had. Perhaps he encouraged you to write to Westminster? Nevertheless, three things secretly reassured him about the rightness of the sentence. The evidence, the verdict of the jury and the fact that the murders had ceased. He would be curious, however: Furrell had disappeared and Sir Louis must have known about Molkyn's reputation, as well as the deep dislike in the area for your father.' Corbett paused. 'And then the murders began again. Sir Louis's belief in your father's guilt was severely shaken. He may have also suspected that the real murderer could have even been responsible, God knows how, for your father's illegal execution. Sir Louis, therefore, decided to take steps. He would carry out his own justice.'

'What are you saying?' Sir Maurice asked. His face had paled. He kept running his fingers round the collar of his tunic.

'Sir Louis,' Corbett confronted him directly, 'you, I believe, are responsible for the murder of Molkyn the miller, Thorkle, Deverell, and, I wager, you know where Master Blidscote's corpse can be found.'

'You say I am a justice.' Tressilyian spoke up. 'And so I am. What evidence do you have for all this?'

'You are a good man, Sir Louis,' Corbett replied. 'Mistaken, but basically good. You suspected a miscarriage of justice had taken place. You felt sorry for Sorrel, Furrell's widow, so you gave her a pension, a silver coin at certain times of the year. Why should such anonymous gifts be given at specific times? Ever the lawyer, eh, Sir Louis? Those dates mark the beginning of the law terms in the courts of Westminster. It was your way of reminding yourself. You looked after Sorrel just as you looked after Sir Maurice.'

Sir Louis smiled, running a finger along his moustache.

'Only a justice could afford such generosity,' Corbett declared. 'As for that attack on you in Falmer Lane, the day you rode into Melford to meet me, it was curious! Why did you come alone? Why did you make an excuse to arrive late? You didn't want Sir Maurice riding with you, did you? You wanted to depict yourself as under the knife, fearing attack because of that dreadful miscarriage of justice. You stopped on the trackway. You looked around. No one was in sight. You cut down that sapling to block the trackway. You walked into the trees, took off your boots and fired those arrows. You then continued your journey.'

'I could have been seen,' Tressilyian pointed out.

'No, it's a lonely place. Two things puzzled me about that assault. First, who was this bare-footed bowman? He struck once but never struck again.

Sorrel, who knows those woods like the back of her hand, failed to see any mysterious archer. Secondly, if this bowman had gone to such trouble, why wasn't he successful? Molkyn, Thorkle, Deverell and probably Blidscote are all dead. All you received were cuts which, of course, were self-inflicted. You got rid of the bow and quiver, ensured all the signs of an attack were visible. You then continued on your way. You muddied the waters. You also left that crude sign pinned to the gibbet and daubed a similar message on the headstone over Sir Roger's grave. All your actions that day would have been easy. A heavy mist had swirled in. The graveyard is a lonely place and, once you were ready, you burst into the crypt as the frightened, aggrieved justice.'

'And the executions?' Sir Maurice asked.

Corbett could tell how the young manor lord half accepted the truth of what he was saying.

'Oh, those were quite easy. Molkyn was well known for his drunken habits on a Saturday evening. Sir Louis went into the mill, he sheared Molkyn's head off like one would snip a flower. Thorkle was the same. Melford, particularly in autumn time, with the mists shrouding a desolate countryside, is ideal for such attacks. Deverell the carpenter was also studied. Sir Louis knew about the Judas squint—'

'Where's the evidence for all this?' Sir Louis demanded.

Corbett hid his surprise at Tressilyian's calm demeanour. He wants to be caught, Corbett thought; he expected to be trapped.

'The evidence, Sir Louis, is tenuous. First, that note left at Deverell's house. Do you remember the quotation: "Thou shalt not bear false testimony against your neighbour"? Most people translate that verse as "You must not bear false witness . . ." You used "testimony" about the statements of witnesses at Sir Roger's trial. You said, in effect: "If they gave false testimony, upon their heads." What a coincidence! Molkyn lost his head, Thorkle's brains were dashed out. The crossbow bolt hit Deverell in the face, piercing the brain. When Blidscote's corpse is found, his death blow will be to the head.'

The justice sat, hands on his knees, staring down at the floor.

'I am going to ask you one question, Sir Hugh.' He lifted his head. 'Have you trapped the real murderer?'

'I know who it is,' Corbett replied.

'Do I have your oath on that?'

'You have my oath.'

Sir Louis took up the edge of his cloak and picked at the threads.

'If I am going to be put on trial, I demand to be taken to Westminster.'

Corbett ignored Sir Maurice's sharp intake of breath. 'Agreed.'

'I am a justice,' Sir Louis continued. He sucked on his upper lip. 'I took an oath to uphold the truth and see that the King's laws were executed. I've told you this before, Sir Maurice. I had little love for your father: he was a lecher, a philanderer. Thank God you are different. Even my late wife . . .' He paused. 'No woman was safe when Sir Roger was around, but I never believed he was a murderer. Why should he kill Widow Walmer, whose favours he enjoyed? Yet the evidence was there, particularly Master Deverell's, not to mention the bracelets and the knife. Nevertheless, I thought the jury would return a "Not Proven" verdict. Sir Roger would be acquitted, but disgraced and be forced to leave the shire. I was surprised when Molkyn returned the hanging verse: "Guilty with no plea for mercy." Justice followed its cruel course.'

He smiled. 'Sir Hugh is correct. I hid my doubts; I recalled the evidence: the jury was responsible. Above all, the murders had ended.' He paused, wetting his lips.

Corbett went over, half filled a cup of wine and brought it back. Sir Louis thanked him with his eyes.

'Oh, I made my own enquiries. I found out how Molkyn had acted the bully in the jury room. I was deeply suspicious about Furrell's disappearance. I felt sorry for Sorrel and for you, Maurice. I did my best. I tried to be the father I had so brusquely removed from your life.' He cradled the cup. 'But when those murders began again I knew I was wrong. Somebody had come into my courtroom. I was no more than a puppet, a seal for the real killer's wickedness. He and the rest had used the law to send an innocent man to the gallows.' He clicked his tongue. 'I felt a fool. I realised why Molkyn would sometimes leer at me or Deverell scurry away like the rat he was. I knew the King would have to intervene. I encouraged Sir Maurice to write those letters but I wondered what would happen if they escaped justice. The rest, Sir Hugh, is as you've said. In my view I carried out lawful execution: Molkyn, Thorkle and Deverell were the ones I held responsible. I might not trap the true killer but I am a King's justice: perjury and bribery are capital offences. I learnt about all their habits:

Molkyn's drinking, Thorkle in the threshing shed away from his hot-eyed wife and furtive Deverell, with his Judas squint.'

'And Blidscote?' Corbett asked.

'Oh yes, our fat, corrupt bailiff. It was no coincidence that Molkyn and Thorkle were selected. He was as guilty as they were. I invited him to meet me near the river Swaile. I wanted to see his fat face crease in terror. I didn't want him scurrying away: his body, weighted with rocks, still lies there.' Tressilyian put the wine cup down on the floor. 'I have no regrets, Corbett. None whatsoever.'

'Why didn't you wait for me?' Corbett asked.

'To be honest, Sir Hugh, I didn't know how keen-witted you were. I didn't want them to escape with their lies. It was my court they had mocked, not yours. I couldn't see them escape. I am sorry about the lies but I wanted to muddy the waters so as to have time to finish the task. Deverell in particular, was difficult to hunt. Despite his protestations in court, he was not a man to go wandering around at night.' He shrugged. 'What more can I say? What is there to say?'

Sir Hugh rose and touched him on the shoulder. 'Sir Louis Tressilyian, I arrest you in the name of the King for murder! You will be taken to London and lodged at a suitable place and, at a time appointed by the Crown, tried for your life.' Corbett held his gaze. 'You expected this, didn't you?'

'I had heard of you.' Tressilyian smiled faintly. 'As the days went on, I knew it would only be a matter of time, but the real assassin . . .?' He spat the words out.

'Oh, he'll be caught. The souls of those he murdered stand before God's court and demand justice.'

'You see yourself as one of the Children of the Light?' Sir Louis taunted.

'No, sir, I don't.' Corbett fastened his sword belt around him. 'But I work for them. Ranulf, Chapeleys can stay with Sir Louis: he is to be lodged in one of the tavern chambers. The door is to be locked and guarded by Chanson.'

'I won't escape,' Sir Louis declared. 'You have my word. Nor will I do anything feckless. You can suspect what my defence is going to be, Corbett? I am a royal judge. Perjury and murder were committed in my court. I carried out the King's justice.'

Corbett paused at the door.

'Not even the King's justice, Sir Louis, is above the law.'

'Where are you going?' Ranulf asked.

'Why, to the church. Join me there, Ranulf. I have a passion for bell ropes and how they work.'

Corbett closed the door behind him and went down the stairs. The market square was now busy, the noise raucous. Chapmen and apprentices roared their prices, enticing customers with Bruges cloth, Spanish leather, fruits brought in by the traders from London, jewellery and ornaments from Ipswich. The relic-seller joined in the shouting, offering a sealed cup which he maintained contained the last breath of St George. Corbett pushed his way through, knocking aside hands and shaking his head as traders blocked his path, offering him a new belt, riding boots or gilt spurs. At last he was free. Grasping the hilt of his sword, he made his way up to the church.

He paused at Elizabeth's grave and noticed the white rose laid on the freshly dug earth.

'Help me,' Corbett whispered.

He walked through the coffin door. Candles were lit in the sanctuary but the place was empty. Swirls of incense from the morning Mass curled and sweetened the air. He went down to the belfry, opened the door and went in. For a while he stood examining the heavy ropes and the weights placed on the end.

'If I knew who the patron saint of bell-ringers was,' Corbett murmured, 'I'd pray to him.'

He took one bell rope, placed it deep into the sloping windowledge and walked back into the church, closing the door behind him. He sat for a while and prayed. He didn't want to do anything but wait to see if his theory worked. He went up to the Lady Chapel, lit a candle and knelt on the cushioned prie-dieu, staring up at the face of the statue.

'You remind me of Maeve,' Corbett whispered.

He felt guilty at such distraction, crossed himself and returned to the back of the church. The coffin door opened. A parishioner came in, an old woman who lit a candle, said a prayer and left. Corbett grew anxious. He was about to return to the belfry when the bell clanged and his heart leapt.

'I thought as much,' he murmured and flung the door open.

The rope bearing the lead weight had slipped off the window recess and, falling, had created a slight tremor, which sent the bells clanging. Corbett lifted the rope up again and placed it further up the window-dowsill. He stood and watched. The weight, made of copper or brass, was shiny and smooth. He noticed how it began to slip very slowly along the ledge.

'And the further up I put it,' Corbett told himself, 'the more time it will take.' Now, he thought, all I've got to do is wait.

He sat on the belfry steps and wondered where Ranulf was. The coffin door opened. Footsteps echoed along the nave. The door was flung open and Burghesh came in.

'What on earth is happening?' he exclaimed. 'Why is the bell ringing?'

He glimpsed the bell rope and its weight in the window recess. He opened his mouth and stepped back.

'What are you doing, Sir Hugh?'

'I wondered,' Corbett replied, 'how the church bells could be rung when no one was up here? Last night when Curate Robert died, nobody was in this church. Do you remember? We all were sitting at the Guildhall feeding our faces, revelling in the civic wealth of Melford. Then the church bell rang. Up you jumped, Master Burghesh, like a hare in spring, and off you ran to discover what caused it. Some time later you come hastening back, all a-bother: Curate Robert has hanged himself for all to see. No sign of violence, no evidence that someone had hanged him. Moreover, up the cuff of his sleeve was a scrap of parchment, a quotation from the Psalms about his sin always being before him. To all intents and purposes, Curate Robert must have been the slayer of those young women. Unable to confront his guilt, or fearful of being caught, he seized the opportunity, when the church was deserted, to come into this belfry and hang himself.'

'That's what happened,' Burghesh stammered.

Corbett leant his elbows on his knees and smiled back.

'That's not true, Master Burghesh. First, why did you leave the Guildhall? Because a bell tolled? Couldn't Curate Robert deal with that and, if there was anything wrong, travel the short distance to the Guildhall to inform Parson Grimstone or yourself?'

'Curate Robert liked his wine,' Burghesh declared sourly. 'It was one thing or the other: whipping himself for his sins, praying prostrate on the cold flagstones or drowning his woes in copious wine.'

'No doubt he did, Master Burghesh. Last night, however, he came here to pray and think whilst you and Parson Grimstone prepared for the banquet. You joined him, all solicitous, bearing a big bowled cup of wine mingled with a very strong sleeping potion. You grow such herbs in your garden. Curate Robert wasn't invited to the celebrations and he probably would have avoided them. He wanted to sit here in the dark feeling sorry for himself. If the wine didn't put him to sleep, the potion certainly did. Whilst he drank, you busied yourself around the church like you always do. You came into the belfry, took one of the ropes and placed it very, very high, as far as you could into a window recess: something you learnt as a boy or noticed over the years. The recess has a slight slope. Eventually, the rope, pulled by its weight, slides off just like a man being hanged. The weight falls and the tremor sets the bells ringing. I've just proved it myself. I suspect it would take,' Corbett pulled a face, 'if pulled right back into the recess, a considerable time before the weight actually fell.'

'Nonsense!' Burghesh exclaimed.

'I can prove it,' Corbett murmured. 'I didn't study the mechanical sciences in Oxford but I know a little bit about weights and measures. Anyway, you had your signal to come hurrying back to the church. The house was all locked up. Poor Curate Robert had drunk the wine and was fast asleep. You then took him into the belfry, up the steps, tied the rope round his neck and released his body. Curate Robert never regained consciousness. Perhaps you tugged on his feet to hasten his death? That's what caused the second peal of bells that night. You hid the cup, an easy thing in a place like this. You wiped poor Robert's mouth with a cloth and gazed around: all was well so you hastened back to the Guildhall to proclaim the sad news.'

'What about the letter?'

'What letter?'

'The piece of parchment found hidden in Robert's cuff?'

'Oh, you put that there. You brought the wine down to Curate Robert. Before you left the priest's house with Parson Grimstone, you searched Bellen's chamber, while he was in the church, and took away anything which might provoke suspicion. You were also looking for such a scrap of parchment. I wager Curate Robert was well known for writing out verses, quotations from the Bible on which to meditate. The one you took suited your purpose though any of them would have done. You put it into your wallet and went along to the Guildhall.'

Burghesh had now recovered his poise. He crossed

his arms as if to show Corbett his hand was nowhere near his dagger.

'But what if the weight hadn't fallen? What if something had happened?'

'In which case Curate Robert would have woken up with a sore head, feeling guilty as usual. You would have enjoyed a splendid banquet at the Guild-hall and waited for another opportunity. True, you had been through Curate Robert's chamber. Perhaps he would notice a few papers missing, some distur-bance. But, there again, he might blame himself. He wouldn't be able to remember very clearly, would he? Or he might blame Parson Grimstone who, in his cups, is forgetful and wanders where he shouldn't.'

'And why should I kill Curate Robert?'

'Because you are an assassin, Master Burghesh. You like killing. You particularly like to watch some young woman's terror as you rape, then garrotte her.'

Burghesh swallowed hard. 'I don't have to listen to this web of lies!'

'Where can you go?' Corbett lied. 'My men are outside the church. They'll arrest you as soon as you leave. Do you want to know why you killed Curate Robert?'

'You have your theories,' Burghesh scoffed. 'Why should I kill a man whom I have lived with for so many years? He was my friend.'

'He was also curate of this church,' Corbett retorted, 'and you were growing very concerned. Parson Grimstone drank a lot, he was becoming forgetful. What really concerned Curate Robert – and I admit I have no real evidence for this – was that someone told him, God knows who, why or how, that sins confessed in the shriving pew were known to others.'

'So, you have no proof?'

'I have proof of sorts. Curate Robert would be mystified by this, deeply alarmed. Did he discuss it with Parson Grimstone who, of course, would tell you? Or, did you go through the curate's chamber and discover that he might be writing to his bishop? Bellen was becoming dangerous, that's why you killed him! At the same time, he could be cast as a possible assassin. In truth, Curate Robert knew little about the murders. However, any priest with a spark of conscience would grow concerned if the seal of the confessional was being violated. I'll wonder to my dying day and so will you,' Corbett added, 'just who this person was. Loud-mouthed Molkyn? His daughter? Or Deverell, our furtive carpenter? Even Blidscote?'

'Are you also going to accuse me of Molkyn's and Deverell's deaths?'

'Of course not,' Corbett replied. 'They were executed, or murdered, by Sir Louis Tressilyian, who realised that, due to their false testimony, an innocent man had been hanged.'

Burghesh started, his agitation obvious.

'Oh yes, Sir Roger was innocent! You killed, Burghesh, and, because of you, others lied, perjured themselves and were finally murdered to protect your sin.'

Corbett got to his feet and moved further up the steps, lengthening the gap between himself and this bloody-handed assassin.

'You've always been an assassin, Burghesh: you

will stand there and hear the truth. You became a soldier to kill. You revel in hot, splashing blood, the stink of death, have done ever since you were a young man on a farm near Melford. How many years ago would that be? Forty? Going back to the reign of our King's father? I have studied the Book of the Dead. It makes mention of two, three young women being murdered decades ago, as well as elliptical references to the corpses of "Unknown". Who were these Unknowns? Poor travellers? Whores? Prostitutes? Runaways with the misfortune to come to Melford? You preyed along those country lanes like a weasel hunting rabbits. No one was ever caught for these murders, perhaps no one even cared. You were safe. To all appearances you were the honest, bluff Burghesh, half-brother to young Grimstone, who was destined for the Church. I wonder if you ever opened that book and looked at your victims' names? Do you ever feel a pang of guilt?'

Burghesh just stared back.

'You trained as a mason but eventually the lure of wars drew you away: an opportunity to exploit your bloodlust. God knows how many deaths you have been responsible for up and down this kingdom. Along the Scottish and Welsh marches, when whole villages and towns were put to the sword, who'd care about corpses?'

'I was a good soldier,' Burghesh sneered. 'Never once did the King's marshals lay charges against me.'

'Oh, of course, they didn't. Armies move quickly. No one would notice. I have met soldiers like you, Burghesh, bluff and hearty, but killers to the bone. You also earned yourself a pretty penny. You plundered the victims of war, didn't you? Not only those you murdered but anyone else you could lay your hands on.'

'The fortunes of war,' came the cool reply.

'And you brought your fortune back to Melford to show everyone how well you had done. You purchased the old forester's house and, once again, became the half-brother and prudent friend of Parson Grimstone.'

'He needed my help.'

'Of course he did! The years haven't been kind to Parson Grimstone, have they? The idealism, the dreams have faded. Lonely, a lover of red wine, Grimstone would have welcomed you with open arms.'

'I told you. We are half-brothers and he was a good priest.'

'Oh, I am sure you did your best to hide your bloodlust. You may have even struggled against the different demons which ravage your cruel soul. But old habits die hard, eh, Burghesh? You are a clever soldier. You know how to muffle the hoofs of a horse. Melford had also grown, become even more prosperous, the countryside more lonely: copses, woods, forests, grass-filled meadows and hedgerows, which turn the narrow lanes into little more than trenches, a place crisscrossed by old footpaths and trackways. Melford is so easy to slip in and out of, no walls or barred gates. So you go hunting again, dressed in your mummer's mask.'

'Mummer's mask?'

'Yes, a mummer's mask. Something you had picked up on your travels or found here in Melford.

Usually you would carry it in your saddle horn, perhaps in a bag or under a cloth. It was your disguise, just in case any of your victims ever escaped. At first you were careful. You preyed on the vulnerable, the weak, the traveller's girl, the tinker's wife or daughter, the occasional itinerant whore. You attacked, raped and murdered. God knows where some of their poor corpses lie, though I'll come to that in a while.'

'If you have no corpses, you have no proof!' Burghesh retorted. 'Sir Hugh, you are supposed to be a King's clerk. All I hear are empty theories, hollow threats. What you say about me could be said about many a man in Melford.'

'True.'

Corbett spread his hands and wondered where on earth Ranulf was. Burghesh had closed the thick heavy oaken door. Corbett hid his disquiet. If Ranulf came into this church he would think it empty, perhaps go looking for him elsewhere?

'You are a hunter, Burghesh, of the soft flesh of innocents. You strut around Melford as the friend and confidant of the parish priest. You sit here in church and study the congregation like a fox eyes chickens in a farmyard. Melford has changed, hasn't it? The young women are better fed, better clothed, have more time on their hands. The market draws them in. You see them there with their pretty faces, swelling bosoms. Your lust grows: no more the tattered traveller, the dirty slattern. But how do you trap them?'

Corbett paused. He watched the weight on the bell rope slide a little further down the recess.

'So you chose Peterkin the simpleton. You lured him into taking messages to this woman or that. Peterkin was used to doing that. You taught him a simple doggerel verse which few young women could resist, especially if Peterkin was so urging, and showed that he had been paid to carry such a message. How could any young woman not be curious? Yet, she'd keep quiet, wouldn't she, lest others find out or the message proved false? She would not wish to be made a fool of. After all, who would blame poor Peterkin? Your first victim rose to the bait. She went to some lonely spot and you were waiting. Most of the murders apparently occurred in the early evening. You raped, you murdered with that damnable mask over your face. You hid the corpse and then slipped back into Melford.' Corbett shrugged.

'The nightmare had begun!'

# Chapter 18

'Don't you suffer guilt?' Corbett taunted. 'In the early hours of the morning, or at night, do the ghosts gather round your bed? Have you no fear of God or justice?'

'I like a good story,' came the mocking reply.

'Elizabeth the wheelwright's daughter –' Corbett continued matter-of-factly – 'her ghost is here. As I came into church I prayed to her. Perhaps she is the best example to use. You approached poor Peterkin, as you always did, gave him a coin, made him repeat the message. Normally Elizabeth would ignore Peterkin but she's young, full of wayward notions. Peterkin is earnest and has been paid to deliver a message. So, on that fateful evening, she goes to her secret place in the copse of woods near Devil's Oak. She meets her death: you, with that heinous mask across your face, the belt-bracelet you wear jingling on your wrist. You attacked, raped and murdered her. Once the bloodlust was past, you carefully removed the corpse to a hedge, near Devil's Oak. Perhaps you intended to come back and hide it. If you had your way, maybe you would have hidden all the corpses, except for Widow Walmer's.'

'So, I am guilty of her death as well?'

'Yes, five years ago, you killed at least three women. You would have killed again but something strange happened. Sir Roger Chapeleys gave the church a triptych. God knows why. A gift? An expression of guilt and remorse?' Corbett undid the wallet on his belt and drew out the crude drawing he had found in Curate Robert's room.

'Do you recognise this, Burghesh? In the background, a picture of Christ crucified; in the forefront, three figures. The central one is a priest, the man on his right looks like a clerk; he might be a curate or perhaps an angel. The one on his left is this figure wearing a mask. Do you see it? Jerkin, leggings and boots and, on his face, a mask similar to a mummer's. You thought Chapeleys was poking fun, hinting at the truth. The central figure being Parson Grimstone, the clerk Curate Robert and this mummer's figure, your good self.'

'True, I never liked the painting,' Burghesh sneered. 'I was glad when someone burnt it.'

'No, you burnt it lest someone read the same message you did. Do you know, Burghesh, I don't think Roger Chapeleys was hinting at anything. Such drawings are quite common in London churches. The man on the priest's right represents the wisdom of the world and the figure on the left its foolishness. It's a reference to a quotation from St Paul. It underlines temptations facing many priests and exhorts them to ignore both.'

Corbett could tell from Burghesh's eyes that he had struck home.

'You are a fool,' Corbett continued. 'It wasn't an

accusation levelled against anyone. You took it as a personal insult, a subtle accusation of your bloody deeds. I wager you realised that later. If Sir Roger had truly suspected you, he would have accused you in open court.'

Burghesh opened and closed his mouth.

'Sir Roger Chapeleys had difficulty with drinking. He was well known as a lecher and a toper. He was an unpopular figure. You decided to destroy him!' Corbett didn't wait for an answer. 'On that fateful night Sir Roger visited Widow Walmer. After he left, you went down. Perhaps you had visited before. You knew her house, Sir Roger's gift of a knife. She allowed you in and then you killed her.'

'I was in the taproom of the Golden Fleece.'

'Oh, of course, you were, both before and after the murder. No one took careful note of your comings and goings. Like Lucifer you sidled up to Repton the reeve. He, too, knew about Sir Roger's visits and was drowning his sorrows. Go on, you urged, confront the woman with her infidelity, tell her about your love. Repton didn't need much encouragement. Down he went but he had the wit to realise the danger when he found her dead. He was terrified. He fled back to the Golden Fleece. He'd make excuses, say he had changed his mind. He really wanted someone to accompany him back. What an ideal opportunity for you. Good friend Burghesh accompanied him down and the rest is known.'

'Has Repton told you this?'

'No,' Corbett smiled. 'But he will do. When we fasten his hands and allow the King's questioners to interrogate him, it's wonderful what he will remember. You were with Repton, weren't you? Good old Burghesh slipping in and out. I suspect it was you who attacked me near the mill on my first night in Melford. You were trying to confuse me. When I reached the Golden Fleece, you were sitting there cradling a tankard, jovial and hearty, beyond any suspicion.'

The weight on the bell rope reached the end of the ledge and fell off. Corbett ignored the jangle of the bell.

'All was now ready. Sir Roger's house was searched. You'd sent the keepsakes of those other victims to Sir Roger. You knew the mind of the man. He'd regard them as gifts or tokens from some of his conquests. He'd throw them in a chest and think nothing of them.'

'And Deverell?'

'Ah, now we come to the rest of your stratagem. I said Parson Grimstone is a toper. He is also lonely. He's a well-meaning man but garrulous in his cups.' Corbett tapped the side of his nose. 'He knows all the secrets of the village, doesn't he? Especially Molkyn's. The death of his first wife, as well as his illicit relationship with his own daughter, Margaret. The same is true of Thorkle. How his wife was planting a pair of cuckold horns with young Ralph? And, of course, about the carpenter Deverell, in truth a monk who'd fled his monastery, enjoying an illicit marriage whilst hiding from the eyes of the Church.'

Beads of sweat glistened high on Burghesh's forehead. 'Those are confessional secrets!' he spluttered.

'Some are, some are not.' Corbett sighed. 'But Parson Grimstone is lonely. He's drinking with his close friend and half-brother Burghesh, who has collected such juicy morsels over the years. You do know about such scandals?'

'I will say nothing,' Burghesh retorted.

'I wonder how you approached your blackmail victims. Was it scribbled on a piece of parchment? Some quotation from the Bible? Like the one Molkyn received, quoting Leviticus, which strictly condemned incest? Was it a personal visit in the dead of night or along some alleyway? Do this, do that or face the consequences. They would all be terrified: Deverell faced ruin, Thorkle ridicule, Molkyn public anger.'

'I didn't choose them for the jury. Blidscote did!'

'Blidscote?' Corbett asked. 'Good God, you didn't have to be a friend of the parish priest to know about Blidscote. He's a byword for corruption, or rather was. He's dead now. Did you learn about his passion for little boys? What united all your victims of blackmail was not only their secret fears but their open dislike of Sir Roger. You, the Mummer's Man, the Jesses killer, had set the stage.'

Corbett emphasised the points on his gloved fingers: 'Chapeleys had been with Widow Walmer the night she died; the knife; his ownership of some of the dead women's jewellery; Deverell's testimony; popular dislike against him and, finally, a jury really controlled by you. What chance did the poor man have?'

Corbett moved on the step. He took some comfort from a sound outside, a slight footfall. He hoped it was Ranulf and not Parson Grimstone.

'The only fly in the ointment was Furrell the poacher. He knew the comings and goings of the countryside. On the night Widow Walmer died, he saw Sir Roger leave her safe and sound. He talked of other people slipping through the darkness to that poor woman's cottage. We know Repton went down twice. I suspect a third was you, the killer.' Corbett leant forward and jabbed a finger. 'And it will be Furrell who hangs you, Burghesh, and hang you shall! He became very curious about what he had seen, the lies told about Sir Roger. I am sure you had a hand in the whispering campaign.' Corbett paused. 'Above all, Furrell had seen that triptych: he began to wonder if the truth was as clear as a picture. So, where does a man go who is troubled?' Corbett pointed to the floor. 'Why, Master Burghesh, he comes to church. I warrant he spoke to Parson Grimstone, or did he approach you directly? Accuse you openly? Whatever, he never left this church alive.'

'Nonsense! Furrell was a drunk. He fled from that woman of his and went elsewhere.'

'I promised Furrell would hang you. Master Burghesh, the busybody around the church, the man who burnt the triptych, who cleans, rings the bells and digs graves.'

Burghesh was now clearly agitated, a hand resting on the hilt of his dagger.

'Where do you put a corpse like Furrell's,' Corbett continued, 'when you have a woman like Sorrel who knows the countryside like the back of her hand? You put him with the other corpses. I'll go through the Book of the Dead again to trap Burghesh the grave-digger. In the evening you dig a plot for a funeral the following morning. Only sometimes, you dig it a foot deeper and bury one of your victims, someone like Furrell or one of the wandering women. I'll get half of Melford up here with mattock and hoe and we'll go through that Mortuary Book. We'll dig up coffins then go deeper. The dead will convict you. The treason of the ghosts, eh, Burghesh? They'll represent evidence you cannot challenge. After all, only you dig the graves. We'll also question Parson Grimstone, search your house, particularly the little stable behind. We'll look for cloths filled with straw to deaden the sound of your horse's hoofs. And, of course,' Corbett knocked the bell rope, 'we'll go back to Curate Robert.'

Corbett got to his feet. 'We'll hold a court here in church. I carry the King's Seal. I'll call on the dead to betray you. How thronged the nave will become! You are a killer, Burghesh. You deserve death.'

Burghesh leant his head back against the door, watching Corbett from under hooded eyes.

'Sorrel called you a weasel, Burghesh. I wonder what's the full tally of your victims. How many secret graves lie around Melford? Furrell and his woman discovered some: that poacher was your nemesis. Do you know what that means?'

His opponent simply sneered.

'It's God's judgement,' Corbett explained. 'I suspect Furrell brought that triptych back from Ipswich for Sir Roger and remembered it after the poor knight was hanged. Furrell certainly suspected you. He made up a song, about being between the devil and an angel, he was referring to Chapeleys' triptych.'

'He was a drunken fool!'

'He was a sharp fool. To quote scripture, Master Burghesh, the foolishness of man is often the wisdom of God. You also dismissed Sorrel as a vagrant but, when I arrived, you changed your mind. You realised how much she might know: that's why you went out to Beauchamp Place to murder her. You would have murdered me as well with that piece of twine stretched across the bridge. An old poacher's trick or, in your case, Burghesh, an old soldier's! I've seen royal archers use the same trap to bring down horsemen. Oh yes,' Corbett watched Burghesh carefully, 'you crept out of Melford and, if I hadn't been at Beauchamp Place, Sorrel would have disappeared. I wonder where you would have buried her? You lured some of your victims back to the woods behind your house and, as with Furrell, buried them in the graveyard.' Corbett took a step forward. 'Let's go into the church, Burghesh. Its nave must be filling with ghosts, all crying to God for justice. They'll betray you, hand you over for punishment, both in this life and the next.'

Burghesh ripped the dagger from his sheath.

'What are you going to do?' Corbett scoffed. 'Kill the King's clerk?' He drew his own dagger. 'My name's not Elizabeth. I am no soft, frightened girl.'

'No, you are not!' Burghesh snarled. 'You are a clever clerk. You don't know what it's like to have demons tapping inside your skull. You are right about one thing: Melford is so easy to leave and—'

Before Corbett could stop him, Burghesh was through the door, turning the key in the lock. Corbett heard a brief scuffle and went down the steps. The door was unlocked and swung open. Ranulf stood there, the hilt of his sword under Burghesh's chin.

'Where have you been?' Corbett accused.

'Looking for you.'

Ranulf's eyes never left Burghesh. He pressed the point of the sword, forcing the man to look at him.

'I couldn't find this creature but I remembered your words about the bell tower. I have been listening for a while at the door, just catching phrases. So, look what we've caught!'

'Tie his hands!' Corbett ordered. 'And, once you have done that, ring the bell!'

Ranulf obeyed. Corbett went and took the sanctuary chair and placed it in front of the rood screen. Parson Grimstone came waddling in, all confused. Corbett told Repton the reeve, when he arrived, to take him back to the priest's house and lock him in. Within a short while the nave was packed with people hastening up from the marketplace. Corbett ordered the Book of the Dead to be brought. He told them what he was going to do and quelled the clamour.

'Is it true?' Repton shouted. 'Master Burghesh is under arrest? He and Sir Louis Tressilyian?'

'Yes,' Corbett replied. 'But I have to discover some new evidence.' He raised his voice and shouted above the murmur. 'Certain graves have to be reopened, coffins and corpses removed.' He paused for the shouting to die down. 'We will discover something evil,' he continued. 'I ask you to trust me.'

'Well, we had best do as you say,' Repton the reeve replied sardonically. He let his hand drop over his groin. 'We don't want to upset our royal clerk, do we?'

Corbett led a party of men out into the graveyard. He discovered when Furrell was last seen and compared dates in the Book of the Dead. One grave was opened, its mouldering coffin removed and wrapped in a sheet. Nothing else was found. The second time, however, Repton, standing in the grave, said he could feel something beneath his feet.

'It's not hard soil either,' he shouted.

A short while later a grisly, decayed cadaver was brought gently out and laid on the wet grass. The flesh had shrivelled, only some hair remained. Corbett put his gloves on, turned the head over and pointed to the crack at the back of the skull.

'It's Furrell, all right,' Repton murmured. 'God have mercy on him! I recognise his belt and boots.'

A woman screamed and Sorrel, hair flying, came running across the graveyard. She took one look at the corpse and, if Corbett hadn't caught her, she would have collapsed to the ground. He let her kneel there, sobbing, face in her hands, and moved to other graves. The day grew on. Sometimes they found nothing but, quite regularly, other unaccounted corpses were unearthed: grisly cadavers, really nothing more than skeletons.

'What is this?' Repton demanded.

'Burghesh would kill,' Corbett replied, 'and bring the corpses in at night. He dug the graves for a funeral Mass either early in the morning or late in the evening. His victim was then buried and sealed in her grave before the consequent funeral. It's all the evidence I need.'

By now a considerable crowd had gathered. The news had spread and Corbett became concerned. The mood of the onlookers turned ugly. Sticks and stones were thrown across the cemetery wall, a threatening group clustered under the lych-gate. Ranulf armed himself, as did Chanson. Corbett swore in Repton and others as members of his comitatus, then went down to the lych-gate and confronted the mob.

'Will justice be done?'

Corbett recognised the burgess who had bored him last night at the Guildhall. Corbett held up his warrant so all could see the seal.

'I am the King's Commissioner!' he shouted. 'I have the authority to hear cases and pass sentence: that will be done!'

'What about a jury?' the burgess asked.

'There is no need for a jury,' Corbett retorted. 'Burghesh threatened a King's clerk carrying the royal warrant: that's treason. However,' Corbett admitted ruefully, 'it would be better if Burghesh confessed.'

The prisoner was brought up from the crypt. He glimpsed the mob and heard their threatening cries. Corbett had him held beneath a yew tree, then brought across the sheets of leather containing Furrell's remains and those of the others. Burghesh stared at them and glanced away.

'Will you confess?' Corbett demanded.

Burghesh breathed in noisily. 'What can I say?' he murmured, and smiled slyly at Corbett. 'It's true what you said, the treason of the ghosts! The dead betrayed me.'

'The dead want you,' Corbett retorted. 'You have a reckoning to make. You and Parson Grimstone.'

'Oh, is that the way this will go?' Burghesh asked.

'He was your accomplice,' Corbett insisted.

'No, he wasn't. He's just weak.'

'Is that a confession?' Corbett asked.

'No, it's not, master clerk. If you want one then you shall have it, but only after I have talked to Parson Grimstone.'

Corbett agreed. Ranulf and Chanson took the bound prisoner into the priest's house. Corbett returned to the church and sat studying the carvings on the rood screen. He tried to pray but found he was tired – a sudden weariness – so he sat at the foot of a pillar and dozed for a while. He felt sickened by Burghesh and the callous cruelty of his murders. He wanted to be away from Melford.

An hour must have passed before Ranulf and Chanson brought Burghesh back into the church. The prisoner now seemed to be in a trance.

'Grimstone's a wreck,' Ranulf murmured. 'He sits there gibbering like a child. He'll be dead drunk within the hour.'

'And the killer?' Corbett nodded at Burghesh.

Ranulf felt inside his jerkin and drew out a scroll. Corbett unrolled it and recognised Ranulf's writing. The confession had been taken in the bleak, elliptical manner clerks used. Corbett asked for a candle to be lit and read it. He went cold at the list of crimes.

'At least fifteen,' he murmured. 'Fifteen people killed!' He got to his feet. 'Bring the prisoner into the sanctuary.'

Corbett stood before the high altar. He took a small crucifix from a side table and placed it at one end, the King's commission beside it. Burghesh stood on the other side of the altar, Ranulf and Chanson flanking him.

'Adam Burghesh,' Corbett began, 'you are accused of terrible murders in and around Melford. The list,' he tapped the confession, 'speaks for itself.'

'I am guilty.' Burghesh's mouth hardly seemed to move. 'I have spoken to Grimstone. I thought he'd forgive me.'

'I have the power to try you,' Corbett declared.

'What's the point?' Burghesh half smiled. 'If it's to be done let it be done quickly. You have the authority, you have the proof and now my confession. My only regret is I never killed you. I should have done. I recognised that the very first day you arrived here. I am guilty as Judas and I couldn't care if I hang like him!'

'Adam Burghesh, by the power invested in me as the King's Commissioner of Oyer and Terminer, I do, by your own admission and the evidence offered, find you guilty of terrible homicides. You have the right to appeal . . .'

Burghesh snorted with laughter.

'You have also drawn a knife against the King's Commissioner and that is petty treason.'

Corbett paused, he felt a deep revulsion at this cold-eyed man who had wiped out so many lives; who had lied and forced others to lie to save his own neck.

'You are sentenced to hang on the common scaffold. You will have the opportunity to be shrived by a priest. Sentence is to be carried out before sunset!'

In the remaining hours Corbett and his men, with the assistance of Sir Maurice and others, packed their belongings. The young manor lord had now taken over proceedings, sending a messenger to bring in armed retainers from his own estate. Corbett and Sir

Louis Tressilyian, guarded by Ranulf and Chanson, met Sir Maurice and the execution party at the crossroads outside Melford. A large crowd had gathered, spilling into the fields around. Burghesh was defiant to the last. He was placed on the ladder, pushed up by two of Chapeleys' retainers and the noose placed round his neck.

Darkness was falling, a cold wind had arisen. Corbett sat hunched on his horse before the gibbet. He hated executions, the logical conclusion of the King's justice, yet this time he felt different: no elation or joy, just a grim determination to see the matter through.

He glanced over his shoulder. Tressilyian, who had given his oath not to escape, sat on his horse, his bound hands holding the horn of his saddle. He seemed to be unaware of anything except the man on the ladder, the noose round his neck. Sir Maurice sat next to him, pale-faced, hard-eyed. Corbett glanced around. Sorrel was standing nearby, a posy of flowers in her hands. He recognised the wheelwright, Repton and others from the Golden Fleece.

'Adam Burghesh!' he called out. 'Do you have anything to say before lawful sentence is passed?'

Burghesh hawked and spat in Corbett's direction.

Corbett pulled his horse back, its hoofs skittering on the pebbled trackway. The clerk raised his hand.

'Let the King's justice be done!'

The ladder was pulled away but Burghesh acted quickly. He leapt and his body shuddered and jerked for a while, then hung still. Nothing broke the eerie silence except for the rustling of the wind and the creak of the scaffold rope.

'The corpse is to remain there for a night and a day!' Corbett ordered. 'Then it can be buried.'

He turned and beckoned Sir Maurice forward.

'Set a guard on the scaffold,' he whispered. 'Make sure that killer dangles as a warning.'

'I'll do that, Sir Hugh. And Sir Louis?'

'I don't know,' Corbett replied. 'He's a clever lawyer: he will argue that he carried out the King's justice. Burghesh is proof of that.'

'Will he suffer the same fate?'

'I doubt it,' Corbett replied. 'But he'll face a very heavy fine: prison or exile for a while.' He took off his glove. 'I wish you well, Sir Maurice.'

The manor lord clasped Corbett's hand. The clerk turned his horse and stared at the now silent figure swaying slightly on the end of the rope. He felt a touch on his knee and looked down. Sorrel offered the small posy of flowers. Corbett took it. She grasped his knee.

'Thank you,' she whispered. 'I now have a corpse to grieve over and a grave to visit. The King's justice has been done.'

Corbett leant down and stroked her face.

'Aye, Mistress Sorrel, and so has God's!'

# Author's Note

Serial killers are not a product of the twentieth century, but our knowledge of them is the result of modern technology. The killings described in this novel represent a composite picture of different murder patterns during the Middle Ages. Enclosed communities like Melford did exist and could erupt in violent and bloody murder. The problem was that, unless the victims had powerful kinsmen or the matter was brought to the attention of the King's justices, little could be done. Judges were bribed and juries bought or heavily influenced, not only in murder cases but even in matters of rebellion and treason. Life could be cheap and, in the fourteenth century, economic prosperity brought displacement and a sharp increase in peasants being driven from the land to wander the countryside looking for work. Such groups were always highly vulnerable, though *The Treason of the Ghosts* is based more on killings which took place in London and Norwich rather than the open countryside.

The changes brought about by the increased demand for English wool abroad led to radical changes in our farming and pasture system. I have often walked the narrow, deep lanes described here; even Edward I accepted that they were a hazard to law and order!

Justice, on the other hand, could be swift, and Corbett's execution of the murderer follows a medieval pattern. The bell tower of St Edmund's and the cunning use of the ropes is also based on fact as well as observation. In the fourteenth century the sons of Cain could be as cunning in their plotting as their modern descendants.

Paul Doherty was born in Middlesborough. He studied History at Liverpool and Oxford Universities and obtained a doctorate for his thesis on Edward II and Queen Isabella. He is now the Headmaster of a school in North-East London, and lives with his wife and family near Epping Forest.

'Vitality in the cityscape . . . angst in the mystery; it's Peters minus the herbs but plus a few crates of sack'

*Oxford Times*

'The maestro of medieval mystery . . . packed with salty dialogue, the smells and superstitions of the 14th century, not to mention the political intrigues'

*Books magazine*

'As always the author invokes the medieval period in all its muck as well as glory, filling the pages with pungent smells and description. The author brings years of research to his writing; his mastery of the period as well as a disciplined writing schedule have led to a rapidly increasing body of work and a growing reputation'

*Mystery News*

'Medieval London comes vividly to life'

*Publishers Weekly*